In the
CASTLE
of the
FLYNNS

a novel

MICHAEL
RALEIGH

sourcebooks
landmark

Sourcebooks and the colophon are registered trademarks of Sourcebooks, Inc.

Published by Sourcebooks Landmark, an imprint of Sourcebooks, Inc.
P.O. Box 4410, Naperville, Illinois 60567-4410
(630) 961-3900
Fax: (630) 961-2168
www.sourcebooks.com

The Library of Congress has cataloged the hardcover edition as follows:

Raleigh, Michael.
    In the castle of the Flynns / by Michael Raleigh.
        p. cm.
    (alk. paper)
        1. Irish American families—Fiction. 2. Chicago (Ill.)—Fiction. 3. Orphans—Fiction. 4. Boys—Fiction. I. Title.
PS3568.A4316 I5 2002
813'.54—dc21
2001032239

Printed and bound in the United States of America.
RRD 10 9 8 7 6 5 4 3 2 1

In loving memory of Catherine Raleigh McNamara

For the Raleighs and the McHughs:
this is not their story—but it could have been

photo from the right, almost as if he has come to visit from an adjoining picture—a role he was to play in my life. The people in the photo are singing, singing badly and very loud, and the ones in the back row, the tall ones, are leaning to one side so that it appears they'll lurch on through the glossy white margin holding the picture together. Even from the old black-and-white I can tell they're red-faced and noisy and sweaty, and several of them, exactly the ones I would expect, have had too much to drink, and not for the last time. There are either ten or eleven people in this photo, depending on whether one counts the blurry figure dashing in from the right. These are the Flynns. I think of the first photo as a portrait of my original family. I think of this one as a photograph of my life. I doubt if a day ever passes that I don't look at it for a moment.

In the center are my mother's parents, Patrick and Winifred Flynn. They are flanked, surrounded, overwhelmed on all four sides by family, including their children: Anne, Michael, and Thomas—my uncles and my aunt. My late mother had been the eldest daughter. Her name was Betty. Entering the photo from the right, a running blur, is my cousin Matthew Lynch, not a member of this family at all but of the even larger Dorsey family, my father's people. I was of course a Dorsey, but for reasons I will explain, I lived with my mother's people. The two families had been close even before my father married my mother, two sprawling clans originally from the same neighborhood, from Old Town, the area of old streets surrounding what is now called Cabrini-Green, streets named for writers—Goethe and Schiller and Scott—but full of working-class people. My mother's family had later moved on and planted themselves in a four-block area around Riverview Park. Cousin Matt is in the picture because the Dorsey family was also in attendance on this day: the Paris-Shanahan wedding, involving families known to both sides, so that for the first time in my limited experience, everyone I knew in life, every single blood

Pictures

I keep the photographs together always. They are framed now, my two family portraits, but wrinkled and faded from my youthful inattention: had I known what they'd someday mean to me, I'd have shown them better care. The first is a studio portrait, on a thick sort of cardboard, of four people: my parents, Mr. and Mrs. John Dorsey, my infant brother Johnny, and me. At the time of this photo, I was a few months short of my fifth birthday. Within the year Johnny would be dead of rheumatic fever. Two years after Johnny, my parents would be dead as well. It is a stiff, posed photo, and I can see my smile beginning to give way to boredom or gravity. I have studied the photograph over the years, looking for some hint that this family already sensed its impending fortune, some dark suggestion of unhappiness in the eyes. I have found none: the faces in a photo reveal only what the subjects hope. Any deeper message is probably in the imagination of the beholder.

The second picture is quite different. I have come to think of it as The Photographer's Nightmare. Taken in 1955, the year after the death of my parents, it is crowded, unfocused at the edges, as if distracted from its purposes by the raucous, manic behavior of several of its subjects. The lighting is uneven, one of the people has turned his head just as the photographer snapped his little button and, as a result, appears to have two faces attempting too late to blend. A person is entering the relative I had on earth was collected in one place for something other than a funeral: uncles and aunts, cousins, second cousins, great uncles and great aunts, both pairs of grandparents. The place was Johnny Vandiver's Hall on Roscoe, a tottering frame hulk just behind Vandiver's tavern and the obligatory venue for weddings in the neighborhood.

I once heard my Uncle Tom say, "You never forget the first time," and I think he had something else in mind, but it is also true of weddings: this one was my first, and it is forever imprinted on my memory. For one short day, all the women I knew were dazzling, the men, at least till they hit the bar, looked like slumming royalty. The air was close with perfume, aftershave, hair oil, the acrid smell of dry-cleaned clothes and the scent of mothballs that clung to the older people. I reveled in the noise, the food smells, the bluish cloud of tobacco smoke that hung just above the tables, the discordant music from a toothy accordion player and his trio of failed musicians.

For the better part of four hours, I was on my own, unsupervised, unchecked, unnoticed, the one child there without parental guidance, an unknown quantity, and I roamed the hall and its fusty corners and dank back stairs like a stray dog. I imagined that I was a spy, an army scout, I played games with my cousins, wrestled with Matt till the grown-ups threatened to throw us both out in the street, talked with an endless succession of solicitous adults who wanted, as always, to know how the Local Orphan was getting on.

But mostly I skulked about and observed how adults in that far-off time after a pair of wars let off steam. What I saw was— to an eight-year-old—glorious. For a good part of my youth, it was to color my understanding of what went on at wedding receptions: the best man went toe-to-toe with the boyfriend of one of the bridesmaids; a woman became intoxicated and began undressing to music until her husband dragged her off the floor; a gray-haired man replaced her until his horrified daughters hauled him away; a teenager threw up on the dance floor. A pair of strangers appeared along the far wall, just a couple of party crashers, and the groomsmen escorted them out to the street without ceremony.

At a rear table, oblivious to the existence of the rest of the world, I saw my uncle Joe, my dad's brother, and his wife Loretta in one in their endless series of fights, hissing and growling like a pair of well-dressed cats, their faces two inches apart: by the end of the evening they would both be drunk, wrapped around one another, and he'd be staring at her as though he'd discovered Helen of Troy on his lap.

Out in the hallway, in a blind corner near the coat check, I came upon the evening's centerpiece: my uncle Tom in a deep clinch with a dark-haired girl I didn't know. She was a slender girl with very white skin, and the thin straps that held her dress up seemed to be coming down. I watched them clamp mouth on mouth and wondered how they could breathe. As I stared, it suddenly came to me who this girl was, a one-year-old family mystery had been cleared up for me, and I understood that there was an element of danger present.

When I went back inside, my grandmother buttonholed me, round-faced and matronly in a new permanent and a dark dress with small white dots. She had doubtless been looking for my grandfather, who was almost certainly in Vandiver's tavern out front, or perhaps Dunne's saloon up the street, but she was willing to settle for me.

"Are you having a nice time, Danny?"

"Oh, sure." And of course I was: thus far the wedding had presented me with violence, humor, drunkenness, jealousy, and my first experience of sex, dimly understood but fascinating. "Can we go to another wedding next week, Grandma?"

She laughed. "Oh, not next week, sweetheart, but soon enough. Maybe both of your uncles will finally settle down with a nice girl." She said this without much conviction and scanned the big smoky room in search of either of her sons. Tom chose this moment to enter with the dark-haired girl, who had thankfully pulled her dress back up.

I stole a glance at Grandma. Worry softened her face, and her dark-eyed gaze followed her favorite child across the dance floor. We both watched Tom take his leave of the girl with a little wink, and Grandma allowed herself a little snort at the girl's expense, accompanied by a brief wrinkling of the nose to show her disapproval. I wasn't sure why she would disapprove: I thought the girl was wonderful.

Eventually I rejoined my cousins and we trooped around the hall, weaving in and out of trouble and managing to be in all the best places: the groomsman and the jealous boyfriend went at it not ten feet from us, and the aforementioned teenager threw up just as we were passing by. Toward the end of the long night we kids all split up and went back to the tables where we belonged. Matt stayed with me for a while; we sat down at an empty table a few feet from his parents, Dennis and Mary Jane. They were arguing, and I could tell by the way he watched them that this was nothing new. When he saw that I was staring, he smiled at me and began talking about the trip they were taking to the Wisconsin Dells the following weekend. When his father got up and staggered away from the table, Matt gave me a little whack and said he had to go. I told him I'd see him around.

A little while after that we took our picture. It took some time to set up: my grandmother wanted her two brothers in it, my great uncles Martin and Frank, and this was no small undertaking, for we had to send out search parties. Eventually they found Martin in the tavern grumbling and making dire predictions of the end of the world to anyone who would listen, and Uncle Frank's wife Rose found him asleep in his car—he came in blinking and licking his lips, and his hair stood up on one side where he'd been sleeping on it. You can still see it in the photo—he looks as if he's modeling a new hairstyle, and one of his eyes is not completely open. My grandmother was relieved to hear that he'd been asleep in the car, which meant that the community was safe.

They all seemed happy. My grandmother had also located Grandpa and he was still coherent—and we crowded together and attempted halfheartedly to accommodate the poor photographer. He was a beefy man with a matted shock of hair and ill-fitting clothes. He chain-smoked and his shirt had come out of his trousers, and he had had a long hard day trying to squeeze dignified photographs out of that sweaty, unrestrained gathering. Somewhere at the periphery I could hear someone singing "I'll Take You Home Again, Kathleen," and then all of them picked it up and I thought the photographer would run outside and throw himself in front of the Damen Avenue bus. Aunt Anne was running her hands through my hair and they made me stand right in the center of them all. Someone, one of my uncles, was patting me on the shoulder and they were howling away like cats on the back fence.

I was laughing, at what I couldn't have said, and if you had told me my life would be frozen at just that moment in time, that I would enter the next world feeling just as I did then, I would have counted myself lucky. I had probably begun to understand that they all belonged to me, and I to them.

The photographer snapped his picture and muttered something and then asked us to stay for one more, something had gone wrong, and as he pressed his button anew, someone bumped him from behind, and this last time just as he took the picture, Matt bolted into the camera's field.

The fat photographer straightened up, said, "That'll have to do," and I heard him add "goddammit" under his breath as he waddled away with his camera, trailing cigarette ash and shirttails behind him. Shortly after that troubled photo session a fight broke out over a coat, and the police were called. I thought my heart would burst.

I rode home with Uncle Tom and Uncle Mike. Uncle Mike was driving, hunched over the wheel as though the car crowded him. He was big and heavily built, and had the red hair of Grandpa's people. Tom was dark-haired and dark-eyed like his mother, and a relatively small man, though I couldn't see it then. They muttered to one another in the voices they usually used when they didn't want me to hear, but I did, I always did, and I knew they were talking about Tom and the girl.

"Playing with fire, Tom. It ain't gonna work."

"We'll see."

"And Philly, he finds out, he'll come looking for the both of you." He pronounced it "da bota you."

"I can't do nothing about that." A moment later Tom added, "He don't appreciate her, he don't appreciate what he's got. If I hadn't had to go to overseas, she'd have been mine. I'm gonna take her from him." Tom said this last with the same tone of absolute certainty he'd used after the death of my parents, when he'd told me that they were all going to take care of me.

"Be careful," Uncle Mike told him, and then sighed. He sat looking out the window and shaking his head.

I waited what I thought to be a respectful moment and then asked, "Are you gonna marry the lady with the black hair, Uncle Tom?"

"Jesus," Tom muttered. He looked at me in the rearview mirror. "You don't miss anything, do you?"

"I don't think so."

"Well, this is between the three of us. About that lady—whose name is Helen, by the way—it's too soon to be talking about that kinda thing. Besides, nobody can tell what's gonna happen in the future. Now crawl back in your hole and go to sleep."

I nodded, my suspicions confirmed: this was the mysterious Helen whose name I'd heard whispered among the family.

"Just be careful," Mike repeated. "He's nuts, that guy."

"Yeah? So what? So am I," Tom said quietly.

I was delighted to hear his intentions. I wanted him to marry the dark-haired girl, I wanted him to have anything he wanted. Just as he was his mother's favorite, he was mine: he was handsome and funny and brave and a war hero, and in the absence of a father, I was convinced Tom had hung the moon.

The Darkest News

For much of the time, though, I associated Tom with bad news; it seemed that he was always the one delegated to give bad news, and on a June morning in 1954 that I will never forget he had given me mine. He had dropped down on one knee to get closer to my level—I'd been playing on the floor of my grandmother's living room, and I'd already come to expect any adult dropping down on one knee to give me a serious talk about something: it had been my mother's habit. He gave me a nervous half smile and put a hand on my shoulder.

I wanted to run away, for I sensed what was coming: something had happened to my parents, to both of them. I'd spent the night at my grandmother's and it was clear that something catastrophic had occurred. My parents had gone out on Friday night and had not come back to pick me up, and then I'd woken during the night to hear my grandmother sobbing in the kitchen and my grandfather trying to calm her.

In the morning she woke me with a forced smile and a stricken look in her eyes and then made me pancakes in an empty kitchen—my grandfather wasn't in his accustomed place, sitting facing the window and filling the air with the blue smoke from his Camels. My grandmother hardly spoke to me during breakfast except to ask if I wanted more pancakes. After five I was full, but she kept making them. I remember that they were perfect, not a one of them burned or irregular.

In a lifetime of making pancakes for me and the others in her family, that was the only day I can remember when she hadn't produced at least one pancake the color and consistency of my school shoes. I watched her silent form and saw her wipe her eyes several times. At one point she stopped and just leaned on the stove with both hands, and I knew what had happened but said nothing, as though I could fend off this evil, undo it, perhaps, if I could but refrain from speaking of it.

My uncle came in just as I'd gone into the living room to play. I remember that he stood with the door half-opened, as if he might leave again, and then he went out to the kitchen. I heard my grandmother begin to weep, and then Uncle Tom came in to see me with the look of a fighter who has just barely beaten the count. Uncle Mike was behind him, big-eyed and looking stunned.

"How you doing, kiddo?" he asked, and didn't even fake a smile.

"I don't know," I told him, and I didn't.

He looked off past me for a moment and then got down on his knee. "Something happened. A bad...a bad thing, kiddo." He broke off and looked away again, and this time he made a faint gasping sound. He seemed to be searching for the words, and I beat him to it.

"Something bad happened to Mommy and Daddy."

He blinked in surprise and then nodded. "Yeah. They were in an accident. And they died. They went to heaven."

"I want them to come back."

He looked away again and shook his head. "No, they... people don't come back. Once they been to heaven, they... they don't come back."

"How do you know they're dead?"

He shot a panicked look at his brother, saw no help, plodded on alone. "I was, you know, I was out there."

"I won't see them?"

"Not till you get up there, to heaven."

"I wanna go now."

"You can't, not yet, anyways, you got to…"

And then I let it all out, and I have no clear recollection of the next few minutes, except that I sobbed against his jacket till his shoulder was wet, and I could hear them all crying, all of them except him. He just hugged me. I had a sudden feeling of terror that was somehow balanced by the fact that the accident hadn't taken him as well. Up close, he smelled of Old Spice and Wildroot Cream Oil and I had always wanted to smell like him.

I remembered our crowded apartment up the street on Clybourn, a cluttered flat above a shop where they repaired radios and fans and had them lining the windows, and I saw myself alone in the middle of it. They were all gone. I was seven years old and they were all gone.

"Where am I gonna live?" I said into the cloth of his jacket, and he patted the back of my head.

"You'll be okay, Danny. You'll be all right." Then, after a brief hesitation, "We'll take care of you."

They attempted to keep the details from me but it was all they talked about, every telephone call was about this terrible thing, and I soon learned how they had died: a head-on collision at the intersection of Belmont and Clark. A drunk teenager had tried to beat the red light on Belmont, the worst and final mistake in his young life, for the collision had killed him as well. My father was dead when the ambulance arrived. My mother, thrown from the car, had died on the way to the hospital.

On nights when sleep came slowly, I lay in bed quaking with a child's rage at them all, at my mother for leaving me, at this dead boy for killing my parents, at my father for what seemed his incompetence—the news bore frequent accounts of other accidents whose victims survived, and I thought he should have been able to save himself, or at least my mother.

There had been a brief, tearful wake for my brother Johnny that I can hardly recall. My sole surviving image from it is the horror of my mother, beautiful and disconsolate in a plain black dress—there is nothing so terrifying to a child as the sight of a parent crying. But my parents' wake was my first real experience of the rituals of death. They all tried to keep me from it as well as they could—my grandmother was convinced it was harmful for me to see both my parents in their caskets—but Uncle Tom insisted that I be present for some of it, and I was glad. I had a brief moment of elation when I approached their twin caskets: I was going to see them again. And I knew it was them: Uncle Mike had made a brief sortie into theology while they were getting me dressed, explaining about souls and spirits but it all sounded like gibberish to a seven-year-old boy, and he gave it up almost immediately. These two figures in the caskets were my parents; it was them but life had left them. I raised a hand to touch my mother's fingers, clasped around a rosary of my grandma's and then I stopped.

"No, go on," I heard Uncle Tom's voice say. "It's okay, they're your parents, nobody else's." He let his eyes linger on his dead sister's face, wet his lips, and then stood back to let me by.

I touched her fingers and they were cold and the skin felt strange, rubbery. I moved over to my father and he felt the same, and for some reason I was consoled by this, that they were experiencing this thing together. I had a momentary urge to climb in with them, as I'd climbed so often into their bed. I wanted to talk to them but was self-conscious. In the end, I knelt down and said an Our Father and a Hail Mary, and stared at them for a while, till my uncle put a hand on my shoulder and said, "Come on, Dan, some of your cousins are here." In the background I could hear my grandmother crying and talking about me.

I watched their reactions as they entered, the Flynns and Dorseys, saw how they embraced one another like old friends and then watched their faces fall as they remembered the enormity of this double dose of the world's trouble. More than once I saw them peer in disbelief at the twin coffins at the chapel's far end.

On the far side I saw my Grandma Dorsey in the protective embrace of her beautiful daughter Teresa, or Sister Fidelity as she was now—widely viewed by the two families as both saint and eccentric because she had already achieved two rare states in life: she was a nun just returned from working in the foreign missions, and she had gone to college.

As nearly as I could understand it, going to college was an odd thing for a girl to do, and the other—"joining the Lord's household," as Grandma Flynn put it—put her on a different plane from the rest of us. In an Irish household one could come no closer to sainthood than to become a nun; it did not bring the glory and neighborhood celebrity conferred on boys who voiced the determination to become a priest, but it was viewed in a different way. Seminarians played ball and boxed, priests went to ballgames and even liked a shot of Jim Beam now and then, but a girl who went into the convent renounced the world, even the neighborhood. We didn't understand them and so they took on a special place in the pantheon, like astrophysicists.

For the rest of it, I was glad they'd let me come, for as near as I could make out, a wake was a family party done up in dark clothing: every relative I had on earth was there, three generations of Irish immigrants, and half the neighborhood. There were even black people, three women and a young man who had known my mother from the big A&P where she worked. They spoke to my grandparents and I saw that both my grandmothers were glad to see these black people, but Grandpa Flynn seemed uncomfortable with them. Grandpa Dorsey was dead, so there was no reaction from him.

All around the long room, wherever I looked, I found adults gazing at me with sad eyes or simple curiosity. My cousin Jeff, five years older, widely read and worldly, explained my situation to me.

"You're an orphan now."

"I am?"

"Yeah. Your parents are both dead, see." Here he gestured to the caskets, lest I forget the cause of the gathering. "So they're all kinda sorry for you, and you're interesting to 'em." He shrugged as though this made no sense whatsoever, and then added, "It's neat to be an orphan, though."

"How come?"

His mouth made a little "o" and a faint gleam of excitement came into his eyes as he warmed to his task. "Well, you'll probably get more presents and stuff on your birthday because they feel sorry for you. When's your birthday?"

"March 27."

"Oh." His face fell. "They'll probably forget by then. Act real sad when that time comes. Christmas, too." I assured him that I would do whatever was necessary. He thought for a moment and added, "Don't eat. They always think something's wrong when you don't eat."

I looked to the front of the room where the Dorseys stood to one side and the Flynns to the other, and visitors and mourners stopped to speak to them all. While the adults were thus occupied, I joined my cousins, especially Matt, and did what children have always done at wakes, namely, played tag, explored the funeral home, and invaded the privacy of other families in mourning.

There was a second chapel in the building, and a wake in progress in this one as well, and we stole in and stared at the deceased in that one, a man named Albert Schuss, according to the sign at the entrance—and I can no sooner forget his name than the occasion when I learned it—a shrunken-faced old man whose funeral clothes bagged on him. We compared him with his wife, a short fat lady who sat a few feet from his casket, and decided that Albert's wife had precipitated his demise by refusing to share her food. For her part, Mrs. Schuss was pleased to see us: she seemed to think we were distant nephews.

When we returned to the proper chapel, I found myself caught in the dour gaze of Grandma's brother, my great-uncle Martin. Despite their humor and love of song, the Irish have a tendency to moroseness; indeed, they revel in it; some would say the pursuit of lugubriousness is a national mission no less important than the cause of Irish freedom, and there is in each Irish family one person who gives himself over fully to the development of this ancient and honored Celtic trait. Uncle Martin's long solitary life had given so fine an edge to his fatalism that his presence at a party was feared, like snow at Easter.

Not a cynic so much as a professional grumbler, he believed—so I had learned both from eavesdropping on my relatives and from Uncle Martin's unprompted ruminations— that the world had come steadily unraveled since the days of the ancient Greeks, that most of the miracles in the Bible were exaggerated or sanitized: for example, he believed that Moses had indeed parted the Red Sea but that the ensuing flood had killed not only Pharaoh's army, but also a good portion of the Israelites, in particular the aged, the slow, and the obese—and that the Earth would be hit at any moment by a comet.

Now he stared at me as though I had been found wanting, and when I met his gaze he jerked his head in the direction of the caskets.

"Not much of a wake, is it?"

"It's not?"

"Well, it's fine for the way they do them now." He gave me a sad look. "Ah, you're too young to know the difference. In my day, we had *wakes*. We knew how to give the deceased a fitting send-off, you see. That's the purpose, after all, to show the dead what you thought of them. My father's wake lasted four days. This was in the Old Country, of course, not here in the land of the Income Tax and the Board of Health. At least if we had a Board of Health, *I* never knew about it. We held our wakes in the home of the deceased."

I shot a quick look in the direction of the caskets and tried to picture them in Grandma's house. This seemed inexpressibly bizarre, and he read my expression.

"Oh, now, we didn't keep them there forever, lest they go a bit ripe on you, but we showed them their proper respect and after you got used to the fact that they didn't say anything, why, they were lovely company. And this provided the mourners with an opportunity to speak their feelings to 'em, you see. They'd relax with a bit of nice whiskey and work up the nerve to talk to them."

"To the dead people?"

"Well, who else? But here in America where we're supposed to be free but still wear the yoke of servitude, why it's against the law to hold the wake of your kin in his own house, and would you mind telling me where the sense of that is?"

I couldn't, of course, but he didn't really want to be interrupted. He went into the next stage of his soliloquy, growing wistful.

"It wasn't always this way. We had our freedom at one time. When I first came here, in 1911, there was no income tax. There's a godless idea, lad, taxing the workingman's wages. Then there was Prohibition." He snorted, then paused for the sake of drama and nodded to me. "Prohibition, that great evil that fell upon the land, and we all fought it, all the people, it was grand how we all rose up."

His face grew serious, he could have been speaking of the Easter Rising at the Dublin Post Office or of Charles Parnell, but I believe he was remembering the days when he and my grandfather had attempted to sell gin concocted in the family bathtub, and a thin, cloudy whiskey that Uncle Frank had devised in the garage behind his rooming house, Uncle Frank's commercial ambitions unfettered by the fact that he was a policeman. It was this ill-advised venture into the world of business that earned Uncle Martin the title of "The Old Reprobate" from my grandma, his sensible sister. He was "The Old Reprobate" and Uncle Frank, who seemed to bring disaster or violence wherever he went, was "The Great Ninny" to his sister.

"It would peel the skin off your arm," I'd heard Grandma say about Uncle Martin's bathtub product. "It would melt your eyeballs. People nearly died of it."

"Oh, they did not," Uncle Martin would say, and Grandma would just say "Billy Fahey" and nod confidently.

Uncle Martin would swallow and look away with a nervous light in his eye, and eventually say, "That was just a coincidence: he always had a bad gut."

Once or twice I'd heard them argue this way and she'd mutter about the repulsiveness of drinking something brewed in a common bathtub. When he said it was just fine, she'd say, "Do you drink your bathwater, then, Martin? What would our mother have said?"

This would end the debate: the mention of their mother, dead under the sod of County Leitrim more than thirty years, was enough to silence any argument, bring quiet and calm, and I'd heard how my grandmother once, when they were all young, had stopped a fierce brawl outside the drugstore up on Clybourn by this magical incantation. No one else ever brought her up: the use of their mother's name seemed a trump card available only to Grandma.

Uncle Tom rescued me from Martin with a wave. I went and stood beside him and watched him greet people, even people he didn't remember. Among these people was a wizened woman I'd never seen before who nodded to us and moved on into the funeral parlor.

"Oh, Christ," Tom said.

"Who is that lady?"

"Nobody knows, kid. She just shows up at funerals." And in truth, during the course of my life I was to see her at a dozen or more funerals, her presence always both amusing and vaguely reassuring to me, like a tired but beloved joke.

The high point, if there could be said to be one at a funeral, was the appearance of the McReady sisters, both of them, including Betty, who had long been rumored to be dying. She did not seem to me to be dying or even contemplating it: like her sister Mary, she was hugely rotund, talkative, loud, and aggressive. They were a year apart, yet so remarkably alike that they were often referred to in family circles as "the twins," though I once heard Uncle Mike refer to them as "the battle-wagons." The reference had confused me.

"Oh, here we go," Mike said.

Tom nodded and I heard him mutter, "Okay, this is just what we needed."

The McReady sisters marched together into the funeral parlor, followed at a respectable distance by Joe Collins, Mary's confused-looking husband—said by my uncles to be the stupidest person in the United States—and Uncle Mike muttered, "The fleet must be in, 'cause there's the *Iowa* and the *Missouri*," and I could see the resemblance to twin battleships, as they steamed through the mourners and forced a parting of the crowd. They wore matching, tentlike blue coats and twin pillbox hats—Mary's was adorned by a single dangling flower, while her sister's had none. In addition to their sizable presence, they brought noise to my parents' funeral, like a benign wind, and I saw amusement and anticipation on many of the faces around me.

My grandfather exchanged a quick happy look with my uncles, Grandma rolled her eyes (they were her second cousins), and the sisters fell upon the happy crowd, engulfing one and all in their massive embrace. They spoke at the same time and in loud barks, chattered and called to people across the parlor, and the wake grew festive in spite of itself.

When I least expected it, they turned to me and I heard Uncle Tom whisper, "No matter what they do, smile. And don't try to outrun 'em."

I did as I was told, though it was difficult. They both reminded me of the loud, mad Queen of Hearts in *Alice in Wonderland*. They squeezed me, savaged my hair, patted me on the head, picked me up, and, inevitably, kissed me, leaving my entire right cheek dripping and lipstick-covered. I shot a glance at my cousin Matt and his wide-eyed horror confirmed my worst fears of how it had looked. Aunt Mary gave me another squeeze and just when I thought my breastbone would cave in, she let me go. The sisters then went on up to the caskets, where there was a tense moment as they put a shoulder into one another for space on the kneeler, causing some to fear an outbreak of fisticuffs. Eventually they came to some amicable division of space and proceeded to sob quietly together. Joe Collins stood a respectful distance behind them and looked uneasy.

"Why does Aunt Mary's husband walk behind her all the time?" I asked Tom.

"He knows it's safer back there."

Toward the end of the evening I fell asleep in a chair and Tom took me home and put me to bed.

The following morning they took me to the funeral. At the funeral home the priest led us in prayers, and when they closed my mother's casket, Grandma Flynn gave in to her grief and sobbed so heartbreakingly I thought she'd die there. It was the deepest, truest expression of grief I'd yet seen in life, and I was horrified. People moved to comfort her but Aunt Anne, my shy, slender Aunt Anne, just shouldered her way to her mother and put a consoling arm around her. Uncle Tom and Uncle Mike stood on either side of me and took turns murmuring,

"It's all right. People cry at funerals," but for the rest of the day I wondered if my grandmother, too, was going to die. A few feet away, Grandma Dorsey stood red-eyed but quiet, flanked by my aunts Mollie and Ellen, and looking small and very old.

At some point they all found people to greet and I found myself standing apart from any of them. I looked around the big, crowded parlor of the funeral home and realized my Aunt Mollie was standing a few feet away, watching me.

She smiled but like most of the others she had been crying and her cheeks were still wet, and she had a tissue crushed into one hand. I didn't know what to say to her so I waved, and she came over and hugged me.

"It'll be all right, sweetheart. It just doesn't seem like it right now." She gazed from me to the casket where her favorite brother lay and just shook her head.

After the mass, I rode with my uncles to the cemetery and watched as they gave Grandma Dorsey the flag that had been draped over my father's casket in honor of his Navy service. When we were done there, we all returned to Grandma Flynn's house, and I experienced my first true Irish wake; that is to say, I attended a party. There was food enough to supply the Chinese army, and liquor, and my grandmother counted herself lucky to have a home after my cousins and I were finished with it.

But it was to survive this and many other traumas in its time, my grandmother's house, just as it had born the hurts of wind and weather, and a small fire that had given some wayward self-taught architect an excuse to tack on a questionable extension: a piece that seemed to butt itself into the rear of the big house as if the two had collided. No matter how one viewed it, my grandparents' house was a singular place, unlike anything else in the neighborhood, a great rambling, drafty, flaking mass of wood that had come together around the time of the Chicago Fire, a frame beehive of rooms and closets and corners, turrets and cupolas and porches, a house that time had passed by. But it sat boldly at the corner of Clybourn and Leavitt and gave itself airs beside a triangular lot owned by someone else, a patch of land given over to weeds and insects and the occasional mouse. My grandparents did not own it, but rented it from a former neighbor who had moved to Evanston.

Whatever its age and tortured provenance, it was the biggest house on the street. A recent repainting in bone white had left it a gleaming relic, and I thought it palatial. At times I played out on the wide porch and pretended it was a castle, and in my imagination, I named it the Castle of the Flynns, and it became a tribal stronghold replete with dungeons and moat and battlements. My grandfather once told me it was haunted, and on more than one summer night I peered into darkened rooms in hopes of espying a ghost.

And on the day of my parents' funeral, this Castle of the Flynns was assailed from all sides by the two families and their retinues.

My grandfather cranked his Victrola and played fiddle music and after a few shots tried to dance to it. Uncle Frank and Uncle Martin joined him, but my grandmother stopped them when Frank fell over a table and just missed sailing out the open window. A bit later an argument erupted between the McReady sisters, so that I thought they might wrestle, and my grandmother commissioned her brothers to intervene, which they did by dragging the massive ladies out onto the dining room floor for a primeval version of a fox trot. The four of them bumped and lurched around the dining room like continents colliding, and the rest of us, Dorseys and Flynns, perhaps from relief that we hadn't been asked to dance with them, formed a tight circle round them and clapped.

The rest of the evening was marked by loud talking, they all talked at the same time, and by their music, which they insisted on singing with, and by smoke, they smoked, all the men and half the women, Luckies and Chesterfields and Camels, unfiltered, of course, for a filter was something in a car engine.

By eleven o'clock the last of the guests had been bundled into cars or cabs and the house grew quiet at last. It was the latest I'd stayed up in years, and I fell asleep on my grandmother's living room sofa.

The Council

Two days later some of those guests reconvened at Grandma's house, for what could only be called a council, involving a dozen or so of my relatives—Grandma and Grandpa Flynn and their three surviving children, and about half of the Dorseys, including Grandma Dorsey, her bachelor son Gerald, her son James and his fiancée Gail, her daughters Ellen and Mollie, and of course Teresa, the nun.

The subject of the council was me, not that anyone said it in so many words, but they all gave me long looks when they clomped in from the wooden porch, as though getting a fresh fix on me, reminding themselves what I was all about. For the first time, I saw that I made them uncomfortable, and several of them looked away quickly when our eyes met. My excitement at seeing all these adults and being at my grandmother's house was soon dampened both by these uneasy glances and by the mordant atmosphere both sides brought to this table. The wake was over; this was life. I was a reminder, after all, of the deaths of two beloved young people, and it had already dawned on me that I was something of a burden, perhaps even a liability.

If I had any doubt what this meeting was to be about, it was soon dispelled when my grandma herded them all into the yellow-painted kitchen and told me to stay in the front of the house and play. She gave me a little wink and a bottle of Pepsi—a clear bribe, and the fact that it came without a glass meant it was an afterthought: she was nervous. I waited a respectable thirty seconds or so to give them a chance to get started and then crept into the dining room and crawled under the table, from where I could hear ninety percent of their conversation.

It was a tearful meeting, and once or twice I heard raised voices, always quickly hushed by Grandma Flynn barking out, "Hush up, will you? The boy'll hear you!" in a voice that could have been heard in the second balcony at Chicago Stadium.

Their talk wandered as they tried to avoid the inevitable, but ultimately Grandma grabbed them and pulled them back to earth. In the end it was decided that no single one of them could be expected to carry this new weight.

On the Dorsey side, Aunt Ellen had three of her own, and her husband, my Uncle Roy, was dead. Uncle Gerald was a confirmed bachelor, Mollie was still single, James was about to marry, and my Uncle Joe and his wife Loretta had their hands full—they had Bernie and his sister Dorothy, and David, a child with cerebral palsy, and I now learned that an orphan was considered a similar sort of burden, for I heard someone say, "They have trouble enough already."

When Matt's parents—my Uncle Dennis and Aunt Mary Jane—were mentioned, I heard my Grandma Flynn quickly say, "Oh, no, no, the poor things." Someone agreed that they were in "money trouble," but I had heard a different kind of trouble in my grandmother's voice, my first intimation that there was something about Matt's house that I knew nothing of.

In the end it was decided that they would all share the responsibility. I would live with the Flynns. On certain days of the week, my Grandma Dorsey would take care of me; on other days, I'd be in the care of Grandpa Flynn. On weekends, my Uncle Tom would help out, as would my Uncle Mike. The married ones expressed their determination to do what they could, to take me out to spend time with my cousins on occasion and give the others a break. I was to live, though, with

Grandma and Grandpa Flynn, which also meant with Uncles Tom and Mike and Aunt Anne.

There had been some talk of my moving in with Grandma Dorsey and, had the deal turned out differently, I might have had an entirely different life, for Grandma Dorsey was a quiet, passive woman worn down by decades of life with the late Grandpa Dorsey, a difficult man who had led his family through disasters beyond my ability to comprehend.

I had heard more than one remark proposing beatification for Grandma Dorsey by virtue of having survived life with Grandpa Dorsey, or, as Grandma Flynn put it, "for not putting an end to that one and tossing the body in the river." It was clear to me that, had Grandma Flynn been espoused to Grandpa Dorsey, it would have been a short, stormy marriage and would have ended badly for the husband.

That night, as I went to bed, I said a small prayer of thanks to God for making me so popular that my relatives felt they had to share me. Half a dozen of them were still out there in the yellow kitchen, relaxed now that a decision of sorts had been made and most of them had dodged this strange new bullet. They cracked open a couple of quarts of Sieben's beer and chatted. The talk turned to the two young ones they'd just buried, and once or twice I heard their voices break, but eventually my uncles took over with funny stories about my mother and father, and then it sounded like a party. I sat up on one elbow and listened to it all. Their voices were reassuring to me: I was literally surrounded by people who would take care of me.

It proved to be the only night in a period of almost five months that I felt reassured about anything. By the following night, when the council with its party atmosphere had already begun to blend into the blurred tangle of recent events, the new terror that I'd come to know at bedtime had returned. I cocooned myself in the covers, burrowed beneath the fat old pillow I'd inherited—it had been my mother's, Grandma told me—and wept. The night after my parents had died, I'd fought sleep for hours, convinced that if I closed my eyes I'd die during the night. Each night the fear returned, and though I gradually came to realize I wasn't going to pass away in my sleep, I became convinced that I lived an unprotected life, that I had lost a sort of mystical shield afforded to each child at the outset of life, and that the love of these grandparents, uncles, and aunts was a poor substitute for the genuine article.

During those first few weeks I spent a great deal of time in small dark places: closets, darkened rooms, under tables. I drew pictures of my parents, dozens of them, scores of them each week—pictures in pencil and pen and in crayon, pictures of my parents and me at the park, at the zoo, in the Wisconsin Dells, where we'd gone the summer my baby brother Johnny had died, at Riverview, at home eating dinner. I crawled under my grandmother's table and drew them obsessively, and one day when I came home from a walk with my grandfather, my Uncle Tom was looking at them with my grandmother. Her eyes were red and she was shaking her head. He looked at me curiously, and I realized he wasn't concerned with the implicit sadness in the drawings.

"You drew all these, Danny?"

I nodded.

"I didn't know you could draw. Can your friends draw like this?"

I shook my head. His reaction puzzled me: it was a well-known fact in school that no one drew as well, but no one ran as fast as Jimmy Kaszak, and Theodore Renzi could play the accordion. As an afterthought I mentioned that Michael Neely could draw airplanes but not people. He nodded.

"You draw what you feel like drawing, kiddo, but next time you draw something besides your...you know, besides people, let me see 'em."

"Sure," I said, and thought no more of it.

Sometime later, I saw a movie on television about explorers in some jungle place where there were still dinosaurs. These were particularly inept explorers, inasmuch as the dinosaurs stomped, chewed, or gored the majority of them, and I fell in love with dinosaurs on the spot. Aunt Anne took me to the crowded library that occupied one wing of the Hamlin Park fieldhouse and I took out all the books on dinosaurs, then spent the rest of that week drawing them. One evening I found my uncles passing my drawings back and forth and shaking their heads.

They noticed me simultaneously.

Uncle Mike frowned up at me. "You trace these, right, Danny?"

"No. We don't have any good tracing paper."

"Freehand he does 'em all," Tom said. "Freehand."

Uncle Mike's gaze went from the drawings to me again. "Seven years old and he draws better than I do." I didn't see his point: anyone drew better than Uncle Mike.

A scene from that time stands out. I was drawing at my grandmother's kitchen table and my Uncle Tom was sitting across from me nursing a cup of tea. He twirled the cup gently in the saucer as was his habit, occasionally glancing at my drawing, once or twice shaking his head as my picture took shape and color.

"You're good, kiddo. That must be fun," he said, and I remember looking up at him in surprise. He caught my look and just said, "Takes your mind off things, I bet."

I nodded but just to please him. For of course it took my mind off nothing, I could draw and pay almost no attention to the drawing or the process. I went back to my picture, secretly watching Tom as he sipped his cold tea and stared off into space, thinking about whatever it was he wished he could take his mind off.

The first weeks were awkward, filled with moments that frightened me, that made me wonder if the whole group of them together would be competent to do what my mother had done largely unaided. I needed haircuts, shoes, new summer clothes, in the fall I'd need school pants, shots for school, I'd outgrown my winter coat, and none of them seemed to have a clear idea where or when to provide these things—I once overheard my Uncle Tom and Grandma trying to figure out the best place to buy my clothes for the upcoming school year.

"I know she liked Wieboldt's better than Goldblatt's," my uncle said in a musing tone.

"But Goldblatt's has cheaper clothes for the little ones," Grandma pointed out. "I used to take her there, and we'd watch the old ladies in the babushkas fight over things in the bargain basement. She thought that was so funny." She sounded as though her voice was about to break, and he said "Ma" in a pleading tone, and then she was herself again. "But she wouldn't go to either of them for shoes, I know that. You can take him to Flagg Brothers, or Father and Son."

They had little conferences about everything, I caught them talking about my clothes, my playmates, about who would take me to the zoo or the movies or a ballgame, and the little talks always ended with one or the other of them making assurances that everything would be taken care of, that they'd do the best they could. But their efforts were not reassuring to me: they had no idea how my mother and I spent my summer days, they'd have no clue about my daily schedule when I came home from school, no notion that I went over to Jamie Orsini's house at least once a week, and that my mother and I went to the library at Hamlin Park on Wednesday afternoons, and at times it seemed that the loss of my parents had also robbed me of all the little things that had made up my life. I watched their awkward attempts to do what was needed and grew furious with them all.

One evening after dinner I hid in the farthest corner of my room and cried. My grandmother found me and wanted to know what was wrong, and I felt foolish explaining that on warm nights like this one my mother would take me for a walk and buy me a Popsicle from a little man with a pushcart.

Uncle Mike loomed in the doorway behind her, looking concerned and puzzled. "You want a Popsicle, pal? Is that all? Is that why he's crying?" he asked, and I hated him.

I don't know what I did or said, but my grandmother just shook her head.

"No, no, it's not the Popsicle. It's the…it's what he did, you know. It's the *walk* and the Popsicle." She got up and tried to brush wrinkles from a lap rich with them. "The walk and the Popsicle and his mother is what he misses. Well, I wouldn't mind a walk and a Popsicle. Come on, sweetheart," she said, holding out her hand. Tears were beginning to form at the edges of her eyes, but she blinked at them and cleared her throat, as though she was about to deliver one of her orations, but all she said, in a tired, preoccupied voice, was, "I like the banana ones."

One night I woke with a bloody nose, and before I'd cleared the sleep from my eyes there were all 'round me in a terrifying Tolstoyan death scene, a wall of my adults, Anne and Tom and Mike and my grandfather, all of them looking as though they were watching an execution.

"Oh, God," Aunt Anne said, as though she'd seen God.

"Bejesus," Grandpa said, "will you look at that."

"There's blood all over the bed," Michael pointed out, and my Uncle Tom was telling me to take it easy when I thought I already was taking it easy, and then my grandmother shouldered her way through the circle and took me by the hand.

"Whattya think, Ma? Does he need a doctor?" Uncle Tom asked.

"For the love of God, it's a bloody nose, not cancer. It's no more than all of you had, and more than once." Reassured and delighted by the attention, I grinned at all of them and thought my uncles might faint.

On another occasion, after a movie and ice cream with Uncle Tom, I began vomiting in his car. My mess was bright red and chunk-filled, and I wondered if I would die of it.

"Jesus Christ," Uncle Tom said, and gave a hard jerk on the steering wheel that sent me flying into the door of the car. He drove me directly to the emergency room of St. Joseph's Hospital, where I was born and where I would now, apparently, die, and carried me in with a wild-eyed look of panic that had me on the verge of tears.

A man sat on a chair, holding one injured hand in the other, and a worried-looking couple stood at a desk, waiting, I believe, to have a baby.

A harried nurse put a hand on my head, muttered, "No fever," sniffed at the mess on my shirt and gave my uncle a look that might have drawn blood.

"*Pop*," she said. "It's pop, and God-knows-what-else." She eyed me and said, "What else?"

"Popcorn and a Mounds bar and Raisinettes. And ice cream."

She gave Uncle Tom the evil eye again and said, "You're not his father, are you?"

It was a statement rather than a question, and Tom just shook his head, then said, "Uncle."

"Figures. I can tell you don't have kids yet, Charlie." She disappeared into a side room, emerged with a wet towel and cleaned me up. Then she told Uncle Tom, "Take him home, give him lukewarm water or apple juice or a little applesauce." Then she looked at me. "Next time this guy takes you to a movie, don't eat so much junk, you hear?"

I Discover Adult Supervision

My grandmother ruled the Castle of the Flynns, but of all of them, the person who was to become my care-taker, putting his unlikely mark on me during that uncertain first summer without parents was not my grandmother, who still worked five days a week, but my grandfather, forced by a bad heart to take an early retirement from the streetcars. I had little idea what "a bad heart" meant, though I noticed that he walked slowly and liked a nap in the afternoon, and it seemed these might be the manifestations of such a condition. Nor did I see significance or connection in his frequent coughing and the pack of Camels that never seemed far from his hand.

In hindsight I feel a special compassion for him: it was to him that the task fell of acclimating me to my new life. My grand-mother worked at a knitting mill on North Avenue "for that pirate, that buccaneer," as she called her employer—correctly predicting that he would one day take his mail in a cell. My uncles both had jobs, Aunt Anne worked as well and was little more than a teenager.

Thus it transpired that my initial babysitter/playmate/sur-rogate parent was my grandfather, Patrick Flynn. Not that he was new to my company: for a time my mother had worked and Grandpa Flynn had occasionally been my babysitter then as well. He was a tall, sad-faced man who asked little of life and whose quiet mien disguised his sense of humor. He walked with one hand in his slacks pocket at a stately pace, like Fred Astaire in slow motion. When he pulled a face or wanted to be comical, he could make himself look like Stan Laurel, and I told him so frequently. He was fifty-eight the year I moved into their home, though in the photographs he looks older.

It was from Grandpa Flynn that I learned about buses and streetcars, boxers and baseball players, of the age and breadth and complexity of the city beyond Clybourn Avenue. He was fond of Irish music, and sometimes on cool afternoons I sat beside him in the living room as he put his old hard plastic 78s on the black Victrola in the living room and gave the machine a few cranks. Frequently these were humorous records, most of them recording the continuing adventures of a man named Casey: "Casey at the Doctor," "Casey at the Dentist," etc.

At other times, he listened to music, music filled with fiddles and tin whistles and pipes, and if the mood hit him, he danced, though his dancing wouldn't have been obvious to an outside observer, for he shuffled his feet slowly, with no hope of keeping time with the music. He also grinned a great deal, which is actually how I knew he was dancing. When he was truly filled with the music, he would yank me to my feet and make me join him, going in slow motion through the steps till I had a vague idea what I was supposed to do. He taught me the jig, at least his abridged version, and something called a hornpipe, which he said was a sailor's dance.

He was also a natural storyteller, that is to say, a shameless liar. He related tales from his youth and embellished them till they shone like the Greek myths, narrated the unlikely adventures of his brothers-in-law Martin and Frank and made them seem like Abbot and Costello. He spoke of the Old Country and filled me with fascination and terror: fascination when he told me of half-human *selkies* and the "little people" who, he contended, lived no farther from his native village than I lived from Riverview; terror when he spoke of ghosts and banshees and undead entities that populated the moody landscapes and roamed the gray skies—Ireland seemed to hold more unearthly beings than people. He also spun outrageous tales of his own indigent boyhood, the tasks to which his hardworking parents had set him on their farm or, when he was having fun with me, "on the fishing boat out on the wide ocean, in all harsh weather," though a glance at the map would have told me Leitrim's water was primarily bogs and rivers, and the odd small lake.

He claimed that the Irish had less food than anyone on earth, less even than the Chinese for whom we prayed in school, and were reduced to eating little else but potatoes, though the English were said to have worse notions about what one could eat: he claimed they were fond of the white, mushy fat on bacon and that they ate it uncooked, with yellow mustard.

"Which," he would say, "explains a great deal about them, you see."

I see now that he was a simple man. Left to his own designs he would have passed his leisure listening to his records or roaming the city on streetcars to the very end of time, stopping for the occasional shot and beer in a cool, dark neighborhood tavern, and watching baseball or boxing on television—which he considered the great wonder of the age. Nuclear power did not impress him and he would have thought the computer the spawn of the devil, but television seemed to him the nation's gift to the man without means.

In our now-permanent association, we found we had things to learn about each other. There were times when he liked to listen to the news on the radio and did not want to be bothered. If I came babbling into the room at such moments, he would wave an impatient hand, always holding a cigarette, commanding me to be silent, and I would slink back to where I came from, my feelings bruised. He soon learned that when I was in the midst of one of my all-day drawings, filled with dinosaurs or knights in bloody battle, I was reluctant to join him on one of his long bus rides, and at first he took this personally.

We also had to learn how to communicate. Once in a while, when he didn't want to talk to certain callers, he would ask me to answer the noisy phone in the kitchen, and he wasn't very specific about what to say.

One morning when he was listening to his music and I was drawing at the dining room table, the phone rang. He looked up at the wall clock and said, "That's Gillis, that crazy fool. Eleven o'clock and he's drinking." Gillis was a loud drunk, as annoying an adult as I was to meet in my childhood, and my grandfather didn't much relish the thought of an afternoon in Gillis's company. So he had me answer the phone.

"What should I say, Grandpa?"

"Tell him anything. Just tell him I'm not here. And tell him I'm not going to be here—for the foreseeable future." He seemed pleased with this last part and laughed to himself.

I found this message puzzling and didn't for a moment think Mr. Gillis would accept it, especially from a boy not yet eight years old, so I manufactured a more logical reason for my Grandfather's inability to come to the phone.

I took a deep breath, swallowed, picked up the phone and said, "Hello."

It was Mr. Gillis, and he asked for Grandpa.

"He's dead."

"*What?*" the voice squawked into my ear.

"He's dead."

"But I just saw him yesterday."

"He died today."

"What did he die of, for God's sake?"

"Ammonia," I said with confidence, for I had heard of many people dying of ammonia, and my grandmother always warned me that this killer illness would take me if I didn't wear a hat on cold days.

Mr. Gillis was speechless, and I took the opportunity to say "Good-bye," and hang up on him. When I told Grandpa what I'd done, he was as speechless as Gillis, and then he began to tell me what an outlandish thing I'd done. When he recounted the moment to my grandmother and Uncle Tom that afternoon, he laughed himself breathless, laughed till he'd started one of his long coughing episodes. I couldn't have been more confused, but I enjoyed the boisterous moment after dinner when a delegation from Miska's tavern came over to pay their respects and make inquiries about my Grandpa's sudden passing.

Several weeks later I was left alone in the house on an afternoon when all the adults were working and Grandpa, who had been coughing more than normal, had to go in for mysterious medical tests. There was no one to watch me, and my grandparents gave me instructions in the most urgent tone that I was to let no one into the house, no one, "Not even the pope," my grandfather said, till one of my uncles came home. I took this injunction as I took all things verbal: literally.

I sat calmly in the silent house with the chain on the front and back doors, holding onto my instructions like a remnant of the True Cross, and drew a large, elaborate picture on my special drawing paper.

And when my Aunt Mollie Dorsey, pressed into service as a last-minute babysitter, knocked on the door, I refused to let her in. She certainly wasn't the pope, and my instructions were clear. She was a sweet-tempered young woman with an unusual sense of humor and a laugh to match, high and joyous, and when it became clear to her that she would not cross that threshold till an adult Flynn came home to let her in, she settled herself on the porch and we had a fine chat through the locked door.

Several times that afternoon I heard her burst out laughing though I could not have said what was so funny. I kept her there for two-and-a-half hours and had to spend the greater part of the next two days listening to both sides of my family giving one another different versions of the story. The consensus seemed to be that I was a good boy but bereft of plain sense, and one had to be careful what one said to me.

On the whole, though, the time I was to spend with Grandpa that first summer without my parents provided me with some reassurance: we did the same kinds of things we had always done together, nothing had changed, at least about these times. My days with him tended to the nomadic: as a retired streetcar conductor, he was entitled to a lifetime of free rides on any of Chicago's transportation systems, whether El train, streetcar, or bus, and he seemed to know every single driver or conductor we ever met—they all called him "Pat" or "Irish."

Sometimes we rode the troublesome trolley buses that ran hooked to a dark tangle of overhead wires: a trolley that came loose from its wire could snarl the traffic to all the points of the compass for a half hour. On our rides, we took a window seat near the driver. Some of them would let me have stacks of unused transfers and the transfer punch they used, and I'd sit and clip and punch away till I was covered in bus-transfer confetti, all the while listening to Grandpa and the old-timers joke and trade tales of the old days, of blizzards and great storms that shut down the city, and fights, and men with razors and guns.

We scoured the city: he took me down to Haymarket Square, where he knew a Greek who ran a produce company, and they fed me strawberries while they talked. Sometimes we went to visit his friend Herb, an embattled instructor at the Moler Barber College. This was a small institution on West Madison Street that took in young men of dubious dexterity, ostensibly to turn them into barbers. Sometimes Grandpa got a haircut or shave, and on rare occasions he let them cut my hair, though my grandmother would raise hell with what they did to my head. These were, after all, young men who merely *wanted* to be barbers.

My mother had still been alive the first time Grandpa had taken me to the barber college for a haircut, and the nervous young barber-in-training had shorn me too close on one side. I was amused by the bizarreness of it but my mother had shrieked when she saw me.

"Good God," she'd said. "What happened to his hair?"

"It's only a haircut," Grandpa said.

"It's all bare on one side. My God, Dad, what did they use, an axe?"

"They're just young fellas learning, and it only costs a dime there," he argued.

"Oh, honey, they butchered you," my mother said, looking at me ruefully. I was puzzled by her reaction: my religion books were peopled by monks with tonsure, and I fancied that I resembled the Norman knights in my book about England. I also wanted to tell her I'd gotten off easily: while I was there, another incipient barber had cut a man's ear with the straight razor and made him howl with the clippers.

Sometimes Grandpa took me to Hamlin Park and watched me play, sitting on a long bench painted a sickly green and chatting with men his age. At such times I believed the world was overrun with old men. When it rained, we settled for a visit to his friends at the firehouse on Barry, and they let me climb all over the pumper truck while they shot the breeze.

He was not perfect. In a family burdened by a love of drink, he was as troubled as any, and as the terrifying prospect of endless leisure opened its dark maw to him, he had developed a more urgent need to drink, even though such a course was bound to involve him in almost constant conflict with my grandmother, which contest he would necessarily, inevitably, lose.

He took me to taverns and bought me cokes with maraschino cherries in them, and little flat boxes of stick pretzels. When she came home from the knitting mill, my grandmother would ask me what we had done all day and I would announce that we spent the whole afternoon in a saloon, and she would upbraid my grandpa in a shrill voice.

"Jesus, Mary, and Joseph, in a *tavern*, Pat? You have to take the boy into a tavern? What on God's earth is on your mind, taking him into those filthy places?"

Her tone troubled me, as did her obvious anger with my beloved Grandpa, but what was most vexing was her sudden renunciation of taverns, since I knew the two of them went on occasion to a tavern on a Saturday evening and more than once I'd heard them come home singing.

One night he stayed out later than usual, and when he returned, his face was flushed and he was sporting a ridiculous-looking smile and a gash over one eye. He had fallen on the sidewalk. She took him into the bathroom to clean him up, assailing him all the while with her opinion of the low estate to which he had fallen. She called him names, questioned his sense, and generally laid down a barrage of verbal artillery that had my head spinning, and I wasn't even the object of the assault. When he'd been patched up, he made his way to the kitchen and sank onto his accustomed chair, where he lit up a Camel and stared out the window, drumming tar-stained fingers on the table as Grandma continued the evening's homily. Finally, he turned and squinted at her and caught her in mid-sentence with "Bejesus, woman, will you shut up!"

Of all the many avenues open to him, this was not his best. I would have pretended to collapse on the table, for example, or claimed stomach trouble and scurried back to the bathroom. But he told her to shut up. And she hit him with a pan. It was a large black cast-iron skillet she used for bacon and eggs and to create the little lake of rendered lard that was required before she could make chicken or pork chops. She took hold of it in both hands and whacked him on top of his head.

Amazingly, it made a loud "bong," as if this were a scene in a Popeye cartoon. He winced, rubbed his head, and puffed on the cigarette. She replaced the pan and left the room, red-faced and teary with anger. For the rest of the evening they said nothing to each other, but after they put me to bed, I was aware that they sat together in the living room watching a show with Julius La Rosa, one of their favorites.

She was vigilant about my budding morals and questioned me about the places where Grandpa took me. Often we went to visit what she called "his cronies" in the neighborhood: a blind man named George who fed me caramels that he kept in a bowl in front of him. I was fascinated by George, for Grandpa had once told me that George had lost his sight in the twenties when a hoodlum had tossed acid in his face. The attack had been a mistake, the acid meant for another man. We also visited a little round Italian man in the projects named Tony. He made his own wine, either in his tub or in the basement, and frequently sent a bottle of it home with us as a sop to Grandma. And we went to taverns.

He considered himself something of a sharpie but was no match for her. Once when I was perhaps six, after we'd spent a lovely afternoon in a cool, dark tavern, him watching the ballgame and me playing with the saloonkeeper's new litter of Dalmatian pups, he coached me on what to say to Grandma's interrogation.

"Don't tell her we went to a tavern."

"But we did."

"Oh, sure, but you can say we visited Gerry. We did see Gerry, didn't we?"

"Yes. He was in the tavern."

"There you have it."

And so, when she came home from the knitting mill, she asked me what we'd done and I announced that we'd visited Gerry. "Did you go to the tavern?" she asked, and when I said, "No," she quietly asked if I'd been able to play with the new Dalmatian puppies at the tavern, to which I answered,

"Yes, I got to play with them all afternoon." It was this and similar experiences which taught me that in this lifelong contest, he might hope to outlast her, but he was no match for her as a tactician.

At times, to avoid dragging me into godless places, my grandpa took to bringing home his liquor, usually pint or half-pint bottles of wine or bourbon. When finished, he would hide the bottles, and it was his choice of hiding place that sometimes made me doubt his sanity. An empty bottle might find itself under the cushion of the big red armchair in the living room, or under one of the sofa cushions, or behind a vase on a shelf in the dining room, and once he hid his spent bottle inside the body of the Victrola.

It is plain that on some level he intended her to find the bottles—"Dead soldiers," he called the empties—that they were his shiny glass emblems of defiance, a skull-and-crossbones trail to show he was still running his own life, when of course illness and boredom had taken it over. So she found his little bottles effortlessly, and each discovery produced a scene that might have been scripted.

"What is this?" she would say, holding the bottle by two fingers like a dead rat and staring at it as though she'd never seen one before.

"Oh, now what does it look like?" he would mutter, looking at the television.

"You've been drinking this poison again."

"No," he would say. "That's an old one."

"I reversed the cushion on this chair last week, and this filthy thing wasn't there then."

"Well, I don't remember when I drank it. I'm not even sure it's mine," he would say with a shrug.

"And whose is it, then? Mine?"

And my grandfather would turn to me and give me a long, slow squint, and this would set her off.

"Oh, for the love of God, you know very well it's not his," she would say, and march off to the kitchen, and then it was her turn to mutter, a couple of people who had learned to communicate both directly and indirectly after thirty years of unarmed conflict. "A moron I've chosen to live my life with," she would say, "an *amadan* I've got for a husband, without the sense to come in out of the rain, pouring poison down his throat and dragging a tiny boy along with him."

There would follow the sound of the bottle being tossed violently into the garbage can.

"A brainless idiot I'm joined to for life," she'd say loudly.

Still facing the television screen he would mutter something like, "A little drink never hurt anybody I know," and she would hear it, as she was intended to, the softness of his voice notwithstanding, and this would launch her like a missile into a short but violent burst of anger and general name-calling, a performance that would in Shakespeare's day have earned her the title of Village Scold.

And then she would be all right. A few minutes would pass, marked by the sounds and smells of Grandma putting dinner together, and after allowing her a short while to calm down, my grandfather would call out, "What's for dinner?"

"God knows you don't deserve one."

"Probably not, but I'd like to know anyway."

"Pork chops and boiled potatoes."

He would nod, pleased with the answer, and I would nod along with him. She was making good things, and that meant she wasn't holding a grudge.

Good things they were, always. She could cook anything and make it taste like food on a picnic, but it was not necessarily the menu a doctor would have put together. The salient characteristic of my grandmother's cooking was lard. "Shortening" she called it, but it was lard, lard from a can the size of a man's head, thick and white with the consistency of new-poured cement, and when it had melted into a pool an inch thick in the big black skillet, she would drop in the pork chops, or the chicken, or the hamburgers. If necessary, she cooked eggs in it, though she clearly felt that the ideal medium for the cooking of eggs was the grease from a half pound of bacon.

She wasn't trying to kill him: she was just a farm girl from the simplest part of the old country, where a breakfast or dinner that "stuck to your ribs" was more than a colorful expression. Once I saw her drop my grandfather's toast in the bacon grease. At first, I thought this was a mistake, but she left it there and when it was soaked through, she slapped it on his plate.

"A little grease makes your insides work," she once told me, thus giving me the notion that lard was the culinary equivalent of a good thick motor oil and suggesting to me that Grandpa was probably healthier than he looked. For his part, however, the old man frequently claimed that after one of her breakfasts he often lost the feeling in his lower legs.

A typical dinner was chicken or pork chops, potatoes, sometimes soup, a vegetable. And Jell-O. In the years we were together she served me Jell-O perhaps two thousand times, and it was always lemon: perhaps she found the color soothing, or had heard lemon Jell-O had magical properties, so that was what we had. With dinner they split a quart of Meister Bräu, and indulged in the fantasy that this small quantity of beer was my grandfather's "ration," ignoring the fact that he'd put away a half pint of Jim Beam earlier in the afternoon.

She made me drink milk, except on Saturdays when she gave me Pepsi-Cola. Fried pork chops, boiled potatoes, green beans, lemon Jell-O, Pepsi. To this day, if I'm served pork chops I expect it to be followed by lemon Jell-O, and I can't think of any of these things, can't taste them, without thinking of my grandmother.

Each morning when I awoke she was already up and dressed for work and tending to the needs of "the two simpleminded children that live in my poor house." She made us sandwiches for lunch, wrapping them in a thick waxed paper, and fixed "eggnog" for him in a tall glass. It appeared to be sugar and a raw egg in a glass of milk, and after it had set a while, the contents separated into layers. Grandpa would hold it up to the light and peer at it, then shake his head.

"Oh, look at that, would you? Something in there's moving."

Then he would stir it and drink half of it down at a swallow, gasping afterward.

"Is it like the eggnog we have at Christmas?" I asked him once.

"Good God, no." He stared at his eggnog and spoke in a stage whisper, "She tries to poison me." Then he pretended to have a brilliant idea. "Here, Danny-boy, do you want it?"

I told him I had cereal, and I did, multicolored balls of cereal that went soggy in milk and dyed it the colors of spumoni ice cream. In any case, I had no need for this glass of milk with disgusting elements of raw egg floating around in it. For his part, he seemed to find my little soggy bits of cereal repellent, and frequently I'd find him grimacing as I fished for the last shapeless bits swimming in the now-colored milk.

After she went to work, I'd play or read and he would smoke Camels at the kitchen table—a practice that seemed to be a male responsibility in most households: my uncles all did it and I remembered seeing my father sitting at our kitchen table smoking and staring out the window.

In the afternoons we went on our trips, and when we came back, he would settle in under the glow of a couple of snorts and take a short nap. As he slept, I would explore the house, unfettered by an adult hand. I went through my grandparents' drawers and studied old photographs, read old mail, explored the dark recesses of Uncle Tom's closet and the dresser where Uncle Mike kept magazines with pictures of girls without clothes. I understood that these magazines had something to do with sex and that I mustn't look at them, and so I rooted them out like a termite on old wood. I went through my uncles' pockets in search of scandal and found loose change, scraps of paper, work-related notes, receipts. I crept into the pantry and drank Log Cabin syrup straight from the little tin chimney atop the painted cabin, I spooned honey straight from the jar, I tried wine, which I found acridly repulsive, purloined hard candy from a hidden jar, stuck a greedy finger into the raspberry preserves and, finally, I sank my exploratory fangs into the wax fruit on grandma's living room table. It was, like most wax, tasteless, and I was surprised that anything so colorful as her wax peach could be so bland. I tried to smooth out the tooth marks and set the peach back in the bowl, then bit into the wax grapes, in case the peach had been set out as a decoy.

Eventually, she was to find the tooth marks, and it happened when I was in the next room, in the dining room, where I had covered the entire dinner table with my toy soldiers. From the corner of my eye I saw her bend over the glass bowl and freeze and I shot her a quick glance. She was holding the wax peach and staring at it open-mouthed. Then she glanced from it to me with the look that she'd probably have used if I'd told her I'd gone dancing naked down Clybourn. In the end, she replaced the peach, bite marks down, and said nothing. As she walked into the kitchen, she was shaking her head.

And on another lazy afternoon in my company, my grandfather set fire to the couch.

He had nodded off with a Camel between his tobacco-stained fingers and I was playing a few feet away on the living room floor with my soldiers. I had noticed the cigarette but was still convinced at that stage of life that adults normally knew what they were doing. A while later, I saw that his hand had dropped down and loosened its grip, and the cigarette was now directly on Grandma's sofa, her lovely flowered sofa, the prize of her living room, the cigarette coal in the center of one of the cushions. As I watched, the cigarette burned a small hole into the cushion, and then the hole grew a bright thin orange glow, and this tiny layer of fire began to eat at the sides of the hole till it was the size of a baseball.

I began to get nervous—not for my own safety, for I thought I could outrun the fire, but for Grandpa's: I feared that my grandmother would kill him. I remember the growing panic in my heart and then I went over to wake him: it took me several minutes and when I finally got him to open one eye, I pointed to what his wayward cigarette had done.

He bounced up like a cartoon character and stared at the burning circle for a moment, and then said, "Oh, Jesus Christ. I'm a dead man."

Then he began to beat at it with his hands. He could do that, beat out fire with his hands, because of something that had happened to him all those years of standing in the open doorway of a streetcar in the cold. He'd lost some of the feeling in his fingertips, and I'd seen him put out matches and unused cigarettes by casually squeezing match head or coal between thumb and forefinger. Now he beat at the offending flame and sent me for a glass of water, and I had to go twice because I spilled the first glass on my shirt.

When the fire was out, the room heavy with the acrid smell of wet, burnt cloth, we sat there on either side of the accusing hole. My grandfather coughed and made an irritated gesture of waving away smoke that I couldn't see. Grandpa didn't speak, he just kept sighing. Finally, we got up and he flipped the cushion so the hole was hidden. Then he looked at me.

"Don't tell your grandma, or we'll both be dead men."

"Why me?"

"Because you were here."

"But I don't smoke."

"It won't make a bit of difference. She'll say you were my accomplice. We're in this together. If she finds out, there'll be no corner of the earth where we'll be safe."

For weeks my grandfather attempted to hide the problem from her by the simple expedient of sitting on the sofa whenever she was home. He spent hours at a time in that one spot, as though he'd become melded to it. I tried to hold up my end of the bargain, planting myself on the sofa when he left it unguarded, but eventually she wore us down.

He was in the bathroom and I was on the wounded cushion, and she came in and announced that she needed to reverse the cushions. She asked me to get up and I feigned first deafness and then an ignorance of English, and she finally grabbed me and pulled me off the sofa. I made it as far as the door to my bedroom before I heard the sudden gasp that told me she'd found the hole.

For a moment it seemed that the power of speech had left her: she made a strangled squawking sound, like an aggrieved duck.

"Oh, what's he gone and done now? I'll brain him," she said between clenched teeth, and then touched the hole as though she could heal it with her fingers. She let the cushion drop, then turned slowly to look for one of us, and found me. Her voice had snared me in the doorway and paralyzed me like wasp sting, and I found myself uttering silent prayers to St. Joseph in his function as Patron Saint of a Happy Death. I wasn't holding out for a happy passing, just a quick one, and then she advanced across the room like Rommel's tanks. Her eyes, normally a soft brown, were red. No, they were glowing.

"You did that to my sofa?"

Without thinking, I blurted out, "I don't even smoke!"

And then she smiled. "ah," she said. That was all she said, but it was a lot. She said "ah" the way Hannibal probably said it when he caught the Romans at Cannae. She said "ah" and I said a prayer for the lost soul of my grandfather.

He came out of the bathroom humming, and when he saw the hot coals in Grandma's eyes the song died young in his throat. He looked from her to me, understood what had happened, wet his lips, and prayed for sudden eloquence or the timely intervention of the Deity.

Their conversation, if anything so one-sided can be called that, is a blur to me, though his mistakes were apparent even to a seven-year-old—the first was the old "What sofa?" routine, the second, his attempt to look puzzled, which instead made him look very stupid and seemed to vex her all the more. She rained invective on him, mixing insults with expressions of disbelief and frequently invoking Jesus or Mary or the other saints, including St. Jude, whom she addressed as the Patron of Lost Causes since she was "certainly married to one."

Much of this oration was English though there were a few words in Gaelic, and when she was done, he was pale and I could have sworn he was shorter. She left the room and went into the kitchen to bang pots and pans together, and he sank onto the armchair, pulled out his smokes, thought better of it, and jammed them back into his pocket.

I asked him if he was all right. He looked at me with his mournful Stan Laurel eyes and shook his head. "My life is over."

She refused to eat with us that night, waiting till we were done before entering the kitchen. The next morning, she made and wrapped our sandwiches for lunch and fixed his eggnog and said nothing till she was leaving. At the door, she gave him a long look and said, "Burn a piece of my furniture today, Patrick Flynn, and we'll need the priest."

My grandfather just nodded and looked like a man who's received the governor's pardon. For several weeks after that, she found no empty liquor bottles in the dark recesses of her home, and he kept his visits to the tavern down to the minimum necessary to sustain life.

More than once I heard them arguing over his cough, his smoking, and there was a different tone to these fights. My grandmother seldom raised her voice in these discussions, my grandfather sounded frustrated rather than irritated, and they kept their voices low, as though these times were somehow private.

Gradually I came to understand that my grandfather's afternoon naps, especially those after a couple of drinks, provided me with an almost perfect freedom: nothing woke him at these times, and it was a short jump from my rummaging through the drawers and cupboards of the house to the realization that I might do more. Shortly after the incident with the couch, I went out alone. I slipped out the back, left the screen door resting against a shoe, and went out into the alley that ran behind the house.

It was a narrow filthy place of cracked pavement with wide holes that collected a brownish oily water after a hard rain and bred mosquitoes. Garbage spilled out of small metal cans and fed mice and, on more interesting occasions, rats. We were just a few blocks from the river, and the neighborhood drew them, and on that first foray on my own, I found a dead one. I poked at it with a stick, gingerly as if it might revive itself. The body was already stiff, and something made me plunge the stick into it.

From the alley I made my way through the neighborhood, pausing at the small playground across from my house, delighted that I alone was unaccompanied by an adult. When I noticed a woman on a bench frowning my way, I left.

I was probably gone no more than twenty minutes, but I felt I'd been adventurous, I'd done something on my own, I had a secret. And when I returned to find Grandpa still sleeping, I experienced a sudden feeling of excitement, as though I'd won a victory over him.

I did little on these excursions but wander the neighborhood, and I returned each time filled with the sense of my own cleverness. Most times I stayed where I was supposed to be, but on certain afternoons I seemed to need the adventure and its attendant risks and rewards.

Most of all, I delighted in this secret that I kept from all of my family.

One evening my grandmother returned from the drugstore and fixed me with an odd look. She said nothing to me but later I heard her whispering in the kitchen to my Aunt Anne, and when I went to bed that night, she told me I must always make certain someone knew where I was.

Another Tribe
Altogether

My father's clan, the Dorseys, were a tougher sort of people than my mother's, having survived not only a greater degree of poverty, but life with Grandpa Dorsey. Though I knew they were my family, I thought of them as Matt's people, and the Flynns as mine. They lived, the better part of them, clustered around Old Town, a neighborhood already aging at the time of the Great Fire. The Dorseys had been there since the turn of the century, when a teenage John Dorsey, my grandfather, had first come up from Peoria to make his mark in the big town, working first as a laborer.

He met and married my grandmother around 1909 or 1910, when both were in their early twenties; they settled somewhere around Division and Sedgwick, married and raised a brood straight out of a Victorian novel, eleven children in all. At one time, all of them were shoehorned into a basement flat on Goethe. Two of her children had died young; a daughter had been born severely retarded and was in a sanitarium, and no one spoke of her.

There was more than twenty years difference in age between the oldest child living, a daughter named Ellen, and the youngest, my Aunt Mollie (Grandma Dorsey had given birth to her at the age of forty-three, and people spoke of Grandma as though she were fecundity personified).

Grandpa Dorsey's death at sixty-six from a heart attack had

come as a surprise to no one. If anything, people were awed that his perennial abuse of his body and occasional consorting with people of a dark, hard type hadn't put end marks to him long before this. He was said to have been quick-tempered, ambitious, smart, flighty, a dreamer; tireless, cocky, irrepressible, a Good-Time Charlie trying to hit one of life's trifectas.

All my life I was to hear tales of him. He'd had his own construction business at twenty-two, a fleet of three dozen cabs on the eve of the Depression, he owned a pair of buildings on Wells Street—all of this gone like dandelion fluff within two years of the crash. He got up onto his feet almost immediately, there was apparently no job he wouldn't take to make a few nickels: his later résumé would have read like a litany of all the day-labor jobs available in the country.

I don't know what kind of money it would have taken in the Depression to raise a house of nine children, but whatever it was, Grandpa Dorsey didn't have it, he was never able to climb back to where he'd been. They moved almost every year between 1932 and 1941, frequently to avoid an eviction. On one occasion he coldcocked the sheriff's man coming with the papers, just to buy them time to drag their belongings up the alley to another place.

I once listened to Uncle Gerald reminiscing about the whole bunch of them, spread out in a long line from their old flat to the newest one, usually no more than a block away, moving from Scott to Schiller, Schiller to Goethe, Goethe to Evergreen, Evergreen to Wells, damp basements to drafty storefronts to attics turned overnight into housing by a couple of men with saws and hammers; a procession of Dorseys, the eldest carrying boxes, bags, and cheap furniture and the youngest pulling toy wagons filled with the family's possessions.

They were perennially poor, their home always crowded; their luck seldom held for more than a year, their lives made complicated by the mercurial nature of the person at the head of the household. I remembered him vaguely as a man with an energetic manner who spoke to me as though he had seen so many like me that he didn't have much time to be impressed—which, in fairness, was true: he'd seen enough of his own. What I remember most about Grandpa Dorsey was his eyes: they were unusually bright, almost feverish, as if he couldn't wait to get on with his next adventure in life. Many things about him fascinated me, not least of which was the fact that he was the sole adult who took no particular interest in me. He died about the same time my brother did.

My Grandma Flynn found it hard to speak of Grandpa Dorsey without a little snarl of contempt creeping into her voice, and my uncles spoke of him in terms that mixed wonder with disapproval. No one could explain clearly to me where his fortune had all gone, but gone it was. I once heard Tom and Mike talking about him in that low murmur adults resort to when they're being secretive but too lazy to whisper, and it seemed to me that they were hinting that gambling was at the bottom of some of it, and what he hadn't lost on the ponies and the fights he'd lost to the Depression. I did not yet fully understand the Depression, nor do many people, in my estimation. As nearly as I could understand, the Depression was for some the equivalent of a hurricane that blows up along the coast and knocks people's lives and fortunes into the drink. My grandfather had apparently been a victim of this sort of bad luck, and had compounded the tragedy by creating more of his own.

I have wondered about him often through the years, not because of any closeness between us—there was none to speak of—but because of the mark he left on my hard-luck Aunt Mary Jane, and through her to my cousin Matt. I'd heard them say that Mary Jane had "a heart of gold and not as much sense as God gave sheep"—Grandma Flynn's words. Grandma also once said that Matt was "his grandfather come back to try life one more time," and the note in her voice said that this was something that boded well for no one.

But once or twice a week I stayed with Grandma Dorsey. I loved my visits there—she expected even less of me than the other side of the family did, and since she wasn't working in a knitting mill she had time for other things: that is to say, she baked. She was a short, rotund woman, much older than the grandparents I lived with, who had at some early, difficult time in her life with John Dorsey decided to take a sunny view of the world. That world had done its best to shake her loose of this notion, but she persisted in her humble happiness. She delighted in a house crowded with people, and she loved to cook. She baked constantly and in large amounts and very well. She hummed when she baked, snacked on the dough, tossed odd scraps of it and failed cookies to her dog, a great unwashed collie named "King," and filled her kitchen with smells that I don't expect to encounter again till the afterlife.

At this time she was already in her late sixties—it was hinted that she'd even lied about her age to Grandpa—and the rearing of her small army of children plus her adventures with Grandpa had worn her down, so that her idea of childcare was what a modern educator might have called "unstructured." In short, she didn't really know what to do with me, and often didn't know where I was. Her most common recourse was to provide me with surplus kitchen utensils and send me outside to dig for treasure. The flat was the ground floor of a red-brick building on Evergreen right next to the El tracks: her "yard" was the dank muddy expanse beneath the steel skeleton of the tracks. It was frequently muddy, and it was into this material that I dug and tunneled, frequently producing great mounds of black dirt that I later turned into forts and buildings that she marveled at.

Her apartment bore the scar tissue of a long, crowded life, and to an inquisitive child, it was a place of delight, a packrat's nest. I'd once heard my father tell my mother that Grandma Dorsey hadn't thrown away anything since the turn of the century, and this seemed a bald statement of fact: her flat was a jumble of furniture and knickknacks and improbable objects that either she or my late grandfather had found reason to keep, including toys, magazines, jars, boxes, bottles, tin cans, and for some unfathomable reason, bottle caps. She also seemed to have coasters from every saloon her husband had ever frequented, and I played with these in great stacks.

It also smelled. Like most children, I did not mind the world's smells, not yet having developed the finicky notions of the adult world, so that today when I encounter those smells, the odors of damp, rotting plaster, ancient wood, primeval wallpaper, dirty rugs, I am nostalgic. These were the smells of a happy place, a place further associated in my mind with her baking, with the odd old toys she was always dragging out of a closet for me, with the generally hedonistic experience of being a seven-year-old boy unutterably spoiled by his grandmother.

I would play on the floor of her small musty living room or crowd her kitchen table with homemade lead soldiers that had belonged to my father and his brothers before him, and from time to time she'd steal a glance at me over her shoulder as she baked or cooked—often she'd make soup or stew or spaghetti sauce enough to feed half a dozen people, with the understanding, no, the *hope* that one or more of her brood would drop by.

A docile, patient woman who hummed more than she spoke—Grandma Flynn said this was the result of a lifetime of speaking to a wayward husband till she was breathless—Grandma Dorsey seldom had much to say to me beyond questions about what I needed and whether I was hungry. I learned early on that the answer to this latter question was always "yes" and it brought swift rewards unknown in the house where I lived. Later, one or another of my uncles or aunts on that Dorsey side might stop by to chat or see how she was, and she'd feed them, and on some nights there were three or four unexpected but perfectly welcome visitors in her kitchen, all of her issue. They were happy to see me, they thought I was just what she needed during the day to keep from going soft mentally, and they liked me, every one of them, but they had grown up in a crowd and most of them were in the process of creating their own, and I was not the center of the universe that I was in the Flynn house.

Late that summer I began to see my cousin Matt at Grandma's house on a regular basis. Aunt Mary Jane had gotten a job downtown at the Fair store, and so he spent most of his days in the care of Grandma Dorsey. Some weeks I was there more than once, and so Matt and I came to count on seeing one another.

He was a handsome boy, blond and hazel-eyed and wild and cheerful, physically gifted where I was clumsy, confident where I was shy. He was adventurous and restless and I thought he was a sort of paradigm of boyhood. With his rough self-assurance, he seemed somehow older to me, so that I had found not only a perfect companion but an older brother. I wished I had his looks, his laugh, his voice, I became irritated with the clothes my late mother had burdened me with, for they weren't like Matt's. I wore saddle shoes to church and he had red gym shoes; he wore blue jeans—the first time I asked Grandma Flynn for blue jeans she said I'd wear them "over your grandmother's lifeless corpse." For his part, Matt thought I was funny: he was not verbally gifted, had trouble expressing himself at times, and had no memory for jokes. And if ever I was to meet a boy who needed to laugh, it was Matthew.

I fed him jokes and one-liners I'd heard from Milton Berle or Sid Caesar on television and had him gasping for breath. I wished we were brothers, and once told another boy that we were.

It was critical that he liked me: he was everything I wanted to be, and more than anything else, he had what I had already lost. He could pepper his conversation with indifferent mentions of his father and casual references to his mother. He had parents whom he saw every day, who took care of him and bought him things, and I didn't quite believe that what I had measured up. I lived with old people, and no matter how I admired him, Uncle Tom was not my father, and I was already aware of their collective difficulty in anticipating the needs of a small boy. Once Matt made a reference to his mother and father fighting: he sounded angry with both of them, he spoke as though he hated his home, and I wondered what there could be about a home with a mother and father that would make a boy sound that way.

Under Grandma Dorsey's attitude of optimistic permissiveness, my days with Matt were an unending adventure. She had a groundless belief in our basic common sense and judgment. Also since there were two of us, she felt we were safe, and so we were allowed to explore "the block"—which we took as license to roam the entire North Side.

We spent whole days in Lincoln Park, roaming the great sprawling park from north to south, from the prehistoric ridge of Clark Street to the lake itself. The park was a wilder, darker place then, with more trees and heavy clumps of dense bushes and undergrowth, and an enterprising child could find a thousand places to hide.

Statues made their home in the park, it teemed with them, and we sought them out, puzzled over their names and then just clambered over them, LaSalle and Shakespeare and Linnaeus, Hans Christian Andersen and the great seated Lincoln behind the Historical Society. We threw stones at the ducks in the lagoon, tried to spook the zoo animals or their attendants, and once made off with the bucket of fish that were about to be fed to the penguins, then stood at the side of the lagoon and threw fish chunks at the young couples in the slow-moving rowboats. We crouched in the little underpasses and listened to the strange echoing sounds of our voices, climbed the high hill at the edge of the lagoon to visit the statue of General Grant; we hid in the underbrush to spy on lovers, tried to push each other into the lagoon, rolled in the grass.

Children are fascinated with the dead, and so we always sought out the graves. The land for Lincoln Park had been reclaimed from cemeteries, the old City Cemetery and several others, and when these graveyards had been relocated in the nineteenth century in an attempt to put an end to malaria epidemics, a few of the unfortunate—or lucky, depending on one's view of a corpse's inalienable rights—deceased had been left behind. The city admits, now as then, only to three, though the park doubtlessly rests on the bones of hundreds of early Chicagoans of all races, particularly the poor.

Foremost of these Abandoned Dead were the Couch brothers, Ira and James, resting for all time in the lone tomb left after this crepuscular relocation, a gray mausoleum just north of the Historical Society.

We would creep up to the tomb—you could get at it then, touch it, climb on it, leave your initials, anything short of entering it to visit Ira and James, and it was always a high point of our park excursions. We worked feverishly to figure out a way to get inside but failed, though Matt was certain we'd eventually crack it. "When we get older, we'll be smarter," went his reasoning.

The other dead man was said to be buried closer to Clark Street and now enjoys quiet celebrity due to a plaque indicating his presence in the nether regions just below the horseshoe pits: this second dead man was David Kennison, the last known survivor of the Boston Tea Party, who had lived more than fifty years after that momentous piece of public lawlessness to end his days in the swamp town at the junction of the Chicago River and Lake Michigan.

On occasion we entered the Historical Society itself and viewed with awe the reassembled cabin where Abraham Lincoln had spent part of his childhood, and the items taken from his pockets the night of his death. I was fascinated by these things and developed the belief, shared only with Matt, that if Lincoln's former home and cherished belongings lived in this old building, then the spirit of Abe himself couldn't be far away.

From the park we would go to the big red-brick mansion where the cardinal lived and where, my cousin assured me, the pope stayed when he was in Chicago on vacation; we prowled shops and gangways in Old Town and ventured west across Orleans into the projects. I found these little treks with Matt almost as interesting as my Wednesdays with Uncle Tom, especially as there was an element of danger present in his company: Matt seemed to delight in antagonizing other boys, he could spot a group of kids on a street corner—white kids or black, it made no difference to him—and say something in five seconds that would have all of them chasing us with blood in their eyes.

Once or twice they caught us, these unsuspecting boys, some of them several years older than we, and then Matt stunned us all by popping one of them in the mouth and taking off before anyone could react. He was quick and devious, and I never saw a sign of fear, though once a taller boy was getting the better of him and Matt, sobbing through gritted teeth, went so crazy, punching and clawing and kicking, that the older boy let him go and took off running. I was to see Matt fight a number of times as we got older, and to see his anger often, though rarely directed at me.

Most of the time, though, we just explored that part of the city, from Old Town to the outer edge of the Loop, from the projects to the lake. Soon we took on followers, three or four of the kids from Grandma Dorsey's block. They liked me well enough but were drawn to Matt: when he wasn't bent on provoking fights with large groups of strangers, he was actually a good companion. Every group needs a child who looks beyond the normal activities and routines, who sees in odd things possibilities for recreation, if not criminal malfeasance, and Matt served in that capacity for us. He was not only adventurous but imaginative, and his peculiar obsession was with gates and bars and barriers, which he read as the adult world's personal challenges to children, sufficient to generate an immediate and urgent need for transgression.

We scoured the city, climbed roofs and roamed cobblestone alleys—most of the old alleys in those days and a good number of the sidestreets in Chicago were still surfaced with smooth red bricks that were picturesque but hell on car tires. We investigated porches and basements, jumped fences, and even broke into the odd building.

Once we came upon a tall, weathered frame building that looked very much like a farm building, a relic perhaps of the days when that section of the city had been unreclaimed prairie. It had the big double doors of a barn and leaned to one side, as though gravity were about to tip it over. Matt took one look at it and decided it was a national treasure.

"It's a hundred years old."

"How do you know?"

"I can tell. The wood's all gray, and they don't build buildings like this no more. Let's go in."

"We'll get in trouble," I said.

He looked at me as though I'd drooled on my chest.

"No, we won't. The guy who owned this is dead, or he would have painted it."

This seemed airtight logic to me, and I told him I was in.

The building sat on a corner lot, surrounded on both sides by what we always called "prairies"—unused vacant lots given over to weeds and prairie flowers sometimes four or five feet high, and thick as the bristles on a brush. Rabbits and mice lived in these places, and small snakes, you could lose or hide things in them, and Matt contended that a dead man had been found in one near his house but no one believed him.

Grandma Dorsey had begun giving me my father's old Hardy Boy mysteries, and I realized that I was poised at the onset of exactly the type of adventure that Frank and Joe Hardy seemed to have every week. Thus the locked doors of the old barn gave me no pause: the Hardy Boys were forever breaking and entering in the name of adventure. Besides, to this day I have no idea where we were but it was a strange neighborhood, and a crowd of small boys far from their homes quickly lose what little moral restraint they have acquired. We bought Matt's line of reasoning without hesitation. Rooting around in the high grass like a scavenger tribe, we found a rotten log and, using this as a battering ram, Matt and I and a boy named Terry Logan pounded at the ancient planking near the back of the building until it caved in with a dry crack. We pulled the shattered plank away and without hesitation crawled in.

A billion specks of dust hung suspended in the bar of gold light from the hole we'd just made, and the rest was darkness. We were vaguely aware of a large dark shape in the center a few feet away but it wasn't till our eyes had adjusted to the darkness that we realized it was a car. It was unlike any car I was familiar with, tall and boxy and odd, and I realize now that it was probably one of the old ungainly cars from the 1920s. More important to us than its strange silhouette were the thick cobwebs that hung from it and dangled from what few corners of the old barn we could see. Matt drew a finger through the dust along the door of the car, then looked up and squinted into the dark.

"There's something up there," he said, and my heart sank but I followed him to the back, where we found a brittle wooden staircase that moved from side to side as the three of us climbed up. "Up" led to a loft that seemed to run along all four sides of the building. It was narrow and crowded with boxes and long or bulky objects that we could not see but which made each step an adventure. At one point Terry Logan almost fell out of the loft, and afterwards I could hear his fevered, terrified breathing.

"Ain't this a ball?" Matt asked at one point, and I almost laughed aloud at Terry's unconvincing, "Sure is."

"Prob'ly spiders up here," Matt said with undisguised joy.

At the front we found a sort of window, matted with fifty years of dust and filth, which Matt kicked in after only a second's moral debate, our earlier assault on the wall having made him a hardened second-story man. Sunlight, blinding sunlight, shot through the hole. Now that we could see around us, the barn lost none of its mystique: we could see old farm tools, ploughs and scythes and a pile of old wood-handled drills, and Matt thought he'd died and gone to heaven.

"This place is great, this is unbelievable. These are from Civil War times I bet."

"Maybe older," I suggested, and we had a brief three-way debate on whether there had been a Chicago before the Civil War, with the others insisting that there hadn't been, and me holding to a position that Chicago was even older than New York.

Our discussion was interrupted by the sound of a car pulling up very close by. We scampered down the staircase, and I was struck by a wave of terror that did not abate even when I tumbled the last three steps and landed on my back with Terry Logan on top of me. Matt was already out the hole. When we emerged into what seemed to be a sun that had moved closer in our absence, we saw a man staring at us. I have since seen shock on many faces, but never, before or since, have I seen shock so perfect, so total, as this man watched three small boys issue from his property through a hole of their own making. His mouth was open and his eyes unnaturally wide, and when he finally spoke, his voice was just a whisper.

"You little bastards!" he said, and then I heard Matt giggle and knew our adventure was entering a new phase. Matt headed through the prairie, instinctively seeking an equalizer for the man's long legs and finding one in the thick weeds.

Terry and I followed with our hearts battering through our chests. I was by turns horrified that my life was about to end in a foreign place where no one knew me, and delighted that we were having an adventure which involved a potentially violent adult who rained profanity on us with a vigor I'd never before experienced. This man had none of the imagination I'd noted among my uncles and some others, but the vehemence with which he cursed us was admirable and made one overlook his lack of a vocabulary.

As I ran through weeds head-high, I could hear the man behind us, panting and still cursing, and I realized I was laughing, and so was Matt. Then I fell. I caught my foot in the tangled stems of the weeds and went down, certain that my life had come to a sorry end. For a while I lay there, holding my breath and peering up at the blue sky with one eye, expecting the tall weeds to part at any moment and reveal the drooling, maniacal face of the cursing man, who would then kill me. He tramped heavily through the grass, gasping now, and then I heard a heavy thud and a groan.

For just a frozen moment in time I lay there wondering if this was the first manifestation in my young life of that most widely debated of creatures, the Guardian Angel. Had my personal angel grabbed the Cursing Man by an ankle, or given him a hard push to send him face-first into the weeds, or just created a sudden and short-lived hole for the Cursing Man to step into? For a second I worried that My Angel had struck the man dead, but even in my nascent and often bizarre theology there was little place for the concept of Guardian-Angel-as-Personal-Assassin. Whatever had happened, I was grateful and eventually remembered that the continuation of my life depended on my escape. I bounded to my feet and took off.

Matt and Terry were waiting for me at the mouth of an alley a block away; Terry was saucer-eyed with fright and Matt had gone pale under his constant sunburn, not because he'd been afraid of being caught himself but because he'd envisioned going home to tell my grandmother he'd gotten me killed or sent to prison.

"Hi, you guys," I said in my breeziest manner.

"Did he get you?" Terry asked.

"Nah. I got by him without him seeing me. I fell though," I added, feeling that I had to account for my tardy arrival. Matt gave me a look that mixed relief and disapproval, and we all made for home at a brisk trot.

Later that day I tried in a circuitous way to find out whether Matt believed in angels. It was a mistake. He stared at me for a moment with a look halfway between skepticism and irritation.

Then he said simply, "There's no angels. I don't believe in none of that. That's make-believe." Something in his face and tone told me that his angel had had more than one opportunity to show up, and hadn't.

Riverview

Looking back at the summer of 1954, my first summer with my grandparents, I can see all the stages but I am unable to make out the seams, as one time blends into another, but I'm certain that within a month of trial and error they'd managed to resurrect as much of my old routine as could be expected.

In the afternoons I played with a boy up Clybourn named Ricky or my schoolmate Jamie Orsini. My days were full, each one reflecting the determination of the adults around me to make up for what they saw as a great yawning hole in my life, and I have little recollection of afternoons spent moping or mourning.

I seemed to have inherited many more layers of supervision than I thought necessary, and that unlike my late mother, who was willing on occasion to let me walk up the street to a playmate's house, my grandparents tended to believe I'd been abducted if I was gone for more than two hours. I sometimes overheard them fretting over the gloriously rudderless Tuesdays I spent at Grandma Dorsey's in Matt's company. As I was to learn later, they feared Matt's influence on me, and they spoke often of Grandma Dorsey's "frailty," though in truth she was solid as an anvil, just not particularly adept at the supervision of small boys.

My nights were another matter: once they were all asleep, all shut up in their little cells in the hive, I lay in bed and told myself I was a lost boy, a child without family. I reminded myself that they all slept in rooms where they'd slept for years, that I alone was a newcomer, and I felt alien and unguarded. I listened to the sounds in my grandparents' house, sounds probably not much different from the sleeping sounds and night noises of my late parents' home, the sounds of creaking wood and loose windowpanes, a cat mousing under the porch, and transformed these simple night noises into ghosts and bats, and danger on two legs. The street sounds were no better, the wind roared and the high calls of the nighthawks unnerved me, and cats fighting sounded like babies left out in an alley.

Sometimes I caught snatches of conversation from people walking home from Riverview or a night in a Belmont Avenue tavern: in the isolation of my dark little room their voices seemed louder than they probably were, harsher, even threatening, they were coming up the stairs for me and I'd have no time to wake someone. For the first couple of months with my grandparents, I stayed awake so long at night I was able to convince myself that I never really slept. Once I made the mistake of sharing this remarkable fact with my grandfather, who simply raised his eyebrows and said I seemed to be sleeping when he came in to check on me each night.

A new fear came to me, for having been visited early on by death, I had come to be obsessed with it. These dark moments in the middle of the night soon accommodated a new worry, that my new family would all die as those before them had.

The first time this thought struck me, I fought it down, but it returned on other nights and soon took on a knotty logic. I had more than once entertained the notion that the loss of my parents was in some way a punishment. At first I could not have said what I was being punished for, though I believe such notions are common to children who suffer a sudden tragedy. I was in some way a bad boy who had been found out and punished. This early feeling of guilt subsided in the face of my more practical concerns and worries about my new life, but now, in the middle of these solitary nights, it found me once more and terrified me. It seemed clear and logical that my family, grandparents, uncles, and aunt, would all perish as my punishment for the many bad things I had done. And where my previous notion had simply been that I was "bad" in some nebulous way, I now saw myself as a child turning to evil. I saw a boy who crept about the house and went where he was told not to go, opened drawers belonging to adults, sampled what he liked in the pantry, and even stole out of the house on his own. I saw a boy who had joined in with his wild cousin to do things for which swift punishment was merited, a boy who broke into barns and climbed roofs, and I saw worst of all a boy who had begun to feel and then to demonstrate in strange ways his anger at his relatives. Such a boy, it seemed to me in the middle of the night, such a boy could expect a terrible punishment. On more than one of these occasions I cried and prayed to God not to take any of them unless He planned to take me as well. In the mornings I vowed to change, but my plans for the defeat of evil were always thwarted by stronger impulses. Gradually the fears and feelings of guilt left me for a time and I thought I was through with them. In reality, they were simply growing tentacles and horns.

In the evenings we often went out as a group, whoever happened to be home, setting in place patterns that would last for summers to come. We went to Hamlin Park and had ice cream bars and Popsicles or to church carnivals, or best of all, to Riverview. To Riverview, the ancient amusement park that sprawled along the river in the heart of the old neighborhood like a walled country of smoke and noise and seemed to be telling me, "Here anything can happen, and it probably will." It was unlike anything I was ever to see again, part amusement park, part dance hall, part circus, acres upon acres of wooden hills and towers that always seemed too frail to support the metal cars, trains, and rockets they carried, let alone the raucous crowds who squeezed into them. To a child's eye, it was the whole gaseous adult world writ large: noisy and smoky, the air thick with tobacco smoke and cooking smoke and burnt fuel and steam, cotton candy and popcorn and women's perfume and the dense mystery of odors that wafted from the beer garden. Attractions were found here to show up the sentimental, the silly, the dark side of the world.

There were rides to terrify the hardiest of street boys, fun houses and parachutes and nearly a dozen roller coasters: the Bobs, the Greyhound, the Silver Flash, the Comet, the Fireball.

And noise, always noise, the clackety racket of the coasters as they pulled stolidly to the tops of the hills just before dropping fifty or sixty feet to the undying terror of the riders, music, laughter, the happy background screams of the people dropping through the sky on the Para-Chutes. Men yelling to one another, kids shouting, the sideshow barker with a voice like a klaxon that reached you long before you could see him.

There were reminders here, too, of my parents: we'd come here often, and one summer my father had worked the gate, two nights a week, to make extra money. On those nights, we got in free, and I felt like a minor celebrity.

In the summer, Riverview took over a child's consciousness. It lay at the place where Clybourn Avenue dead-ended just before the river, and when the sun was high overhead I could see the park up the street, shimmering in the whitish glare like a magic kingdom, something that might be gone in a high wind.

On hot dull afternoons, my friends and I lay under the trees in Hamlin Park and spun lies and folktales about the rides: that a boy had died of fright on the Bobs, that a man had pushed his wife out of the Greyhound, that lovers had taken a long suicidal dive from the topmost car of the Ferris wheel, that a child exactly our age had tumbled from the Comet and been sliced like summer sausage beneath the coaster's wheels.

We repeated overheard fragments of adult conversation, embellished them, improved them, stretched them to their proper size and gave them new form: fights became brawls, muggings became murders. A purse snatching became robbery at gunpoint. None of us had yet been allowed to go into the Freak House, and so it too became fodder for our imaginations: the "tallest man in the world" became ten feet tall, the fat lady had to be rolled into the park, the fire-eater farted flames. Matt said there was a child inside who was actually half-wolf, and my own contribution was the two-headed man, whom I claimed to have seen any number of times. I said he looked like Buster Crabbe, on both of his faces.

And on the hottest nights it seemed as if my entire world had conspired to show up at Riverview. I entered with my family and promptly ran into friends, neighbors, cousins, other uncles and aunts, schoolmates. Everyone had ride coupons they didn't need: I had extras of the Ferris wheel and the neighbors up the street always seemed to have extra coupons for the Greyhound or the Comet, and I never tired of riding them. But more than the free coupons, I learned to watch the crowd for familiar faces, to wait for the old creaking park to pull its little surprises on me.

To a child obsessed with his place in the world, Riverview sent me constant reminders that in fact I'd inherited a great tangle of family that could pop up anywhere, and that my neighborhood literally had no end. One night my uncles took me and I was delighted to see Grandma Dorsey and Aunt Ellen and her children; another time I was standing in line waiting to get on the Bobs when someone slapped me on the back of my head. I spun around to find my cousin Matt grinning at me.

On still another evening, an unearthly shadow seemed to fall upon me, only me of all the people standing in line for the most nightmarish coaster of them all, the Bobs: I turned to find my Aunt Teresa, now Sister Fidelity, beaming down at me. I was intimidated by the good sister, blood ties or no, not only by her billowy habit but by her lovely face as well, and I didn't want any of the other kids to see me talking to a nun. I smiled and wished that I had a hole I could crawl into, or that her new assignment among the poor on the West Side could begin immediately. A few feet back, I could see two of my schoolmates, eyeballs bulging, their schoolboy assumption being that I had done something wrong and that a nun had come all the way to Riverview to bring me to justice. She asked me how my summer was going and then admitted that she didn't like to ride a roller coaster by herself.

"If I die," she said, "no one will be able to tell Grandma Dorsey." I knew I would never die on a roller coaster, but I had no such confidence in the constitution of a nun, and so I allowed her to ride with me. We spent the minute-or-so of terror howling and laughing at one another. On the second hill I thought she'd lose her habit but it didn't budge. After that, we went on the Tilt-A-Whirl and the Ferris wheel and became fast friends.

Poised in the topmost car as the great Ferris wheel took on a fresh load of passengers, nothing around us but a sky bleeding purple, we chatted, this nun just back from the Lord's Missions in Guatemala and I, and for an adult she made incredible sense.

"This is my favorite place in the whole park, Danny, the top of the Ferris wheel. From here you can see your whole life spread out down there. I can see where you live, and I can almost see my mother's house over on Evergreen, and I can see the houses of all the people for miles."

I agreed with her that this was a wonderful place, and she nodded happily, then surprised me with her next question.

"Do they make you feel like an oddball?"

"Who?" I asked but I knew who.

"Your family—well, mine, too. Our families, then. Do they make you feel a little strange?"

"I don't know. Maybe." I was unsure how to answer: she was an adult, after all, and Grandma Flynn had once said she was the smartest one on either side of the family, though the men had been unwilling to go so far.

"They make me feel like one of those poor souls in the freak show," she said.

"Are they poor souls? Will they not go to heaven?"

She laughed. "Of course they will. Maybe sooner than a lot of us. Anyhow, we're different from the rest of the family, you and I. I'm different because I became something…something not so strange but people don't understand why a girl does it, and so they'll never again treat me like a normal person. I'm not a member of the family anymore, I'm a *nun*. My first Christmas back home after taking my vows, my own brother Gerald was calling me 'Sister' like I'm some character out of the *Lives of the Saints*. I could have brained him."

I blinked here and gave myself away.

"You want to call me that too, don't you? When I'm home with my family, I'm Teresa. Aunt Teresa to you."

"What does Uncle Gerald call you now?"

"Nothing. He's afraid to call me 'Teresa' and he knows I'll do him an injury if he calls me 'Sister' again. He always was a little slow," she said under her breath, but I heard her anyway.

"And you're different because they can't quite bring themselves to treat you like any other small boy. You're a special problem for them, and they're going to treat you like one. Just don't take it to heart. Don't *think* you're a special problem. None of it is anyone's fault, that's the thing to remember." I must have shown some reaction to this mention of fault, for she turned toward me, but she had misunderstood. "They all…they all mean well. You're a lucky boy to have so many people love you. Just don't let them drive you crazy."

"I won't." We'd begun our slow descent now, and she was quiet for a moment. "Are they nice? The people there?"

"The people? In Guatemala, you mean? Oh, sure, they are, they're grand. You'd like them—they're like the Irish." This seemed to strike her as a fine joke, and she put her head back and laughed, and I found myself chuckling along with her.

When the ride was finished, she patted me on the head and asked after Grandma Flynn.

"She's fine," I said without thinking.

"Oh, Lord, no, I'm sure she's not fine. She's lost her daughter, and they were great friends, your mother and Mrs. Flynn, great friends. Be very good for her."

"I will."

She nodded, then looked away in distraction, and I remembered that she had lost a brother. After a moment she fished a half dollar out of some secret compartment in her habit.

"You're a nice boy, Danny. I enjoyed our rides together."

"Me, too, Sis…Aunt Teresa."

"Well done. Here." She handed me the fifty-cent piece, made a brisk turn on her heel, and walked off, tall and handsome and self-assured, ignoring the many curious faces that took a moment to gawk at her. My Uncle Tom had once remarked with a rueful note that it was "too bad *that one* became a nun." Uncle Mike had simply said, "Yeah, what a waste," and though I didn't understand what either of them meant, I knew I liked her, too.

In Riverview I entered a tiny porthole into the adult world. I was a watcher of people, I studied strangers the way I eavesdropped on my uncles, and the rickety old park rewarded me with dark glimpses into the behavior of the species. I saw fights there between older boys and once between two very drunken men outside the beer garden. They were both fat, both bleeding from scalp cuts that exaggerated their injuries and made the scene wonderfully lurid. The police came rushing over from the little police station inside the park and collared them both. As they pulled the men away, someone clapped, whether for the action of the police or the quality of the fisticuffs, I wasn't sure.

There were other tensions in the park. I always stopped to watch at the place where you tried to make a man in a cage fall into a tub of water by hitting a target with a thrown ball. The men within the little cage were usually black, the ones outside were white, sometimes cocky young ones with good aim, but usually older men, sweating, grunting drunks. The black men sat on little perches like dark-skinned birds and laughed at the efforts of their tormentors. The more the men threw and missed, the angrier they became, muttering threats and racial epithets at the black men, who responded with loud doubts about the white men's manhood. Once as I watched this little two-headed rite of racist hostility, my grandmother grabbed my arm and yanked me away. Behind me I heard my uncles chuckling at the scene, then a loud shout as one of the black men went into the drink.

On a humid night toward the end of that first summer, I was patrolling with my cousin Matt when we came upon a scene that struck me as something from a movie. Two groups of young men had come upon one another, four or five on a side. One group included my uncles, Tom and Mike, and a pair of their friends. The other group was led by Philly Clark. Perhaps someone had put a shoulder into someone else in the crowded midway, perhaps there had been a choice remark tossed over a shoulder. Something had already happened, I couldn't tell what, but it was clear from the way the men had formed a pair of facing lines, and from the way they all watched Philly and my Uncle Tom, that these young men all expected trouble.

We moved closer till we could see the angry faces—some were angry, though a tall thin guy behind Philly looked nervous, and my Uncle Mike simply looked like a man who has found himself in an unpleasant situation out of his control. In truth these two groups had faced each other before over other matters. From opposite ends of the neighborhood, they viewed each other as rivals, for jobs, for girls, for status. Matters usually crested during the summer, for both groups fielded baseball teams that faced each other in the various men's leagues in the parks. There had been individual fights, and at least one group effort.

I had heard Philly Clark's name in my grandmother's house. My uncles talked about him and my grandmother had called him a "hooligan." From what little I'd been given, I pieced together that there was trouble between Philly and Uncle Tom, part but not all of it over a girl. At that time, I knew no more about her. More than this, they detested each other. Philly was tall and handsome, had been a star athlete at Lane Tech and, it was said, was well-connected, and not only because his father was a precinct captain.

Now, he stood just a couple of feet from my uncle, head thrust forward belligerently. He was speaking to Tom, pointing to emphasize his words, and his finger seemed to come within touching distance of my uncle's face. Tom stood back on his heels and looked up at him—he was four or five inches shorter than Philly. He had an oddly satisfied look on his face, as though the whole scene was amusing him. If it was, he was alone in his amusement.

"Oh, boy," I heard Matt say. "They're gonna fight!" We moved closer so that I could make out some of Philly's words.

"I stay away from what's yours, you keep away from what's mine, you got that?" When my uncle said nothing, Philly poked him in the chest with the finger. "You got that?"

Tom ignored the finger. "How can she be yours if she's with me? Answer me that, Philly."

"She ain't gonna be with you, not ever, not if you want to live a long time. You got that?" Philly jabbed him again with the finger, and I thought he might throw a punch. My uncle just took a half step back and looked at Philly's hand.

"You tired of that finger?" Tom asked. He sounded very calm. "You tired of that nice shirt, those slacks, those fancy shoes?"

"Oh, tough guy, I'm terrified," Philly said with a mirthless smile.

"No, you're the tough guy. Everybody shits green ink when you walk by, but if you don't step aside and let me pass, I'll give you enough trouble to last you for a while."

"I can take you, Flynn."

"What're you, sixteen, Philly? You still think the girls like a guy who can knock somebody around. Now get out of my way or you're gonna wish you had."

A long moment passed as Philly considered whether to take things up a notch. People can smell a street fight coming, and a small crowd had formed around my uncles and the other men.

"I kicked your ass before, Flynn," Philly said so that he could be heard over the park noises.

"Long time ago. Ancient history, kid stuff. And you never wanted to fight me in a ring." Tom grinned at him. "Tony Zale gave Graziano a rematch, Philly."

"Oh, you'll get a rematch all right," Philly said, but he was moving away, giving Tom a path.

My uncle walked straight ahead, looking neither left nor right, and his group followed him.

"Just remember what I said, Flynn," Philly said to my uncle's departing back. Then he and the others broke into a little circle, chattering all at once. One of them was patting Philly on the back, but I could see Philly Clark's eyes, and I saw that the big handsome man in the good clothes had lost face.

Later that night as we walked the two blocks to my grand-parents' house, my uncles muttered to one another about the incident and I kept a respectful silence. Uncle Mike was urging Tom to be cautious.

"Watch your back door with that guy," I heard him say.

Tom's voice was so low I almost missed his answer. "I ain't worried about Philly. Jesus, Mike, I was overseas, people tried to kill me over there, for Christ's sake. What's that punk gonna do to me?"

"Just be careful, is all I'm telling you."

"I got no interest in a beef with Philly Clark. I couldn't care less if I can take him or he puts my lights out. I just wanta take his girl away."

Uncle Mike growled in irritation and seemed to give up. I thought that made it my turn, so just as we reached our house, I tossed in my two cents' worth.

"Are you gonna have a fight with that guy, Uncle Tom?"

They both spun around and Uncle Mike looked irritated.

"You're not supposed to listen to our conversations," he said, but Uncle Tom looked amused.

"How's he supposed to do that, huh? We're both jawin' away like he's not here. He supposed to put gumballs in his ears, or what?"

He paused at the broken gate, hands in his pockets, looking calm and confident. "No. I don't fight with street trash no more, I'm retired, like Joe Louis. That guy gives me any lip, I'll sic you and your cousin Matt on him." He shot a quick grin at me and then led me into the house. My grandmother, after her perfunctory mutterings about how late they'd kept me out, put me into bed. I was exhilarated by what I had seen, and bothered by it as well, with its hint of potential danger for yet another of my loved ones, and the one I already prized most. I went to sleep that night daydreaming about a heroic encounter between my uncle and Philly Clark, and in my version, the big man in the fancy clothes took a fearful drubbing from my uncle to the cheers of hundreds of onlookers.

A later version, edited and refined many times, had my uncle lying temporarily stunned on the ground as I administered an incredible beating to his assailant.

Uncle, Hero,
and Film Critic

I was baffled that my uncle had an enemy, that any adult would harbor hostile feelings for him. The moment that Tom had broken the news to me about my parents, he had moved into the center of my universe. This was no dramatic shift in my feelings: he'd long occupied a spot just behind my parents in my pantheon of adult heroes. It was a natural spot for him: my father had been a quiet, reserved man uncomfortable with noise and childish craziness. My father worked two jobs and had little time of his own, but Tom had been a frequent visitor to our house. Tom was outgoing and charming, and what was more amazing than anything else, he seemed to find me good company. "He's found another little boy to play with," my Aunt Anne kidded. Early on, before I understood the concepts of family and relatives, I was fond of telling anyone who would listen that my uncle was "my special friend."

None of this changed when I moved into my grandparents' home. I looked forward to the moment when Tom returned from work, and though he never showed irritation with me, I know that I followed him through the house like a stray dog, assaulted him with my questions and news of my day, and hung on him like a second skin.

He worked at the Borden Dairy in what was always called "The Old Neighborhood," over near Grandma Dorsey's flat. Once Grandpa Flynn took me to visit him at work and he gave me little bottles of chocolate and strawberry milk. In the evenings he went out with his friends or with my grandfather, sometimes to watch a fight or a ballgame at one of the countless taverns in the neighborhood—there seemed to be one on every corner, adults apparently drank their way through life—and at other times I knew he was going out, inexplicably, with girls.

His personal routine and habits fascinated me: he listened to music a great deal, sang when he was working on a task around Grandma's house or drying the dishes for my grandmother, and at times I caught him talking to the singers on Grandma's yellow radio: "Sing it, Frank, show 'em how it's done," he'd say to Sinatra. "Ah, you're beautiful, Peggy," I heard him tell Peggy Lee, and then he caught me watching from the next room, and grinned. "She gives me fever, kid," he told me, and I was embarrassed. And when Rosemary Clooney invited him to "Come on to My House," he'd laugh. "Oh, I'll come to your house, all right, Rosie."

Sometimes at night my grandparents would turn on the big GE in the living room and listen to the Barn Dance or Tennessee Ernie. "You're turning into a couple of old hillbillies," he'd tell them, laughing, but he liked the fiddle music and the sad songs, and after my many hours listening to Grandpa's Irish music, his songs of lost loves and country, I could hear the similarities and thought it was all Irish music. Tom even sang along with some of these country singers. He'd get serious when the girl singers sang their sad stories: "I'd take care of you, honey," he'd say.

I felt sorry for the sad girls, I wished they could meet my uncle. He didn't have anyone special that I could see, and after the incident at Riverview I shared Uncle Mike's hope that Tom would forget about the unnamed girl I'd heard them talking about. Whoever she was, she meant trouble for him, one way or the other.

Once I saw him break into a jitterbug to Grandma's big yellow kitchen radio. They'd told me about his dancing—Aunt Anne told me he was the best dancer in the neighborhood. "Oh, he's grand," Grandma agreed. The dancing part made me uneasy. It was one thing to sing in the kitchen, but I wasn't sure a boy was supposed to like dancing, let alone excel at it. But it was fascinating to watch him and, in the end, I decided that if Uncle Tom liked it, there had to be something in it. I tried it myself once, alone in the kitchen with the music, and fell over one of the kitchen chairs. Grateful that I'd had no audience, I decided it wasn't for me.

It was also through his example that I learned the rewards of reading in the bathroom. He was fond of reading in the bathtub—no, that doesn't come close to it: he was unable to get into the tub without a paper or magazine. Once when my grandmother upbraided him for the time he took in the tub— "You'll get pneumonia," was one of her arguments, "You'll get your death of cold," and, "It's bad for your skin to soak so long in warm water," were others—I heard him play his black ace: he told her that this was the result of Korea.

"I sat up there on that hill, Ma, and I thought about getting out of there like anybody else, and I thought about you, Ma, and I wanted to be warm and clean someplace, I wanted to be home. But the thing I kept thinking about was a hot bath. A hot bath. And I promised myself I'd never hurry through one again—just in case…you know, in case I get sent back to Korea."

"Oh, God forbid!" she muttered, but she left him alone after that.

Also—and predictably—he read on the toilet. I learned this one morning on his day off, the morning that was to keep him forever associated in my mind with blood. I was in the living room rifling through my box of lead soldiers trying to find enough men with heads to make a squad and he emerged from the bathroom looking like a leper. Tiny pieces of tissue were stuck to his face and blood seeped through each one. He seemed unmoved by this predicament.

"Hey, Butch. You got some comics around, don't you?"

I must have been staring, for he repeated the question and I responded with another.

"What happened to your face?"

"What? Nothing happened to me...Oh." He laughed, a short little bark. "I cut myself shaving. It's nothing. Some day you'll be able to shave and then you'll get all these little cuts on your face."

"Do they hurt?"

"No, but if I'm not careful, I could lose enough blood to die."

"You could?"

"Nah, I'm just kidding." He surveyed the living room for a moment and a tiny patch of bloody tissue came loose and fluttered down to the floor like the last red leaf of autumn. If I close my eyes I can still see him coming out with a dozen patched cuts, looking like something out of an old Ed Wood movie—*The Bleeding Men from Outer Space*, perhaps, or *Attack of the People with Open Sores*.

"So how 'bout some comics? Man needs some reading material when he sits on the throne."

"He does?"

"Sure. Some things you should never be in a hurry for. Going to the can is one of them."

"They're by my bed." In the tiny half room at the front of the house where I slept, I had just enough room for my bed, a small dresser, a toy box and two cardboard cartons, one for my soldiers and the other for my comics. I had hundreds, I bought them constantly or people bought them for me and I never threw them away: at the Certified on the corner of Barry and Leavitt they sold old ones without covers, three comics to a pack for a dime.

I had Archie and Walt Disney comics, Superman and Blackhawk and the occasional bloodthirsty war comic like G.I. Comics, horror comics I didn't even understand and nearly fifty Classics Illustrated—all purchased by my grandmother lest Archie and Jughead cause an atrophy of my young brain.

Tom disappeared with his leprous face into my room for several minutes and I heard him exclaiming at my collection. He emerged with the Classics Illustrated version of *Ivanhoe* and told me he could be found "in the library." From that day on, I seldom spent more than five minutes in the bathroom without one of my comics, his purloined habit becoming my custom for life and occasioning many fierce debates between me and my grandparents, who contended that I now took half an hour to do thirty seconds' business.

Sometimes on his day off from the dairy, usually Wednesday, my uncle took me places, and on these days I bounded out of bed in excitement, and when he staggered down from his room with his hair stuck up on one side of his head like a black rooster's comb I followed him through the house like a deranged puppy.

He was, as I have said, my favorite, as he was everyone's. He was the shortest of my uncles but the best-looking, handsome in a dark way that suggested something other than an Irish background, though I'm assured that there are many like him in the old country. Like many small men, he moved with a briskness that suggested efficiency, capability, self-assurance, and he seemed to me gifted in all these ways. He was the most talkative of the family, the wittiest, he laughed loudly and easily, as though he'd been expecting the opportunity and you'd come along and provided it. Uncle Mike had played football at De Paul Academy, but Tom was the family athlete and had once drawn scouts to his sandlot baseball games. In those days, however, it was believed that small men couldn't stand the rigors of the long baseball season, and nothing ever came of his baseball skill.

In his youth he was said to have been quick-tempered and fearless, had tried his hand with modest success at CYO Boxing and the Golden Gloves, and from what I pieced together over the years from overheard conversations and careless comments by the other adults, I gathered that he'd been something of a street-fighter before his military service. I once heard my grandmother worrying aloud about him, and Uncle Mike tried to reassure her, saying, "Don't worry, Ma, he's a different guy. Korea took all that tough guy out of him. It changed him."

Of course, the first chance I had, I asked him if it were true.

"Uncle Tom, did Korea change you?"

He put down the paper he was reading and peered at me, perfectly aware that he was being afforded a rare opportunity to eavesdrop on a conversation he hadn't been in on.

"Where did you hear that?"

"I don't know."

"Your uncle Mike or your grandmother, or the both of 'em, I think."

"Did it?"

"Yeah. Made me taller."

Unfazed, I hit him with another one. "Were you a tough guy before you went into the Army?"

"Everybody thinks he's tough. Then you grow up and find out the truth."

"Uncle Mike says you were."

"He's got too much time on his hands. Nobody my size is tough." He thought for a moment and smiled, and I knew he'd found a way to make light of the subject. "Well, there's exceptions, of course: Mickey Walker was real tough. He gave away forty pounds when he fought Schmeling. Beau Jack was tough. Ike Williams. Barney Ross. Henry Armstrong, of course, but he's before my time." He got up from the couch and made his way toward the kitchen.

As he was walking away I tossed out with, "Did you get shot in Korea?"

He stopped and turned, fixed me with a look that said I'd stepped onto dangerous ground and then relaxed. "Do I look like I got shot?"

"No. I just heard…that you got hurt there."

"Only my feelings. Now knock it off about Korea. I don't want to talk about that." A look of clear annoyance crossed his face, and then he remembered his audience. "I didn't like Korea. None of the girls would go out with me." He went to the kitchen, shaking his head, leaving me alone and uncomfortable in the living room.

But, my verbal assaults on his private thoughts notwithstanding, most Wednesdays we were inseparable: he took me downtown, to the movies and out for a hamburger and a malt, he took me to the beach and the zoo, to museums to learn about the world. He seemed to know every interesting place in a city overrun with them, some of them little-known: we visited the train yards, watched boats, wandered in neighborhoods where we were the only white people, ate in restaurants serving food I'd never heard of. I believe he knew the location of every hot-dog stand within the city limits and had eaten at all of them.

He was in love with movie theaters, with the smell of fresh popcorn and the sight of a glittering lobby filled with overwrought pseudo-Grecian sculpture and dominated by a candy counter the size of a small ship. Chicago in 1954 was a city of movie houses, great and small, they fed off one another, crosspollinated and gave birth to new ones, it was impossible to go four blocks without coming across one.

My uncle knew every one of them and took me to them all: to the grand palaces downtown like the Oriental and the Roosevelt and the Chicago and the Loop, and all over the North Side, the Century and the Belmont, the North Center and the Crest, the DeLuxe and the Covent and the Will Rogers and half a dozen others so small and shabby that they weren't listed in the papers—I still find the ruins of these little shows, their empty husks and boxy skeletons on used-up streets. He introduced me to the Bugg Theater at Damen and Irving, where old movies came to live out their last days as part of a double feature that changed three times a week. He taught me that there were no movies like the old ones, and that there was never a good reason to watch a movie without a box of buttered popcorn and some candy. His combination of choice was popcorn and a Mounds bar, and I adopted this vice without hesitation.

This was truly the Age of the Western, and in the period between 1954 and 1956 I'm certain we saw every oater made in the English speaking world, and knew the complete canon of each small-time star who put on a stetson: Rory Calhoun, George Montgomery, Joel McCrea, Audie Murphy, Sterling Hayden, MacDonald Carey and John Ireland, Lloyd Bridges and Randolph Scott, Frank Lovejoy and Guy Madison and John Payne. He was fond of historical films as well, and at the Bugg Theater he introduced me to the collected works of "Cousin" Errol Flynn, including *The Charge of the Light Brigade* and *They Died with Their Boots On.*

This was also the period when Hollywood fed off the common man's paranoia and fear of science, and buffeted the moviegoer with the perils of space travel, the dangers of science, and the evil intentions of our celestial neighbors: I saw the earth attacked by robots and flying saucers with death rays, by giant crabs and grasshoppers that came to town and behaved badly, by beasts living in the bowels of the earth and mutant sea creatures, including a memorable octopus that tried to eat San Francisco.

One day as we headed home after a movie in which malevolent beings from Mars attempted to take over the earth, I commented, probably with a note of hope in my voice, that it was good that such things weren't real.

He said, "Yeah, that's for sure." A moment later he laughed and looked down at me. "No, you know what? I don't think so. The people in this movie, they have their attention focused on one problem. They don't have time to worry about anything else. They got no time to worry about money or their wife or their job or school; they have to worry about the Big Problem. You see? You're out there fighting a giant octopus, it don't make a lot of difference if your boss is mad at you." A moment later he said, "The world's full of problems, kid, that's what life is made of. Give me the giant octopus anytime."

I laughed, and not till years later did I fully understand what he meant, and what is more important, that he was right.

High Art and Baseball

We visited the museums, all of them, and my uncle stunned me with the things he knew: I decided he was brilliant. With the hindsight of forty years I understand that he just wanted me to learn what other kids were probably learning, and that he didn't want me to think he was stupid. He had a fair knowledge of animals and geography and astronomy—at least to the point of knowing the basic constellations. I knew no other adult who could point out Mars or Venus on a clear night, and took this to be a manifestation of a singular mind.

Most of all, I enjoyed the Art Institute, and I've told a thousand people over the years that the day he first took me there was the day that changed my life forever. It's not true, of course: the day he took me under his wing was more likely the day that actually changed my life, but the other way still makes for a good story.

At the Art Institute I fell in love with the paintings and the cheery lighting immediately, but it wasn't so much the art that made it special for me, it was what happened between my uncle and me. At all the other museums, the Field Museum and the Museum of Science and Industry, the Aquarium and the Planetarium and the tiny, almost unknown Academy of Sciences, he knew things, many things, and I spent a good deal of my time listening to him, trying to learn. At the Art Institute he was a little lost, off-balance, we were equals, a pair of lost explorers in a foreign place.

"This one I don't know much about, Dan," I can remember him saying as we stood just inside the big front doors. "I never studied much about art in school." He spoke quietly, I can still see him looking self-consciously around us at the people entering the museum. If it made him uncomfortable, I was sure I wouldn't much like it.

"Do you like it here?" I asked him.

"Do I like it? Oh, sure. It's great. Art is great. C'mon, let's make your acquaintance with these painters."

I can't think about those long elegant halls without seeing him, standing there with his hands on his hips, wearing a blue silk jacket with a map of Korea on it—thousands of servicemen returning from the Korean War came back with those gaudy jackets.

In my mind's eye, Tom is squinting at Monet's waterlilies or his haystacks, at Manet's picnickers, at Seurat's park strollers, at portraits and crowded scenes from the Dutch and German masters, at the harsh, powerful Americans, and he's talking, constantly talking of what he sees.

"Wow, look at that! See, Dan? See how they make it look like snow? Look up close, it's just white paint, globs of it with blue paint for the shadows. Up close it's just globs of paint, now step back and you see? See what he did here? How 'bout that, huh?"

He liked to peer close-up at a painting to see the brushstrokes and then back away to watch the transformation of the artist's daubings into an image.

I wanted to like what he liked but I wasn't impressed: I stared at an entire wall of Monet's haystacks in a field and wanted to know why Monet couldn't think of anything else to paint; I looked at the little dots that formed Seurat's lovely scene and asked why he couldn't cover all the canvas like a real painter; I looked at the Renaissance portraits and thought we had once been a race of fat people. It seemed that Manet had blurred vision and van Gogh painted only boring things: flowers, empty rooms, his own face. And confronted with abstract art, with distorted faces and bodies from the Riverview funhouse, two-headed humans and flat squares of one or two colors, I couldn't shake the feeling that someone was pulling my leg.

"What's that one supposed to be?" I asked of an abstract filled with geometric shapes and accented near its middle with a single eye.

"Beats me, kid. I knew a guy in the service that drew like that, but he was nuts."

"Uncle Mike says all artists are nuts."

He snorted and said, "He would. Your Uncle Mike, he's got his heart set on making it in the world the way people usually try to, in business, wearing a suit and driving a nice car. You tell me, kid: a guy wants to make nice pictures all day in a sunny room—if his luck is running, maybe he actually makes a living making these nice pictures. Is that nuts?"

"It sounds okay."

"Of course it's okay. If I could draw…" And I remember him looking down at me in an odd way. "*You* can draw. You could be one of these guys if you wanted. You could be anything you wanted."

I told him I wanted to be an FBI agent or a jet pilot and he just shook his head absently.

"Nah, you'll find something better than that. You want to do something that's…enjoyable. That's what you want."

I don't remember saying anything to him, but he had shown me a new possibility in life—though painting still seemed a pallid option compared to the FBI or the Texas Rangers or jet planes.

We quickly developed favorites: Tom liked El Greco, whose people seemed to have stretched limbs or blue skin— "This guy was wild, huh? They look like giants in a B movie."

He liked Ivan Albright, whom I found rather frightening, and was fond of *Nighthawks*, by Edward Hopper.

"See, I actually think I understand this one," he said the first time. "I know all the people in it." When I asked him who they were, he just said, "The kinda people we know. Maybe that's me someday."

I hated the painting: there was something frightening about the idea of these people whiling away the night in this sterile place, and for a moment I felt terribly sad that he thought this might be what was in store for him.

He saw that he'd given me a shock. "Nah, Grandma won't let me stay out that late," he said, and led me away. The day was not lost, however: he took me to a room I fell in love with, a long gallery of gore and bloody wounds, the work of German Renaissance artists ostensibly bent on visual reverence for the early Christian martyrs but in actuality obsessed with violence and blood, perhaps letting off the steam of a repressed age, or of emerging modern man in love with his own bellicosity: there were gory scenes of early saints pincushioned with arrows, people broken on the wheel, people mauled by savage beasts or roasted alive. It sold me on the high-art concept.

But of all those artists, living and dead, one stood out in a small boy's opinion, a painter whom I have long remembered as the Nameless Impressionist: she was a middle-aged woman we found bent over her easel in the same corner each time we visited the Art Institute, scratching and daubing away at a painstaking recreation of one of Monet's landscapes. The first time, I watched her do one of Monet's small flower studies and announced to my uncle that she was doing a better job than the master had. I thought I was whispering, but several people laughed and I was embarrassed until Tom said that he thought so too. The woman gave us a distracted look, blew hair out of her eyes, and went on with her incipient Monetism.

In warm weather we went to ballgames and a strange calm

seemed to come over him that brought with it long silences. At times I would look up at him and see him surveying the park or the crowd with a dreamy look on his face, and I wondered why he wasn't paying attention to whatever was happening on the field. These were dark days in Chicago baseball: the White Sox were good but never good enough to get past the Yankees or Indians, and the Cubs were awful in ways only they could devise. "Beautiful Wrigley Field" was frequently empty: the upwardly mobile middle class hadn't discovered the attractions of ivy and day baseball yet.

But what was mordant for baseball business was wonderful for a kid and his uncle who just wanted to hang out at the ballpark. We'd find our seats and stretch out, and two or three innings later we might move and try out some other seats. Toward the late innings we'd hit the upper deck, and one breezy day when the Milwaukee Braves were shelling the bleachers we moved to the very top row of the ballpark. It seemed that I could see the ends of the earth: at the very least, I could see Riverview, and what I thought were the twin steeples of St. Bonaventure Church.

Then Tom showed me his knowledge of the wind currents. From a vending machine we had bought a pack of cheap black-and-white baseball cards featuring the current Cub crop, including both the phenomenal black rookie named Ernie Banks—for it was true that, years after Jackie Robinson and twentieth-century reality came to baseball, the Cubs discovered black people: now they had Banks and Gene Baker. I held up a card showing the pitcher whose offerings were at that moment being deposited in center field by the Milwaukee hitters. Uncle Tom took the card, bent it, leaned back in his seat so that his head and arm were actually outside the upper deck and then flicked the card up into the jetstream. The card disappeared over the upper deck roof and Tom slid back into his seat, his eyes quickly scanning the area for the acne-struck teenager who was our Andy Frain usher.

"Watch the field," he said, looking straight ahead. "Pretend you're watching the game."

I feigned interest as the next Brave batter fouled off a pitch, and then I saw the card. It was floating to earth like a tired bird, making a long, slow descent, and it landed mere inches from the shoes of the Cub second baseman. The fielder looked at it, stared up at the stands with what could have been a frown, and then picked up the card and tried tossing it away. The card flew seven or eight feet and settled a little closer to the pitching mound.

It was a simpler time: today if a kid—or his uncle—tossed a piece of paper onto the field, it would be retrieved by the groundskeepers, who would wash over the field like the locusts that ate Brigham Young's crops, forty of them retrieving the offending card while a crew of security people with headphones swept through the stands looking for Alger Hiss.

But that first time nothing happened, and so we repeated the process with the remaining five cards, and when we were finished, all six, including Ernie Banks, were littering the infield grass. My uncle was particularly proud that he'd sent the last card, a photo of the Cub first baseman Dee Fondy, within a foot of the real Dee Fondy. His effort also earned us a visit from the dreaded Andy Frain usher: this one was perhaps sixteen years old and might have weighed 110, and he informed us that we could not throw things on the field and that if we persisted in our degenerate behavior, he'd have to ask us to leave.

My uncle who had been shot with guns on frozen Korean hillsides and brawled with grown men looked the kid up and down with a "so what?" in his brown eyes, and just when the usher started to look nervous, decided to be a good guy about it. He looked down at me and said, "Cut that stuff out. You want to confuse our infield?"

"No, sir," I said, delighted to have a speaking role in the performance.

"He won't do that no more, sir," my uncle told the kid in

the blue uniform, and the guard went away, his body language proclaiming to the crowd that he'd behaved honorably.

My uncle looked at me. "He's just doing his job. He probably don't even like it, his ma probably talked him into making a couple dollars for the summer. All over the country there's people just doing their jobs, and most of 'em don't like their jobs. Worst thing about the country."

"Do you like yours?" I asked him.

"No," he said and watched the meeting in progress on the mound, during which the Cub manager presumably told his pitcher to let Eddie Mathews hit the ball four hundred feet if possible, because that is what happened next. After the home run he looked down at me, and he was laughing. "Hard to believe the Pirates got a worse team, isn't it? Listen: most guys try to find a job that pays the rent and a little more, and they're happy when they get that because they know there's people that don't have even that. That's how I am: I got a decent job and I make a fair buck, but there's a difference between making money and having a good job."

"What would be a good job?"

"The one you don't mind getting up for every day. The one that makes you *happy*. That's the one you want, Butch, the one that makes you feel good about how you spend every day. They can pay you a lot of money, but if you're on your feet in a factory every day and you know it's never gonna change, it's not much of a job. Not a real great life."

"What would be a good job for you?"

He looked out over the field and pointed with his chin. "What they do, I'd do that if I was any good. Greatest job on earth, playing ball and having people cheer you and pay you money—only most of these guys don't know it. And it don't last long for them. And there's guys that write about baseball for the papers, now that would be a good job but that's a college man's job."

"Writing about baseball is a job?" This made as little sense as anything I'd heard.

"You bet it is. And when the season's over they write about the Bears or they cover the fights. They get in for nothing and then they tell people what they saw and how much they liked it."

He raised his eyebrows at the significance of this, and it did seem like a fine thing.

"Maybe I'll work at a dairy," I told him.

"Nah, you don't want to work at a dairy. Buy your milk from a dairy but don't work for one."

"Why do you work in a dairy if you don't want to?"

He gave me an amused look. "It pays the rent, it's better than standing on the corners wondering where the next nickel's gonna come from. Which is where a lotta guys are right now. No, you see, sometimes you have to take what people are willing to give you. When I was a kid, I thought I was hot stuff, I thought I had all the answers, and then I found out, yeah, I was smarter than the average guy but they don't give out medals for that, kiddo. They don't knock your door down trying to give you fancy jobs. I should have gone to school when I got out of the service. But I didn't, and now I'm a guy in a dairy."

"Is it a bad thing to be a guy in a dairy?"

"No, but some guys have a different idea what kind of guy they are, and I'm one of 'em."

I wanted to ask him what kind of guy he was but was prevented by another Milwaukee home run, this one by Joe Adcock, and it left Wrigley Field and soared far over Waveland, and I tried in vain to follow its flight.

"I couldn't see it come down," I said.

"It didn't. Some of 'em just stay up there in the sky forever." He laughed and said we should go get something to eat. I wanted to ask him my question but that part of our talk seemed finished. We took the bus back to the neighborhood and he spent most of the ride looking out the window over my head. On that day I was eager to get home, to curl up in a corner of my room with my toys or a book and get away from the feelings that had come over me in the ballpark: I knew without fully understanding that he wanted a girl who belonged to someone else, I knew he didn't have a lot of money, and now I understood that he was not happy with what he was. For the first time, I saw that other people might not view him as I did, that they were unaware of what a special person he was, and I was saddened. That night I prayed for his life to get better.

But there are few relationships so simple. He was more attentive to me than anyone could have expected, generous with his time, with himself, but it was not enough. All children are demanding and my needs were great. I hated to share him, resented all things in his young bachelor's life that competed with me for his attention: his girls, his job, his friends, his baseball team—features of his world by turns fascinating and hated.

On weekends when he couldn't spend time with me I sulked and wandered around the house with my head down in what I hoped was a fine display of anger and would say nothing when my grandparents wanted to know what was wrong.

One night he came home late from a date and I crept out of my room while he was in the bathroom. I hadn't seen him in two nights. The following day was Wednesday, and I hoped he'd offer to take me somewhere, so I was giving him the opportunity to tell me about it. When he emerged from the bathroom in his pajama bottoms I was waiting for him in the hall. He came out looking preoccupied, and he was almost on top of me before he noticed me.

"Whattya doing out of bed?"

"I was waiting for you."

"Oh, yeah? Your grandma will have your hide, and then she'll have mine 'cause it'll be my fault that you're up somehow." He spoke sternly but patted me on the head. "Now go to bed. You need a drink of water or something?"

"No. Are we going anywhere tomorrow?"

He shook his head quickly. "Uh, no, not tomorrow. I got something I gotta do tomorrow. Maybe Saturday or Sunday, okay?"

I nodded and mumbled something in what I hoped was a clear display of disappointment.

He said, "Saturday or Sunday for sure, all right?"

And I nodded again and went off to bed.

The following day I went into his room and closed the door behind me. I opened the top drawer of his dresser and stared at his private things. To that point I had gone through only my grandparents' dresser and the drawers and shelves of the pantry: the two identical dressers in my uncles' bedrooms were off-limits, like their wallets. Grandma had once told me it was very impolite to go through a woman's purse, even for money, and that a boy found rooting around in a man's wallet could be up to no good. Their drawers seemed logically to fall into that same forbidden category, so that when I opened Tom's top drawer that day, I understood that I was crossing some sort of line.

I took my time going through his things: there were cuff links and tie pins, and I found a small plastic box with a half dozen or so military buttons. At the back of the drawer I found an old Morgan silver dollar, and I took it. As I closed the drawer, I noticed a small photograph of Tom and a group of his friends. I stared at it for a moment and then picked up a pencil stub and made a long dark line across the front of it. By the following day I was filled with remorse for what I'd done. I used an eraser to remove some of the pencil line, and then put the silver dollar back.

New Year,
New Troubles

At summer's end I went back to school at St. Bonaventure's. My teacher would be a nun new to the school, with the exotic name of Sister Polycarp, and I was nervous about her, and about school in general. First grade had been an uneasy time for me. My teacher had been Sister Augustine, a stern old nun who could not abide a wise guy, and my inability to remain quiet or even seated for long periods of time had brought me into frequent conflict with her. So although I was excited to see my friends, I entered the second grade with some foreboding. My feelings worsened on the first day, when I noticed all my schoolmates being brought to school by their mothers, or in some cases, mothers and fathers. I was brought to school by Aunt Anne, which did not seem the same thing at all.

My fears about my new teacher proved unfounded, at least for the time being, for Sister Polycarp knew about my parents and was quietly solicitous of me. I soon found that my "situation" had given me a kind of celebrity among the other children. School and the little landmarks by which a child notes the time on his calendar eased my terrors and after a couple of weeks I had settled in. Our school mornings were punctuated by prayers for the conversion of Russia and, precisely at 10:30 every morning when the siren went off, a bizarre exercise in which all the students slipped out of their seats and took refuge beneath their wooden desks—for our protection, it was said, against nuclear attack.

During one of these exercises I peered over the edge of my desk to see if Sister Polycarp had, as she was required, forced her sizable form under *her* desk. She was in her chair, staring out the window and shaking her head.

In truth she seemed kind enough, and if I had allowed her to be herself, I'd have encountered no trouble from her at all, but it was not to be.

In general, though, the first few weeks of that new school year passed without major incident. I managed to focus my attention on my toys, my friends, my adventures at Grandma Dorsey's house with Matt, and most of all the new kind of family life I'd begun. In the late afternoons I watched television—the year before, Grandma and Grandpa had bought a wonderful new Stromberg-Carlson. It had a blond wood cabinet that Grandma wiped and polished like a religious relic, and a small grayish screen like Cyclops's blind eye.

I watched cartoons and *Kukla, Fran and Ollie*, *Elmer the Elephant* or *Garfield Goose*, and *The Little Rascals*, and when my uncles and Grandma came home from work the house filled with noise I'd never really experienced in my parents' small, quiet flat. We chattered and laughed over dinner, and in the evenings if it was warm, we all walked over to Hamlin Park, and Uncle Tom or Uncle Mike bought me an ice-cream bar or a Popsicle. On Wednesdays and Fridays we watched the Gillette Fights, often televised from a place inexplicably called St. Nicholas Arena, though it had no apparent connection with St. Nicholas's more important life's work.

I can still see myself at those times, sitting back while all the adults around me focused their attention on the radio, the television, or each other, and watching them, telling myself I now had a new family and my year in school would be like anyone else's, perhaps even better, for Aunt Anne was normally there to help me with my homework to a degree that my late mother would have found indulgent.

But my days soon brought me reminders that my situation was forever altered. After a short, unimportant fight in the playground with a third grader named Henry, I was hauled into the principal's office, where I received, along with my opponent, a stern lecture from the most universally feared individual in the building, a tall thin nun whose name I believed to be "Sister Phillip-the-Principal." The older boy was able to make her see the fight as my fault, and she sent me on my way with the admonition to improve my behavior lest I cause shame to my family. She started to say "your parents," and then caught herself.

Shortly after that, I was sent home with the first of innumerable notes from Sister Polycarp to my grandparents, a succession of urgent sounding epistles that before year's end would rival St. Paul's, in number if not in complexity of message.

My grandmother took that first note from me as though I'd handed her a dead insect, and when she'd digested the message from Sister Polycarp that I'd developed a great love for the sound of my own voice, she made her disappointment in me clear. I had nothing to say in my own defense, for it seemed there was no audience for anything I could have brought up. That night I lay in bed and told myself that my mother would have understood the situation and handled it much better than these people who had no idea what they were doing.

A few days later, a third incident occurred that underscored for me the truth of my situation. I was walking home alone, having missed Matt, and I must have dawdled long enough to allow most of the children to get ahead of me, for there was no one else around.

I had stopped just past the viaduct on Diversey to watch a fire truck rumble by when a boy ran by me, grabbed my cap, and dashed up the street. I yelled and gave chase. He appeared to be older, and he was faster, but I caught him at the corner when he had to stop for a truck that was making a turn. Without thinking, I ran up to him, demanded my hat, pulled it from his hand, and shoved him. He staggered a couple of steps and smacked me a perfect shot in the nose, and I went down on the sidewalk. I got up, crying, and went after him, swinging with both hands, and he laughed.

I remember that he was a strangely disheveled-looking boy with odd, close-set eyes, and his jacket bagged on him as though bought for someone else. There is nothing quite so urgent as a child's need to get at a tormentor, and I can still see myself chasing him up and down the sidewalk, sobbing over my injured nose as I attempted to land just one blow. The older boy eluded me easily, chuckling as I threw long roundhouse punches with no chance of landing. In the end he tired of the game, dropped me with another punch, and ran off. He turned the corner past the Stewart-Warner factory and was gone.

My experience shocked me. I had had fights on the playground and seen Matt provoke several, but no stranger had ever struck me without provocation. I was frightened, and all the way home I looked over my shoulder to see if he was following me.

Aunt Anne was waiting for me at Clybourn and Diversey, a concerned look on her face, for by now I was quite late. I touched my nose and saw that there was no blood. I was on the verge of blurting out my story when something told me to keep it to myself. I saw my uncles telling me to stand up for myself, and my grandmother and grandfather wanting to know why I was alone in the first place, and decided it was no use.

That night in bed I imagined coming home to my mother, imagined her instant reaction of concern and anger. I saw her pursuing the older boy down the street, confronting my hard-hearted principal, and tearing Sister Polycarp's notes in small pieces and throwing them at her. But there was no mother in my life, and I told myself it made a difference. I told myself I was, in some fundamental way, unprotected, and that the new arrangement of my life had failed in its first tests.

Other tests came and I waited expectantly. Halloween approached, a different sort of test in my new life: anybody, I thought, could give me a bed and clothes, but what would my holidays be like? Would they understand what a small boy needed in order to celebrate a holiday that had already taken on as many of the mystical trappings and connections as Christmas? Perhaps it took the combined intelligence of all four adults in the household and a bit of prodding and advice from the other relatives who had children in the household, but in any case the adult complement of my new home managed to display an understanding of what Halloween meant to a child. For the first time in my memory, the front windows of the big house were filled with cardboard pumpkins and witches, and my grandmother came back from Lincoln and Belmont with a big bag of Halloween candy, with which she filled a glass bowl in the living room—ostensibly for the trick-or-treaters but in reality for my consumption. She took me to Woolworth's on Lincoln for one of our little shopping trips: we ate at the long lunch counter dominated by the smell of hot dogs steaming in glass cases at either end of the counter. For a while I looked at toys, and she bought me a pair of plastic pirates, then took me to pick out a costume.

"Your grandfather wants to paint you with burnt cork and dress you in old clothes like a hobo, it's his idea of a Halloween costume, but I'll not have any of that. We did that with Thomas and Michael and you couldn't get the cork off their faces without taking some of the skin off. They sell costumes in the stores now," she said, heading toward the costume section. "Burnt cork!" she muttered, moving on ahead of me. "People will think we can't afford to buy you a decent costume."

I selected a Casper the Friendly Ghost costume replete with flat plastic mask and counted myself a lucky boy.

On the grand day itself my Uncle Tom took me out trick-
or-treating right before dinner. The sidewalks were crammed
with kids in costume, the air heavy with the smells of burning
leaves from the big cottonwoods and oaks, and the dry, dead
ones that carpeted the sidewalks like paper. On Leavitt we fell in
with a schoolmate and his father. After dinner my uncle took me
over to Grandma Dorsey's house and I went trick-or-treating
with Matt and Aunt Ellen's two sons, my older, more worldly
cousins Jeff and Billy. By day's end I had enough candy to slow
down a freighter, and my family had convinced me that at the
very least, my new life would include a normal Halloween.

A Tale of
Two Fir Trees

The year dragged on toward the holidays—for most of 1954, it seemed to be November—but finally December arrived and my family fell all over one another in their determination to show me a "normal" Christmas, with the result that nothing about it seemed normal at all. At first I had thought I might not have much of a Christmas, not having parents any longer—I had wonderfully dramatic visions of myself sitting by the window alone on Christmas, without presents, in an empty house—but then common sense reared its head and I realized that these people had all been a part of my other Christmases, so that it was unlikely this one would pass by unremarked.

I made a few of the normal remarks a small child makes at the beginning of the season—dry, subtle hints such as staring for long moments at the calendar and then exclaiming, "You mean it's almost Christmas?" or the more manipulative, "I don't know how Santa will be able to find me now."

They took my hints as verbalized doubts that I'd have a Christmas, and they panicked. Several of them, notably my grandmother, broached this subject with the tentativeness of a first-time brain surgeon, dancing all around the subject and letting fly with leaden hints that I need not be concerned about my holiday. I tried to make them understand that I had no real worries about Christmas, but they were determined to see me, at least at Christmastime, as The Orphan.

"Poor little thing," I heard my grandmother say one night. I was believed to be in bed; in reality I was crouched down beside my door, ear to the wood, using my radarlike hearing to eavesdrop. She said "poor little thing" again and I heard something else there as well, the remembrance of her daughter, the realization that her daughter would not share this Christmas.

"Ma," Uncle Mike said, "it'll be okay."

"It won't be okay," Grandpa said, and I could almost see his wife beaming at him for this rare moment of public support. "It's easy for us all to say it's Christmas, but the boy has never faced the holidays without his folks."

"*We're* his folks," Tom said, and he sounded irritated.

"We're no replacement for his mother and father," Grandma said, "and that's the God's truth."

"I know, Ma. But we'll…we'll just make an extra effort, we'll do it, and he'll have a good Christmas."

"Does that mean you'll go to Mass?" I heard the little musical note in her voice that said Grandma, ever the counterpuncher, had caught him at a weak moment.

"Come on, Ma, I usually go to Mass on Christmas. Lot of other times too."

"Funny, I don't remember seeing him at St. Bonny's lately, do you, Patrick?"

"Dad? He wouldn't know, Ma," Tom said, laughing. "He's not there either."

"He goes more than you do."

"We were talking about Danny, and, yeah, I'll go to Mass like I always do on Christmas."

"Have some more tea," she said, pleased with the way things were going. I was pleased as well. It seemed that my Christmas was assured, and I set about tending to my own responsibilities in the matter.

One after another, they asked me what I wanted for Christmas, conferred with one another, got on the phone with

Grandma Dorsey and various representatives of the other side of the family. Eventually it struck me that if so many people were interested in my Christmas lists I should have more than one. I sat down one afternoon when I got home from school and made three—one for each household and an extra one, labeled "For Uncles and Aunts" and intended to be shared by all members of that group.

Several times I overhead them talking about what they planned to get me, and to me they made heavy, pointed references to what Santa himself might come up with. I was reminded that Santa expected a certain standard of behavior, and I pretended to believe this, but I was certain that he'd go easy on a kid who had just lost both parents.

From the first of December, it seemed to snow all the time. It piled up in great fluffy drifts and blanketed the streets, buried up the sidewalks and made foot travel an adventure. The grown-ups looked out the window after each new snowfall and moaned about it. In the morning when I was ready to leave for school, my grandmother bound and gagged me in layers of clothing thick enough to repel bullets, including a snowsuit made for a child with longer legs. I looked at myself in the hall mirror and saw a small Aleut with lumpy legs and little or no face. Still, it kept me warm. I had that snowsuit, a pair of black rubber boots with steel buckles, a cap with ear flaps that made me look like a trooper in the Red Chinese Army, a scarf wound some fifty times around my neck and mittens. Many mittens: I lost one a week for the duration of the winter, and my grandmother eventually gave up trying to help me keep them and simply bought me duplicate pairs.

Nor were my mittens the only things I lost; when I look back upon the various stages of my life, each has a salient characteristic. The hallmark of this one is that I lost things, all sorts of things: my rosary, a tie, my books, my boots, my mittens, socks and underwear if I went swimming at the Hamlin Park pool, toys and school supplies, the myriad accoutrements of youth—I lost them all. I developed a half-serious belief that somewhere in the universe God was collecting the things I lost in a huge pile that would eventually rival the pyramids, that someday many years from now I'd happen upon this trove and be rich as Croesus.

A couple of weeks into December, Grandma entrusted me with my first task: she gave me a quarter and sent me to the corner grocery store for a quart of milk. The store was less than three hundred feet from our house, as the crow flies. I lost the quarter before I was halfway there. I returned, sobbing, and she gave me another quarter.

That night she and I laughed over my incompetence. The following day she sent me to the store with a dollar. I lost it while scratching my name in the snow with a mitten, which I also lost.

In spite of the steady drain on their income caused by my habit of losing money as soon as I made it past the door, they managed to put together a Christmas. We had a tree, though not without controversy, as my grandparents reenacted a little drama I'd once witnessed between my mother and father.

On my last Christmas with my parents, our tree had been the cause of no small discord between my mother and father. As nearly as I can understand it, my father had stopped for a few drinks at Liquor Town with his cronies and then gone out to select a Christmas tree—normally, for him, a complicated task rich in the essential matter of American business: that is to say, it involved cutthroat negotiations between two parties intent on swindling one another if given a chance.

He never bought the first tree he liked, never agreed to the price written on the tag, never accepted the word of the tree-seller about the age, variety, or health of the tree. As a result, he always came home with a magnificent tree and beamed as he told my mother what he'd paid for it. On this occasion, however, fortified by whatever he'd consumed at the saloon, he went on down to the lot in front of Riverview Park, lost his reserve and most of his judgment, and bought a tree.

In fairness to my father, it was a singular tree, even a small boy could see that: primitive people had worshipped trees like this, the Vikings had made great ships of them. As we stared, my father wrestled with its weight, falling against the doorjamb twice. It was perhaps eleven feet tall so that its spiky top was bent double against our ceiling. It was dark green and long-needled and wrapped in thick brown twine like an arboreal mummy, and when my father cut the twine, the lower branches sprang out in a green explosion and the Viking tree revealed its true dimensions: it was bigger than the living room, it consumed the living room. And, joy to a small boy, it had pine cones, it was festooned with pine cones, they dangled like little treasures and dropped from its upper branches and went bouncing across our floor as I scurried around to collect them.

"Good God," my mother said, and the tone in her voice said she wasn't praying. My father was ready for her, he'd prepared a brief speech while dragging the great tree down Clybourn Avenue that might have been effective if he'd been sober enough to pronounce even a handful of standard English words. The gist of it was that he had taken one look at this tree—from nearly a block away, he said, so easily did it stand out from its hundreds of fellows—and fallen in love with it. There was also something about buying it for her, to please her, and I saw right off that this was ill-advised.

I looked up from my pinecone collecting and saw my mother staring at him. My father was red-faced and his eyes bulged slightly and from the way he kept wetting his lips, I thought he must be thirsty. I remember him trying to hold the tree still, not realizing that it was swaying because he was, and when he was finished with his little address, he turned and bestowed a fond look on the tree. My mother watched him for a moment and pronounced the tree "a monstrosity."

"A mustrosophy?" he responded in his newfound language. "Wha's wrong with it?" My mother had then cleared her throat, put a sweet look on her face, and launched into a detailed and comprehensive listing of the tree's faults.

"It is too big for our living room," she began, speaking in a very precise way, like a grown-up giving unpleasant news to a very small child. "It is crooked, it is uneven, the trunk is too thick for our tree stand, I think it's too big for any tree stand I've ever seen, it's got more bald spots than Eisenhower's head, it's losing needles. It is ugly, very ugly. And it has pinecones. I hate pinecones."

"They're kinda nice, hon."

She shook her head. "Not in my house."

"Aw, now, just gimme my saw and I can cut 'er down a little and she'll look just fine up against the front window there." I tried to picture this leviathan of trees in the living room and decided it might work out if we could manage to live in the back half of the flat for a month.

"It'll look real nice," he went on, never knowing when to stop.

"If you put that shaggy thing in my living room, you'd better count on sleeping in there with it."

He gave her a long look, blinked twice, wet his lips again and shrugged. "Well, what can I do now, sugar? I can't take it…"

She nodded. "Yes, you can. Take it back. He'll give you another tree for the money. How much did that…no, wait, I don't want to know, if you tell me, I'll die. Just get it out of here."

My father gave the big tree a moonstruck look and then caught my eye. He raised his eyebrows in a mute request for my personal assessment and I just smiled, aware that my mother was looking in my direction now. I scuttered out of the room and, at the doorway to my bedroom, stole a glance at them. They stared at one another from across the great tree and my father was no longer smiling, not at her, nor at his beloved tree.

Eventually he buttoned up his topcoat and prepared to wrestle the tree back down the stairs. Now that he had cut the twine, it no longer fit conveniently, and it sprayed dead green needles like a machine gun when he forced it out into our hall. By the time he had it out, the floor was covered with them, he was sweating and muttering and even daring the occasional profanity. I wondered if we would have a Christmas after all. From the hall he yelled in that he had lost his hat, his new fedora that had come in a big round black box with the word "Stetson" on it. I could tell he was yelling to make my mother feel bad, but she just yelled back that the hat was caught in the top branches of his dear tree and not to stop at any more taverns before he came home. At one point I think he and the tree fell on the stairs, and I heard him cursing as he struggled with his sylvan opponent, but my mother was already humming as she began sweeping up the needles. Whatever had suddenly brought her the joy of the season had escaped me, and then it occurred to me that my father would not be back. I began to cry.

"What's wrong? Are you scared because Mommy and Daddy had a little argument?"

"No. Daddy's gone. I want Daddy to come back."

"He's coming back. People...people just have arguments, more at Christmas than any other time. I read that in the paper but I would have known it anyway. All families have arguments at Christmastime. Except the Jewish people," she said in a more musing tone. "Maybe they're lucky they don't celebrate Christmas. Anyway, he'll be back. And when he comes back, he'll have a *nice* tree."

And when he came home an hour later, sobered and holding up a more modest specimen of the conifer family, she nodded and complimented him on the return of his usual excellent taste in trees. She turned to me and said, "Nobody knows a Christmas tree like your father. I'll bet that's the most perfect tree on the lot."

He snorted, but after a few minutes a satisfied smile appeared on his face and eventually he found a moment to give me a wink and nod in the direction of the new tree, an eight-foot balsam that filled the small flat with its Christmas perfume. My mother crossed the room and pretended to be fiddling with the needles. She turned slowly and gave him a long look, and I couldn't see her face but I'm now certain what the look said, and my father wasn't drunk anymore, at least not so one would notice. She gave him a fast kiss and stepped back just as he grabbed for her, saying, "You'll drop the tree."

For the rest of the night they wrestled with the tree and the tree stand, dug out lights and ornaments, helped me hang tinsel. They had put on music, Bing Crosby and some other people, and each time I looked at my mother it seemed that she might break into a little dance, and I wondered if she could be this happy over a simple tree.

So, too, I was to learn, my grandfather apparently made the occasional misstep in this annual ritual; perhaps this was a lapse in sense that occurred in all men. The tree that Grandpa Flynn brought into his home my first Christmas in his care was a far cry from the Viking tree. It was four feet tall, listed to one side like a rowboat taking water and bore the many signs that in a human being would have indicated a hard life. It had several bare branches and a spot on one side where it had nothing at all, neither branch nor needle nor stump to indicate that any had ever been there.

I was to go more than thirty years before seeing another tree like my grandfather's, and when I did, it would be in a picture. It was in *National Geographic*, in an article about radiocarbon dating, and the role in this process of a tree called "The world's oldest living thing," the bristlecone pine. Thunderstruck when

I came across it, I studied the photograph for ten minutes to be sure, and there is now no doubt in my mind that what my grandfather had unwittingly brought into the house that December night in 1954 was a three-thousand-year-old pine tree. And, like my father in that earlier time, he stood in the doorway with his purchase and struck a proud pose for his wife.

But unlike my mother in that previous conflict, my grandmother did not say anything. She made a little squawk and my grandfather actually jumped. I sniffed at the tree from a foot or so away and detected a well-known smell but not the smell of balsam or pine sap. My unfortunate grandfather had gone to Miska's tavern on Belmont before going out to choose his tree, and what he'd done there had dulled his mental acuity, and he had come back with this gnarled little denizen of barren climes.

He frowned at her and said, "Now what's wrong with you?"

"With me? What's wrong with me? No, sir, what's wrong with you? What have you brought into my house?"

"It's a Christmas tree, for God's sake."

"It isn't."

"'I'tis." He regarded the tree for a moment and then came out with what the years have taught me is the clearest admission in the language that a Christmas tree is in some way deficient: he pronounced it "a cute little tree."

"Driftwood, someone's gone and sold you."

"It only cost a dollar."

"Who got the dollar, you or him?"

"Now what do you think?"

"I think if I live to be a thousand I'll never see an uglier tree, nor a man with less sense."

"Ah, you're never satisfied," and Grandpa punctuated his statement by thumping the tree's gnarly trunk onto the floor, an act which precipitated a green flurry as it snowed needles onto Grandma's carpet. I feared that if he did it once more, the tree would be naked.

"If you get one more needle on my floor, Patrick, I'll brain you with that scrawny thing."

"Fine talk for Christmas."

"Christmas is not for ten days, and you may yet live to see it, but not if you thump that thing on the floor again."

"And what would you have me do with it, then?"

"Throw it into the lake, and you riding it like a broomstick."

"Ah, you'd know about broomsticks."

"Or maybe you and the snake that sold it to you can both..."

"Woman, give me some peace! I'll take it back."

For some reason, this response seemed to mollify her and she just stood there, studying the tree and squinting at it.

"I'll get my money back and get you something bigger," he said, then muttered something about her "always needing the biggest, nothing is ever good enough for her ladyship," but he was already backing into the doorway, like Lee's defeated infantry.

"Oh, bring it back in, Patrick. It's here and you don't need to be out hiking around in a blizzard for another tree." I was about to point out that it really wasn't snowing at all but caught a certain look in her eye and thought better of it. "We'll fix it up and no one will know you've been sold a pine walking stick and thought it was a tree." With that, she left the room.

That night, we worked on the tree. We did not so much decorate the tree as camouflage it—with lights, tinsel, my grandma's treasured ornaments, decoration enough for a tree four times the size of this bristlecone pine, and then my uncles constructed a little wooden "extension" below the tree stand. We covered this with the cotton batting that my grandmother used as a tree skirt, and when we were done, the tree was not only closer to five feet tall but dressed up like a grand duke. When this miraculous transformation was finished, Grandpa turned off the light and we stood there in a little cluster, my uncles and grandparents and me, and we went through the ancient, silent ceremony that occurs for a least a minute or two in every house that takes in a tree at Christmas, no matter how the rest of their life is going. After a while, I watched them.

I had seen this little rite in my parents' house but never here, and as I glanced from face to face I saw the play of different emotions on them: I saw the same childlike glow that had crossed the faces of my mother and father, and more complicated things as well: I saw hope and worry and regret, and understood perhaps for the first time that this holiday would be different for them as well, try as they might to make it like all the others.

But try they did. For the next two weeks they nearly killed themselves in the daunting task of putting together a Christmas that would allow me to forget that my parents were dead. This was impossible, of course, though if there was a season when a newly orphaned child could suspend knowledge of his reality, it was Christmas. Dark fearful moments still came just before I dropped off to sleep, and on some afternoons when I was home from school and my grandfather fumbled at my mother's task of putting together a snack for me in the empty kitchen, I understood that for me everything had changed, that my parents were truly never coming back.

At times this knowledge frightened me, at other times I cried quietly and hoped no one would notice—I understood that my tears would cause them pain and did everything I could to avoid that. Even so, several times my grandparents or my uncles found me crying in a room by myself, once in a bedroom with the light off, and at these times they treated me as a fragile, wounded creature. The first couple of times, I enjoyed the extra attention, but I soon grew to hate how it made me feel.

Christmas 1954

Eventually we had Christmas, and it was in its way as memorable as any. They did their best to keep to my parents' routine, so that on Christmas Eve, Uncle Tom brought me over to Grandma Dorsey's house, where madness reigned in the basement flat on Evergreen Street. We crept down the worn stairs and he knocked on the door. Inside we could hear a dense murmur of many voices and occasional laughter, and for a moment it seemed that this was how we'd spend our Christmas Eve, standing outside Grandma Dorsey's little flat and listening to others celebrate Christmas. Uncle Tom persisted, each time rapping a little harder and finally kicking the door and yelling, "Open up! Police!" The noise died as though shot, and I heard someone mutter something. Then the door swung open and my Aunt Ellen, the oldest of the Dorsey children, stepped into the doorway and squinted out at us.

"A couple of strange men," she said in her pretend-hard voice, and then she came out and hugged Uncle Tom. She planted a dark red kiss on his cheek and then bent down and did the same to me.

"Merry Christmas, sugar," she said.

Aunt Ellen led us in and yelled, "Hey, look what Santa left on Ma's doorstep," and everyone laughed and yelled, "Merry Christmas," a woman's voice called out something about the big one being homely but the short one being "kinda cute" and

I saw my cousin Matt waving at me. I couldn't see the room for the wall of people.

There were almost two dozen of them crammed into Grandma Dorsey's little flat by the tracks, all my father's brothers and sisters and their families—my cousins, some close, others little more than acquaintances—more people in that tiny cluster of subdivided rooms than anyone could imagine, and it was all perfect. I tried to ignore the way they looked at me when I came in, as though they were just now recollecting why their brother would not be there. But it was Christmas Eve among the Dorseys, the looks passed quickly, and then it was just as I remembered from the years before, nothing had changed. I heard music, they all seemed to be talking at once, and it smelled of food—there was a ham and a turkey and platters of half a dozen other things, cakes and trays of tarts and a mince pie and huge bowls of the cookies Grandma Dorsey made day and night during the month of December, like a baker on piecework. And it was hot, from her tiny radiators all clanking and hissing and from the two dozen bodies, and the air was almost wet with ladies' perfume and men's aftershave.

Grandma came up and hugged me as though we hadn't seen each other four days earlier, and she thanked Uncle Tom for bringing me over.

"Oh, sure," he said. "Wouldn't let him miss this. Wouldn't let myself miss it."

"Nice to see you, Tom," the woman's voice said again and this time I was able to place it, my Aunt Mollie, the youngest of the Dorseys, my father's kid sister.

"Hi, Mollie," he said. After a short pause, he added, "Merry Christmas."

She was leaning against the big round oak table in Grandma Dorsey's house of clutter and she seemed for the evening to have undergone a minor transformation from slacks and sweaters:

she was wearing a dark green dress with a little gold pin of a Christmas tree, and lipstick, rare for her.

"You look sharp, both of you," she said.

"*You* look real nice," my uncle said, and I wondered what she made of the slight note of surprise in his voice.

Grandma led me into her cluttered living room and I made the appropriate noises about her tree, just a tabletop tree but hung to the groaning point with ornaments and bubble lights, wonderful bubble lights. On the floor below the table was a jumble of presents, and I stared at them till I thought I could spy one with my name on it.

Eventually we ate, all of the adults standing because there was no other way fifteen or so grown-ups could get at the tables simultaneously. I stayed with Matt and we each had a small helping of turkey and potatoes and approximately three hundred cookies. My uncle told me to go easy on the cookies and was set upon by Aunt Ellen and young Aunt Mollie for having no Christmas spirit. I filled my mouth with Grandma Dorsey's cookies—her own version of *pfeffernüsse*, her butter cookies, sugar cookies, cookies frosted in half a dozen colors, gingerbread men and women and candied dates—and watched the grown-ups: Uncle Tom seemed to be enjoying himself with the women, though he kept his eyes almost exclusively on Aunt Ellen while Mollie watched him with a sly smile and I told myself I had no idea what was going on, and it didn't matter.

Matt and I each drank the better part of a quart of orange soda and after we ate, Grandma led us and the other cousins, older and younger, over to the table with the tree, where she commanded her oldest son, my Uncle Gerald, to take charge of the passing out of presents. Someone had put a Perry Como Christmas record on my grandmother's boxy record player and the noise in the room softened but did not disappear.

When Uncle Gerry came to my package, a heavy cylinder in silvery paper—"Feels like a mortar shell. Is that what you asked

Santy Claus for, *a mortar shell?*"—I noticed that it was an exact duplicate of the one Matt was tearing at like a wolf on fresh meat. Around the room an unbroken row of smiling, sweating faces watched the kids open their gifts, and Uncle Tom winked at me when I caught his eye. My present was a set of Lincoln Logs, a big set, with Indians and a couple of frontiersmen, and it didn't matter that I already had Lincoln Logs. You could never have too much building material for your toys. I grinned over at Matt, who beamed back, and as Uncle Gerry called out the names in a voice like the priest giving a blessing, we spilled the logs out onto Grandma Dorsey's floor and began building.

The rest of Christmas Eve at Grandma Dorsey's was a welter of noise and song and food smells and a half dozen minor disasters: someone dropping a glass of wine onto the plate of sliced turkey, one of my younger cousins bawling over something, my cousin Elizabeth being sick and throwing up strawberry pop on her Christmas dress. At one point I realized I hadn't seen Matt's dad, my Uncle Dennis, and I scanned the crowd, finding only Matt's mom, my aunt Mary Jane. I heard my Uncle Tom's laughter from across the room and located him, scrunched into a corner with Aunt Mollie. Someone had changed Perry Como for something faster, a big band with a lot of horns, and Aunt Mollie seemed to be dancing in place while my uncle talked to her.

I have no idea how long Uncle Tom kept me there, but we left to a chorus of voices saying "good night" and "merry Christmas," and I fell asleep in the car before we went four blocks.

I woke in the morning to a quiet house, remembered the hot raucous party at Grandma Dorsey's and for just a sliver in time my heart sank that it was over. Then I realized it was Christmas, and I was home, and wonderful things were likely to happen here as well, if on a less epic scale. I lay back and indulged myself for a moment, reliving Christmas Eve, and then I remembered my parents—my mother mostly, for it had always been she who woke me in the early morning to tell me we'd all just missed the visitor in the red suit. I remembered the way she'd watched me as I opened my presents, the look on her face, and my throat seemed to close. Somewhere outside my door I heard the slow scuffing of slippers and my grandmother humming in a low voice and I knew I couldn't let her see me cry. I stayed there till I felt completely composed and then, allowing curiosity and youthful avarice full rein, clambered out of bed to greet the morning.

"Merry Christmas, sunshine," my grandmother said. "First we have to see if Santa brought anything, and then we'll have pancakes." The house smelled of bacon and pancakes already, and her eyes begged me to be happy. I was glad to oblige.

It was a long day, quieter than Christmas Eve had been, and included the ritual savaging of carefully wrapped presents, a breakfast no one was much interested in, a long song-filled mass, the ritual playing with presents—that is, the scattering of one's newfound wealth throughout the house, like Hansel leaving himself a trail to follow through the woods—and a Christmas dinner of great weight attended by a dozen or so of us: Uncle Mike and his girlfriend Lorraine, Uncle Tom, my grandparents, my Great-Uncle Frank, sober and serious-looking in a blue suit, along with his long-suffering wife Rose, Uncle Martin, and my Aunt Anne and her current boyfriend, a thin, quiet fellow named Roger who fawned on Grandpa and stole nervous glances down the table at Grandma, who clearly thought him beneath her daughter but held her tongue because it was Christmas. I found Roger fascinating, for I'd never seen a person whose face so clearly revealed the depths of his discomfort. The poor fellow couldn't possibly know that he was to be the first of many young men whom the family found unworthy of Aunt Anne.

I rushed through dinner as I'd dashed through breakfast, in order to play with the new toys—the new Lincoln Log set, a set of plastic spacemen, a Gene Autry cap gun with its own holster, and the prize of the day, from my grandmother, a set of lead cavalrymen from England in a burgundy-colored box, lancers they were, with red plumes and gold helmets, and the grandest set of toy soldiers I'd seen in so short a life. I knew deep inside me that I'd have the heads off half of them in a week, and in six months you wouldn't be able to tell they'd ever had lances, or even arms for that matter, but right now they were the gaudiest thing I'd found under my tree.

There were books as well, colorful books about history and a book of Greek myths, and one I'd gotten the night before from Aunt Teresa, the nun. It was a spellbinding book about children who became saints by meeting a violent end, utterly fascinating because of the blood and gore that the color plates captured so imaginatively. I played and read and snacked on the pies Grandma had bought from Heck's bakery and the cookies Grandma Dorsey had sent along with us the night before, I drank far more pop than I had thought possible, and with one ear I listened to the adults in the next room.

Uncle Martin was proclaiming that Christmas had, as a concept, deteriorated rapidly in recent years, and Uncle Frank wanted to talk politics, and several members of the family were interrogating Roger, presumably on his goals in life but really on his intentions toward Anne, and it was clear from Grandma's tone that she thought Anne had brought home an idiot. When their voices dropped to a low murmur I knew they were speaking of me, wondering and worrying whether it would all be enough to get me through my first holiday without parents.

"Poor little thing," Aunt Anne said. "God knows what it's like for him."

"Heckuva thing at Christmas," Uncle Mike said, and I knew the lugubrious side of his nature had roused itself.

"For God's sake, you talk like he's dead instead of in the next room," Uncle Tom said and my grandmother told him to watch his language. I decided this was as good a time as any to join the grown-ups, and so moved my belongings to a corner in the dining room, feigning complete disinterest in their talk.

Their later discussions were far more uplifting. My grandmother had had a glass or two of champagne, and quart bottles of Edelweiss and Meister Bräu had appeared on the table, leading to a turn in the conversation, to old family characters, including but not limited to the exploits of my Uncle Frank who, if these tales were to be believed, had done well to stay out of jail all these years, in spite of his long service as an officer of the law.

One of these adventures had apparently involved the transport, in the paddy wagon he drove, of a politician's wife and a racehorse, though it was unclear whether the lady and the horse rode in the wagon at the same time.

Uncle Frank stared at his cigarette for a while and they discussed him as though he was not present, and he made no sound till they got to the story about the horse.

"It wasn't how it looked, and that's all I'll say on the matter," Uncle Frank said, which meant he was about to expound at great length. "A simple misunderstanding," he added, which was also his explanation about a donnybrook at his own wedding and about a fiasco involving an abortive business deal involving a huge amount of rotting fish purchased down at South Water Street. I later learned this was Frank's explanation of almost every kind of trouble he had ever made for himself. Uncle Tom pressed Frank for details involving a man Uncle Frank had apparently met in a bar, and one or the other had been wearing a dress though it was unclear to me which one, but Grandma said we'd have no talk of *that* at Christmas dinner.

They laughed and told one another story upon story, and Uncle Frank sat there sipping beer and muttering to himself. I heard him say "plagued by bad luck and a soft heart," and this made them all laugh harder.

There was talk of my grandfather's late brother James, who had managed to be sought by both the Irish police and New York's finest, and then someone, perhaps Martin with his need to peer more closely at the world's dark side, brought up his own younger brother Terrence, who had fallen to his death in a construction accident, and "the twins" as he called them, brothers named Emmett and Peter—one had died and the other, his inseparable companion, had simply disappeared. Grandma reclaimed her table and her holiday and forced a change in topic to the current generation and, fortified by most of a three-dollar bottle of champagne, began declaiming about the amazing length of time it took Irish young men to settle down. I stole a glance at them and she was staring at her sons. Lorraine, Uncle Mike's girlfriend, found this amusing, but Mike studied the foam on his glass and Tom began fishing for his smokes.

My grandmother fixed her steely gaze on them and it came at last to rest on her favorite. He mumbled something to the effect that he hadn't found the right girl yet, and she began to remonstrate with him about his fussiness when the world was absolutely overrun with nice girls. It suddenly seemed that for once I had something to add to an adult discussion, and I yelled out that I thought he should marry Aunt Mollie Dorsey. All sound died in that house.

I swear that the winter wind rolling up Clybourn Avenue and rattling the loose panes in our windows chose that exact moment to cease and desist.

I looked up to reassure myself that my entire family hadn't been assumed into heaven like the Blessed Virgin and found them staring at me with facial expressions that varied from amusement (Aunt Anne's) to shock (Uncle Tom's). The silence stretched itself and threatened to settle in for the duration, and then my grandmother uttered a single word.

"Mollie." She said it with wonder and amusement, said,

"*Mollie Dorsey*," and I heard the speculation there, and then she was looking at Uncle Tom, whose neck and cheeks had gone dark red. He was no longer staring at me, having seen a more immediate need to defend himself from frontal attack.

"What about her?" he asked. "She was there. The kid saw her last night at the Dorseys."

"Of course he did. She used to go out with that Swede, didn't she? Was he there?" It didn't seem to me that there had been anybody there who looked remotely like a Swede, not that I would have known a Swede from an Apache, but I knew that Grandma already had the answer to this question.

"Now how do I know? I mean, I didn't see him."

Grandma looked at me and raised her eyebrows.

"No, he wasn't there." She looked very pleased with me and I added, "I think he's dead."

Tom shot me a look rich in irritation and I heard Uncle Mike chuckle, but I didn't care. I remembered how they'd looked, my Aunt Mollie and Uncle Tom, my favorite uncle and easily the cutest aunt if one did not count Teresa the inaccessible nun, the two of them tucked back in a doorway just a bit removed from the rest of the party. And I remembered he'd looked happy, and she'd been dancing, bopping to the music and smiling up at him. I saw no reason why they couldn't be in love, why they wouldn't be.

Uncle Tom said, "Now why would you say that? He's not dead, that guy."

"She's a nice girl. And pretty, too."

"Well, sure she is, Ma, but…"

"But nothing. For a time back there, before you went into the Service, I thought she was setting her cap for you but she was still a schoolgirl, a bit young, I suppose."

"She's not in high school now," Uncle Mike said with a serious expression, and I understood from the look Tom gave him that Mike had decided to have fun with this. "Nice girl, too. Sense of humor, got a personality." He looked at Lorraine. "Don't you think?"

Lorraine nodded eagerly. "Oh, sure, lots of personality. She's real nice. Smart, too, I think."

"And how is she doing?" Grandma asked Tom.

"She's fine," he said in a monotone. Grandma did the eyebrows with him now and he added, "She's a nice girl, I like to talk to her. We're just, you know, friends."

"Friends?" she said, as though this was an alien concept. "Friends. Not good enough for you, though."

"It's not that, Ma. I'm not getting mixed up with one of the Dorseys, I mean, it just wouldn't feel…"

"Oh, who cares how it feels? It happened once, there was nothing wrong with it, God Bless both their souls…" Here she seemed to recollect me and caught herself. "She's a nice girl, a pretty girl, for heaven's sake." She seemed genuinely irritated. "You've got your mind set on something else, that's all. People always want what they can't have."

I looked down at my toys, not wanting to see whatever turn this would bring in the conversation, but apparently she'd said what she felt like saying. I heard her getting up and clearing the table, and then Tom dropping silverware in his haste to help her, and so to forestall her anger. A couple of minutes later all was normal, and the men adjourned to the living room to doze. I cringed as Tom passed me, but he patted me on the head.

Enemies and Allies

For all their stress and madness, the holidays hide things, they preoccupy us so intensely that we forget our life's troubles. It is that first bleak stretch of January that often reminds us of the true nature of things.

The winter of 1955 promised to last forever. It pursued us on the streets and breached the walls of our houses, so that boilers failed, sinks coughed up water dark orange with rust, pipes froze. It seemed to me that I walked each morning bent over into the same gales that scoured Clybourn Avenue, stepped onto the same ice sheets and plunged over the tops of my boots into black water, stumbled over the same drifts that piled up on the corners. I was always cold, always arriving places tired from fighting through the thick snow on the sidewalks, it seemed that the Ice Age had come again. In the mornings Aunt Anne or one of my uncles would march me up Clybourn. At the corner of Damen and Clybourn, we'd meet up with cousin Matt and his mom, and the adults would let us walk to school together.

School soon became a torment, not for any harsh treatment or difficulty with subject matter but from a kind of restlessness that seemed to come over me when the holidays were over. I drew constantly, and when I wasn't drawing I was staring out the windows and wishing for the snow to go away.

And now I began to notice another pattern, one that I found most painful. The school day was rich in references to parents, and activities involving them seemed constant. In the first half of the year we had drawn Thanksgiving pictures of our family at dinner, and we'd made Christmas cards from construction paper and paste, and a tissue-and-coat-hanger wreath "for your mother," the art teacher had said. These small injuries were offset by the imminence of Christmas itself, but there was no such balm for my feelings in the second half of the school year. I saw my schoolmates' mothers walking them to school, heard the principal's announcement over the loudspeaker of parent-teacher conferences, and listened to the art teacher wax enthusiastic about the Valentine's card we'd soon be doing "for your Mom and Dad." When we were to describe what our fathers did for a living, Sister Polycarp invited me to talk about Uncle Tom or my grandfather, and the other children seemed interested but I knew it could not be the same.

Without seeing a connection, I grew short-tempered, I spent little time on homework assignments and forgot half of them; my answers in class were frequently wrong, and when my classmates began to laugh at me, I discovered a new role. I went out of my way to say and do stupid things, reveled in their laughter, and in a short time taught them to expect the bizarre from me. Through it all, the big moon-faced nun at the front of the room stared calmly at me, like one waiting for a long-winded speaker to finish. Sister Polycarp had taken the name, I learned, of an obscure martyr and bishop of the early church, and we called her "The Carp," not from any personal animus toward her but simply because she was there, and a nun, and a teacher. We had names for them all.

In quiet, measured tones she corrected my responses, silenced the class, steered the lessons back on course. When possible, she ignored me. Other times she kept me after school. My disruptions were constant and my nervous energy mounted through the week till I was a mass of tension come Friday, my antics hit a peak and I had to be disciplined.

I seem to recall standing for at least part of each Friday in a corner, or facing the blackboard. She led me to my place without comment, resumed her lessons as though I did not exist. Her serenity enraged me. One afternoon she put me in the corner and I simply refused to shut up, so she taped my mouth closed. It was just paper tape and I licked through it in twenty minutes, to the delight of my fellow scholars. Sister put me out in the hall and I remained there till school was over.

She kept me there as my classmates went by and then handed me a note to give to my grandparents. The note invited them to come and see her. This meeting took place the following evening and when my grandmother and Aunt Anne returned, they were not angry as I had expected but very quiet. They sat me down in the kitchen and told me the gist of their conversation with my teacher, which was that I seemed to be going out of my way to become the class clown.

"She's trying to be patient with you, Danny," Aunt Anne said, and my grandmother muttered something about what Sister Polycarp was going to think of the family that was raising me.

"She says you act like a little crazy man," Grandma added, "like you lost your mind."

"I think she likes you, Danny," Aunt Anne said, and I nodded though I was fairly certain my teacher had taken a deep dislike to me, and I was not at all surprised. I promised them I'd try to do better. When I saw my uncles, I expected new lectures from them, but Uncle Mike just told me to "settle down," and Tom asked, "You gonna try to do better, kiddo?" while his eyes asked other questions.

I was taken aback by their chorus of disapproval and it bothered me greatly that I had no explanation for myself. More than anything, I was frustrated at my inability to call up any of what seemed half a dozen good reasons for the way things happened, it seemed there were things I could say that would make them all shut up, but I could think of none of them. They were disappointed in me and it seemed unfair. After all, I never began a school day looking for ways to disrupt my classroom. I didn't intentionally forget my homework or what little I studied. It merely happened. I convinced myself quickly that they understood nothing of my situation, that it would be fruitless to try to explain my side. I decided that I would do better, but I believed not much would come of it, for I'd made an enemy in the classroom.

After about a week of meticulously forced good behavior, Sister Polycarp sent home another note, saying that I was doing well, and Grandma and Aunt Anne congratulated me, unaware that even a child bound for a life of crime will manage a week of good behavior after a serious parent-teacher meeting.

As I was leaving the kitchen with a handful of pretzels, my aunt stopped me.

"Matt's still having trouble, Danny."

"He's in trouble all the time," I said, then added, "He's got Sister Charles Boromeo," certain that this was explanation enough for Matt's more difficult time. There were two second grades and Matt was in the other one, and though Sister Polycarp and I were embarked on a course of strife, I wouldn't have traded places with Matt for anything.

Anne opened her mouth and seemed to catch herself. She wanted to tell me something and couldn't seem to bring herself to do it. In the end, she nodded. "Yes, he's in trouble a lot, the poor kid. He's not…school's not a very comfortable place for your cousin." This seemed to me to be a rather stupid observation, and I was disappointed in her: of course he wasn't happy, none of us were, we were all schoolkids at the mercy of teachers with unclear goals, capricious temperament, and medieval notions of discipline.

It was true enough that Matt was in trouble "all the time": we had entered into a tacit competition to see which of us could range farther outside the pale of civilized behavior in school and, irritant though I may have been in my own class, I was not in Matt's weight class. He had given some indication in first grade that he'd be trouble in a classroom, but had gone on to outdo himself in second, turning his school days into a sort of war between himself and Sister Boromeo and the principal, and anybody else who took their side.

It did not help matters that Sister Charles Boromeo was aged and frail and irascible, a tiny black-robed curmudgeon who scuttered back and forth with little feverish movements and lost her temper and her concentration at the slightest disturbance. She thought he was incorrigible, and announced it to anyone who would listen; she further held to the unshakable notion that Matt and I were brothers and shared a sort of miscreant gene pool that had already determined our fates.

Eventually I was to learn that the rickety nun had also taught my father and Uncle Gerald on Matt's side, and Uncle Mike and Uncle Tom on mine, and that these experiences had taught her no good could come of our bloodlines. It was a time of physical punishment, in the classroom as well as in the home—small wonder that we fought constantly in the playground, on corners, in the alleys, picked senseless fights, and displayed what seems to me now to have been a random cruelty—and the ill-tempered little nun was quick to use her hand on her unruly charges.

And so, when my well-meaning aunt tried to tell me that school was a difficult place for Matt, I had the odd new experience of knowing things my adults could only guess at.

She could not know, none of them could, what Matt and I talked about, what I knew about him. On those rare occasions when neither of us was kept after school, we walked home together and I listened in surprise and admiration at his fulminations, his raging youthful tirades about school: he hated it, hated the nuns, hated the subjects, worthless subjects that were of no practical value—"What good's religion, tell me that, huh?" he would ask. He was bored nearly to madness and had begun to spread his frustration in the classroom. His frantic teacher had taken to hitting him with a ruler and pulling on his hair, and he plotted her demise. He told me if she hit him once more, he'd punch her in the nose, he'd chop her head off, he'd throw the body in the North Branch of the Chicago River which flowed just a few yards past Matt's home in the projects.

On afternoons when his rage was at low ebb, we made a game of it, allowing our comic-book-filled imaginations to devise ingenious ways to rid our world of Sister Charles Boromeo: we would tie her across the streetcar tracks on Western Avenue, drop her out of the Para-Chutes at Riverview, drown her in the murky water of the lagoon in Lincoln Park, stuff her lifeless corpse in the cold stone sarcophagus in the Egyptian room at the Field Museum, toss her in with the piranhas at the Shedd Aquarium.

Week in and week out, Matt was disciplined constantly, his parents called in. The mornings after these meetings he was sullen and subdued. On one occasion, I was late and they were already waiting for me, my Aunt Mary Jane and Matt, tight-lipped and pale. He refused to say anything and she sent us on our way. For several blocks he said nothing. Looking at his angry profile, I saw that Matt had a red welt on the side of his face and another on his forearm.

"Where'd you get those?" I asked when we were a block from school.

"Where d'ya think? My old man." After a moment he added, "He really gave it to me."

"With what?"

"His belt. That's what this is from, the buckle on his stupid belt," he said, holding up his arm. "I hate him."

For some time I couldn't say anything, he'd given me so much to think about: I couldn't imagine anyone in my family hitting me with anything but the flat of a hand on my behind, and that rare enough. And I'd never heard a child speak with such pure hostility about a parent.

"He's not happy, Danny," Aunt Anne said. "There are things in his life…" she began, and I saw her confusion. She had things to tell me and wasn't sure how, wasn't sure how much, and in the end she just gave up and repeated, "He's just not a happy kid."

"I know," I said. I thought of Matt's anger at his father, of the beatings and the angry red marks on his face and arms, on the face of this boy whose life at times seemed perfect to me, and wondered.

After school sometimes I went to Hamlin Park with my local playmates, and more often than not we ran into Matt. Sometimes he was wandering alone and fell in with us, but most of the time he was with other boys, frequently boys I didn't know from the far end of the neighborhood beyond Riverview or from the section of the projects along the river where he lived. Once or twice I saw him with older boys, and on these occasions he barely acknowledged me. I wondered how he knew so many different children from the far corners of the neighborhood.

One afternoon he was in a fight. He was matched with an older boy and taking a beating. They boxed and the older boy used his reach to throw long rights that caught Matt coming in and bloodied his mouth and nose, and he kept coming in. I yelled that they had to stop it and the other boys ignored me, I told them my uncle was coming to break it up and they finally stepped in. The older boy backed off and they had to hold Matt off him, he was crying and panting through his bloody mouth, his breath making bubbles through the blood and saliva. When it was over he stalked off down the street, head down, hands clenched in tight little fists. I ran after him but he wouldn't talk to me.

For a time I believe I actually worked at my truce with Sister Polycarp though an observant witness would have seen the fragile fabric of the thing unraveling. In the other second grade just down the hall, however, nothing had changed. Matt was still embroiled in his undeclared war with the entire adult world. He was punished constantly, sent home with notes. His parents were called in again and again to conferences with his teacher and the principal. At one of them the old nun informed Matt's parents that he would never amount to anything, that he was just like all the other males from our family that she'd had the unpleasant task of teaching, and Aunt Mary Jane would have gone for the old woman's throat if not for the intervention of the young assistant pastor, who calmed her down and brought the meeting to an uneasy close.

In the mornings when we walked to school together I was no longer subjected to his high-pitched rages. Frequently he was silent, and at other times he just spoke of what he planned to do that day after school. He talked frequently of the older boys he'd taken up with at the park, particularly one named Joe Kunzel, a tall, handsome blond boy several years older who had a little gang of younger children that he led through the neighborhood. Several times they'd engaged in fistfights with other groups of boys at local schoolyards, and once Matt told me in gleeful tones that they'd begun regularly to steal pop and gum from the small grocery store on Damen and George. I went along with them on a couple of their raids through the area but Joe Kunzel made it clear he wasn't much interested in me becoming part of his gang, and the feeling was mutual. I didn't really want to be there when they had their adventures: I preferred not to see what they did.

February closed with snow and March brought in cold and sleet, and then surprised us with our first warm day of the year. That morning we were walking to school when Matt shocked me by stopping at the viaduct on Diversey and announcing that he wasn't going any further.

"You're gonna be late," I pointed out.

"I'm cuttin', nitwit."

"You can't."

"Wanna bet?"

"You'll catch it."

He gave me a cold look and then snorted. "Oooh, I'm so scared. You think I don't catch it already, Dan? Whattya think happens when I get home with those stinkin' notes? And if I lose the notes, they call my ma, and my old man comes home and beats the crap outta me. I ain't goin', and I don't care what they do."

"Okay."

"Don't say nothing to nobody."

"They'll ask me what happened…"

"Tell 'em I stopped here to pee on the tracks and we were late so you went ahead."

I did as instructed, went through my studies and eventually forgot about Matt. At lunch, the principal caught me on the playground and interrogated me. I gave her my story and she watched me for a long moment, clearly suspicious, then let it go. That night Aunt Mary Jane called and they put me on the phone, informing me that I was never to let my cousin run off again, that he could have been in danger, that anybody could have grabbed him and thrown him in the river. When she was through I felt as if the whole affair had been my idea, and my grandmother looked at me as though I'd robbed the church. My Uncle Tom took me aside.

"You got caught in the middle here, see? You let him get you into this. Next time tell him he got you into trouble and you're not gonna lie for him. That's what your grandma is mad about. That's all that is."

"Aunt Mary Jane is mad at me, too."

"Aunt Mary Jane is mad because she's worried about her kid." He sighed. "And she's got good reason," he added, and I wondered what he meant.

The Roaster

It was to prove a difficult March for me, but a Saturday early in the month provided a brief interlude in my life, for it was on that day that my grandmother made the mistake of sending Grandpa for a chicken.

We were in the living room, the three of us, and Grandpa was reading the sports section, and affected not to understand Grandma's request.

"A chicken?"

"Yes, a nice one for dinner. A fresh one. I'll make dumplings."

He grumbled and snorted, and after a moment said, "Where do you want me to get a chicken?"

"Go to the German over there on Belmont. He'll give you a nice bird. I didn't like that bird I bought at the A&P."

"That was a chicken, was it?"

"Now what did you think it was?"

Grandma berated him for his inability to be serious and then he gave her an odd look, then looked again at me. He smiled and I experienced one of those moments when another person's thought is actually visible to the beholder. His face froze and a glassy look came into his eyes. He grinned now, looking just this side of demented, and then he nodded to his wife.

"A chicken, is it? All right, I'll go buy a chicken. Can I take this fellow with me?" He pointed to me.

"All right." She gave me a pointed look. "A roaster, tell the man."

I recall that I had a lovely time, tempered slightly by my realization that, two hours into our journey, we had ridden buses, bought snacks, and stopped in several taverns but we were no closer to finding a chicken than a cure for cancer.

I knew better than question him about our direction, so I rode the buses with him and listened to him chatting with the other drivers. We got off the Roosevelt Road bus at Racine and he stood there on the corner for several seconds, hands in his pants pockets, looking up the street at the low-rise projects.

"This was my neighborhood a long time ago." A dreamy look had come into his eyes and I had the notion that for just a moment, he'd forgotten I was there.

Coming up the street, was a huge green wagon full of loose vegetables and crates of them, pulled by the most massive horse I'd ever seen. The driver sat impassively and looked straight ahead, as though unaware that he'd left his own time and entered ours.

Grandpa saw me watching the great horse. "You like the horses, do you?"

I told him I did.

"Well, I'll have you know, when they made me a foreman on the Illinois-Central railroad, I rode a horse."

"You rode a horse?" I gaped at him, unable of course to see him as the nineteen- or twenty-year-old he must have been.

"I did," he assured me, and he might as well have told me he'd fought dragons.

"I rode all day, up and down the line to see that the men worked and make sure there was no trouble. I had long sections of track to cover, and no one but me to cover it. I rode that horse all day in whatever weather there was." He tried to make it sound arduous and wearing, but I heard the little sigh in his voice that said it had been a grand thing to be a young

Irishman in the new country riding a horse under the warm sun and giving orders to other people. "A chestnut mare, I rode."

I tried to relate this image to my life. "Were you with your mother and father?"

"Oh, no, no. My father was dead by then, and my mother stayed in Ireland with my sisters. She died in 1932. Twenty-three years she's been dead," he added, with a note of surprise. "That first year, I had a room on O'Brien and my brother lived on Parnell, I thought all the streets was named after Irishmen. He's gone now, you know."

"He died in a fire."

"Yes," my grandfather said, and offered nothing more.

"Did you know Grandma then?"

"Ah, I did and I didn't. I knew her, knew *of* her, you know, back in the old country. Our families knew one another. Her people are from Leitrim, the same as mine, and my brothers and I knew Martin and Frank and the twins, all of them. My oldest brother actually had some notions about marrying your grandmother's older sister, but nothing came of it. Then I come to the States, about the same time Martin came here, and after I'd been here awhile, Martin brought over your Uncle Frank and your grandmother, and the twins, and the poor fella that fell down the elevator. Martin had more sense then, you see. And it was Martin who decided I needed to meet a nice girl and settle down."

"You were lonesome?"

"Oh, you know, you miss the people you left behind, and you're in a new place and you don't know people enough to talk to. I didn't know many girls, that's for sure."

He puffed at the dwindling cigarette butt and then put it out by squeezing it between his thumb and forefinger.

A group of children ran by us and gave him a look. Several of them were black, and I was fascinated.

"Were there colored people?"

"Not many, at least not right here. But there were colored people. And Jews over there on Maxwell Street. 'Jewtown,' we used to call it. And other kinds of people, every kind you could think of, really."

"Did you like them?"

He seemed on the verge of an easy answer, then stopped himself. "I did not. I…we didn't like the colored. Young men don't like anybody different. There is trouble all through life, and you want to blame somebody for it."

"Grandma says there's good people and bad people in all the races."

He made a snorting sound. "She would. But she's right about that. Just don't tell her I said so. I don't want to start something I'll regret."

"Are women as smart as men?"

"Well," he said, and his eyebrows shot up in what I knew to be the sign of significant thought. "I suppose some of them are. Your grandmother—and don't tell her I said *this* or I'll say you just made it up—she's smarter than most of the men I've ever known, and your Aunt Teresa Dorsey that's the nun, well, she's as smart as anybody you're likely to meet." He frowned and for a moment his thoughts occupied him.

"You see, Danny, most men are utterly stupid. It has been a shock and a disappointment to me, but it's true. Now, you happen to come from a long line of intelligent men, and the Irish are known for it in general, but you'd be surprised how many men are too dumb to come in out of the rain."

"Like Aunt Mary's husband Joe?"

This seemed to strike him funny, and he laughed aloud.

"You've been listening to your uncles again."

"Yes."

He patted me on the head. "Your Uncle Michael thinks you hear everything, no matter where you are. But, yes, old Joe Collins, he's a prime example of what I'm saying."

"But he's Irish."

His face clouded. "There's people born with three arms, there was a cow born with two heads over in India, two complete heads. Yes, Joe Collins is Irish. The world is a place of strange things, difficult for us to explain. I think it's God showing off his sense of humor."

"Oh."

We wandered by the beautiful old Holy Family Church, which had survived the Chicago Fire, stopped in a saloon on the corner of Roosevelt and Racine, where many of the faces at the bar were black, some white. He had a shot and a beer and bought me a coke with a cherry in it.

We wandered over to Maxwell Street, where many of the vendors were doing their business a day in advance of Sunday's weekly free-for-all of street capitalism. He bought me hot dogs at a smelly stand where onions sat in an ominous brown pile at the end of the grill. A tiny, wrinkled man tried to sell him a green suit, another offered him a fedora, and a dark-haired vendor sold him a small religious statue that appeared to be a saint—"Holy thing," the vendor said in troubled English. He was short and grim-looking, with nose hair and bad teeth, and he watched Grandpa warily. Then they engaged in twenty seconds of spirited haggling and Grandpa got the little statue for fifty cents.

"Which saint is it, Grandpa?"

"I don't know, but we'll tell your grandmother it's St. Patrick."

We wandered farther and farther away from the main street, ending up at a viaduct, where he sat down on a piece of concrete. "To catch my breath," he said, but it seemed he'd stopped to cough.

Our seemingly purposeless wandering had begun to worry me.

I waited till he'd stopped coughing. "Are we lost?"

"No, no, of course not. You can't get lost in Chicago."

"Are we going to get a chicken?"

"Oh, we are, indeed. We're going to give her a bit of the Old Country."

With that, he got to his feet and announced that it was time to see "Barney." We returned to Racine Street and a squat brick building that seemed to have sunk down below the rest of its block. At the bottom of a short staircase, we pushed our way into a long low room filled with people and cages, noises and smells, a hot, roiling, crowded place that was part market, part circus and probably never knew a quiet moment.

People stood at a counter babbling with a fat man and a tall woman while others peered into the small metal cages that lined three walls of the shop, cages piled one on top of another and filled with chickens, rabbits, ducks, and a few birds of, to me, mysterious provenance. Some of the chickens had seemingly freed themselves, for there were at least half a dozen strutting around the sawdust-strewn floor and pecking for food, and no one seemed to mind. I looked up at my grandfather and saw that he was laughing soundlessly at my reaction.

The fat man behind the counter boomed out, "Hey, Irish!" and the woman clapped her hands as though my grandfather's appearance was Christmas come early. They hugged and shook hands and Grandpa pulled me to the counter by the elbow. He introduced them as Dora and Barney.

"This is Daniel, my grandson," he said.

The woman clapped her hands together again and said that I was handsome. She had an explosion of gray hair like old steel wool but a very young-looking face, a pretty face, dominated by an amused pair of blue eyes. The man was red-faced and dark-eyed, with huge hands, and I noticed that, like my grandfather, he'd lost a fingernail or two to the vicissitudes of manual labor. He winked at me and said, "So you're the crown prince, huh?" and I laughed at the oddness of the idea. I held out my hand and he engulfed it in his dark, calloused fingers.

"Go ahead and look around, look at the critters," his wife said, and my grandfather added, "Find us a chicken."

I turned and found myself facing a big one that eyed me with impertinence and blocked my path.

"Except that one," Grandpa said. "That's a rooster."

"Thinks he owns the joint," Barney said, and they laughed as I stepped gingerly around the glaring bird.

I was in heaven. For what seemed ages, I wandered around the shop peering into the cages and making the acquaintance of the rabbits, chickens, ducks, and pigeons—at least there were a number of what appeared to be pigeons, though I was unsure what anyone would want with a pigeon.

While I was making overtures of friendship to a large brown rabbit, a door opened out of the back wall and a younger version of Barney entered the room. He was puffing on a cigarette and wearing a bloody apron, and I assumed he was somehow connected with a local butcher shop and had come to visit Barney or see the interesting animals. When he noticed me at the rabbit's cage he made a curt nod.

"That's a good one there."

I smiled and nodded, impressed at his taste in pets.

Eventually my grandfather called out to me that it was "time to pick the prize roaster," as he put it, and I selected a reddish-brown hen that seemed particularly friendly. Somehow I had lost all sight of our mission, and I no longer realized the impending fate of whatever bird I chose, or of all the birds in the shop, for that matter. Barney brought me back to earth with a jolt, taking the bird from its cage and calling out, "Hey, Lou!" in a voice that shook the walls and startled some of the animals.

The blood-stained man reappeared from the back room, cleaver in hand, and then I understood that I'd passed a death sentence on this hen. Barney was handing the bird over when my grandfather said, "No, hold on there, Barney. Gonna have a little fun with the old woman." He didn't say what the fun was, but the nature of it seemed clear to Barney and his smiley wife, for they both laughed, and the woman called Grandpa a scoundrel.

The upshot was that Grandpa paid Barney some money—a dollar and a half, I think—and we left the store with the bird shut up in a cardboard carton. At my insistence that the bird would need "fresh air," Barney had punctured the sides in a couple of places. Delighted with our new companion, I waved to Barney and Dora, promising to look after Grandpa and to come back and see them sometime.

We walked to Ashland, and by the time our bus came, the chicken had gotten its head outside of the box, so that it seemed my Grandpa was carrying a box decorated with a chicken's head. The chicken made frequent squawks so that my grandfather kept telling her, "Pipe down, you," and seemed annoyed, but I thought that for a creature confined to a cardboard box she was surprisingly well-behaved.

We boarded the bus, but the driver was a young man who did not know my grandfather, wasn't impressed by the brotherhood implicit in his streetcar man's card, and seemed to feel that a chicken on a public bus was an abomination. He curled his lip, exchanged a sour look with the chicken, and shook his head.

"Can't bring that on a bus, Mac."

"It's the boy's pet, pal. Can you go along with me here?"

"Nah, they got rules, sanitation and like that."

He started to give Grandpa a lecture on public behavior, telling him people didn't need to see a filthy chicken sitting on the bus. Grandpa listened patiently to his spiel, then pointed to the comatose drunk sprawled halfway into the aisle in one of the front seats.

"My chicken's not as good as this bum here?"

The driver shot an unwilling glance at the snoring drunk, who had begun drooling down his shirtfront, then looked at the chicken. The bird seemed to sense that this was a pivotal moment and made neither movement nor sound, meeting the driver's eye till the man shrugged.

"Ah, go on. It's all the same to me. You know, that's not even the first chicken I've had on this bus today." He sounded disgusted.

My grandfather patted him on the shoulder and told him he was "a good egg."

The Ashland bus smelled of food, and I would have sworn someone was eating fried chicken, but the upshot was that somewhere around Chicago Avenue the chicken made a break for freedom. For several minutes she struggled at the confining flaps of the boxtop, and then she had it open. She burst up like a cresting whale and cleared the box before I could grab at her, then went scuttering and squawking up the aisle of the bus to the consternation of my grandfather and the amusement of the other passengers.

The bus had come to a stop, and from the front I could hear the driver cursing, though whether his words were meant for the chicken or my grandfather was impossible to say. It had been a long day, with a great deal of walking and no small amount of liquor, and my grandfather was frankly not quite in the chicken's class when it came to a footrace, so the bird made it to the front of the bus before Grandpa was anywhere near it.

Then it made a small error, circling back and slipping past him, only to run into me. I was certain that the bird would peck my eyes out or work some other birdish horror upon me, but I grabbed it and clutched it to my chest in terror. My grandfather held his hands out and I thrust the bird into his arms. Then the light apparently changed, the bus lurched out into traffic, and Grandpa lost what little balance he'd begun with. With the bird tucked uncertainly under one arm, he fell back against a pole, grabbed for it, and missed, falling onto the lap of a man with a lunchbox.

The chicken also landed on this man, her startled-looking face no more than an inch from his. He had apparently been dozing, and now awoke to find a strange man on his lap and a chicken staring into his eyes, and quite understandably he screamed—in Polish, Grandpa later told me—and this shook the already-terrified chicken, who pecked once at the man's nose and bolted up off him in a burst of noise and feathers and avian terror.

By now the aisle of the bus was filled with passengers trying to get a better look at this urban drama, so that the chicken had no way out except to go bounding up onto the laps of still other travelers, and from their surprised bodies to the metal seatbacks. I saw what she had in mind and tried to head her off, with my grandfather exhorting me not to let her get away, and even in my confusion and panic I heard amusement beginning to form in his voice, though I couldn't have said why. People were yelling and laughing, and one man was cursing and yelling that the chicken had beaked a hole in his *Daily News*.

I pushed and squeezed my way to the front, where the driver was yelling at us to get "the goddamn chicken" off his bus, but he could have saved his breath because at that moment the bus pulled in at Ashland and Clybourn, our stop. Grandpa had his hand around the chicken's neck. He yelled at me to grab the bags, and then we were off the bus.

A few minutes later we were on the Clybourn bus, the blessed Clybourn bus that would take us to within a few feet of our house. This new bus was almost as crowded as the Ashland bus had been, but with the difference that most of the earlier bus's riders had been either sober or sane. Our new bus was one of those urban adventures that come together by fluke or the sardonic humor of the Deity, when the unbalanced feel one another's pull like gravity and are drawn to a common place. I was to encounter such full-moon gatherings in many Chicago locations during my life—Bughouse Square, the Jackson El, the old Pixley & Ehlers cafeterias—but in this case, the odd and mentally infirm had collected on a simple bus, the Clybourn bus.

At least a dozen drunks occupied the bus. In the very middle of the bus a man was playing the harmonica, occasionally interrupting his performance with an *a cappella* version of his tune and in the long back seat that stretched from one side to another, a crazed-looking man sang out greetings to the other riders. In the front, closest to the driver, an ancient woman eyed the newcomers and commented to herself about them. Our chicken proved to be beyond her depth, and she stared slack-jawed as we moved past her with the bird. We sat and I looked around uncertainly and saw here and there the dangling legs or arms of riders who had seen no reason to stay conscious during their ride.

The chicken did not like the Clybourn bus. Whether exhausted by its exertions in the name of freedom or irritated by the music on the bus, it soon made its feelings known. The bird gave voice to a long, plaintive shriek.

"He's hitting that little boy," I heard a woman call out.

"Ah, you shut your trap, you old busybody, it's a chicken, for God's sake," Grandpa yelled back at her. After only a few moments the other passengers seemed to acclimate themselves to the chicken's presence and its unearthly noise, and returned to their various amusements. The din was awful, my ears were pulsing, and my grandfather put his face in his hand and shook his head. After a while he looked around, then at me.

"You know we're the only ones on this bus that aren't crazy?"

I nodded, and our neighbors, as if encouraged by this attention, burst into a hydra-headed rant of chatter and music that provoked in the terrified chicken an answering wail.

The strange man in the back seat and the beady-eyed little woman in the front had somehow discovered each other and plunged into a verbal duel of insults and crazed accusations.

Around them people sang, laughed, joined into the debate, or snored.

My grandfather surveyed the little self-contained capsule of human madness and made a slow shake of his head.

"When I was a streetcar man, I always imagined that there was a streetcar to hell. That people going to hell went there on a streetcar, a slow one that made you wait a long time and then was too crowded for you to sit, and had a driver that barked at you like a mad seal, and I always imagined that it would sound just like this." He paused and listened for a moment. "Save yourself, Daniel, for we have boarded the express to Hades." He laughed and looked out the window and muttered, "Serves me right."

It was growing darker, and I had a sudden fearful thought.

"Are we going to be too late for dinner?"

He thought for a moment and then decided to face the ugly truth. He let out a long sigh. "For today's dinner, yes, we're too late." He eyed me for a moment and then added, "But we're very early for tomorrow's."

He grinned and I laughed with him, and then he put his face in the palm of his hand again and his voice came out muffled: "Why am I laughing? I'm dead, you're dead. I wouldn't give you a nickel for our hides when she gets hold of us."

I smiled and looked around me, and when I glanced back his way, I saw that he was watching me. My grandfather had looked at me this way before, but now I could read other things in the look, and one of them was sadness. I had not yet understood the reasons for this sadness, at least I had not allowed myself to admit to them, but at that moment I knew I felt something of what he was feeling, and bus ride to hell or no, I didn't want it ever to end. I began to cry, silently, looking away or hiding my face in the collar of my jacket, and when he saw, he put an arm around me and hugged me to him. That he did not ask what I was crying about told me that he knew, and that I did indeed have something to cry about.

The chicken came to my aid. With one arm around me, Grandpa couldn't keep the tired flaps of the box in place, and the wily bird saw one last chance at freedom. Once more it launched itself out of its confinement and then went cackling in terror up and down the aisle of the bus to hell as the driver snarled at it to shut up, and when the bus finally pulled in at the corner of Clybourn and Diversey, the chicken alighted with a young woman and we followed.

We pursued our errant dinner across the street, watching it weave in and out of traffic, and then it spotted the doorway to Liquor Town. A man was coming out and our chicken saw its moment, ducking inside before this portal to freedom could close. I realized we would be known by half the patrons, but Grandpa pushed on in, exhorting me to follow him. I felt that if Grandpa could handle the embarrassment, then I was his man.

Sure enough, we did know a number of the startled people lining the stools of the long bar. Several were friends of Grandpa's, and there were even several women there, this being Saturday. They gave us a shocked look and then Grandpa galvanized them into movement.

"Help us catch that damn thing," he yelled.

"You can't bring that bird in here," the bartender yelled.

"We didn't *bring* 'im in, he come in by himself," Grandpa pointed out, and when the bartender continued to protest Grandpa said, "Ah, pipe down."

We pursued the bird into the back room of Liquor Town, where two sweating fat men made pizzas. There were more than a half dozen of us now, but the chicken was neither impressed nor cowed, it gave no hint of ever tiring, and the two fat pizza cooks chose to cheer it on, which seemed to give the bird renewed heart for the struggle.

In the end, perhaps from exhaustion but possibly from boredom, the chicken sought out the dark wedge of space between the two pizza ovens, a dead-end, and Grandpa stuffed it back into the box. Grandpa told me to follow him, and we went back out onto Clybourn. Then he set down the box and stood back, bent over with his hands on his knees. He was sweating, and a pair of red spots had appeared high on his pale cheekbones. He coughed, a long cough that took his breath for a time, but when it subsided, he was laughing silently. Inside the box, the bird was silent, motionless; then I saw the beak through the flaps, and soon one dark beady eye appeared to assess us and our intentions.

"What are we doing, Grandpa?"

He gave me an odd look. "I dunno. Maybe we'll let it go."

"But why, Grandpa?"

"Well, we've had so many adventures together, the three of us, seems a shame to kill it. I've come to think of it as an old friend. I think you've developed a fondness for it as well."

I considered this for a moment. In all our time with the chicken, I hadn't envisioned the probable end for this unhappy bird, and now that I could, it didn't seem at all fair. Then I pointed out the problem with this notion.

"What about Grandma?"

"Ah, that's a horse of a different color. She didn't have no adventures, did she? No, she'd look at this stupid bird and just see a nice dinner, while you and I, we see a...a companion." He thought for a moment, then said, "Ah, well, if she kills me, at least I'll die with a clear conscience." He bent over and pulled back the flaps of the now-tattered box. The chicken eyed him, then thrust its head out into the air like a feathered periscope and surveyed the street.

"You're free, you stupid thing, you can go," Grandpa said, "but stay away from the gray house up the street, that's Old Lady Gorski, that old Polack'll eat you raw."

The bird sniffed at the air, then leaped out of the box and took off at a brisk but unpanicked, even dignified pace. We watched it marching off up Clybourn, in the general direction of the now-closed Riverview, and I had no trouble imagining the chicken finding its way inside the darkened park and living off old peanuts and popcorn and having a fine life for a bird once destined for a dinner platter.

Then we went back inside Liquor Town and my grandpa took me to the phone, put in a nickel, and let me explain the situation as I saw it: namely, that the chicken had escaped and had last been seen heading west, and that Grandpa was distraught. "Distraught" was his word, and I felt it to be a fine word for the circumstances though I had no idea what it meant.

"He's *what?*" my grandmother asked.

I gave her the fine word again, then explained that my grandfather was even now sitting at the bar of Liquor Town, too mortified to come home, too shamed to face his wife without the dinner he'd been sent for. I didn't actually feel this was a lie, for his discomfort was manifest, and we'd both seen her lose her temper.

She paused at the other head for a long time, then said, "Is he sober?"

"Oh, yes," I said, though I wouldn't have known.

"It escaped—you mean it was alive?"

"Yes."

"What in the hell was he thinking about? How were we going to kill it?"

Grandpa had explained this to me: we were going to beat the life out of it with a hammer, though I now realize he was pulling my leg. At any rate, this was the explanation I gave to my grandmother, who then muttered predictable things about the proper use of a hammer.

She paused then, and for a moment I thought the line had gone dead. Then she sighed into my ear and said, "Tell the old fool to come home, and if he comes in with the drink in him, he's as dead as the chicken would've been."

As if reading her mind, Grandpa whispered, "Tell her I've only had one."

"He's only had one, Grandma."

"One? *I'll* give him one," she said. Then she repeated, "One," and told me to come right home.

He was silent on the walk home, and when we reached the porch I went up first and he struggled over the stairs. I could hear him panting.

"She'll be waiting with a frying pan," he said. "You have to protect me."

The door opened, and instead of my grandmother in her battle fury, we were met by Tom. He was putting on a clean shirt, and the bloody pieces of tissue clinging to his face told me he'd also shaved. He looked from me to my grandfather, his eyes worried.

"I thought maybe you guys got thrown in the slammer. Dad? Anything wrong?"

Grandpa shook his head. "No, no, just…we had a long day, we had adventures, and I'm bushed. Didn't we have adventures?"

He looked at me and I nodded on cue.

"We had a chicken but it got away. It was red, but I think it didn't like the bus."

He gave me the longest look anyone has ever turned my way, a look that assessed me and judged my mind to be feeble. I could almost read his mind, I am certain he thought my grandfather had gotten me drunk. Then he looked back at his father.

"It was alive?"

"Well, it's how they start. They're all alive to begin with, for God's sake."

"I know that. How come you were…"

I looked up at them and saw the new look come into my uncle's eyes, and then slowly he began to laugh, that same laugh my grandfather had, a silent laugh where almost no sound escaped, so that the humor seemed even deeper, more profound, because it had rendered them speechless. Now my grandfather joined him, and Tom put an arm on his father's shoulders and shook his head, and then Grandpa was patting Tom on the back.

"Time to face the music," he said, and walked toward the kitchen. My grandmother met him in the doorway, blocked his path for a second, wrinkled her nose at him, and then he handed her his purchase.

"What in the name of God is this?"

"Oh, a holy statue for you, a lovely thing—St. Patrick, I think it is." She stared at him for a second, then moved aside to approach me.

"Danny, are you all right, sweetheart?"

"Sure. I got hot dogs and cokes and cheese popcorn. And the man that sold Grandpa the statue thought it was God. Grandpa thinks he was an immigrant. And we had the chicken but it got away. I think it's at Riverview unless Mrs. Gorski got it."

She watched me without blinking or saying a thing, just shook her head, then moved back into the kitchen.

"Grandpa's okay?" Tom asked.

"Yeah. I think he feels bad about the chicken."

Tom nodded and we both listened to the voices from the kitchen.

"For the love of God, where have you been all day?" She tried to sound irritated but succeeded in sounding worried. He answered her in a tired voice and I heard him cough. She said, "You need a cup of tea," and began bustling around her kitchen to make him some tea.

She asked him something else and I heard him say he felt a thousand years old, and my uncle sat me down beside him on the sofa on the pretext of asking me to tell him about our adventures. I kept looking out toward the kitchen, and a cold-ness came into the pit of my stomach.

My grandparents were in the kitchen together for a long time, and when their conversation was finished, Grandma came out and gave me a tired smile. Beyond her, I could see my grandfather sitting at the kitchen table, looking toward the back window, drumming his fingers on the table.

She and my uncle exchanged a quick look, and then she put on a smile for my benefit. "Well, there's no chicken for supper because of you two *amadans*, and if there was a chicken I wouldn't have time to cook it. You have to pluck them, you know. So Tom, you call up the Chinaman and order chop suey." She wrinkled her nose and feigned annoyance at the idea of chop suey—her catchall name for all Chinese food—being suitable for dinner, but she'd turned the occasion into a party and we all knew it: egg rolls and paper-thin wonton and food clever enough to disguise the vegetables.

Tom grinned at me. "Hey, hey, kid. Chop suey!"

I smiled back at him, perfectly willing to let them put this gloss on the evening.

Forty-five minutes later a skinny Chinese man came with our food. He stood and listened to Grandma's complaint about how long it had taken. Through it all, he smiled and nodded, his lack of English manifest.

Uncle Mike showed up with his perfect timing for food and we spread it all out on the dining room table. Tom opened each container and Grandma peered in and muttered, "What in God's name is that?" And then our Chinese dinner took for us its accustomed form: bathed in steam, noise, strange and wonderful smells emanating from the chaotic array of white cartons and small packages of waxed paper. Each of my family stepped into his role: Uncle Mike eating his methodical way through everything and Uncle Tom warning us there would be none left for the rest of us, my grandmother rhapsodizing over the shrimp in garlic sauce and declaring, "Oh, they're grand, the Chinese people. They're just grand." Grandpa squinted at a small dark piece of meat and pointed out that the dog next door was missing. Aunt Anne showed up in the middle of everything, chattering about how cold it was for March, and they seemed all to be talking at once.

Lizards and War
and Lost History

On cold Saturdays, I accompanied my grandmother to what we called "Lincoln Avenue," the miniature downtown that spread out like the spokes of a grand commercial wheel from the intersection of Lincoln, Belmont, and Ashland. Half the North Side shopped here, some of them never in their entire lives entering the Loop with its more famous and pricey stores. The neighborhoods then were small cities, self-contained and self-sufficient: there was another centered around Division, Ashland, and Milwaukee; one at Six Corners; a couple more along Sixty-Third Street. We rode a trolley bus up past the wonderful marble façade of the Belmont Theater and into the heart of our "city," and Grandma led me though Wieboldt's, Goldblatt's, and Woolworth's.

She complained for most of the morning, about how it made her feet hurt and how hot it was in the stores, about the rudeness of people who nearly knocked you over without acknowledging your existence, about gouging merchants, unfathomably slow elevators, shifty people lurking in corners to snatch a purse, and the "hidden danger of the escalator," which she believed to be an instrument of death.

She groaned and grumbled through every inch of it and I paid no attention, for I knew she lived for her Saturday shopping. She loved it, she waited patiently through five nine-hour shifts at the knitting mill for it, inside she was smiling through it all. She bought me candy and nuts, chatted with clerks and shoppers she'd never laid eyes on, cluck-clucked at the strangeness of it all, and wouldn't have missed it for a papal audience.

A favorite spot was the bargain basement at Goldblatt's, where cut-rate merchandise was piled high on long tables, bright-colored bait for the bargain hunter. She bought nothing here, content instead to stand a few paces away from the tables and watch expectantly as wild-eyed shoppers grabbed and clawed at the piles and the competition degenerated into a wild melee. We watched women tug at opposite ends of discounted underwear till it split, saw shoppers pilfering items from other people's piles, even occasional acts of force: a woman throwing an ample hip into a competitor who had cut in front of her at the table.

Grandma Flynn would stare with a look of fascination and shake her head, occasionally murmuring, "Like wolves they are." She looked down at me. "A lot of them are foreigners, you see," she said in her rich brogue.

Once we saw two women in babushkas start fighting; we watched, rapt, as they tore at each other's clothes and yanked the purchases from each other's hands, and then my grandmother collected herself and led me away, muttering, "Well, now they've gone too far!" in a delighted tone that said she'd just seen the Dempsey-Firpo fight.

We looked at everything, it seemed, rode escalators and elevators and climbed stairs, and I knew the day could have only one possible end: we would find a couple of stools at the long lunch counter at Woolworth's, and I'd watch the hot dogs sweating and blushing on the big rotisserie and I'd have to have one; she'd order a club sandwich and we'd both have cake for dessert, chocolate cake with icing an inch thick and to this day I don't think I've ever had anything in its class.

The first time she took me by myself to Woolworth's she looked around her as though something was missing. For a time we sat at the counter and she was quiet. Eventually she mentioned that she'd taken my mother there when my mother was my age. I looked away and nodded; I wanted to hear no more sudden references to my mother lest I shame myself by public crying. I was irritated with her.

Then one afternoon I came in from the alley and she was sitting alone at the kitchen table with a photo album. She was crying silently over pictures of her daughter. I think I actually took a step into the room on some vague impulse to comfort her, then stopped myself; I thought it would embarrass her. I backed out of the kitchen, returned to the living room, and made enough noise to herald the approach of the Fifth Army band so I could come back to the kitchen. She was wiping her eyes and smiling at me.

"Hi, Grandma."

"Hello, sunshine," she said. "I cut some onions before," she said, and I nodded as I was expected to. After that I tried not to be irritated when she brought up the subject of my mother.

She was a farm girl, my grandmother Winifred Flynn, from just outside a town in Leitrim, a town named for a pig, a poor place from what little she said of it, it seemed that both sides of my family had come from poor places and generations later still made their lives in poor places. She had little interest in talking of Ireland, spoke of her family, though, the Dunphys, of a mother who had died young of influenza, of a whitewashed stone cottage full of brothers and sisters: seven had made the ocean pilgrimage to America, two had stayed in Ireland.

I'd heard the many tales of her brothers' exploits, but as I grew older I was to put more pieces together, to ferret out what she did not give freely, and I found that there had been tragedy enough in her life for several. Of those seven who'd made that voyage between 1915 and 1921, four had survived their new country's ministrations. The youngest, Terrence, was the unlucky lad Martin had spoken of on Christmas, who had died from a fall down an elevator shaft in 1926. Another, Mick, had died in World War I, at Château-Thierry. I heard her speak once of the unfairness of it.

"Hadn't been here long enough to know the street names and they had him in the Army on a big boat going right back in the direction he come from. He was twenty years old and he wasn't in America two years, and they sent him overseas and he was killed."

Something about the vehemence in her voice suggested this brother, the only one spoken of with a nickname, had been her favorite. The four survivors were my grandmother, the troublesome Martin and Frank, and "the sad one," she'd once called the last brother, the surviving one of a pair of twins. This was Peter. The twins had lived all their lives together, a pair of Irish bachelors who'd never seen their way clear to settle any farther into the new country than New York.

I had seen them once, long ago: I had a faint gray recollection of a pair of identical red-faced men who'd come to visit one Christmas when I was two or three, both of them quiet men who smelled of tobacco. The lost twin was named Emmett, and he'd died, this quiet uncle, and left his brother alone and disconsolate. Peter had notified the others of the brother's death and then dropped off the face of the earth.

Grandma was a chattery woman who bustled about her house creating noise wherever she went, as though the silence offended her, but I knew she sometimes had a cup of tea in the afternoon or late at night, once the rest of the house had turned in, and sat at her table in her small kitchen and thought about her life. She was proud of her work at the knitting mill, it pleased her to work with wool as so many had done in the Old Country. She bought me sweaters at her employee discount and took obvious delight in the ones she herself had worked on.

She rode two buses each way, worked a nine-hour shift, and still came home expecting to cook dinner, and I never heard her complain of the rigors of her life. More than once I awoke in the middle of the night to see her looking in on me. I had no idea how much of her time she worried about me.

On certain afternoons my curiosity about my family burst from me like an ill-timed belch and I peppered her with questions—sometimes taking her lead and asking about my mother's childhood, her friends, what my father was like when he first came calling. At these times I felt a desperation to know everything I could about them, I felt as though someone had stolen my history. I was careful to pick times when she was in high spirits—as careful as I could be with a need for truth that sometimes made me feel as though I were carbonated.

And she would sit endlessly stirring her tea and conjure up a time that I never knew. Uncle Martin had once called her "the family *shanackie*," and it was true there was a lot of the storyteller in her. She was the custodian of the family's tales and she took care with them, filled them with color and life, and I could see all of it. If she loved a story, she took her time with it, drew it out, and gave it its proper length and attention, and that is how she told me of the courtship of my parents.

They'd met, my mother and father, in the old neighborhood when both families lived on the same crowded block of Goethe in Old Town, then as now a place where poor families danced on the edge of disaster a stone's throw from the mansions of the rich. Childhood acquaintances, then, a dark-haired Irish girl and her tall skinny neighbor boy, just two of the neighborhood mob of children of that earlier time when most families, especially the poor, had many children. Eventually the Flynns had moved away, settling near Riverview, the Dorseys had clung to their little "patch," and my mother and father had not seen each other again until they were teenagers and the country was just months from its entry into the Big War.

"She didn't see your father until one day in 1940. She was working in the A&P on Ashland. Afternoons and Saturdays, she worked there. He came in for milk and saw her for the first time in years. That's what she told me, anyhow," Grandma said, and her voice took on a musing tone that told me she wasn't certain about the truth of this. She paused and I looked up and saw that she'd forgotten me as she wrestled with this memory. Then she gave a shake of her head like a dog shaking off water and returned to the moment.

"The first time they went out, he spent all his money and after he brought her home, he had to walk all the way back up Clybourn Avenue to the old neighborhood, too proud to ask for a dime for a streetcar, and it started raining before he was halfway home.

"They went out all the time, sometimes a whole group of them, boys and girls together." She nodded and I could tell she approved of this whole group thing.

"When the war came they were already talking about getting married and I told them they were daft, she was seventeen, for the love of God! And then the war came and he went into the Navy." She couldn't conceal her relief at this development. Then she added, "We've got pictures, you know."

"I know."

"We've got all the pictures he sent back from the Pacific, we've got him with his friends and playing ball with the other sailors and in his white uniform and the dark blue one, too, one for summer and one for winter. And we've got him with the lizard." A quick look of horror and revulsion crossed her face.

"Have you seen that one, with that...*thing* in it?"

"Yes," and of course I had, for it was my favorite, my late father posing with the corpse of the largest lizard I ever saw, before or since. Like Betty and Mary McReady, The Lizard was in its own way a family legend. My father and The Lizard had made each other's acquaintance on Guadalcanal, where The Lizard had made his home in the bush just outside their camp. From what I'd been told, The Lizard proved a difficult neighbor, breaking into the camp food supply and spending its nights making unearthly croaking noises, becoming thereby an object of even greater animus than the enemy troops. My father had mounted a short, clever campaign against the beast, eventually trapping and killing it, making himself a hero to his fellows, even if he never saw action.

In her mind's eye, Grandma studied the picture of my sunburned father standing hipshot and windblown on a low hill with some of the other men grinning behind him, and next to him the unfortunate lizard, trussed like a primitive trophy to a sort of tripod. My father smiled into the camera. The dead lizard gazed off in the general direction of New Guinea, stoically reflecting on its fate.

Grandma shuddered and took a sip of her tea to calm herself. "They say God makes all the creatures of the world, but I can't believe he made that one."

"I want to see one."

"Oh, Good God, you don't want to see something like that. I'm glad I never saw one of those things. He said the islands are full of them."

"Was he a hero in the war?"

She started to shake her head and caught herself. "Oh, well, they were all brave, you know, but some of them didn't get into the fighting." She was obviously disappointed not to have anything better than the lizard for me, and then she brightened.

"You could ask Grandma Dorsey, she'd know more about it. After all, he wrote her letters all through it. Not as many as he wrote to your mother, of course. A great letter writer, he was, he'd send her pictures and postcards, jokes, words from songs. He did that a lot, sent her the words from songs that reminded him of her." She shot me an embarrassed look. "It's what people do when they're in love."

I nodded. I'd heard this before from my mother. I had been watching a movie: Dorothy Lamour was singing in one of the Hope-Crosby road movies—"Moonlight Becomes You" was the song—and she'd come into the room where I was watching it. She stood looking at Dorothy Lamour for a moment with a strange, moody look on her face, and when the song was over, she'd smiled at me.

"Your dad sent me the words to that song when he was overseas."

"Why?"

"Oh, we were in love, that's why. Someday you'll do stupid things for some pretty girl."

"No, I won't," I remember telling her.

The following Saturday my grandparents were invited to an anniversary party and I was to spend the day at Grandma Dorsey's house. I made a mental note to get hold of my father's letters, to talk to Grandma Dorsey about his wartime heroism.

"About the war?" Grandma Dorsey said to me.

"Yes. But not about The Lizard. I know about The Lizard."

"Oh," she said, disappointed. "It was bigger than a man. It was like an alligator."

I nodded and held my tongue. I'd looked at the picture again and learned that the beast was perhaps four feet long, not even a Komodo dragon, but if Grandma Dorsey remembered it as an alligator, if she remembered it as a *brontosaurus*, I wasn't going to disabuse her of such a colorful recollection.

She was kneading dough for biscuits of some sort, and paused with her chubby fingers embedded in it. "I don't think he was in any of the fighting. Your Uncle Gerald was in the fighting at Midway because he was already in the Navy when the war came. And Joe was there at the end when there was all the fighting in the Philippines." She looked at me and I tried to seem knowledgeable about the conflict. "But your father wasn't in the fighting. He was on the *Tulagi*, that was his ship. The only thing he was in was, you know, that time with the big lizard…and, oh, that one big fistfight."

"Fistfight?" I straightened up at this, my head already aswim with visions of my father duking it out with the Japanese soldiers.

She shook her head sadly. "With the marines. It was the sailors from the *Tulagi* against the marines on Guadalcanal. Such silly things they did when they were bored. At least they didn't kill each other in the fight." She paused and then added, "I don't think they did, anyway."

I sat at her table and she fed me bits of the dough and then made me bacon and eggs. I watched her shuffle about her kitchen and bathed in her serenity, my peaceful grandmother whom I had never seen cry, even when she stared at me and told me I was the spitting image of my dad when he was eight.

It wasn't until years later that I learned about Grandma Dorsey's life, not just the poverty and uncertainty of it all, but the other things she'd seen: a baker's daughter from Missouri, coaxed across the big brown Mississippi to marry the mercurial John Dorsey, who'd dragged her through times she'd never dreamt of.

It was well that she bore him so many children, for she'd buried two of them early on in her life, one an infant girl. The other had been a boy named Edward. He'd died of pneumonia during an uncommonly harsh winter more than forty years earlier. Edward had died in his sleep, in bed with his brothers, in a cold crowded flat on Scott Street. He would have been her eldest if he'd lived.

Later that afternoon she called me into the house and I saw that she had a shoebox waiting for me on her jumble of a kitchen table. She watched me shyly, and when I opened the box and saw the letters and photos I grinned at her and she nodded, satisfied.

Many of the photographs were duplicates of those I'd seen already, or similar shots, but a handful were genuine treasures, photographs of my father as a boy. Whether from their tenuous existence at the very brink of poverty or a large family's simple lack of interest in such things as cameras and photographs, the Dorseys didn't seem to have many photos of the early days, so that I'd seen few pictures of my father's life. His very existence before meeting my mother seemed something to be imputed from stories and testimony.

But here were photographs of him as a boy, a blond boy who squinted into almost every picture and amazingly had done some of the very same things I did: went to picnics, posed at Lincoln Park, stood in line at Riverview, swam in the lake, and buried his brothers in the sand. In one picture he posed in front of the Belmont Theater flanked by two extremely pretty girls, and it took me several seconds to understand that I was looking at my Aunt Mollie and their stunning sister Teresa, just short of her taking of vows. One photograph I picked up and studied repeatedly: my father at eighteen or nineteen, at a wedding, possibly in his first suit. He stood in front of St. Bonaventure Church with one hand in his trouser pocket and the other hanging at his side, grinning at the camera with exactly the look I'd seen in photos of my Uncle Tom Flynn, a look I came to understand as an archetype of life, the grin of the cocky young man who believes the world is his oyster.

Eventually I turned my attention to his letters and forgot all about photographs, for here was my father's voice.

The letters to his mother were as carefree as the young man in the photo, a boy's recounting of his adventures, and I was too young to see that this was his way of easing some of her many terrors—half the people she knew were in the service, including all her sons. The letters included jokes and funny stories, and his sentences sang out with self-assurance and confidence in the future:

"Don't let anybody tell you we're going to lose this War, Ma, because we've got them beat. Before you know it, I'll be sitting in your kitchen asking what's for dinner. I swear I haven't had a good meal since I enlisted. Navy chow is not so bad but it's not like what I'm used to. I tell all the guys my ma's the greatest cook in the USA. Of course, they all think their ma's the best. Then I tell them what you cook on a regular Sunday, and what you make for Christmas, and that shuts them up."

I read several more like that one, convinced that my grandmother was probably wrong about his service record, that if I read far enough I'd discover his acts of bravery in the face of the enemy, of great ships shelling one another at point blank range. And a couple of them did report on battles, he wrote of listening on night watch from the deck of his ship to some distant battle between battleships and cruisers, tense and frightened, and not knowing how the battle went till the early morning reports of American victory. I read on through his reports from the Pacific, his funny stories and hearty greetings to his mother, until I found one at the bottom of the box that was quite different. It was written to my Aunt Mollie, his favorite, and though the opening paragraphs spoke with easy bravado, the second half of the letter was more honest, and must have been unsettling to both writer and audience.

"I tell you, sis, sometimes it makes me crazy thinking about what's going to happen. In the daytime, when we're all busy doing our jobs on the ship, there's no time to worry, and it seems like everything's gonna be fine. That's when I'm sure I'm coming home to you and to Ma and to my Betty. But at night, when it's too hot to sleep and you can't keep your head from doing funny things to you, I think to myself, doesn't every guy here think he's coming home, and every guy all over the war? Isn't every one of them sure he's going to be the guy that makes it home? But we can't all make it home. That's the thing, sis. And if I make it

back, will Gerry and Joe and Jim? So what's the chances that all four of us are coming home? That's what I mean. When I think about that, it makes me crazy. This whole war makes me crazy. But everybody here is in the same boat. Ha-ha, in the same boat, get it?"

I laughed at his small joke, for the letter had been written aboard the *Tulagi*, and told myself of course they'd all made it home from the war, the four Dorsey boys, and I almost said to him, "You made it and so did your brothers, Daddy," but my grandmother was in the room. Then I noticed the date: August 1944. On the day he'd written it, he'd had less than ten years to live. For perhaps the first time in my life I had a glimpse of him not as my father but as a young man with a life of his own, and dreams, and troubles on his horizon. And for the first time the sorrow I felt was for him. Something seemed to make my heart beat faster, and I put the shoebox aside and read no further.

I told myself I wanted nothing more to do with these old photographs and letters of the dead, but when it was time to go, I asked my grandmother if I could take some pictures with me.

"Oh, sure, that's what I put them out for, Danny."

I took most of the photos of my father, and at the last moment, his letter to his sister.

I found Grandma Flynn's photograph album and the big box of the later ones, pictures that had never made it into an album. I took the ones I was looking for and spread them out in a long straight line across the brown oak rectangle of the dining room table, starting with a picture of my mother as a young schoolgirl and adding to it one of Grandma Dorsey's pictures of my father at the age of twelve or thirteen. Then I set down a shot of the two of them at the zoo, another at Riverview—his arm around her waist now and a different look to him, something older in the eyes—a picture of them with half a dozen or more people at a picnic, a group shot at the beach, a picture of them with two other couples at dinner in Math Igler's, where the waiters wore lederhosen and sang to you, then a shot of my mother sitting on the hood of a great hulking Dodge while a couple of girlfriends looked on, another of her and the same girlfriends dancing down Clybourn for the photographer.

After this I set two pictures of my father, one of him in his Navy whites, standing on Clybourn Avenue and appearing to talk to the photographer, and the picture of him and The Great Lizard. Then a photo of my parents in their wedding clothes, another of them at the reception, my father's eyes already going glassy with drink, then the two of them with me, and a tremor of panic began to replace my curiosity. I lined up half a dozen pictures of them with me, and the panic became a small hard knot in my stomach. I added more pictures of my parents with me, then a single photograph of me and my small brother John. I wanted to finish the whole project with a picture of me by myself, but when I lay the photo down on the table I hated the way it looked, with no hint of my family in it, only me against a dark brick wall. I took it away and just stared at the line of photographs from one end to the other, breathing faster, and I'm certain that I was about to cry, so that I never heard my grandmother come in.

I had no idea how long she stood there watching me, but gradually I became aware that I was no longer alone in the room. When I noticed her I gave a start, looked quickly at my row of pictures and wanted to hide it, to sweep it all onto the floor, but she'd seen it. Her eyes said she understood exactly what I was doing.

"Grandma likes to look at the pictures too, sunshine. We'll look at them together tonight if you want."

"Okay," I said, still embarrassed, irritated with her for intruding into this moment, but when the time came that night to look at the pictures together, I was glad for her company.

A Cold Week
in March

Eliot called April the cruelest month, but he never had a March like mine was to be. Looking back, it seems to have been a month of rain, of cold mornings and low dark skies promising to burst, and it seems to have been a month that brought me nothing but trouble.

At night I fought sleep and my old fears returned. I lay in bed and conjured up the worst horrors life could send my way, told myself I probably deserved no better. They would die, these people I loved, one at a time or all at once, by accident, fire, or act of a vengeful God—the method changed from one night to the next, but in the twisted logic of the solitary dark, the result seemed almost certain to me. They would die as a logical consequence of the incorrigible, truly bad child I seemed to have become. In no time, these night terrors fixed themselves on the most logical candidate for death, the one I already understood on some level to be dying.

School became unbearable. Whether it was the long winter or my situation, I don't know, but I could no longer concentrate on my work, and I began having trouble with math, I began forgetting my homework, and I became once more a cause for disruption in Sister Polycarp's class. At odd times I would look up and find her watching me even as she spoke to the class about a lesson. I thought she was looking for opportunities to punish me. Toward the end of the month, just before my birthday, I gave her several.

She sent a sealed note home to my grandparents about my missing work and my behavior, and I threw it away without opening it. When she asked me about it, I lied and said I'd delivered it to them. She frowned and said, "They were supposed to sign it."

I had no answer to that and she gave me a second note. I opened and read this one, which said very much what I expected it to say. Having opened it, I could not reseal it, and so threw it away as I walked home. A boy who was walking behind me picked it up and began running toward me, thinking I'd dropped it, and I was forced to run from him till he gave up pursuit.

When Sister Polycarp called my home later in the week, I saw that my trouble had fed upon itself till it was now a disaster. My grandmother was furious and asked if I was losing my mind, my grandfather muttered about my lack of sense, and even my Uncle Tom was upset. It seemed that everyone in the house leaped at the opportunity to demonstrate displeasure, and when dinnertime came I could hardly eat for the great dull knot that had grown in my stomach. After dinner, my Uncle Tom took me aside and told me that I'd disappointed everyone in the house. He told me if I didn't find a way to do better, I'd be expelled, I'd go to Schneider School and I wouldn't see any of my friends. At bedtime I heard a renewed chorus of admonitions to do better, and climbed into my bed feeling like a criminal. I lay in bed crying for a long time before sleep came.

I greeted the new morning with dread, hated the thought of facing Sister Polycarp, and wished I had the nerve to cut school like Matt. That morning I glanced up from my spelling book and she was studying at me, shaking her head. When our eyes met, she looked away. At the end of that day she called me to her desk and gave me a written punishment to do for having thrown away the two notes, and the back of my neck felt hot. I felt twenty-seven pairs of eyes on me, I was suddenly self-conscious about my clothes and the cowlick at the back of my head, and I told myself there wasn't a person in the room at that moment who actually liked me. I wanted to make myself disappear.

For the rest of the week and part of the next, I faced a cross-examination by my uncle or my grandparents each evening to see if I'd begun to turn things around, and it seemed I was no longer trusted by anyone in the house. On St. Patrick's Day my grandparents and Aunt Anne accompanied me to the annual party held in the school cafeteria, and for a time I stayed with them and behaved as though a very stiff sort of alien life form had taken over my body. I waved surreptitiously to my friends, spoke only when spoken too, and had a dreadful time. Eventually they turned me loose with the admonition to behave, and for an hour or so forgot myself. I did what all children must do at a school party, I ran wild with my friends. We ate too much cake with green frosting, drank too much punch, and wrestled in the boys' room till the principal sent in an eighth grader to drag us out.

We finally decided upon a game of hide-and-seek requiring one team to find and physically drag the other team's members to a sort of jail, and looking back on that time I can see unconscious statements being made in our games about the way we all saw our world. Predictably this game erupted into a sort of random and purely impersonal violence, and we had two casualties before we'd been playing for ten minutes. When I tripped my friend Jamie and caused him to hit his head against a table, the game was over. I received a short, hot lecture from my grandmother that included dragging me over to examine the large lump miraculously growing from my friend's head, and a while later we left, and my grandmother was pointedly not speaking to me.

March 27 should have been the high point of the month, for it was my eighth birthday, and I'd produced extensive lists

almost as long as the ones I'd given my relatives at Christmastime. Measured by almost any yardstick, it should have been
a fine birthday: I received presents, I ate things that were no
good for me, and there was even a small party with my family there and cousin Matt, and even a surprise appearance by
Grandma Dorsey and Aunt Mollie. Somehow, in the very
midst of the celebration, it struck me that my seventh birthday
had been celebrated in another place, attended by my father
and presided over with self-assurance and efficiency by my
mother. I suddenly noticed how hard they were all trying to
make this party work, and how unaccustomed they were to
throwing a child's party. They forgot things and then rushed
around to make them right, things my mother would have
handled without effort. Suddenly this seemed an unhappy imitation of that one, and I know that it was because I could not
feel my mother's presence in that room. I did what I could to
pretend I was enjoying it, but that night in bed I conjured up
memories not of that day's presents and attention but of the last
party given for me by my mother.

At school I simply came undone. One afternoon that week
I received two tests back and found that I'd failed one disas-
trously and barely passed the other. I sickened at the thought
that I'd have to show these to my family. During the reading
lesson I began to draw, whether doodling absently or intentionally avoiding work, I no longer remember, but Sister Polycarp
caught me and confiscated my drawing.

"Pay attention, young man. No one excused you from
school." I tried to find my reader and couldn't, and when she
asked me what I was waiting for, I heard a boy snicker behind
me and I told him to shut up. Sister Polycarp told me to watch
my mouth and I began to cry, and I told *her* to shut up. She
sent me out into the hall and told me she'd be speaking to my
grandparents that night.

I did not come home from school that afternoon.

When the bell rang I put on my hat and coat like everyone else, trembling and near to vomiting with fear. I left the building in line with my class, but when we filed out onto the corner where dozens of mothers were waiting, I turned east and began walking fast. I was not running away, I had no destination in mind, I simply wanted to put some distance between myself and my family. There seemed no good reason to go home.

For a time I lingered at Wrightwood Park, then I went to the local public school playground where I was eventually chased by a trio of bored boys. For perhaps two hours I wandered the neighborhood, convinced that I was having a very dark day in a generally dark life. Something in the gray sky and chill air seemed to put me in mind of my grandfather, and I reflected first on our encounter with the chicken and then on that moment on the bus when he'd begun coughing. I saw once more the look in his eyes and I think I began to cry, then quickly turned up a side street so no one would ask me what was wrong. The sky went darker and I knew my family would have missed me by now, and my fear became terror, for I realized I'd nursed trouble into a calamity. Eventually I made it to Clybourn, but I turned the wrong way and soon found myself among unfamiliar sights. I mistook the first railroad tracks I encountered for those close to my house, and it was some time before I realized this couldn't be right. I began to panic. Somewhere along Clybourn, I sat down on a fire hydrant. I can remember the dull feeling growing in my chest, the tightness in my throat, my fight, my unsuccessful fight, to suppress tears. The image of my grandfather came to me, and then for some reason a picture of my parents, and then I was sobbing, a lost boy in a strange place. A man stopped in front of me and asked me if I was lost but they'd always told me not to talk to strangers and I got up and walked away with my head down. I heard a woman ask me if I was wandering around alone but I said nothing to her.

Sometime later I went up Clybourn the other way and after what seemed hours saw the big Hines lumber yard in the distance and realized I was nearing my neighborhood. Just short of Diversey, a police car pulled up along the curb and a pair of older police officers got out. One asked me if my name was Daniel. I said yes and he just jerked a thumb in the direction of the squad car.

"Get in, Daniel. You got people looking for you."

They drove me to my house and I suffered the time-honored embarrassment of the child returned to his family by the police.

Inside my grandparents' house they all crowded around me, Tom and Mike and Anne and both my grandparents, and they all started talking at once. Aunt Anne hugged me and I was grateful because everyone else seemed to have other measures in mind.

"Where you been?" I heard Tom asking over and over.

I didn't actually know so I was unable to give him an intelligent answer, and then Grandma put her hands on my shoulder and demanded to know what I was thinking.

"For the love of God," she said. "Why would you run away?"

"Bejesus, what's got into you?" I heard Grandpa say, though it wasn't clear whether this was meant for her or for me.

"I got lost," I finally blurted out.

"How could you get lost?" Uncle Mike asked.

I wanted to explain it to him, it seemed I could calm them all if I could just make them listen. Then, and not for the last time, I looked from face to face and saw that there weren't enough words to explain it, that they'd never give me the chance to get my story out, that they had a hundred questions and were asking them all at once.

I started to answer, began to cry and went on, talking louder and louder and sobbing till I'd lost all control and the day's disasters spilled out one upon the other, and when I'd finished I realized no one was saying anything and that I was still crying. They seemed to have taken a step back, so that I remember standing there with my hands at my sides crying, and then my nose was running and Grandma was wiping it with one of her small dainty handkerchiefs that smelled of lavender.

"Jesus, Mary, and Joseph," she was saying but only to herself.

They waited for a moment and then launched into a new set of questions, each of my family zeroing in on a different item from my song of woe.

"Somebody chased you?" Tom demanded. "Who chased you?"

"Oh, Danny, you told your teacher to shut up?" Anne asked.

"She's gonna call here?" Grandpa asked, as if this made no sense.

There was a slight pause and I heard my grandmother's voice, quieter than the others. "You were afraid to come home? To us?"

I looked at her and knew which of the day's many transgressions was the worst. Tom began asking me about the boys who'd chased me and Anne was saying something, but I could look only at my grandmother's face. She shook her head slowly and spoke in an odd way, as though I might not understand otherwise.

"This is your home, and we're your family, and you should never be afraid to come home to my house, I don't care who you told to shut up, not the Holy Father himself." And she walked out to the kitchen to leave the rest of them to the sorting out of my confused state.

"We'll talk to your teacher," Aunt Anne said.

"I'll talk to her," Tom said, and Aunt Anne shook her head.

"No, you won't. You'll take a swing at her."

He shrugged as if this was no surprise to anyone and for the first time that day I laughed.

"That what you want?" he asked.

"No."

"She's nice, really, his nun." Anne gave me a look that dared me to contradict her and I was forced to nod agreement. Polycarp was nice, she just hated me.

They dragged me into the kitchen and fed me one of Grandma's little fat hamburgers and a Pepsi in honor of my tragic encounters with my world. I sat there and picked things out of my hamburger—she had a repellent custom of putting little balls of bread dough into the ground beef to make it go further—and my grandmother and Uncle Tom sat there and watched me. I was too hungry to mind. As I ate, they asked me what they wanted to know. Tom seemed to be concerned that gangs of boys might be attacking me on a daily basis, and my grandmother wanted to know if the two tests were about things I couldn't understand.

When I was finished eating everyone but Tom left the room and he just sat there watching me eat. I looked up at him from time to time but he seemed content to watch me till I'd finished everything, and then he leaned forward with his elbows on the table.

"So you had a pretty bad day."

"Yeah."

"Probably seems like everybody's picking on you all at once, huh?"

"Yeah."

"So what else? I want you to tell me. What else is bothering you?"

"Nothing."

"Yeah, there is. You look mad. You mad at us?"

I remember that I started to say, no, there was nothing wrong, I wasn't mad at anyone, but he'd managed to loosen the logjam inside me and I just sat there with an Oreo cookie in my hand weeping and blubbering about the very empty world that was Danny Dorsey's. It all came out, things unplanned as well as intended: I told him I hated school and didn't want to go back there, that no one in the house would listen to me, that nobody cared what happened to me, that I was in trouble all the time, and somewhere in all of it I thought of my parents and immediately afterwards my grandfather. I began to say things I'd never thought to say, I have no clear idea what, but it all came out, and I know I said I wanted them back, my parents, and I must have blurted out my grandfather's name.

My uncle said nothing, never moved except at one point to make a sharp wave of his hand at whoever had come back into the room. He waited me out in silence, his eyes telling me he thought he was witnessing my total breakdown. I saw a slight nod at the mention of my parents and then his eyes widened slightly at the mention of his father.

In the end I exhausted myself. I couldn't see through the tears and my throat seemed to have shut down, and I'd said all I could ever say.

Still he waited me out and then after a moment he raised his eyebrows and said, "Got it all out?"

I nodded without really knowing what he meant.

"If you wanna cry some more, it's okay."

"No."

He wet his lips and I saw him take a deep breath like a man about to dive into cold water. Then he lowered his head till our eyes were level and said quietly, "You said Grandpa. What about Grandpa?"

I thought, "He's going to die," and for a moment I feared I'd blurt out my peculiar form of haunting, that they were all going to die on me. What I said was, "He's sick," but I knew he'd understood.

He nodded. "Yeah, he's a sick guy."

I had cried so much and so hard that evening that now I had the hiccups and couldn't stop, but eventually he made me laugh about them and then he spoke to calm me down.

"You gonna go crazy on us, Dan?"

"No."

"I didn't think so. But you're having a hard time and I think there's gonna be times when nobody can keep you from being, you know, sad. And probably every once in a while it seems like we forget about you, kiddo. And I guess we do—no, I don't mean we forget you're alive, but we forget we have new, you know, new things to think about, to worry about. Everybody wants to make sure you're okay and so we run around and try to make sure you've got what you need, and then we all go back to livin' our usual lives, and sometimes we forget that we don't have those lives no more. Nobody knew you were having trouble with anything in school, and I guess we all thought since we haven't heard from your teacher, we thought things were better about you behaving."

"I threw away the notes."

He sighed, "Uh, yeah, I think you said that. But the point is we didn't know. We didn't know you were having any trouble and we didn't know you were feeling bad. And once in a while, you're gonna have to say something to somebody, to me or your grandma or your aunt, you got to let us know, we're not mind readers."

He let out a long slow breath. "So. So now we got things to do. We got to make it right with your teacher, and—these punks, they're somebody you know?"

"No. I never saw them before."

"Well, anybody at school pushes you around, older kids, especially, you let me know. And..." He looked around and I realized he had come to my grandfather.

"You live in a house full of people, kinda forgetful people, maybe, but you're like the star of the show, you're the most important person in the place, and everybody will take care of you no matter what. And nobody"—he looked down at the table and began playing with a pack of cigarettes—"nobody lives forever. But there's always gonna be somebody here to take care of you."

"I don't want anybody to die anymore."

He paused with his mouth half open, clearly not knowing where to take this, what he could promise me. "Everybody dies," he said, quietly. "But…we're all gonna be here for a while, you, me, everybody else here. Nobody's gonna die tomorrow. Unless maybe your nun heaves you out a window."

I laughed and he pointed to my hand.

"Look what you did with that cookie. That's what babies do with their food." I stared at my Oreo and saw that I'd squeezed it into a brown paste. I laughed and he directed me to "get another one and start over," and then he got up and left the room. When he left I heard him let out a long breath.

That night I lay in bed and relived the endless list of my humiliations, and worst of all the smothering moment when I'd faced their group disapproval. It seemed the worst thing I'd done was what I'd done from fear, and I knew I'd wake with more of the same, for I had yet to face Polycarp, and there might be other afternoons when the world's bad boys would be waiting for me and I might not get away. Perhaps my grandparents would keep me home if they thought I'd caught pneumonia or something grave on my wanderings, mumps, perhaps, there was a small outbreak of mumps that month. But they'd seen through my symptoms before, my faked cramps and imaginary headaches and dizziness, and I knew they'd send me on to my fate. For a brief moment I thought it would teach them all something if I died in the night. But I remembered my uncle's face and his voice, and I believed that I might survive this time after all.

The last thing I saw before I closed my eyes was my grandmother's head peering around the door at me. There was worry in her face, and something else, a preoccupation, as though one part of her was trying to sort something out even as the other part came to check on me. I think I said "hello" to her and she gave me a troubled smile.

"Good night, sunshine," was all she said.

Nuns and Reckonings

At breakfast the next morning Aunt Anne announced that she was taking me to school, and then Uncle Tom cut her off in mid-proclamation.

"Nah, I'm takin' him. I'll go in to work a little later."

And so I walked proudly up Diversey that morning holding my uncle's hand. Tom kept up a stream of chatter till we got to school. He led me to the line where my friends waited. Children know when another child is in trouble, they smell it the way a shark knows his dinner is nearby, and so I was the center of attention.

Uncle Tom seemed to be waiting for something, my teacher, I thought, but when the front door of the school opened, it was my aunt, Sister Fidelity, who emerged. She came down the stairs looking as radiant as one can look in a black habit and every eye was on her. When she saw me in line she broke into a smile and she made directly for me.

She gave Tom a brief hug and I thought he blushed a little, and he smiled at her the way you'd smile when Ted Williams emerged from the dugout to sign autographs. Then she turned to me and gave me a longer hug.

I stole a look at my companions and felt myself grinning. They were shocked speechless at this unearthly display of affection from a nun, at the fact that she knew me, that she was undeniably the most beautiful nun any of them would ever see in life. Then she led me a few feet away and asked me how I was doing, though it was clear she knew.

"Are you here because I'm in trouble?"

"I'm here because both my favorite boys are in trouble."

"Did you see my teacher?"

"I did," she said, and then before I could ask what they talked about, she added, "And I'll see you after school. We'll go for a Coke. Okay?"

"Sure."

She led me back to the line and exchanged a few words with Tom. It was odd to see how shyly he spoke to her, how he seemed almost physically uncomfortable even though his eyes never left her face. Then the bell rang, they both waved to me, and I had to go into the school.

It proved to be an uneventful day, but I passed it in great tension, almost at the edge of my chair, for I was just waiting for Polycarp to find something wrong with my work or my attitude or my looks, and I was by now half convinced that I was possessed by some impish spirit that sought to bring my ruin by making me talk when I was supposed to be silent.

Then at the end of the day, Sister Polycarp came over to my desk.

"I'd like you to stay for a couple of minutes after school."

"Yes, Sister," I said, as though I had a choice.

I watched my schoolmates marching out to freedom and felt the old knot growing in my stomach. Sister Polycarp asked me to take a seat up in the front of the room near her desk, and I moved while she made neat piles of the papers on her desk. The desk I'd chosen belonged to a classmate named Philip who had trouble seeing the board; I noticed that he had written his name in ballpoint pen along the edge. He would be in trouble for that.

Eventually I realized she was looking at me. I folded my hands and sat straight-backed and, holding my eyes open as wide as I could get them, gave her my most earnest look of attention, tried to look like one of the bloody-faced saints in my book. Unblinking, she returned my gaze till I began to squirm in the hard wooden chair. Then she shocked me by laughing. It wasn't a deep, loud laugh like my uncles' but a soft, rueful chuckle, and then she looked out the window, rubbing her eyes and shaking her head. When she turned back to me, she was smiling.

"Daniel, you look like a little maniac. Relax, and stop doing that with your eyes." I did, and then she sighed. "Daniel, I have been trying to be patient with you. It probably doesn't seem that way, but I have. Other sisters have different ways of providing discipline..."

"Sister Augustine pinches," I offered.

Sister Polycarp blinked. "She *pinches*?"

"Yes."

Another sigh, another, longer look out the window. "Well, she's small and..."

"Old," I helped.

This time she nodded. "Yes, she is very old. And old people have their ways, don't they?"

"Yes."

For a long moment she said nothing, and I studied her. At the time, all nuns seemed old to me but I recognized that Sister Polycarp was younger than any of the others. Bigger too, a hefty farm girl, from Minnesota, she'd once told us, with a chubby face and large brown eyes. We had no idea what color her hair was under the habit.

"We're not doing so well together, you and I."

"Because I'm bad," I offered.

"No, not because you're bad. You're not bad. You seem to be having trouble paying attention in class, and you have trouble being quiet. And...I don't like the way the other children are beginning to think of you. They think you behave the way you do, like a clown who can't quite keep up with the rest of the class, because you have no parents and don't know any better."

"They do?" I felt my face going red.

"I think so."

"Well, they're wrong."

"Of course they are, but you seem to want very badly to become the class clown and troublemaker. I know that it's hard for you to take school seriously, I know you're probably not very happy right now. It is very bad to lose your parents, isn't it?"

"Yes," I said, and wondered why I felt like crying.

"This is something I understand. Both my parents died when I was in grammar school. They didn't even get to see me graduate, they never even saw me become a nun. And I was very angry at the entire world. I was angry at God."

"You were?" I heard the shock in my own voice.

"Oh, yes, I was. As you probably are sometimes but don't want to admit it. It's all right, though, He's got a thick skin. But I was angry, I was very irritated by all the adults that wanted to help me, and most of all I hated the idiot teachers in my school. I hated the nuns," she added quietly. "I hated *all* the nuns."

I made a show of distancing myself from this notion, I put on a facial expression suggestive of extreme reverence, slavish devotion, near worship, then asked the obvious question.

"Did they throw you out?"

"No. Someone was patient with me. And I am trying to repay the favor. I'm also…" Here she faltered, and seemed uncomfortable. "I'm looking for some help. I have very little experience with smaller children, I was trained to teach the higher grades. I try to do a good job…"

"But you do." It was true: everyone liked her, though we sometimes made fun of her round, fat face and big body.

"Well, thank you. But I still need some help sometimes. And if you and I are going to get along, we're going to have to become partners. I need an ally, Daniel. You've probably noticed you're not the only child who has trouble behaving in class."

This was true: a boy name Albert Martino was in many ways worse than I was, a boy named Henry got up and roamed around when he was finished with his work and she had to physically put him back in his seat, and one of the little girls frequently called the rest of us names. So I chanced a subtle nod here in tentative agreement.

"Some days, Daniel, some days I need somebody I can count on to lead by his good example. I need you to do that, Daniel. I'm just not sure you can."

"Well, I think I can."

"Good. I would really appreciate it. Because you and I have something in common that other people don't need to know about. And I know," she began, and I thought with disappointment that she would tell me how proud my deceased parents would be, but she had a good hole card and she played it now, "it would make your aunt proud of you."

"My Aunt Teresa, you mean. You met her today..."

She shook her head. "Oh, no, I didn't meet her today. We're friends, she and I. We met in college." Sister read my shock in my face and gave me a small proud smile. "That's right, I went to college, just like your aunt. She used to write me letters from Guatemala. She's a great person."

"Yes, she is," and I was on the verge of telling how my uncles thought it a waste for Teresa Dorsey to have become a nun, but for once my instincts showed me the course of good sense.

"If I can tell her that you're settling down in school, it will be a load off her mind."

"Well, you can."

"Good. I'm sure you'll do just fine. You like to draw, don't you?"

"Yes."

"Well, we'll have to find a little more time for you to do that."

"That would be real good."

"But now that we've had our talk, I'm going to expect you to try a little harder."

"I will."

"And also, what I told you about my parents? That is a secret, just between you and me."

I was too delighted to speak: life held few pleasures more thrilling than keeping a secret.

When she let me go, I found my Aunt Teresa waiting for me outside. She took me by the hand and we went up to the drug-store on Ashland and sat on the glossy red stools at the counter.

"What do you want to drink, Danny?"

"A Coke, I guess," I said without giving it much thought. She said she'd take me for a Coke and I was a literal child.

She frowned. "A regular Coke?"

I shrugged to cover my confusion. A middle-aged black man who sometimes manned the counter came over to see us.

"This man here," she said, "can make you a cherry Coke or a chocolate Coke or a phosphate—a chocolate phosphate or..."

"Vanilla phosphate," the man helped, "cherry phosphate, orange phosphate, lime phosphate, lemon phosphate, straw-berry phosphate..." and they both laughed.

In the end I settled on a chocolate Coke—the notion of chocolate syrup poured into a Coke was just perverse enough to capture my attention. My aunt ordered a vanilla phosphate and gave me a taste. It was like a very sweet cream soda, and I filed the knowledge away for a future order.

"So you know why I was at your school this morning."

"To see about me and Matt."

She pursed her lips. "Danny, I told you a fib. I was actually there because three people I'm fond of are having trouble. The third one is my friend."

"Sister Polycarp."

"Yes. She's a very dear friend, she's just a wonderful person. She's very kindhearted, and it may be hard for you to see your teacher this way, but she can be very funny, too."

It was true that Polycarp had a certain dry wit that she trotted out for us on rare occasions, but in general she was usually too intent on her work.

"You were in school together," I said.

"Ah. She told you. Yes, we were. And you'd be surprised how smart she is, Danny. She's just brilliant, she should be teaching in a college."

"Really?" Even from Aunt Teresa, this seemed a bizarre notion.

"Yes. Anyway, she likes you very much, but teaching your grade is proving to be very hard for her. And I was really hoping the two of you would work everything out. She needs somebody in that class to be…she needs a very trustworthy boy. I thought maybe that could be you."

"It is," I said without any doubt.

"Good, if you two got along well, that would make me happy."

"Okay," I said, for if she'd asked me to dash in front of the Ashland bus, that wouldn't have seemed much of a sacrifice.

When we were finished with our drinks she walked me all the way home, had a brief visit with my grandparents, and then left, and as she walked out the door, she winked at me.

Young Men
and Love

O n Friday nights I stayed up and watched TV with my
grandparents, comedies and detective shows, and the
Friday night fights. Sometimes my grandmother made popcorn.
But the salient memory for me of each of those Friday nights is
of my uncles going out.

"Where are they going?" I would ask, and my grandmother
would just say, "Oh, they're going out, young men go out on
a Friday."

Most of the time they went out together, but there were
times when one or both of them had dates. I could usually tell
when Tom had a date: there was a slight tension about him that
I didn't understand. He went out with a number of girls, frequently from beyond the known universe of the neighborhood,
but it was understood by all those around him that some of his
dates were with a girl named Helen, and I could tell these nights
from the others, for he was unable to conceal his excitement. On
these nights he sang while getting ready, he made jokes, he even
managed to shave himself without suffering great loss of blood.

I was always asleep when he returned, but some nights
I would waken to hear my uncles speaking in that peculiar
softened way adults speak late at night about their nights. It
took me some time to understand what I was hearing: they
spun great peripatetic narratives, they spoke in code, they said
everything but what they wanted to say, and there seemed to

be many unfinished sentences punctuated by soft laughter. One would ask something inane like, "How'd you make out?" And the other might say "I did, you know, I did okay."

"How okay?"

"Real okay."

If something had gone wrong or the date proved to be a mistake, they reverted to recognizable English: "She's not my type, she likes longhair music and stuff like that," Uncle Mike might say, or, "A little out of my class, Mike," Tom would say. I was baffled, unable to fathom anyone being out of Uncle Tom's class, but he seemed unshaken by it.

Eventually their conversations would turn to the two main females on their horizons. One night I heard them talking about this faceless girl called Helen; Uncle Mike muttered something about Philly Clark, and I realized who this girl was. I strained to hear more, to hear Tom's explanation, but I couldn't make out any more of it.

They spoke, too, of Uncle Mike's best girl Lorraine, a sweet-faced young woman who waited tables at a place across the street from Riverview. I'd once heard Uncle Mike say that he intended to marry Lorraine some day, but their relationship was marked by long periods of acrimony, when sweet-faced Lorraine would slam the phone down in Mike's ear and refuse to acknowledge his existence if they met on the street.

I witnessed one of these moments one Saturday afternoon when I was out with both my uncles. Lorraine was hurrying up Clybourn to her job and we were heading south to do some shopping. I could see Lorraine squinting at us, and her face quickly froze into an expressionless mask. When we were within earshot, Mike gave her a breezy, "Hello, babe. Got time for a cup of coffee?"

She ignored him, nodded at Uncle Tom and just said, "Tom," but favored me with the vague beginnings of a smile and said, "Hello, Danny."

"Hi, Lorraine," I said, and a moment later caught a jealous look from her offended swain to my left.

On several occasions I asked Uncle Tom about Mike's trouble with Lorraine and he managed to make a muddy situation even more confusing.

"Ah, kid, when men and women get together there's no telling what's going to happen."

"Don't they like each other anymore?"

"Oh, I guess so. I think your uncle's in love with Lorraine, but don't tell him I said that."

"Then why do they fight?"

"Because they're in love and they don't like it."

"Why not?"

"I'm not sure. See, everybody's different. Some people, they fall in love and they're happy all the time, you never see 'em fight. Although I never understood people like that, because it's not normal. Most people, they fight with the person they're in love with. Maybe they think this is not the person they hoped they were gonna get, or maybe they thought their, you know, their romance was gonna turn out better. Now, some people, they fight because they like it. Your Aunt Mary McReady, her and her husband been fighting for sixty years."

He laughed. "Sixty years, and old Joe's never won *one*. And Aunt Mary loves it, she picks on the poor guy constantly, it's like her hobby. Yeah, some people just like to have fights. But you're probably not old enough to understand that, 'cause I barely understand it myself."

I thought about cousin Matt, and perhaps I didn't fully understand his motivation, but I certainly could say I knew people who liked to fight.

"So why do Uncle Mike and Lorraine fight?"

"Beats me, but if I had to bet, I'd say it's 'cause your uncle don't really want to be married yet, and Lorraine...well, Lorraine comes from a poor family, see. Her dad died and she had to go to work all through school, so she's a little older than other girls her age. That make any sense to you?"

"I guess."

"And I kinda think she's always hoping some guy is gonna come into the restaurant when she's working, and he's gonna take her far away from this whole neighborhood and all her troubles. And what she got instead is Mike. Which is not bad because he's a solid guy, he's a stand-up guy, she couldn't want a better guy than your Uncle Mike. But she's not sure what she's got is what she wanted, or even *if* she's got him. And I'm sure she gets impatient with Mike, he kinda drags his feet about whether he wants to get married, and you can't do that with a woman, you got to fish or cut bait."

"You do?"

"Absolutely."

"And why does he drag his feet?"

"Irish guys are never in a hurry to get married."

It sounded like a recipe for disaster to me. After a while I asked, "What's gonna happen to them?"

"They're gonna get married." He grinned at me. "They are, and they don't even know it. Probably take 'em awhile to get around to it, but they will, and they'll be fine. They'll settle down and she'll realize she's got a good guy there, guy that'll bring home a buck and doesn't drink much and won't run around on her. He won't, I know that. He'll be decent to her and she'll have what she needs and if she wants to go back to school—see, she never finished—he'll let her. And he'll be happy." Tom chuckled to himself. "Some guys, they think they want to be single but they just hang around with other guys on Friday nights and complain about how bored they are. And your Uncle Mike's one of 'em. Half the time, you say, 'Let's go one more place, let's go get a sandwich,' and he's the one that wants to go home. Goes home every time with nothing but the newspaper."

"What does that mean?"

He shot me a quick embarrassed look and said, "It's just an expression, something I say, don't mean nothing. Anyhow, he's bored being a bachelor. He'll be married before you know it."

"Do you fight with...your girlfriend?" It wasn't the question I wanted to ask but it was something to lead with.

"I don't have a girlfriend, kiddo." He shot me a quick look, saw that I wasn't buying it and then just said, "This one girl and I, sometimes we fight, yeah."

I'd rehearsed half a dozen ways to say what came out next and it still came out raw and blunt: "What about you and your...that girl? Are you gonna get married to her?"

I could see I'd managed to embarrass both of us, so I added a quick, "Never mind."

He stopped and gave me a long look. "No, it's okay. I just don't have nothing to tell you on that score. I don't know if I'm gonna get married to her or somebody else." He saw the questions in my eyes and shrugged. "This is something, I don't know how to explain it to you. Maybe someday..."

"When I'm older."

He laughed. "No, bud, when *I'm* older. Maybe I'll understand it then, 'cause I sure don't right now." He patted me on the head and said, "In all the songs, they say, you know, 'when you're in love, the world's great,' and that's true, but what they never say is when you're in love with somebody, it's the *strangest* thing you'll ever feel. I think sometimes it's close to being crazy, you're half-nuts when you're in love—you've seen how Mike and Lorraine act, you've seen your poor Aunt Mary Jane and Dennis Lynch. They love each other, those two, and they're never happy. Don't tell anybody I said that, but...see what I'm trying to say here?"

"Yeah. I'm never gonna fall in love."

"Oh, you won't get off so easy, kiddo. Nobody's immune."

I wondered how he could be so sure.

Other People's Business

I had to know my uncles' lives, their personal secrets. I already knew more than I ought from the countless times I stood with my ear pressed to the cold wood of my bedroom door, or the evenings crouched under the dining room table, ostensibly playing with my toys and feigning ignorance of their talk but soaking it all in like one of Grandma's yellow sponges. I was tireless, I was shameless. Having already established the precedent, I stole into their rooms like bad luck and rooted around in their drawers, their closets, the stacks upon stacks of shoeboxes piled in the back of these closets.

I was never alone in the house for more than a short time and so learned to use every moment of opportunity—a long phone conversation, my grandfather's naps. I found pictures, ticket stubs, notes, once a maudlin letter from Lorraine to Uncle Mike. I found the sentiments disgusting but was elated to have come across something so personal. In Uncle Mike's drawer I also found a small stack of magazines featuring sparsely clad women in provocative poses. "Tomatoes," I had heard Uncle Mike call these women once, in his baffling slang. Tomatoes.

In the bottom drawer of Tom's dresser I found a small stack of letters. They'd all apparently been sent to him in Korea. Two seemed to be from old girlfriends, one was from Mollie Dorsey, a cheery letter telling him how everyone was doing and how much they all missed him. It seemed so obvious I wondered

what the point of writing it had been. One letter interested me
most of all: it was from my mother. It was brief and to the point:

Dear Tom,

*I've decided to stop reading the papers because they make me nuts.
Dad says the talk is that there will be an armistice soon, because the
Reds are losing too many soldiers. Ma is making me crazy: if you don't
come home soon, I may have to brain her. She really misses you. You
should write her again and this time more than five sentences. There's
a present for you with this. A nice loaf of <u>bread</u>. Ha-ha, just what a
guy who's stuck on a cold hill in Korea fighting a war needs. But this
bread is special!*

Stay safe.

I understood their private joke, for I'd once heard my
mother tell a friend about it: she'd sent him a large loaf of bakery bread, hollowed out to conceal a bottle of Jim Beam. Uncle
Tom and his buddies had killed the bourbon on the spot, then
they'd eaten the bread crust because they were half-starved.

I folded my mother's letter neatly, fought the impulse to
pocket it, and put it back.

Whatever I found in a drawer that was wearable, I tried
out: I posed in Grandma's long hall mirror in the accoutrements
of manliness, trying to get some idea how I'd look at twenty-
two. I was in love with their hats, it was a time of fine hats with
wide brims and colorful hatbands, and I modeled every hat I
found. In the drawer where Tom kept his underwear I found
a jockstrap. Its purpose escaped me, but I noted the twin loops
formed by the side straps and concluded these were earholes in
a very odd sort of headgear—had someone come in at just that
moment and seen me parading in front of the mirror with a
jockstrap on my head, I would have been scarred for life.

I played with their jewelry, tried out their razors, several
times cutting my fingers so that I had to make up plausible lies
to my grandmother. A cut on my chin proved to be a challenge to my mendacity but I got away with it. Unable to resist

the many bottles in the crowded bathroom, I tried on small amounts of each, of Grandpa's Clubman aftershave, his talcum powder, my uncles' Old Spice aftershave and toilet water, and two kinds of hair oil—Mike liked Wildroot and Tom favored Vitalis. One day I decided to do something more dramatic: I mixed something from each bottle in a plastic bowl and splashed the resulting concoction on my face and hair.

That night at dinner I sat at the dining room table like a man of the world. Each of my uncles frowned in my direction, and Aunt Anne was laughing. My grandmother came in sniffing at the air.

"Good God, Danny, what do you have on?"

My grandfather, his senses honed by a mid-afternoon nap, came into the room, squinted, wrinkled his nose in my direction, and told me I smelled "like a French hoor with no taste," and Grandma told him to watch his language.

But as fascinating as their things were, it was the private lives of these adults that I most needed to learn about, and I would not be put off, I was as inevitable as night. I assailed them with questions and shook off their blunt suggestions that I mind my own business. When they circled the wagons, I pried through my grandmother, who refused to speak of anyone else's business, but I quickly learned she would open up if I spouted misinformation and seemed in need of setting straight.

"I know the names of everybody's boyfriend and girl-friend," I announced one afternoon when we were out shopping. "Everybody except Aunt Teresa who can't have one," I added, and I saw that I had her attention. She listened, nodding and occasionally favoring me with an amused look, smiling at people passing by, and when I got to her boys, she stopped smiling. I mentioned Lorraine as Uncle Mike's intended and she just said, "Ah, who knows about those two, sweetheart?" Then I announced that Tom had a secret girlfriend named Helen and my grandma looked away.

"Indeed he does not. She's not his girlfriend. He goes out with lots of girls. He doesn't really have what you'd call a girlfriend. Where did you hear such nonsense?"

"I heard him and Uncle Mike talking. He said she's the one he wants, it's what he said."

"He was just talking. They talk and they don't mean half of what they say, especially about girls, young men talk a lot of nonsense about girls, and *you're* not supposed to be listening to all of it." She slowed down slightly and gave me a look of concern. "Do they talk about their girlfriends in front of you?"

"No. I was in bed and I could hear them talking."

"Well…well, you need to be sleeping, not listening to your uncles talk their silly talk about girlfriends." She made a snorting noise and said "girlfriends" again and then she was off and running about the subject closest to her heart: "They're a couple of big ninnies, your uncles, and they need to be settling down with nice girls. Your Uncle Michael needs to sit down with Lorraine and talk some sense to her and forget about all these other things they argue about. And my son Thomas, who doesn't seem to have the sense to come in out of the rain sometimes with his foolish notions, he should just pick a nice girl—he's got his pick of anybody he wants, you know, he's got dozens of girls that would be happy to marry him, and why not? He's a fine boy and he's handsome and he brings home a decent paycheck and he's got a good future, he'd make a good husband and a fine father and who wouldn't want him, so he should forget this nonsense about that other one."

"Helen?"

"Yes." Then she grudgingly added the name, "Helen."

"Is she bad?"

"No, no, of course she's not bad, for God's sake. Hah, and it's not the girl who's bad most of the time, sweetheart. Anyhow…no, she's not bad, she's just…not right for him."

"How come?"

"I'm sure I don't know," she said with a special tone usually reserved for ending unpleasant discussions, but like much of what I heard in those days, it went over my head.

"Why don't you like her? Is she ugly?"

"Oh, no. She's...she's quite a pretty girl—not like that Josephine he was with at the parish picnic, ugly as mortal sin, that one was," she muttered. "She's just not...for him."

"Why not?"

"Oh, they're different, that's all, they've got nothing in common."

"Is she Irish like us?"

"I think they're German, her people, but that's got nothing to do with it."

"Is that bad?"

"Of course it's not. God made the Germans, too."

"We fought a war with them, right?"

"We fought lots of wars with lots of people but when they're finished, they're finished, and these are American Germans. We didn't fight them. Now give me some peace so I can keep my mind on my shopping. And when we're through, we'll go to the drugstore and get a cup of tea."

"Okay, Grandma," I said, perfectly comfortable that she'd bought me off. "A cup of tea" was a euphemism. There might be a cup of tea consumed, but with it there would be a slice of cherry pie for her and a hot fudge sundae for me, even in the morning before I'd had a lunch. Shopping days, she always said, were different, not bound by the same rules of behavior as normal days.

She was right about the women available to my Uncle Tom. I was to see him with a number of girls: there was a tall, good-looking athletic girl named Elinor, whom my grandmother fell in love with. Elinor was sweet and laughed easily and was known to be a great cook. Grandma called her "The Polack" but made it clear she thought Elinor was a prize for any man with his head on straight. There was a slim redhead that everyone said looked like Hedy Lamarr. I didn't like Hedy Lamarr so I took a dislike to this girl, and for her part, she never had much to say to me or anyone else in the family. Tom came to a parish Christmas party with a thin blond girl named Estelle: she was well-dressed and polished-looking, and I heard someone say her family had money. Grandma pronounced her "homely as the day is long," but didn't say it to Uncle Tom's face. There was also a short, chattery girl with very long brown hair named Nora, and Uncle Mike seemed to think she was the ideal mate for Tom because of her sunny disposition and her sense of humor, but Tom was uninterested in any of them—at least in the long run, he was interested in none of them. I thought this was unfortunate, for Elinor the Polack seemed a prize to me, too, and Nora brought me comics.

Some evenings Grandma would make him tea and sit down with him in the kitchen and talk about these girls, and I'd sit up in the next room and memorize the details of his life. I'd listen for her to make the same tactical errors each time—the brilliant general of the many campaigns against my grandfather somehow disappeared in these dialogues with her favorite son, and she made mistake after mistake so that the whole thing was predictable. They were strange conversations to me, starting as whispers and quickly rising as they grew agitated, their talk peppered with quick exchanges and then marked by long silences as they sipped their tea and prepared to renew their respective assaults. She offered one opinion after another and he rebuffed her meddling.

Gradually I began to notice that no matter what they spoke of, there was another topic in the late-night talks, something hinted at rather than stated. For her part, Grandma spoke only of the girls she approved of and Uncle Tom talked in the abstract about the kind of person he was looking for, but I knew who they were both talking about.

In the other conversations I heard between them—I seemed never to be asleep when I should have been—my uncle spoke to her in a low voice of his plans for his life, his dissatisfaction with work at the dairy. He wanted to get away from it, to start his own business but he didn't know what kind. More than once I heard him tell her he wanted to buy a tavern and she would tell him he didn't need that kind of trouble.

"A gold mine, Ma. A tavern's a gold mine."

"Ah, they're a world of trouble, too much liquor, too many drunks, people handling your money."

"I'll handle my own."

"Then you'll be there all the time, in a saloon, and that's no good, either."

"Ma, what kinda businessman stays out of his own business?"

"A smart one, if he's in that business."

In spring that year the dairy sent him to New York for two weeks to be trained on new machinery. It meant a promotion, that he'd be doing something a little more interesting, and he was excited. The house was curiously silent without him and my grandmother seemed uneasy.

"He's fine, Mother," Grandpa told her. "It's not Korea with the Reds, it's New York."

But New York was a great dark sore on the map where her brother Emmett had died, where her brother Peter had disappeared, and she would have been happier if Tom had been sent to Munich. When he came back I was sitting on the front stairs waiting for him and he laughed at me and handed me a box of toy soldiers, Romans with a chariot, and lions to eat the Christians.

For the next few weeks he was rejuvenated. In the mornings he seemed excited, chatty and joking at breakfast, and he made a point of being the one who walked me the two blocks to Diversey where I met Matt. After work he came home happy, and I heard him mention that he might soon supervise a whole section of people operating the new machines. A month after his return, his union forced his employer to have my uncle train another man on the new machinery, a man with seniority. After he trained the older man, my uncle had to give up his job.

The dairy owner hated the union. Two months later, he sent my uncle to Cleveland to be trained on another machine being introduced into the dairy business, and when my uncle returned to work, he was once again asked by the union to train an older man, then step aside and give up his new job.

That spring, three of his friends found a small moribund tavern for sale on the far side of Riverview. They invited him to come in as a partner; he put up almost his entire savings and became part owner. At dinner on the night he made the announcement he received a mixed reaction. His mother frowned and said she didn't like the idea of him getting involved in a tavern. He'd already taken Uncle Mike into his confidence, indeed, Mike had put in a thousand dollars of his own, and now Uncle Mike explained to her that this was a good opportunity for Tom to have his own business.

She sighed and said, "But a *tavern*, boys. A public house."

Tom shrugged and said, "There's ten thousand of 'em, and people are always gonna want more, Ma. It's just an investment."

"Are you going to work there?"

"Maybe I'll help out once in a while, but I'm no bartender."

He took me to see it on his next day off. It was a low flat building not far from the river, and the heavy cagelike wire that covered the windows seemed to hint of past troubles. Paint flaked off the wooden eaves and doorway, and I could see that tarpaper was peeling off the roof. On one window was the name "The Riverside Inn."

"We didn't buy the building, kid," he said. "Just the tavern, just the business."

He took me inside and introduced me to Marty Polk, the partner who was tending bar. It smelled like all the other taverns I'd been inside, and to those odors had been added the smells of new paint and fresh varnish. It was smallish, with a handful of wooden tables and chairs and a straight bar that curved at each end. It was darker than most of the taverns I'd seen, so that it was night inside the bar. There was no dog in this one, no one who turned and greeted us as we entered, so that it seemed there was a distance between owners and customers.

I didn't like it, but for his sake pretended to be impressed, and honestly tried to imagine it on a Friday night, crowded and bustling and filled with working class people having a nice time.

The tavern began to occupy a certain amount of his time: he filled in as bartender on occasion, made appearances on weekends when friends were going to drop by, and tried to keep an eye on what he jokingly called "the bankroll." Once or twice I saw him when he came back from the Riverside Inn and he had a preoccupied look on his face.

Of Madmen, Science, and the River

I was walking home from school, distracted because I thought I'd lost my hat, rooting around in my schoolbag, and I caught myself about to walk into a boy standing in the middle of the sidewalk. Tough boys from the public schools sometimes roamed the stretch of Diversey between the projects and the tracks, and for a moment I was afraid. The boy was tall and skinny and red-haired, straddling the sidewalk so that I'd have to stop or run into him. I recognized him then: his name was Rusty Kilgallen and I knew him to be in fifth grade at my school. He was rumored to be bright, willful, and a little crazy. His teacher, a youngish nun, seemed to think he was a budding genius. The verdict from at least one earlier teacher had been different: Sister Augustine had thought he was the antichrist.

My search for the hat had dropped me behind the children of my class, and I wondered if this odd older boy meant me harm.

"You're Danny Dorsey," he said. "You know who I am?"

"Sure."

"You can walk with me. That kid Lenny is up there." Lenny was a local tough, twelve or thirteen years old, a cause for terror among those of us who had seen him picking fights and stealing milk money from those smaller than he.

"You're safe with me, see, because Lenny won't push me around."

"Why? Are you tough?"

"No, but I'm smart, and those kids all think I'm crazy. They're afraid of what I'd do to them. They oughta be."

I took this with a grain of salt but had to admire his style. Later, I learned that his assessment had been nothing more than the simple truth.

"So what do you like? Do you like baseball?"

I didn't, not yet at least, but I said, "Oh, sure."

He gave me an amused look, then said, "How 'bout science? You like science?" and his grin took over his face. "You like to explore places and discover stuff?" and I was able to give him a more enthusiastic answer. He nodded, gave me a little pat on the shoulder, and said, "Come on."

I was to learn that he lived less than a block from us, in the projects with his mother; he was almost twelve, quick on his feet and unfettered by adult supervision or a conscience. There was no harm in him and I never saw him lose his temper, and I was fascinated by what seemed to be his essential "otherness." In truth, he had been granted equal parts intelligence, imagination, and restlessness, and he prowled the neighborhood like a Molotov cocktail in Keds. From the vantage point of age, I can see that, except for me and one or two other boys who came to idolize him, Rusty never quite "related" to those around him: children were either his audience or obstacles to his ceaseless quest for diversion. He woke up looking for interesting things to discover, things to try out.

He spent a part of almost every day in a painstaking search of the neighborhood for pop bottles that he turned in for deposit; as a result he always had a pocketful of change. He was generous with these funds, and I was his most frequent beneficiary, trailing him into the little store across from the Hamlin Park pool, where he would buy me a Dr. Pepper and long paper rolls coated with little colored dots of candy. His pockets were jammed, his pants weighed down to bagginess

198 ᴥ Michael Raleigh

by the enormity of his private treasures: marbles and coins and odd stones, the headless corpse of a lead soldier he considered a sort of talisman.

Frequently his pockets held one or more little bottles of flammable or otherwise questionable substances, for his doting mother had bought him a chemistry set—the true danger to American security in 1955 was not the blustering Soviets half-way around the world but the hundreds of thousands of children, many of them future criminals, who owned these little private munitions systems. With a chemistry set a child could set fire to his mother's kitchen, could melt her Bakelite dishes, could render the local water supply undrinkable, could stain his skin a cherry red, could take the paint off walls, and, with the assistance of a sympathetic pharmacist, could even make that dark, dusty grail of childhood, gunpowder. Rusty had these frightening little vials and all the other hallowed weaponry of childhood as well, including a pen knife, matches, a magnifying glass, tacks, nails, and a single-edged razor blade.

Sometimes we sat under a tree at the park and talked, or rather he chattered and I listened, much as Matt and my younger friends did when I regaled them with my stories and ideas and comic impressions. He had no fear that I ever discerned in him, and this puzzled me, for he was skinny, poor, had no father to protect him, and when he wasn't with me, he frequently roamed the streets alone. I knew that he often went into other neighborhoods and children took to him immediately, sensing perhaps that he was different.

As he had assured me, the worst toughs in our neighborhood seemed to have little interest in bothering him—they cut him a great deal of slack, as though he were the neighborhood holy man, touched by the gods with an insanity that awed them all. The violent, evil-tempered Lenny was manifestly terrified of Rusty. I was puzzled by this, for I'd seen Lenny fight, and he was not only mean but strong and quick, and a dirty fighter.

One day Rusty and I sat on the stairs outside the park swimming pool, drinking Birely's orange soda and chewing penny candy. It seemed a propitious moment to dig for gold.

"Why is Lenny afraid of you?"

"'Cause he knows what's good for 'im."

"Did you ever fight Lenny?"

"Yeah, he gave me a bloody nose, that shit."

"Then why is he afraid of you?"

"I got him back the next day." He paused with red string licorice hanging from his mouth, looking as disturbed as a child could possibly look.

"What did you do?"

"He came after me again like I knew he would and I was ready. I had my snake."

My mind went blank for a second. "Your snake?"

He nodded and slurped in the remaining licorice. "I put him down Lenny's shirt. He's scared of snakes."

"Wow. Did it bite him?"

"Nah, they don't bite, unless you're a frog. But he was scared, I knew he would be. And I told him if he ever pushed me around again, I'd put it in his desk at school, and in his lunchbox. I told him I'd crawl into his house at night and put it in his bed. And he knew I would." He smiled at a sudden recollection. "I told him they crawl into your ears at night, and he believed it, what a stupe!" Rusty leaned back, contented, having apparently conquered most of the known universe without throwing a single punch.

The snake, as it turned out, had passed away under Rusty's erratic care, to the delight of his mother. He maintained that he could find one in a "prairie" in ten minutes, but his mother had bought him off with a gigantic scale model of the USS *Forrestal*, for model building was another of his weaknesses. Of all the odd children I was to come to know, he was the most singular. In my own life, there was never a day when I didn't experience some sort of fear: fear that eventually I'd be alone again, fear for my uncles, fear for cousin Matt, fear of the strange kids and stranger adults that peopled the city. And Rusty was the sole child I was ever to encounter who seemed to have put such things behind him.

More than anything else, though, he was as entertaining a companion as I ever found. He knew about snakes, caught spiders and centipedes, could pelt an alley rat with a rock at twenty paces, and believed that much of the known world existed for our amusement: on a very hot day at summer's end, at the parish Labor Day picnic, I was to see Rusty put on a display of his talents that would make him a neighborhood legend.

Later, in January of 1959, as a high school freshman, Rusty was to prove that these demonstrations were neither accident nor fluke: this time he detonated a porcelain commode in the second floor bathroom of De Paul Academy. The explosion blew out two windows and embedded pieces of the toilet in the ceiling. The explosion was attributed by the puzzled school authorities to a buildup of sewer gas, this explanation provided on-site by Rusty and his companions, and accepted by the good Vincentian Fathers because Rusty was the prize student in their science classes. On that day he passed into high school folklore. Three years later he graduated from the academy with high honors, riding a full scholarship to Illinois Institute of Technology. I envisioned him becoming a sort of free agent in the arms race.

One warm afternoon Rusty brought me up into his house for Kool-Aid, and we drank half the pitcher out of little metallic tumblers. It was a small apartment like my cousin Matt's, with hard black floors made of some sort of tile that looked like rubber and felt like marble. Their kitchen window looked out onto the Chicago River, and I stood there watching the water while Rusty went to the bathroom. When we were leaving, I noticed a little table set right beside the door, so that people would see it when they entered or left. On the table was a photograph of a serious-looking man in a tie and suit. Next to the photo was a wedding picture of the man and Rusty's mother, whom I had met a couple of times on the street and seen at church.

"That's my dad," he said.

"What'd he die of?"

"He had a heart attack," Rusty said, pulling open the door. "He could carve stuff from wood and stuff like that."

"Really? What kinda stuff?"

"Animals, planes, boats, anything." He pointed to a shelf holding a couple of small wooden ships.

I nodded. "You got gypped."

Rusty shrugged. "So did you, right?" I nodded and then I followed him out into the hall.

More than once we attempted to fish in the river, garnering a striking collection of odd objects for our efforts, but no fish. We caught a wet cardboard carton, a piece of raincoat, a section of hose, and a dead rat which Rusty examined at great length.

"This is tremendous. I oughtta take him home," he said.

"Your ma."

"Yeah, I know. Grown-ups have no interest in science." He looked off into the distance and I knew his thirst for knowledge had temporarily taken over his common sense: this was when he was most dangerous. "I can wrap him in tinfoil and put him in the freezer. I'll dissect him later."

"Can I come?"

"Oh, sure, you can be my assistant."

I had seen enough of the "science" movies with my uncle to realize that the assistant was always in the very eye of the hurricane, he was essential, frequently being sent out to secure elements vital to the operation, such as human body parts, spare eyes, and the like. I felt honored.

Tragically—to our way of thinking—Rusty's embattled mother found the rat in her freezer before we had a chance to practice science on it. She didn't punish him, from what he said, she had never laid a hand on him, but she didn't talk to him for three days. He said she was letting herself get carried away, that the rat was so frozen it couldn't even smell, but she thought the mere presence of the rat was crime enough and, for reasons neither of us understood, seemed to think the matter was aggravated by the fact that the dead beast had been fished out of the Chicago River.

"Least we didn't find it in a dirty old alley," Rusty said, and I agreed, for like all the children of the neighborhood we thought the Chicago River a splendid thing indeed, no matter what adults thought of it. We spent the rest of that day hunting rabbits in a prairie a mile west of our neighborhood, where he said he'd seen one. He clearly felt that a frozen rabbit would not be nearly as objectionable to his mother as the rat had been, and here again I thought he made great sense. His mother proved intractable in the matter of science: I later learned that she felt the same way about frogs in her freezer as she did about the rat.

My association with Rusty that spring and the following summer was not only my first taste of science but the beginning of a career in general malfeasance. I understood, if somewhat dimly, that he was not totally conscious of the concepts and constraints that bound other people to a certain code of behavior, but I couldn't see how that might affect me. We didn't actually break into anyone's private property as I had with Matt and Terry Logan, but we went where we wanted, welcome or not. Unaware of his proclivities, my grandparents allowed me more independence in Rusty's company because of his age, so that I was able to range far and wide with their blessing.

I followed him across the North Side and witnessed his endless experiments with fireworks—he blew up dead fish with a small firecracker, atomized an old suitcase with a cherry bomb—and I thought I was simply being an apostle of science.

We went "fishing"—using a large piece of nylon mesh to catch alewives and smelt off the rocks at Belmont, and had a joyous time pelting passing cars with our catch on the way home, stopping to stuff a couple into a mailbox and deposit the remaining pair in the frozen food cooler of a small grocery store on Diversey.

We invaded the Chicago Historical Society—Grandma Flynn was pleasantly surprised to hear that we were visiting a museum instead of instigating a public disturbance. Once inside the little museum, we learned that the Civil War field piece could indeed be wheeled about and its barrel elevated by turning the screw mechanism below, and we were treating the other patrons to an imaginary shelling when the security guard chased us from the building. (Much later in life I visited the Historical Society and, when I was sure no one was watching, attempted to elevate the cannon's barrel: the screw had been cemented in place, and I took this as a silent memorial to a pair of wayward boys who knew few limits on a warm spring day.)

We stole into Wrigley Field after school and found box seats on a day that found the Cubs and the Pirates already locked in the most serious contest of the season, the traditional battle for sole possession of last place. There were no more than two thousand people in the park, and the Andy Frain ushers wouldn't have noticed if we'd set fire to the Cub dugout.

At night I would proudly recount my exploits to my uncles, and they would blink and say, "You what?" or, "Don't tell your grandmother." Uncle Mike in particular, with his more narrow view of normal behavior, was fond of asking, "Tell me something. Is that kid nuts?" whenever Rusty was mentioned. Uncle Tom would put on his most pontifical expression and say, "Whatever you do, champ, don't get put in the slammer."

First Communion, Against All Odds

May came along and with it one of the milestones of a Catholic childhood, First Communion. This was an eagerly awaited moment, the earliest of the numerous hallmarks of civilization in an Irish Catholic house, and despite threats to the contrary from our teachers and principal, Matt and I were relieved to hear that we would be included. I had never really thought I wouldn't be allowed to make Communion, but there had been grave doubt about Matt's chances. The ceremony and Communion Mass took place on a sunny Sunday afternoon, and St. Bonaventure Church was packed with hundreds of well-dressed, sweaty Catholics.

The female communicants were dressed in white dresses with veils, the boys in white shirts and ties, so that we looked like a mass wedding of very short people. My classmates looked so outlandish in their once-in-a-lifetime finery that it was a shock to see some of them. One boy was unrecognizable, never having been seen before with his hair combed out of his face and his shirt tucked into his pants. We surrounded him in wonder and examined his new persona, seeing him literally for the first time.

It was warm in the church, and you could smell the dozens of kinds of hair oil, Wildroot or Vitalis or VO5, struggling to assert themselves amid the cloud of perfume, cologne, and talcum powder. I had shown a penchant for fainting during long, hot church services, and when I saw that this was to be a solemn High Mass, I knew I'd probably be on the canvas for at least part of it. My classmates were aware of this unfortunate proclivity, had been present for a couple of my more notable swan dives, and I became one of the minor attractions of the service. I saw my friends grinning at me, pretending to swoon, and I snarled at them all.

Once we had been corralled into our pews in the front, I took a nervous look around for my family and saw them, crammed into a single pew in the center of the church, with a half dozen or so of the Dorseys right behind them, waving to both Matt and me. They all looked hot, several of the men looked mildly annoyed, and Matt's father Dennis looked sick. The women were either happy to be there or putting the best face on it, all except my grandmother, who was manifestly worried. I'd caught a whiff of her anxiety on the ride over to the church, and Uncle Tom had explained it all for me.

"She's worried."

"About what? About me fainting?"

"What? No, I forgot about that. No, you're not gonna faint. No, see, she remembers *my* First Communion. There was trouble." He said "trouble" but sounded delighted.

"What happened?"

"After the Mass, my dad and Uncle Frank and Uncle Martin and half a dozen of these Irish old-timers went down to the gin mill on the corner, where they run into about a hundred other fathers and brothers, and they've all been in church working up a thirst.

"And Uncle Frank, he was still a cop then, and he never waited in line for anything in his life, so he bulls his way to the bar and a couple guys didn't like it, and one of 'em shoves Frank and he decks the guy and pretty soon he's managed to start a brawl. They wrecked the saloon. An hour later, him, my dad, Uncle Martin, and about thirty of these other guys are all in jail. The rest of us are at home where my ma has cooked this big dinner, and there's no men at it because they're all in the slammer."

He put his hand over his eyes and laughed silently for a moment. "If I live to be a hundred and ten, I'll never forget seeing them come home after the cops let 'em out, the three of 'em slinking into the dining room. It's full of my aunts and my sisters and the McReady sisters and a couple other people, and your grandma is standing there staring at 'em like she just seen roaches coming in under the door."

"'On your son's First Communion day, Patrick,' she says in this kinda whisper that she wants everybody to hear, and he just points to her brother. And Uncle Frank's looking like he needs a good lawyer, and she says to him, 'Francis, if you weren't my brother, I'd brain you with a chair.' And old Frank had the good sense not to say a thing."

He looked around us at the congregation and let his amused gaze rest for a moment on the vexed face of his mother. "Oh, she's getting worked up now. No Frank yet. He could be anywhere."

"And Grandma's afraid Uncle Frank won't show up?"

"No. She's afraid he *will* show up."

"Oh, boy," I said, and he nodded.

"'Oh, boy' is right, kiddo. Uncle Martin's not here either." He beamed and looked around the crowd filing into the church.

Now, our long, painfully slow procession at an end, we communicants stood more or less straightbacked in our front pews and grinned at our families, and Mrs. Lonigan the organist was waking up the big organ in the choirloft. The principal, Sister Phillip, whispered to us to sing loud, and just as we were poised to launch ourselves into song, I saw my Great-Uncle Frank. I shot a quick look at Grandma, and the horror in her eyes told me she'd seen him. I saw Uncle Tom elbow Uncle Mike.

Uncle Frank emerged from the church vestibule at the regal pace of a mourner at a state funeral, literally the sole person there who didn't realize how plastered he was. Carefully, gingerly, head held high, as though he were in communion with the saints painted above the altar, he made his way into the church. He looked at no one, did not wobble over much, not even when he walked into the statue of St. Bonaventure at the back of the main aisle. Unfazed by this collision, he altered course slightly, marched up the aisle, found the correct pew, made the merest imitation of genuflection, entered the pew of his family, and proceeded to sit on my grandmother's lap.

She hissed, "For God's sake, Frank," and he let out a surprised, "Oh, is that you, Winnie?" in the voice of a man calling out to a friend at a Bears game, so that the entire congregation heard the exchange and cracked up.

We were delighted at the diversion, and I acknowledged my family's performance with a worldly shake of my eight-year-old head.

"That's my grandma's brother," I explained. "He used to be a policeman before they had guns," and the kids nodded, impressed at his great age and grateful for his presentation.

Beyond whatever damage he caused to Grandma's purse, which had been on her lap, Frank engaged in no further violence, for he went directly to our flat after Mass, took off his shoes, and fell asleep sitting atop the burn hole in my grandmother's sofa. The ceremony itself was uneventful: I did indeed faint from the heat, sometime during the endless sermon from Monsignor Roarke, who was possessed with a marvelous speaking voice but devoid of any sense of time.

One of the girls also fainted, as did my friend Jamie Orsini, but I think he was faking. One of the fathers fainted as well, at least that was how it sounded, the great heavy thud of a large body hitting a hard floor, and there was a murmur of concern from the people around him. A few moments later Uncle

Martin fell asleep and landed in the aisle, and Father Roarke talked on without losing his cadence or his train of thought.

Afterward we stood out in front of the church while an endless succession of relatives took photos. A few feet from me, my Uncle Gerald Dorsey was taking a picture of Matt and his parents. After the picture was snapped, Matt's mom gave Matt's dad a look rich in malice, and I knew Uncle Dennis had done something wrong. He was sweating profusely and after a while I noticed that he was weaving slightly.

"Your Uncle Dennis's got a load on, huh?" Tom asked.

"I guess so." I hadn't heard that expression but guessed what it meant.

Tom patted me on the shoulder. "You gonna drink when you grow up?"

"I don't know," I said, afraid to tell him that I planned to adopt every habit he had, including tobacco, liquor, and dark-haired girls belonging to other men.

He gave me a long slow look. "Look at your cousin."

Matt was staring down at the ground as his mother spoke urgently, angrily, into his father's face. He stood in a peculiar slope-shouldered way, as though he were sick. I saw him shoot a quick look from his mother to his father and then look down again.

"You decide to be a boozer, kiddo, okay, but don't have any kids." I caught the note of anger in his voice and looked up. My uncle stared at me till I nodded.

Uncle Mike came up just in time to catch the tail end of our conversation. "You shouldn't tell the kid that stuff."

"You think he don't see? He ought to know."

I knew that Uncle Dennis had recently become a regular at the Riverside Inn, a development that made no one happy and had apparently brought trouble on more than one occasion.

"Do you like Uncle Dennis?" I asked him.

"When he's sober, Dan, he's a great guy, he's funny, he's

got the gift of gab, he's smart. He just shouldn't have got married. Guy like that can't do a kid any good."

We began walking to our car and I shot a last look over my shoulder at Matt. His parents were still arguing and he was watching them now, and when he caught my eye, he gave me a halfhearted wave.

For the rest of the day I enjoyed behaving like a visiting duke. My grandmother baked a ham and a chicken and the long narrow table in her dining room was covered with side dishes and baskets of rolls. I was allowed a Pepsi with my dinner, and afterwards there was a chocolate cake from Heck's Bakery. In the afternoon, my uncles and grandfather went out for "a beer" as they always put it, though they never seemed to settle for one, and beer frequently had nothing to do with it. My grandmother watched a movie with my Aunt Anne and Uncle Frank's wife Rose.

I made a little house for myself under the dining room table, setting the chairs on their sides to give the illusion of privacy and set up some soldiers behind a barricade of Lincoln Logs. As I played I found myself wondering about Matt, wondering what his day had been like. I hoped there was a dinner like mine in progress at the Dorsey house. I hoped his dinner would be at Grandma Dorsey's, for it didn't seem that his own house would be much of a place for celebration.

A Tale of a
Serving Spoon

One Saturday morning later that May, I awoke to a somber house. My grandmother was in the kitchen performing her rituals, which on Saturday included a pot of coffee for my uncles, a pound of bacon, and what seemed to be a hundred pancakes. I dressed myself, then crept to the bathroom to slick down my hair and splash water on my face as my grandmother had taught me. I remember that a couple of her dark hairpins were lying on the sink; I held them up to my lip to see if a mustache would help me look like that most famous of all the world's Flynns, "Cousin Errol."

While I was admiring myself I noticed a small reddish spot on the mirror. Soon I saw others, on the lip of the sink and behind the faucet, and when I looked down at the floor, I saw that someone had wiped it badly, managing to make dark orange smears below the sink. My first thought was that Uncle Tom had had a particularly harrowing encounter with his razor the night before, but I knew those cuts didn't drip blood. Someone had bled here and been unable to hide it.

When I went out to the kitchen, my grandmother greeted me with her customary, "Good morning, sunshine," but wouldn't look at me.

"There's blood in the bathroom, Grandma."

"Oh, that. Well. Sit down, your pancakes are ready. You can be first this morning." I watched her turn four pancakes and realized that she wasn't going to say anything more. Behind me, one of my uncles shuffled into the bathroom and I saw her dart a quick look in that direction. It was a worried look and something turned in my stomach. I stared up at her as she set the pancakes on my plate and then gave me four pieces of bacon.

"What happened?"

She shook her head and turned away, and a few seconds later just said, "Oh, there was some sort of a fight. They're all just wild men nowadays, and there's too much drink. If there's a fight between these young bloods, then you can be sure there's drink involved in it somewhere."

She pushed the Log Cabin syrup container toward me and I unscrewed the cap from the tin cabin's chimney and buried my pancakes and the bacon in a half-inch pool of syrup. I was in love with pancake syrup: when no one was around, I crept into the pantry and drank it straight from the can. I considered it my secret crime against the family. Eventually Uncle Mike shuffled in, refusing to look at anything but the table. When my grandmother saw him, she let out a groan and said, "For the love of God, Michael." His right eye was monstrously swollen, a lump of tight purple flesh where there had once been a normal eye, the eye itself now reduced to a dark, wet slit. He also had a red mark on one cheekbone.

"Does it hurt, Uncle Mike?"

He nodded slowly. "Yeah. It does a little."

"It's good for 'im," his mother muttered without looking at him.

About five minutes later, Uncle Tom came in. A dark gash, almost black, split the bridge of his nose, and the skin around it was swollen, as was the left side of his lower jaw. He looked everyone in the eye, gave me a bright, "Hello, kiddo," and patted his big brother gently on the back. He kissed his mother and ignored the angry look she gave him in response.

She stared at them both for several seconds, then turned her back and resumed making their breakfast. A moment later she fixed me with a quick look whose meaning was unmistakable, and I got up and brought my empty plate to the sink.

"Did you have enough?" she asked, in spite of the fact that we both knew I'd been dismissed.

"Yes, Grandma." I looked at Uncle Tom, who was stirring his coffee and looking as though he'd been caught at something terrible.

"Does the cut hurt?"

"Nah, it's not as bad as it looks. I been cut worse."

My grandmother wheeled on them. "Yes, he has, he's been cut worse, only he told me that was the last time! You should be ashamed of yourself, Thomas Flynn, and your brother that's older than you, he should have more sense. I thought we'd had the last of this fighting after that night."

"Ma, this was nothing like that. Take it easy."

Predictably, she said, "I won't take it easy," which is what I have heard people say every time in my life someone told them to "take it easy" when they were upset. "I hoped that was the last time, that night you were drafted and you went out with that Billy Drey and got into that terrible fight." She looked at me again. "They were in their best suits..."

"Now he don't want to hear about that."

She waved an angry hand in his direction and went on, unstoppable. "Your uncle was in a brand-new suit, a white summer suit, it was, and they got into a fight with some hooligans in that restaurant on Belmont, the Marquis Lounge it was, and they all got arrested. I had to go to the police station to get him, and there he was with blood all over his new suit, gallons of blood..."

"You don't have gallons of blood in a person, Ma," he said, and I knew he made a mistake.

"And that—that *thing* sticking out of your head, I don't even know what it was..."

"It was a spoon," Uncle Tom muttered. He was looking down at his coffee and this made it seem as though he was speaking not to my grandmother but to his breakfast.

She turned to me again and held an open hand out in his direction. "A spoon in his head, a big steel spoon that they use to serve you in a restaurant. What a sight for a mother: her son losing his life's blood, and a *serving spoon* sticking out of his head!"

"Ma, the kid don't need to be hearing this."

She ignored him and directed her homily at me. "A serving spoon. And blood all over him, he looked like Dillinger when they shot him by the Biograph. That's what I saw when I went down to get him out of the jail." Abruptly, she showed him her back, though we could hear her continuing to mutter about the serving spoon. I was fascinated.

"Did it hurt?"

My uncle gave me a sour look. "What do you think? What do we send you to school for? Of course it hurt. If you had a little pin, like a hairpin, stuck into your head, it would hurt, wouldn't it?" I nodded. "All right, then. Of course a serving spoon would hurt."

"Sure, it would hurt," Mike agreed.

I was unfazed by his anger. "How'd they get it out?"

Tom sighed. "A doctor took it out. That's what you have to do, a regular person doesn't have the..."

"The training," Mike helped.

"Right," Tom said.

"Danny, go out and play," my grandmother said through her teeth, and it was not a suggestion.

Still, I lingered, taking a long time in the bathroom, which had thin walls and a warped, ill-fitting door that allowed a person to experience passively any conversation in the kitchen.

"A lot of brawling filthy drunkards," my grandmother said in a growling voice I'd never heard before.

"No. We weren't drunk and it wasn't a brawl. It was Dennis

Lynch, he was in trouble. Some guys had him in an alley and they were working him over."

My grandmother was silent for a moment, then made a little "tsk-tsk" of pity and said, "Dennis again?"

"Yeah. Three guys there were, Ma. And so Mike and me and Gerry Shea…"

"Oh, *him*," my grandmother spat. "I never liked him."

"Come on, Ma, you did, too. You told me he was a nice kid."

"I changed my mind."

"Anyhow, we're coming back from the movies and we see these guys and they're clobbering Dennis, so we jumped in."

"And they clobbered you," she said, but her voice had changed.

"No," he said quietly, and there was an admirable certainty in his voice. "It looks like it, but you should see the other guys," he said, and it sounded as if he was smiling.

"They beat Dennis up pretty bad, Ma," Uncle Mike was saying. "We took him to St. Joseph's in Gerry's car."

There was a long pause and I heard the sound of their forks scratching at the plates and my grandmother sliding the long thin spatula under the fresh pancakes. Finally I heard my grandmother sigh.

"Will he be all right?"

"Yeah, he's all right," Uncle Mike offered, but he didn't sound convinced.

"They didn't break anything," I heard Tom say, "but he's marked up pretty good."

"The poor thing. He's always in trouble, that one. Why in the world were they beating him up?"

"Money, Ma, what else? He owes a guy money. Always owes some guy money. He gambles and then he borrows and he can't pay it back."

"Should we loan him a few dollars?"

"Ma, the kind he borrows and loses, we don't have. And

if he keeps borrowing it from this kinda people, they're gonna find him in an alley some night and his borrowing days will be through."

There was a long silence and she said, "What kind of people?" in a quiet voice.

"People I wouldn't borrow money from. I don't know who he owes this time, but he borrows and bets with that guy Pender who sits at the far end of the bar at Liquor Town. I wouldn't do business with him."

"Will they be after the two of you now, these men?"

"I doubt it. We didn't, you know, give 'em our names and phone numbers. Far as they're concerned, it was just three guys comin' to help a guy, that's all it was. It's Denny they're after, or his money, anyway."

"Do you need a doctor?"

"Nah."

"Michael?"

"No, it's better."

"'Better?' What's better about it? It's a nicer color than it was last night?"

"Ma, it's all right. Lemme eat in peace, for God's sake."

"Watch your language at my table," she snapped, but it was just for show, and I could hear in her voice that she'd accepted their explanation.

Later that week I saw Matt at Hamlin Park, and we made a circuit of the park, climbing the smaller trees and dashing across the outfield of the baseball diamonds to the irritation of the older kids playing softball. I wanted to ask him about his dad but it seemed like something that shouldn't be discussed. Finally I just asked him how Uncle Dennis was.

"He's okay. The other night, though, he got a shiner and a fat lip from a fight."

We were in a small hawthorn tree, Matt looking down on me from a high fork in the smaller branches. His eyes were alight.

"What happened? Somebody beat him up?"

"No, somebody *tried* to. Two of 'em," he said, beaming, "but my dad took care of 'em. My old man can take care of himself."

I didn't know Uncle Dennis the way I knew my other uncles and aunts. There was always a distance to him, as though he had his mind on other things. On several occasions he took Matt and me to the movies, and once he took us to the parish carnival. He didn't have much to say to us, though he frequently pointed out things to us that he wanted us to notice. One night he drove us down North Avenue after a movie, and pointed out a corner to us.

"I had a paper stand there when I was your age, you guys." We looked in vain for the stand. "Had to get up when it was dark and cold and be on that corner by five. You guys think you got it hard," he muttered, and the faint smell of alcohol filled the front seat.

"You know who one of my customers was?" We shook our heads on cue and Uncle Dennis smiled. "Bugs Moran."

"The gangster?" Matt asked.

"That's right, same one Capone tried to hit on St. Valentine's Day, though this was, you know, years after that."

"Was he a nice guy?" Matt asked.

"Oh, yeah, he was a class guy. He used to tip me a couple dollars sometimes, just for a newspaper that cost a couple cents. That's the kinda spender he was. I like a guy that knows how to spend money. When you guys grow up, make sure you know how to spend a dollar."

I was struck by his revelation, by any hint about his background, for Uncle Dennis was largely a mystery to the family on both sides. No one knew his family or anything about them, except that there had been many of them. When he first met

Aunt Mary Jane, Dennis had just come back to Chicago from St. Louis. He rarely spoke about his childhood, never mentioned his parents. He'd been seeing Mary Jane for several months before anyone knew he was originally from Chicago, and longer still before he dropped hints that he'd actually grown up in the old neighborhood around North and Wells. I'd once heard Uncle Mike complain that Dennis had a way of changing the stories he'd told about his early life, as though he were reinventing himself. Nobody he talked to, Mike said, remembered a big family named Lynch around there.

In June, when we'd all been turned loose on an unsuspecting populace for summer vacation, I began spending one or two days a week at Grandma Dorsey's house. On the first of these days, I amused myself with Terry Logan and a couple of the other kids and waited in vain for Matt to show up. When it became obvious that he wasn't coming, I asked my grandmother if he'd be here the next time.

She turned away quickly and said, "Oh, I'm sure he will," but her tone said something entirely different. I didn't see him for the entire month of June, nor did I see anything of his parents. When I asked my uncles about it, they exchanged a quick look and Uncle Mike shrugged.

"I don't know if you're gonna see him there for a while, champ. I think his folks made some kinda other arrangement."

"Why?"

He looked irritated, and Uncle Tom stepped in.

"I think it's just more convenient for them this way," he said, and changed the subject almost immediately.

I was sitting in the dirt just outside Grandma Dorsey's door. I had dug small trenches and filled them with my toy soldiers, and I was sitting there in the hopes that one of the other kids would show up and join me, bringing new blood to the battle. Grandma Dorsey was in the kitchen peeling onions and talking to Aunt Ellen.

"Anything I've got, she can have, she knows that," Grandma Dorsey was saying.

"Mom, what they need, you can't give 'em, and it's not the money. If it was, we all woulda got together and come up with it. You know it's not the money. Whatever we give them, he'll find a way to spend. Money just…it goes through his hands like water, Mom. We give him money, he'll gamble with it. He's always got some goofy idea about making money, and it never pans out for him. He's nuts."

"Oh, now, he's not any such thing."

"Yeah, he is, and I could *kill* him for marrying her, and sometimes I'd like to give *her* a punch in the nose for…for falling for that crazy man." Ellen was the oldest in her family, a widow at forty, with a house full of children; she was tall, tough, and good-looking in a humorless way, and I had the impression that she took care of her mother. "That broad doesn't miss a thing," I once heard my Uncle Mike say, and he was probably not far off the mark.

"He doesn't seem to have much luck, the poor boy," Grandma said.

"You make your own luck, Mom."

"Not always, you don't. Some things just happen," Grandma Dorsey said, and I was struck by how different she sounded. This was the voice of knowledge, of experience, not my sweet-tempered grandmother mouthing platitudes and homilies about life's dangers and rewards, and it silenced Aunt Ellen for a time.

At last she spoke again, quieter this time. "Mom, they're too proud to come over. We won't see them till they're out of this jam. When Dennis has a buck in his pocket again, that's when you'll see them at your door."

"I'd like to see Matt, at least. They could bring him over sometimes," Grandma Dorsey said in a soft voice, and Aunt Ellen growled, "Aw, Mom, come on."

It was weeks, perhaps months, before they saw him again, but I saw him the following week.

There was a photographer in the zoo at Lincoln Park, stationed just outside the big brown building that housed the cafeteria. You could have him take pictures of you sitting on or standing in front of a stuffed bear. Terry Logan had just angered this man by slapping his hand across the camera lens just as the photographer was taking a shot of a mother and her little boy. The photographer, a thin man in suspenders, gave chase and we tore off in the direction of the big figure-eight–shaped pond we all called "the lagoon"—Terry and I and two German boys named Otto and George.

The photographer probably gave up the chase within the first fifty paces, but a bystander with time on his hands had taken up the cause for a while and so we kept on running. We rounded the lagoon, went on past the dark, spooky little islands where Matt told us someone had once buried a dead body, and we didn't stop till we got to the hill with the statue of General Grant on it. We scrambled up the hill through the dense underbrush that sprouted everywhere in Lincoln Park in those days. The hill was crowned by a high granite edifice that held the bronze general and formed a tunnel-like arcade with windows that allowed a view of the lake a few hundred yards to the east. It was a dank, shadowy place favored by teenagers with romantic inclinations, and we had found used condoms in the bushes around it. We made it to the top and, satisfied that the men had lost the interest or energy to continue their pursuit, collapsed against the damp wall to catch our breath.

As we gasped and giggled at one another, I became aware that we were not alone. A few feet away someone sat in one of the big stone windows and watched us with his arms folded across his chest. I was spooked, and I poked Terry and pointed. The figure in the window was backlit but I could see that it was a child. He said nothing till all four of us were turned in his direction, then slid down onto the floor of the monument.

"You guys are scared of your own shadows."

"Matt?"

"No, Santa Claus! Of course it's me, dummy. Who'd you expect?"

He stepped toward us, coming out of shadow and into the light from the setting sun. I looked around the monument and saw no one else.

"Who you with?"

"Me, myself, and I. Who am I supposed to be with?"

"I don't know."

He looked at Terry and the others. "I saw you running—what'd you guys do, steal something?"

"No, Terry made the photographer mess up a picture." We all laughed and Matt smiled at Terry Logan.

"That one guy almost caught you, Terry."

"I know."

"I could see the whole thing from up here," Matt said. "I come up here sometimes." He gave me a little smile and I nodded. He folded his arms, and I saw things in his face, pride in this display of his independence, and something else, just the faintest hint of hostility.

"What are you doing here by yourself, Matt?" I asked him.

"Who am I supposed to be here with? I don't need to be with anybody else, for Christ's sake. I can go anywhere I want to. My ma calls in from work and checks on me, and then I can go anywhere I want, long as I get back home before she does."

"What if she calls again?"

"She won't. She only calls once, to see if I ate lunch."

He regarded us with a superior air and smiled. "I got to get back. I got a long ways to go. And you're gonna be late, too, Dan. I think you're already late."

"I don't know."

"I do. You're late. See you guys." He started down the dirt side of the hill, hands in pockets, and then stopped. "Hey, Danny? Don't say nothing to anybody, okay? Don't say you saw me."

"All right," I said, not really knowing what difference it made but willing to keep his secrets. He nodded and kept on trudging down the hill.

Death of a Dreadnought

Having survived an entire year of my "second" life, I looked forward to that summer of 1955 the way a child should. It was to be in its way as full of incident as its predecessor had been. If someone had told me that, I'm not certain I would have believed it possible. The first landmark of that summer was a wake and funeral. I was already fearful of them, given the bleak circumstances of the first one I'd experienced, but this one proved to be different, for it marked the passing of my grandmother's cousin Betty McReady, the unmarried one of the McReady sisters.

I was sitting at the kitchen table having Kool-Aid when my grandmother took the call. She hung up the phone on the wall and looked at Grandpa.

"Betty McReady died, Pat. God bless her."

Grandpa looked at her, raised his eyebrows and just said "God rest her soul." When I asked what she'd died of, Grandpa looked at me and said, "Her great weight."

"Oh, don't be telling him nonsense like that. For God's sake, she most certainly did not die of her weight."

"Ugliness, then."

"Keep a Christian tongue in your head, Pat, for the boy's sake. She was a grand old soul," Grandma insisted, and eventually wore Grandpa down because he had long since learned which fights he could not win.

The formal visitation took place at Larsen Brothers Funeral Home on Belmont. Uncle Tom brought me there, dressed in my sole white shirt and a clip-on tie that gouged my neck, and Grandma squired me around the room, where people fussed over how grown-up I looked. Then Uncle Tom led me up to the casket, where I viewed the deceased with great interest.

My parents' funeral was a blur to me still, a hectic, crowded tearful two days of terror and noise and sadness, and I really noticed very little of it, other than the way people all seemed to be watching me, and how different my parents looked in death. The wake of Aunt Betty was therefore an excellent occasion for a boy to experience the Irish interpretation of the funereal ritual. Freed from the dark restraint of actual mourning, I was able this time to watch and learn, and there was much to note. For one thing, her passing flew in the face of a widely held belief among her acquaintances that the McReady sisters couldn't be killed. This notion was born of the fact that these two women had for eight decades ignored all the modern notions of health, exercise, proper diet, and kitchen hygiene and still managed to reach the age of eighty-one (Mary) and eighty-two (Betty). Mary was known to serve leftovers weeks after their original appearance on her table, and Betty became a cooking legend for her belief that if she found something in her freezer, it was good for soup. For this reason her soups were a cause for dread, morbidity lurked in each teeming spoonful, and one lived in terror of the moment when he might find himself at Betty's table and see her coming with a tureen of soup containing animals and vegetables that had last seen the light of day when Roosevelt held the White House.

It was believed by the more educated in the neighborhood that her freezer was a wellspring of meiosis and mitosis that had more than likely produced microbes hitherto unseen in the world. She once actually admitted to guests that she could not identify the meat used in a particular batch of soup, but that she'd "come across it in me freezer, so where's the harm in it?"

Grandpa said that food acquired immortal life once it reached Betty's freezer, and he claimed he'd seen Mary scrape what looked like fur from a hunk of roast beef before carving it up for sandwiches. No one ever died of anything he ate at Betty McReady's house, or at the matching table of terror in her sister Mary's, but it was widely believed that this was because people ate sparingly at their homes, washed their meals down with scalding Irish tea to boil the bacteria alive, or doused them with unwatered whiskey to poison them.

All the neighborhood waited patiently for the day when the tiny beasties would work their fatal magic on one of the rotund sisters. We watched them ingest everything in sight, and nothing happened.

In the end, however, while Betty's ancient system proved impervious to the unseen onslaughts of microbes from old meat and murky soup, her heart had given out. In death as in life, she was the subject of much talk, though now she elicited comment and conjecture of a different sort.

There was, for example, much discussion of the peculiar demands of her funeral. I overheard my grandfather opining that she'd be an easy one for the Larsen brothers to handle, because her corpse was already preserved almost to the point of calcification. What he actually said was that "her innards are damn near cement by now," and Grandma had told him not to speak disrespectfully of the dead.

On the other hand, I learned that her weight presented certain challenges to the Larsen brothers, this according to the semi-hushed conversations I overheard in the funeral parlor. For one, they had some difficulty fitting her into the casket. For another, the clothing brought to the Larsens by Aunt Mary had not been worn by Betty for more than forty years, and there was some doubt whether the dress in particular had ever fit her.

Her size evoked considerable comment among my uncles: "Where we gonna get pallbearers?" I heard Uncle Mike ask.

"We can find six guys here easy," Tom answered.

"Six?" Mike repeated. "What six guys you know could carry Betty McReady *and* the box she's in without one of 'em droppin' dead?"

"Okay, maybe we go with eight."

Uncle Mike shook his head. "Eight guys and a draught horse. Eight guys and an elephant, maybe."

"Hey, show some respect for the dead."

Tom nudged Mike with an elbow and they looked in my direction. I pretended to be interested in the deceased, and Tom suggested we go up to pay our respects.

I spent several minutes studying the late Betty McReady and for years to come my impressions of the embalmer's art were colored by this experience. In repose, her heavy features had given way to gravity, so that her face was both flat and enormous. Also, the combination of the natural stiffness that overtakes the flesh after death and the liberal application of powder and makeup had given Aunt Betty a look quite unlike anything I'd ever seen in a living being. I thought she resembled nothing so much as my grandma's waxed fruit. I made this observation to Uncle Tom and he told me not to say that in front of Grandma. He suggested that we kneel down and say a prayer, and as we did so, Aunt Mary chose this moment to waddle up to the casket to have another look at her sister.

"Ah, doesn't she look grand?"

"Sure she does, Aunt Mary," my uncle said.

She moved past us and the air was perfumed with the scent of mothballs. As always, she was in her heavy black coat—weather made no difference to her—a thick dense coat covered with dog hair. There seemed to be many kinds and colors of dog hairs on her coat, and I once commented to my grandfather that I'd seen her dog and he was black.

"Ah," he'd said, "those are from dogs long dead, Danny-boy. That coat hasn't been cleaned since V-J Day."

Along with the black coat and its patina of pooch hair, she wore her hat: I cannot to this day remember seeing her without her pillbox hat, not even in her own home. It was black and flat and bore a single yellow flower that never moved, bent, nor swayed in the breeze, and as the years wore on the hat grew dusty and battered and misshapen. Now, as she leaned over to look at Betty, the hat opted for freedom and dropped onto the bosom of her sister. Mary immediately grabbed it back and jammed it on her head, unaware that the solitary flower had become entangled with the rosary clasped between the deceased's hands.

Aunt Mary turned to us and saw that she was caught by something. She spent a long moment trying to shake loose, during which a look of total befuddlement crossed her face. Then Mary tossed her head to free herself and the rosary came loose, swinging freely from the yellow flower so that Mary now seemed to have added a new ornament to the hat. The rosary moved to and fro like a beaded pendulum and the old woman was utterly unaware of it. She looked back at her sister, then frowned.

"Oh, someone's gone and taken her rosary, for the love of God. Nothing's safe anymore, people'll steal the pennies off your eyes after you're gone."

This last expression made no sense whatsoever to me and I was going to ask where the pennies were, but she was just warming up.

"It wasn't like this in the old days, people were honest unless they were trying to sell you something, and we didn't have this communism. No communists then, or if we did have them, they kept quiet about their nonsense. And these murderers you have now, why we didn't have anything like that at all."

I wanted to do something helpful, so I pointed at the rosary dangling from her hat. "It's…" I started, then felt Uncle Tom's hand squeeze my arm. "…gone," I finished, and she nodded.

"People will take anything that's not nailed down." She studied Betty's serene countenance. "Ah, she's at peace now, poor thing, her suffering is finished." She turned a beseeching look on us.

"She was so homely, poor thing, and look how they've fixed her up. Not that she's a beauty now, of course—it'd take the hand of the Lord Himself to do that, but still…"

I looked incredulously from Mary to the deceased, a matched pair if the Almighty had ever made one, and said nothing. Mary bent over, examining the work of the funeral home and nodding sagely.

"There, you see?"

I didn't see at all. She appeared to be pointing to a large, terrifying growth at the point of her sister's chin.

"That mole? She used to have a long ugly hair growing out of that mole, and they've cut it off or shaved it or something." She examined her sister, managing to look more like Betty than ever, and my uncle turned away and put a handkerchief to his face. He coughed earnestly into it but I wasn't fooled. Mary waddled off again to greet newcomers, and Tom and I said a quick prayer for the deceased.

After the trip out to St. Joseph's Cemetery, we went back to Aunt Mary's house, a small bungalow near Belmont and Kedzie. People had brought food, "enough to feed starving China," Aunt Mary told us when we arrived, and so it seemed to me. There were cakes and platters of homemade cookies, a ham and a corned beef and a smoked butt, some chicken and cold cuts and all the various salad things, and four kinds of pop, including cream soda, which I had just discovered.

Joe Collins, Mary's overwhelmed husband, met us at the door. He was an addled-looking gentleman, fidgety and skel-etally thin, and immediately I thought of Jack Spratt and his wife, and wondered if there was a small bit of truth in all fairy tales. He smiled and blessed us for coming. He pointed the way to the kitchen and then went past us to greet someone else with a distracted look on his face. I realize now that long association with the sisters probably explained the distracted facial expression, but Tom insisted that Joe's feeble wit was also a factor. I heard him tell Uncle Mike that Joe had "retired from the police force after forty years as a patrolman and still signed his name with an X. Came here not knowing how to read and write and he still can't."

A while later, Mary sent Joe out for more liquor and, as soon as he was gone, she scurried over to a hall closet and produced a quart bottle of Jim Beam, then waddled around "freshening" people's drinks, whether or not they had been drinking bourbon. She paused at my glass and was moments from adding bourbon to it till Uncle Tom said, "Cream soda, Aunt Mary."

She frowned at me and Tom said, "Aunt Mary, he's *eight*," and then she nodded. She returned to her big red stuffed armchair, where she "freshened" her own drink till it was the color of a chocolate phosphate and sipped at it, making little noises of contentment. By the time her husband returned, she was singing Irish songs along with a John McCormack record, in a flat croaking voice like a bullfrog calling for its mate.

The adults chattered away as though it was Christmas come early and I ate my way through the dessert table. Then someone put John McCormack away and turned on more lively music, and Aunt Mary's house rocked with fiddles and flutes, tin whistles, bagpipes, and the thump of the *bhodran*, and the party went tribal. It was a warm afternoon and everywhere I looked I saw sweating, flushed faces, some of them literally inside blue wreaths of cigarette smoke—they put me in mind of little mountains climbing up into the clouds. Now people were singing and clapping. My grandfather, his quiet soul taken by the music and a couple of whiskeys, lurched out into the middle of the living room and began to dance.

"Oh, Dad's got his party hat on," I heard Uncle Mike say, and Tom looked delighted, but the look on Grandma's face was exactly the one I'd seen when she found ants on the kitchen table.

Everybody clapped and whooped and tried to sing, and then my grandfather was pulling me out on the floor with him, whereupon we produced our unique version of the jig, though in truth I knew no more of the Irish jig than I did of brain surgery, but an Irishman is a tolerant audience for his dancers, and most of the attendees were willing to suspend their disbelief and pretend they were seeing the genuine article. They clapped and exclaimed and said I was cute, and my grandfather made them play the record again, and we danced till my grandfather and I fell over each other.

"Easy, Dad," I heard Tom say. "Remember Jake Cooley."

Grandpa waved him off and said, "For God's sake he was getting on to be eighty-five, and I'm not sixty-two yet."

I asked Uncle Tom about Jake Cooley.

"Ah, he was an old guy, like your Grandpa says, and he got a little too energetic on the dance floor and had a heart attack. Not that that's a bad way for a guy to go, dancing in front of his friends with a smile on his face. Most people don't get to die at a party, kiddo."

He patted me on the head and watched his father with a look of good-humored tolerance. I looked around and even Grandma was smiling. A few moments later someone put on another old record, a fox trot, and Grandpa had Grandma out there with him. She was laughing like a young girl. In a few moments the floor was crammed with old people dancing to Mary McReady's record player and I thought I had never seen anything so funny in my life.

Later, Grandpa and I danced again, but he tired quickly this time out, and he went out into the kitchen. I followed him out to get another pop and found him sitting at the table, coughing into his handkerchief.

Tough Guys

It was a plain fact of life that if you walked through a pack of boys who weren't your friends, anything could happen and probably would. Stranger-kids might call you names, ask for money, trip you as you went by, chase you down the street and, on the worst occasions, get close enough to throw punches. A boy was well-advised to keep his head up, cross the street to avoid certain corners, and be aware of who was walking behind him at all times. Like most boys, I had to learn these things.

There were older boys at Hamlin Park who frequently tormented us, largely from boredom. One afternoon after swimming in the crowded Hamlin Park pool, I was coming out of the candy store with my friend Jamie and we encountered a group of older boys, including Lenny, the terror who during the school year seemed to live under the viaduct like a dark-haired troll. They stared at us as we came down the concrete steps. Lenny was sitting on the bottom step, and when I reached it, he tripped me. I landed on my elbow and my knee, bloodying both of them.

"What're you, clumsy?" Lenny said.

I got up angrily and without thinking swung at him and grabbed the front of his T-shirt. He laughed and slapped me in the face, then walked on, staring at me over his shoulder and daring me to retaliate. My friend Jamie watched in fear and whispered that Lenny'd cream me if I did anything more.

At home, my new injuries were noticed, but I told everyone I'd fallen while running along the concrete edge of the pool. Predictably, my grandmother told me I could have broken my neck. I told myself I'd simply try to avoid Lenny in the future.

The next time I went to the library I found Rusty there, rooting around in the adult section for books on explosives. He set a couple of books down on a table and beckoned me to sit down. He made a pretense of paging through one of the books and then looked up suddenly.

"Lenny beat you up?"

"Who told you?"

"Jamie."

"He knocked me down and slapped me in the face. I'm gonna get him, I'll hit him with a brick," I said, though I had no intention of ever getting close enough to hit Lenny with anything.

"No, I'll take care of him, that shit, him and those big tough guys with him." He gave me a serious look. "You're my friend."

"What're you gonna do?" I asked.

"You'll see tomorrow. He always comes to the park on Saturdays. I'll find 'im."

The next morning Aunt Anne wanted to take me to a movie, but I told her I was meeting my friends at the park. She made me call up Jamie so that I wouldn't be roaming the streets alone.

When we arrived, there were already dozens of kids there, some chasing one another, some heading to the tiny gym for basketball, some making their way to the cramped library in the fieldhouse. The center of the park was a great round depression, as though an alien spaceship had landed there, burned a hole into the ground and left four baseball diamonds in its wake. Several dozen boys were already occupying the diamonds, armed with tattered baseball gloves, cracked bats, and well-taped league balls, and Lenny was on one of the smaller softball diamonds.

Jamie and I took a seat on one of the benches and watched the players.

"Rusty's not here," Jamie pointed out.

"I know." A cold fluttery feeling began to grow in my stomach. Already one of the boys with Lenny had chanced to look my way, and when he noticed us, he'd said something to Lenny. Lenny gave me a look of menace and went back to his game.

I was preparing to retreat to the library when Rusty finally arrived. His red hair, impervious to the comb, it seemed, blew in the wind. He had high points of color in his pale cheeks, he was breathing fast, and there was a distant look in his eyes that I was to see a number of times in years to come. He was carrying a bag.

"Hi, you guys. Is he here?"

Jamie and I pointed as though a single string controlled both of us, and Rusty looked down at the ballfield and nodded.

He hefted the bag and said, "I got something for Lenny."

It was a shabby, much-used paper bag, the type you'd put a kid's lunch in, and it was wrinkled and folded in a hundred places because his mother, living on poverty's near edge, had told him to fold it and bring it home after using it. And today Mrs. Kilgallen's only son had filled it with something that was clearly not lunch, for at that moment as he raised the bag, it moved.

Jamie and I gasped together, and Jamie said, "What's in there?"

"He's got a snake!" I said.

"Nah, my snake died. But I got good stuff anyway."

"What?"

"Small stuff," Rusty said, and gave me his grin.

As we were talking, Lenny and several of his friends had moved closer and begun making remarks intended for the three of us. One of the boys held that we were a bunch of sissies who sat around on benches while other boys played ball, and then

Lenny, who I see now as a boy without basic good sense, noted the lunch bag and asked if the three of us were having a picnic.

Rusty wheeled around as if just noticing them. He looked from them to his little bag and back to them, smiling.

"Yeah, that's right, we're havin' a picnic. You want some? You want some, you guys?"

And with that, he was striding down the sloping side of the ballfield, bag in hand, a skinny, pale-skinned child whose pants were two inches too short, unaware that he was, for better or worse, painting a childhood legend in broad strokes.

He was still six or seven feet from Lenny when he reached into the bag and said, "Here, Lenny," and threw what appeared to be a small gray ball of fur at Lenny.

Lenny screamed, one of the other boys said, "Shit!" and all of them jumped back. Lenny caught the gray thing on his chest, screamed again and made a batting motion with his hand. The gray thing bounced off him and landed on the ground, then scuttered away quickly.

"Is it off me?" he asked his friends.

Rusty laughed and put his hands on his hips. "Big tough guy, afraid of a little field mouse. Bet your friends think you're real tough, Lenny. A little mouse, for cryin' out loud."

A dark look came into the other boy's eyes and I told myself Rusty had overplayed a scant hand. Lenny took two steps in Rusty's direction and said something I couldn't hear. His fists were clenched, he'd survived the mouse, and Rusty was finished. One of the other boys said, "Punch 'im in the mouth, Len," and a third boy moved just behind Rusty, cutting off that avenue of escape. Lenny and Rusty were almost nose to nose and I was about to yell some warning to Rusty when he froze them all by reaching into the bag once more.

To his credit, he'd never moved an inch when Lenny came at him, and now I understood that along with his other gifts he had patience.

He pulled a small white bundle from the bag, something in a common kitchen napkin, held it up to Lenny's face and watched the bigger boy's eyes go wide. Then he unwrapped it and flung its contents in Lenny's face.

Lenny made a harsh squawking sound, flailed with both hands at his face and hair and began running. Rusty spun and tossed the napkin in the face of the kid behind him, and this second boy ran across the diamond wailing like a lost soul.

Rusty faced the others and they shrank back. Rusty shook his head theatrically.

"Bunch of tough guys and they're afraid of a couple centipedes."

He took a step toward them and they moved back, and then he launched what can only be described as a battlefield oration.

I couldn't make out the first couple of lines, but then I caught up with him, following a respectful pace or two behind him as he stalked them all, one skinny maniacal little boy in his battle fury giving chase to six, and casting threats and maledictions on their heads like a hot rain.

"You want to pick on my friends, right? Go ahead, and then I'll be looking for you. I can make gunpowder and I got cherry bombs. I can make *shrapnel*, I can make Greek fire, I can burn your houses down with you in 'em, and I got spiders and centipedes, Lenny, I got a tarantula, I got a snake that's four feet long. You pick on my friends again and I'll put things in your bed, and I'll…I'll put things in *your ma's* bed."

They had begun to slow down and now Rusty put on a burst of speed and they all tore off into the distance, and I could neither keep up nor listen to his steady litany of the vile things he would do to them all.

When he returned, he was grinning, and I gave him a roll of Lifesavers.

"You had centipedes?" I asked.

"Yeah. Three of 'em, one was real big. And a spider. The spider was dead but I knew they wouldn't notice." He sighed like a man after a large meal, crunched down on a lifesaver and beamed at us.

"What's Greek fire?" I asked.

"It's some kinda liquid the Greeks used to shoot at people to set fire to their ships."

"And you can make it?" Jamie asked.

Rusty shrugged. "I dunno, but I got a chemistry set."

"He's got the real big one," I told Jamie. "With like sixty bottles of stuff."

"Wow."

For much of that month, I feared that the other boys would not let their humiliation go unanswered, and I imagined them ambushing him in an alley and beating him bloody. But gradually I realized that their fear of finding a bedful of centipedes or black widows in their underwear drawer, or of a deadly rain of shrapnel and Greek fire descending on their homes and loved ones easily outweighed any need to get even. He was safe, we were all safe.

That second summer proved to be different from the first in several ways: not only was I seeing less of Matt, I saw less of Tom. The early days of that summer wore all the gaudy colors of a new vacation, and this time I had a life and a home that I thought of as my own. I had my local friends and playmates to keep me busy, eventually my sporadic encounters with Matt, and long, eventful sorties through the neighborhood with Rusty.

I understood that my uncle was now working two jobs, his regular one at the dairy and the new one at the bar. What started out as an occasional weeknight visit to pitch in behind the bar became a substantial drain on his time, partly from need—people couldn't cover their shifts, somebody responsible had to watch the cash register—and partly from the novelty of being a bar owner, playing big shot on a minor scale and buying drinks for everybody the wind blew in. At our noisy dinner table I caught hints of problems at the bar but thought nothing of them: near as I could tell, there was no corner of the adult world, no matter how insignificant, that was not fraught with trouble, and I was constantly making mental notes to myself to avoid certain circumstances, certain jobs. Given half the chance, I would have avoided adulthood itself.

But there was trouble at the bar, and though the nature of these problems at times puzzled me, they were the classic worries of the saloonkeeper: the difficulties of dealing with liquor troubles among one's friends and even relatives, the need to anticipate problems or break up the occasional barfight, the confrontations with patrons, especially belligerent strangers, and their troubles, troubles about money. When they talked of these things, my family let their voices drop, their references became masterpieces of circumlocution, they seemed to watch me as much as each other, and I feigned a native stupidity while soaking up as much as I could. There was money missing, there were conflicting ideas among the partners as to how they should deal with profit, there seemed to be an almost constant need to pay off one or another of the city inspectors, till I developed the notion that local government was a gaping maw into which one tossed money.

Other troubles were there as well, more serious ones: a partner or bartender with his hand in the till, and a partner who had lost control of his drinking: he'd begun to start fights, there had been angry scenes with this man's wife. My uncle's early exuberant moods during those first few weeks as a bar owner, what he clearly saw as his first step toward giving himself a chance at independence, soon gave way to reality, and he became more subdued when he spoke of the tavern. It had become work, he had begun to see the dark side of running a tavern, of protecting what little one has, of doing business with friends. He stopped bringing the tavern up in conversation, responding when asked a direct question but little more.

One night over supper, I heard my grandfather ask, "How's the saloon doing?"

"It's a pain in the ass, Dad," Tom said.

"*Thomas*," my grandmother said, and they were all looking in my direction except Tom.

"Sorry, I'm just tired. Tired of the gin mill, too."

"Ah, it'll all work out for the best," Grandma said. "There's good money in a tavern," doing her best to show her conversion. She didn't sound as though she believed it.

"Well, four months into this one, I haven't seen a dollar. And I'm good and tired of it."

I was still losing my grandmother's money when she sent me to the store, but not quite as often, so she gritted her teeth and handed me bills or coins and probably said a silent prayer, not only that I'd make it to the store with the money intact, but that I'd find the store: she'd sent me to a butcher's on Belmont one day, and I'd turned the wrong way and walked for thirty minutes before it dawned on me that I had probably missed it. My one achievement was that I had never yet had trouble going to the bakery for bread: she always let me buy a cookie, and this seemed a benediction on my mission. I never seemed to lose her money when she sent me to the bakery.

Two Weddings, One
of Them Inevitable

It was also a summer of weddings, that roiling, tumultuous summer, and I was to attend two of them. The first was the wedding I have described earlier, the wedding of Charlie Paris and Evelyn Shanahan: half the neighborhood was there because almost everyone knew Charlie Paris, ambitious, glad-handing son of a former alderman, and those that didn't know him knew the Shanahans, whose tribe seemingly numbered in the thousands. It was, as I have said, a freewheeling affair, and it colored my notions of weddings for all time, so that over the years I have often been disappointed by the tameness of most of those I've attended. Not the least of my disappointments was the discovery that weddings open to children were few and far between.

The second wedding proved memorable in its own way though not as rich in strife, discord, and violence, real or potential. First, it had a greater personal significance, involving as it did my Uncle Mike, the indecisive bridegroom, and Lorraine, former spinster, now triumphant. This meant that my entire clan would be present once more, no matter what implications that had for the safety of the neighborhood. The Dorsey side of the family were of course invited, all of them, including several I'd never seen. On the Flynn side, shadowy relations going all the way back to third and fourth cousins were summoned to this grand gathering, and this meant there would be people attending who were known only to my grandparents, if at all.

Grandpa Flynn, for example, was preparing himself to greet his storied Uncle Pete, the brother of my great-grandfather Flynn and a man my grandmother had once described as "a lightning rod to disaster." When she had seen Uncle Pete's name on the guest list, she'd made a little croaking sound.

"Peter Flynn? Oh, for the love of God, Patrick, Peter Flynn at the wedding of your firstborn?"

"He is my uncle, the last one left alive," Grandpa had said, drawing himself up in a fine display of injured sensibilities.

"He is misfortune incarnate, Patrick."

I had of course immediately asked Tom what she meant.

"Oh, Uncle Pete? Oh, boy," he said in his way that said he knew stories and only some of them were fit for a boy's ears. He yelled out "Uncle Pete" to Mike, who was lost in his normal half-hour ministrations in the bathroom.

"Uncle Pete?" Mike said. "Oh, boy."

"Sit down," Tom ordered, and I did.

"Okay, Uncle Pete, first off, is a good guy, nicest guy in the world…"

"Nicest guy in the world," Mike called out through the door.

"But things happen to him."

"Around him," Uncle Mike corrected. "A building fell on him once."

"Well, yeah, but let me tell the story myself. So things happen around him, wherever he goes." Tom looked at me with raised eyebrows and repeated "*Wherever*. So a building fell on him once, and he fell into a well once, and one time he fell asleep in a museum and got locked inside for two days. When he was a boy in the Old Country, he was riding a cart full of sheep to the market town and it went over the side of a hill. Killed all the sheep."

"But not him."

"No, be a shorter story then, wouldn't it? Anyway, so he survived the Great Sheep Slaughter, as somebody called it."

"They had kind of a funny song about it," Mike added, emerging from the bathroom smelling of aftershave.

"Anything bad happens in Ireland, they write a song about it. So automatically he's got a reputation as kind of a screw-up, and then he grew up and left the Old Country, came here like all of 'em, like your grandma and grandpa, to see if they could start a life for themselves. Anyhow, Uncle Pete comes here, and he's a walking disaster. He gets a job in a factory, the factory burns down. He gets a job driving a truck, he drives it into a wall over on Twelfth Street. He joins the Merchant Marine in World War I, and twice his ships get torpedoed and once his lifeboat hits a rock and goes down and now he's what the other sailors call a 'Jonah.' When the war is over he goes into business and that's a disaster, he invests money in all kinds of stupid things…"

"A place that builds wagons," Uncle Mike said. "Everybody's buying cars and he invests in a place that still makes wagons."

"Then he becomes partners with a guy that's gonna make pianos cheap, and this guy, he's sixty-five and he falls for an eighteen-year-old secretary and they run off to Brazil or someplace, and Uncle Pete is left holding the bag."

"Did he get to keep the pianos?"

"Weren't any pianos, kid. The way he put it was, 'The pianos were still in the planning stage.'" They both laughed and then Tom said, "So Uncle Pete is coming to the wedding." He winked at me. "Your grandmother thinks in another life Uncle Pete was Job, you know, in the Bible? She thinks the roof'll fall in on us if he's with us for more than ten minutes. Well, big brother, your wedding is shaping up to be real entertainment."

Uncle Mike gave him an insider's look and said, "Guess who else is coming."

"Who?"

"*Seamus Corcoran*," Uncle Mike said, saying the name slowly and dramatically, the way he might have said "John Wayne" or "General MacArthur."

Uncle Tom was clearly one-upped. He stood gaping at his brother, then wet his lips. "He's not *dead* yet?"

"No. Dad thinks he might die at the wedding, but, no, he's not gone yet. He's gonna be there. We're thinking of sitting him across from Ma. Him and Uncle Pete."

"Who is Seamus Corcoran?" I asked.

"'The Last Bold Fenian'," Uncle Tom said.

"World's oldest person," Uncle Mike said.

"What's a Fenian?"

"Don't you know the history of your people?" Uncle Mike asked sternly, but I could tell he was having fun with me.

Tom shook his head. "Oh, Ma's gonna croak. The Fenians, Dan, the Fenians were Irish rebels that fought the British. They wanted to make Ireland a free country. They had kind of an uprising. Over here, some of 'em invaded Canada."

"Canada?" I said, for the connection eluded me.

"And they fought them over there, in the Old Country," he said to head me off.

"In the Easter Rising," I said, proud to show my knowledge.

Tom raised his eyebrows again. "No, kiddo, the Easter Rising was 1916, this...oh, this must have been fifty years before the Easter Rising."

I plunged into calculations, fifty years before 1916, and gave it up almost immediately.

"They don't teach math in that school?" Mike said. "You can't get by without math, Dan," the family accountant began.

"Hey, give him a break. It was in 1867, Dan. 1867."

I felt the breath leave me: the oldest people I knew, Mary McReady and her slow-witted husband, were eighty or thereabouts. It was almost inconceivable that a person would still be alive in 1955 who had been old enough in 1867 to bear arms.

"He fought the British in 1867?"

"He thinks so. We don't know."

"How old is he?"

"Could be a hundred—nobody knows for sure."

"He remembers the fighting," Uncle Mike added.

"Ah, he could've seen a movie about it in 1920. Who knows?"

I chose to take a higher road and accept this ancient Gael as a hero who had taken up arms for his people. "Did they beat the British in a battle, the Fenians?"

"Not exactly. These weren't Irish warriors, Dan, they were farm boys that somebody talked into fighting against British soldiers, so it didn't turn out real well for them. I think most of 'em were killed or tossed into prison. Anyhow, Uncle Seamus Corcoran, who is your grandmother's great uncle, is a thousand years old, and all he knows is he thinks he was a Fenian and he's pretty sure there aren't any other ones left."

"So he is the Last Fenian," I pointed out. I fell in love with the idea of Seamus Corcoran, of a person of my blood having been involved in something as romantic and desirable as pitched battle with red-coated soldiers. I couldn't have been more impressed if they'd told me he was the last of the twelve apostles.

"That's what he says, and God forbid anybody shows up wearing a red jacket."

Uncle Mike chuckled and Tom reached over to pat him on the shoulder.

"It's shaping up, big fella. Now if we can just keep Lorraine from changing her mind, we're in for a good time."

Uncle Mike blinked and a watery look came into his eyes as he pondered this heretofore unconsidered possibility.

"Just kidding," Tom said. To me he added, "It's your Uncle Mike we're keeping an eye on."

In the end, bride as well as groom showed up, the priest gave them no chance to back out, and the ceremony ended without incident unless one counts my Uncle Frank's unfortunate venture into song: unaware that Mrs. Lonigan had launched into one of her great warbling solos, completely unconscious of the fact that no one else in the church seemed to think she needed any help, Uncle Frank opened his mouth and bellowed his version of "Ave Maria" into the stuffy air of the church, producing a stiff-backed silence in the congregation that he apparently took for awe at his song stylings. I looked up at him in wonder, for he was right behind me, eyes shut, nose pointed at the ceiling of God's house, his hoarse voice bending, spindling, and mutilating one of the most beautiful of Catholic hymns till it sounded like the death rattle of a wild animal.

The second time through the refrain, my grandmother could take no more, and leaned back, threw a sharp elbow into his chest and silenced him, killing the final note in his throat, and with it Uncle Frank's incipient singing career. To my knowledge, he never again ventured into the lofty climes of liturgical music, content instead to sing along with tavern jukeboxes.

The highlight of the ceremony itself was not the exchange of vows, usually enough to bring tears to most eyes, but the sermon Monsignor Roarke had prepared for this occasion. In length and complexity it resembled not so much a homily as a religious saga, a cleric's version of *Finnegans Wake* or *The Odyssey*. As he spoke to the stunned gathering, his oration was punctuated by the sounds of bodies crashing to the floor as we took our turns at fainting.

Both the legendary Uncle Peter Flynn and the Last Fenian made it to the church, Uncle Peter occupying the back booth and peering nearsightedly at proceedings that had to be explained to him by a woman who seemed to be either his daughter or a caretaker, sent perhaps by the penal system. Seamus Corcoran, on the other hand, terrible-eyed and only half-shaven, arrived with his son, the son *himself* seventy-five if he was a day and looking more like The Last Fenian's brother than his offspring. Their entrance drew every eye, it would have been impossible not to notice them, for they entered in the very heart of the monsignor's epic and proceeded up the center aisle of the church, all the while muttering irritably to one another about the lack of proper seating.

I marveled at this ancient Irish freedom fighter, having never in my born days witnessed a creature of such age, not even in the animal kingdom, nor seen a human being move so slowly. He scraped along the floor, never actually lifting his feet and covering ground at the same pace as the Wisconsin glacier. They made it to the front, stared blankly at the priest, turned around, and repeated their painful procession, and the Last Fenian could be heard asking, "Where the hell is everybody?" At last they made it to the back, where a young couple gave up their seats. Down the pew from me, my grandmother made a little mewing sound, as though in pain.

The couple having been joined in the eyes of God and man, we all repaired to the hall, Johnny Vandiver's hall, of course, and occupied the selfsame tables we'd used one month earlier at the joining of the Shanahans and the Parises. In fact, there was little difference between the two weddings: the same bar selections, the same food, the same band, and many of the same guests, but I thought it was grand.

It was my party, the wedding belonged to me because it was my family involved, my uncle and of course Lorraine, whom I had long since come to think of as an aunt, even at the most acrimonious moments of their courtship. The big room was filled near to bursting with Flynns and Dorseys and Dunphys, though we'd lost Grandma's brothers to the bar as soon as we arrived. Even my Aunt Teresa was there, released from her duties for the occasion. And for my grandparents it was clearly a great day. My grandfather went around patting people on the back and telling jokes, and my grandmother's face was incandescent. I watched her smiling and chatting and waving—she wore little blue gloves to go with her first new dress in years—and eventually she caught me at it.

She gave me my own personal smile, patted me on the cheek with the gloved hand and said, "It's a grand day. Finally we've married off your Uncle Michael. Now we've got to do something about the other one."

Before I could agree, she got up to greet recent arrivals and I wandered off in search of trouble. There was apparently none to be had, at least not yet, and I settled for an orange pop from Uncle Tom and made a happy circuit of the hall, returning to the table when Vandiver's squadron of waitresses brought out our dinner. Food there was in plenty, simple unimaginative wedding food—roast beef, chicken, and Polish sausage of uncertain provenance and strange color.

"Don't eat the sausage," Grandpa told me. "It's gray."

"Oh, don't be telling him that. I'm sure it's fine," Grandma countered.

Grandpa shook his head. "There's no meat that's supposed to be gray. No gray sausages, not even for the Polacks."

"Now keep still with that nonsense, Pat. Eat it all up, Danny, or the bride's family will be insulted."

I assured her I'd do my best, and I ate a little of everything except the sausage. I took some, cut it up and then buried it beneath a mound of mashed potatoes. I was in a hurry to be finished, to find Matt, to explore the hall and spy on grown-ups and observe their bizarre idea of a good time. Peering around the big room, hardly recognizing some of the adults in their unaccustomed finery, I spotted Matt. I asked to be excused and left, with my grandfather adjuring me to stay out of Vandiver's saloon in the front of the hall.

On the other side of the room I greeted the Dorsey half of my family, joined up with Matt, and took off in search of adventure. All around us was evidence of a rare good humor, even Uncle Dennis seemed genial and clear-eyed, ruffling Matt's hair as he sent us on our way with the admonition that it was high time we found a couple of nice girls and settled down. Almost immediately we found crisis, for it seemed that old Seamus Corcoran had met his end. He lay face down on the table and drooled, and it was several seconds before anyone realized that what would have passed for a coma in a younger person was simply a nap for the Last Fenian.

Not far from this scene we happened upon a similar tableau, in which several adults pounded on the back of the unhappy Peter Flynn in hopes of dislodging the sausage that had stuck in his windpipe. Happily, their lusty whacks freed the errant sausage and sent it rocketlike across the table, where it bounced off the bosom of a distant, equally aged female cousin. This was not to be Uncle Peter's only brush with misfortune that day but the only one that put him in harm's way.

Matt and I made a long circuit of the hall, mocking the grown-ups, shamelessly cadging pop from all manner of relatives and creating a minor nuisance. We talked of our hopes for the afternoon, wondered how late we'd be able to stay up, and hid from our respective guardians.

When dinner was finished, the band took over Vandiver's stage, four neighborhood men, one armed with an accordian, all of them seemingly tone-deaf and devoid of any sense of rhythm, and their appearance precipitated a general migration from the tables to the dance floor. The band started with a ballad and then launched into some swing, and more dancers, the younger ones this time, made their appearance. Once caught out on the floor, the dancers remained and the band mixed ballads to keep them there and the faster things to keep the party going. I saw my Uncle Tom dancing with a succession of partners, including the bride and my grandmother. The bar had reopened, and the point had arrived that comes to all weddings, when the music gets a little dramatic, the dancers become just a bit more intense, looking deeply into one another's eyes and forgetting themselves. I remembered this moment from the Shanahan-Paris soiree and found it mildly amusing or repellent, depending on who the partners were.

I saw my uncle try to leave the dance floor, heading for the bar and suddenly returning, being pulled out onto the floor by a new partner, my Aunt Mollie Dorsey. For a moment I found this pairing odd, and then the possibilities presented themselves, forgotten possibilities I'd seen as far back as Christmas Eve. Just as they began to dance, the music ended but he made no attempt to leave. They talked, their faces close to hear over the noise, and then the music picked up again, a butchered version of a Tommy Dorsey tune with the accordian man now wielding a trombone, and they were dancing once more.

They moved across the floor and attracted notice: Tom was wearing a tuxedo, Aunt Mollie a pale yellow dress that did fine things for her coloring, and I saw that they looked somehow suited to each other: suited, and enjoying themselves. Like Tom, she was a born dancer, and it took no gift of imagination for me to forget that he was the younger brother of my mother, that she was my father's baby sister. A circle seemed to form around them, other dancers leaving them space, and they moved into it, using all of it. They jitterbugged and improvised, and he swung her in the air and caught her as though they'd practiced the movement for months.

Beside me, Matt gave me a nudge and said, "Hey, he likes her. He likes Aunt Mollie."

"No, the one he likes isn't here. Her name's Helen. She's not here."

"Oh," he said, accepting my insider's knowledge. I thought of Helen and wondered whether he'd be dancing with her instead, if she'd been invited. I was fairly certain he would, but he wouldn't have been able to convince me he wasn't enjoying himself right now. A couple songs into their dance they seemed to hit a new stride, their faces changed. They weren't staring meaningfully at each other, but something had happened: for one thing, he seemed relaxed, and Aunt Mollie had a look in her eye that I'd seen once before, when she bandaged a cut on my knee, a look into which I read competence and confidence. I was watching them when I heard my grandfather speak.

"That's the one he should be chasing," he muttered.

"Yeah, she's just right for him," my Aunt Anne said. "They look perfect together."

From nowhere Aunt Ellen appeared, took a quick look at her little sister out on the dance floor and then back at us.

"Uh-uh. Forget about it," she said.

"Why?" Anne asked.

"Because he's got eyes for somebody else and she's not waiting for somebody that's not interested. She's got plenty of guys."

"Things can change," Aunt Anne said.

"That won't," Aunt Ellen said. She smiled at Anne and added, "because men are stupid," then winked at Grandpa and was gone.

Her certainty seemed to take something out of the moment, and neither Grandpa Flynn nor my Aunt Anne said anything more about the two dancers, but I saw that they watched all the same. After a while I scanned the room and found my grandmother. She was standing with a group of women her age, cousins and second cousins, ostensibly having a conversation with them, but her eyes never left her son for long, her beloved son.

After several more tunes, Aunt Mollie and Uncle Tom found themselves with new partners, and still others after that, and they seemed happy no matter whom they danced with, but I watched them, even when I was scouring the room with Matt, and I thought I saw something: several times, I thought I saw her look for him, and I caught him watching her from the side. He had that odd look in his eyes that I'd seen on Christmas Eve, the look of a man who has just noticed something.

The band slipped into a slight polka version of "The Irish Washerwoman." Matt said, "This is where they all get crazy," and I nodded agreement. My Uncles Frank and Martin appeared from nowhere, shoulder to shoulder in an impoverished, lead-footed jig, as though honor-bound to demonstrate the accuracy of Matt's observation. The others gave them room, and took to clapping and cheering them on so that the old men were forced to continue. They shuffled and scuffed, arms stiff at their sides, eyes straight ahead in the formal style of the Irish step dancer. Uncle Frank's face had gone a dark wine color, and Martin's eyes were beginning to cross with his heroic effort, and we were relieved when the band stopped playing, and cheered the fact that they had survived their dance.

A new song started up and Aunt Mary stalked out onto the floor, her bony husband in a grip that made indentations in the back of his jacket. She led him more or less across the other dancers, moving with the inevitability of a cruise ship coming into port, of an iceberg, a cold front, and they succeeded in doing what nothing else had accomplished at this or any other wedding, they called forth silence.

My grandmother materialized a few feet from me. I heard her groan, "Oh, for the love of God," and then I heard my grandfather cackling. After all, his Terrible Fenian had done nothing worse than pass out, while *her* family was providing entertainment on a grand scale. He cackled louder and winked at his friends across the floor, and she gave him a whack in the stomach but as far as I could see it did no good. Aunt Mary and her husband made a stiff turn like a three-master tacking before the wind, and then he dazzled us all by swinging her to him, then bending her ample form over his arm. We waited for him to collapse, or at least for his arm to break, but neither happened and the audience showed its delight when they finished.

Shortly after this memorable display, Matt and I followed a staggering gray-haired man into the men's room to see if he'd do anything bizarre. What we found was a new drama: the staggering man was attempting to come to the aid of Uncle Peter Flynn, who was stuck into the commode. It appeared to us, in part from his profane tirade against those with boorish manners, that someone had left the seat up and the old man had come in without noticing, had dropped his trousers and lowered himself onto the throne and thereupon plunged into the opening, which seemingly fit his large hind end perfectly. The gray-haired man struggled to free Uncle Peter, but age and his condition required him to steady himself with one hand, thus leaving him with limited leverage. They groaned together like a Welsh choir and then Uncle Peter noticed us in the doorway.

"Here, you lads, come here and give us a hand, won't you? I've had an accident."

We approached and took his hand, Matt and I, and tried to pull but he was wedged in like a cork, and we succeeded only in irritating him.

"Oh, Christ, get me out of this thing. Pull, George," he said, and the gray-haired man strained again. "Oh, my ass is freezing and that's not all," Uncle Peter said, and I shot a quick look at the ceiling: if he could become this stuck in a toilet, then perhaps Grandma's worst fear might come true as well.

We gave him another pull, but Matt was starting to giggle, and the old man sent us for help.

"Go, go on with you, get some of the men, get your uncles in here, Thomas and Michael and…oh, I don't know, those other ones, go on, get them," he called after us. And when we were in the act of pulling open the door, he bellowed, "Keep still about this, now, don't say anything, just bring them." But outside a small crowd, drawn in by his great air horn of a voice, was already assembling.

We fetched my uncles and led them to the men's room.

All the way, Uncle Mike kept asking, "He's stuck in the *toilet*?" and Tom just said, "Sure, where else?" Five minutes later, aided by a Greek chorus of perhaps forty men and a dozen boys, my uncles and their friends pulled Peter Flynn from ignominy. We had a brief moment when it seemed he would never come out, and there was talk of running to the drug store up Roscoe for a jar of vaseline, but eventually they had him out.

Matt and I were disappointed.

"I thought he'd make a noise," Matt admitted.

"Like a popping sound?"

"Yeah. I hope my butt's never so big I get stuck in a toilet," Matt said, and I couldn't have agreed with him more.

We spent the last hour roaming around, talking, sitting on the stairs, spying. At last we returned to the big room and saw that people had resumed something like their everyday personalities. The older dancers had retired from the field, and Mary McReady was fanning her husband with a napkin. Aunt Mollie was on the dance floor again, dancing to a song and mouthing the words: her partner was a tall thin young man named Roy, whose sister was one of Lorraine's bridesmaids. I scanned the room and found Uncle Tom. He was in a hearty conversation with three other men, but his eyes returned to Mollie more than once.

I said something to Matt and saw that he was watching something; I followed his gaze and saw his parents, my aunt and uncle. Aunt Mary Jane had an arm around Dennis's shoulders and was speaking earnestly to him. Uncle Dennis had both hands cupped around a smoke, and he was staring ahead as though what she said made no impression on him. Matt glanced at me from the corner of his eye and saw that I was watching them. He looked casually around the room and then gave me a soft right to the midsection. I doubled over and he scampered away, and when I could breathe again I went off to hunt him down, and we played at one variation or another of this chase scene till the wedding broke up, which is to say, till the bar closed and the band came up with "I'll See You in My Dreams" and "I'll Take You Home Again, Kathleen," back-to-back.

Aunt Mary Jane called Matt, and I watched him go shuffling off, head down, after his parents; his mother made her good-byes to people around her, but there was something frozen about her smile, and when they made their way to the door she was watching Uncle Dennis. For his part, Dennis looked straight ahead as he walked and spoke to no one.

They were intercepted at the door by Sister Fidelity. She smiled as she spoke to them, and her sister returned the smile, but Uncle Dennis barely acknowledged her. I saw her pat Matt on the head and give him something. When they left, she turned and looked me in the eye from twenty feet away, as though she could feel me watching her. I started to move away in embarrassment but she was faster than I was, habit and heavy shoes notwithstanding.

"A pair of serious-looking little boys I have," Aunt Teresa said and tried a smile.

"I'm okay," I said.

"Did you young terrors have a good time?"

"Oh, sure."

She started to say something and I could see her change her mind. In the end, she just said, "You and Matt are still good friends, aren't you?"

"Sure."

"I'm glad. He's lucky to have such a good friend. My friend Sister Polycarp says you're doing well in school." Without warning, her eyes grew wet, and she said, "Your father..." and then she caught herself. "I'm sorry, it's difficult for me to be at these family parties without remembering my...your dad. I'm proud of you. And I'm happy that you're a good friend to Matthew. Did you like the party?"

"It was neat. I had seven pops."

"Don't tell your grandmother. Seven?" She looked mildly horrified. "Are you going to be sick?"

"I don't think so, because I had cake, too."

"Cake helps?"

"Sure. It soaks up the pop."

She gave me an amused look, then produced a dollar for me from the hidden compartments of her habit.

"Good-bye, Daniel," she said, and then she was gone in a swirl of black.

I called out good-bye to her and went to find my family. Uncle Tom was driving Mike and Lorraine to their new flat, and then he was going out. One of the groomsmen drove us home and I sat wedged between my grandparents, feeling inexplicably let down. My grandparents exchanged rosy opinions about how everything had gone, and the talk turned to the family eccentrics on both sides.

Grandpa ventured first onto this perilous ground, indicating that Frank and Martin had nearly outdone themselves this time.

"I was waiting for the two of them to come out wearing the lampshades," he said, and compounded his error by chuckling with delight.

"Lampshades indeed," Grandma said, and weighed in with "what a great *amadan*" Uncle Peter Flynn was. "Grown man getting his behind stuck in a toilet, at a *wedding*, for God's sake. A man without the sense to come in out of the rain. We're lucky the roof didn't fall in on us."

"Ah, it could have happened to anyone," Grandpa said, but there was a note of doubt in his voice.

They were silent for a moment and then Grandpa filled it with a counterpunch. "I thought for a minute there your cousin 'The Fenian' was gonna die on us."

She was too serene to be baited. "Ah *that* one, that old crazy man, he should be in Dunning. 'Fenian,' indeed. Asleep in his food, for the love of God."

The Bold Fenian had been revived several times during the night, eventually carried off and driven home, along with his amazingly old son, by solicitous relatives. After a moment Grandma remembered how happy she was and added, "The poor soul. Ready for his reward. Whatever that might be."

I nestled in between them and remembered how my uncle had looked dancing with Aunt Mollie. I remembered him watching as she left with a large group of friends, all of them going out somewhere. He caught her eye and she waved. He waved back, and when she was gone, he shook his head as though to clear it. I wondered what was wrong with his head.

A Trip to
the Country

The next morning I woke to a gray day, heavy rain, and a chill wind blowing in from the lake. Everyone in the house seemed tired, quiet, preoccupied, even my grandmother. She put on Sunday airs, fussed and banged pots around her kitchen, made scrambled eggs and bacon enough to feed Ireland, and even forced herself to hum along with the music on the big yellow radio, but there was a slightly stunned quality to the performance. A son had left home, and I think she was having trouble believing it, even as she pointedly ignored his empty seat at the table. She seemed to be fussing over me more than usual, practically dragging me to the table before I was fully awake and then force-feeding me. A pile of eggs grew on my plate, and she began forking slices of bacon on top as though she'd lost count. Uncle Tom squinted at me.

"Did you enlist?" he asked.

"What?"

"Did you enlist? The last time she did this was when I got drafted. Is he going to Korea, Ma?"

"Good God, don't even talk about that," Grandma said. "Korea, indeed. He needs his food. He didn't eat anything at all at the wedding. I watched."

I knew she hadn't had eyes for anything but the doings of her two sons, but I could tell this was no time for debate, and I began cutting divots in my mound of eggs as my family tried to muster conversation. They all spoke in low, congested voices as though fearful that they'd wake someone. Grandpa said over and over again what a fine affair the reception had been, and Tom made them laugh as he reminded them of Aunt Mary's stone-footed tango.

Halfway through breakfast Grandma put her fork down and sighed.

"You all right, Ma?" my uncle asked.

"Of course I'm all right. I'm fine, I'm just tired."

He looked at me and winked. "I think everybody's tired. We had a little too much party and now we pay for it. How about you and I go someplace?"

"Sure."

In the end we decided that the rain made it a perfect day for a museum, a day for dinosaurs and mummies. We made our way down the Outer Drive to the museum. The Drive curved past the Field Museum, creating the little illusion that the great Grecian building waited at the very end. My heart always started thumping at the sight. This was my place, a building overflowing with treasure to a small boy, with its own smell, never encountered anywhere else, that must have been a mixture of polish, the faint odors of taxidermy, and food smells from the cafeteria.

The same fighting bull elephants greeted the visitor as today, and we always stopped so that I could feel the piece of hardened elephant hide placed beside the exhibit, but inevitably we would find ourselves in the Hall of Dinosaurs, where time lost its hold and reality blurred. I never tired of this place with its massive skeletons on steel frames and the glorious Charles R. Knight murals overhead that took the viewer through all the ages of the earth. We had been there so many times that I'm not certain we actually looked at the individual exhibits and cases—it was enough to be walking slowly through them.

As always he took me to the cafeteria for a hamburger and a piece of cake. The hamburgers were passable if you put enough layers of ketchup and pickles on them, but the cake was worth the trip by itself, dark and moist and top-heavy with frosting.

"A kid baked this," he would always say as he stuck a fork into his piece. "You can tell: no grown-up ever put this much frosting on a cake. A kid got into the kitchen and went crazy."

We sat and ate our cake and he sipped the Field Museum coffee, which he contended was among the worst he'd experienced, and then I found myself blurting out, "Do you want to get married?"

He gave me a long amused look and then shrugged. "Yeah, I do. Your grandmother thinks I'm a confirmed bachelor. And sometimes I think it'll never happen. Seems like something that would happen to somebody else but not me. But someday maybe that'll happen. Why?"

My motives were perfectly clear to me and I saw no reason to hide them. "Because Uncle Mike got married and moved out." To a place not far from his parents but not close either, and Grandma had said he was already looking ahead to another place, the ultimate goal of all of them, never realized by most, to own a home.

"And you think—what? That I'll get married and move away too, right?"

"Yes."

"So? Grandma and Grandpa would take care of you. You'd be okay. And Annie will be there for a while, she's young..." He broke off, realizing he'd reminded me of a third person who would eventually leave me.

"I know." I nodded energetically to hide the fact that my eyes were tearing up. I tried to say something casual, but a hardness had come into my throat and I just looked away.

He put his hand on my hair and I hoped I wouldn't cry.

"Listen, nobody's leaving you yet. For one thing, we'll still see Uncle Mike, you'd never get rid of him that easily, and now you'll see him with his new boss, Aunt Lorraine. And I'm not going anywhere. You have to have somebody to get married to, and I don't, and I don't think it's gonna happen soon."

The disappointment in his voice distracted me from my own worries and I stole a quick glance at him. I was confused: I already knew all I needed to know about him and Helen, I knew what I'd seen that night at the Shanahan wedding. He was stirring the evil coffee and his unhappiness was clear. I bit back my impulse to ask him what was wrong with Helen and then fell back on safer ground.

"Grandma says lots of girls would like you."

"She talks too much." He kept on stirring the coffee and then said, "The thing of it is not getting married, it's the part that comes before. Falling in love, that's the hard part. Boy, talk about a pain in the a…"

"Is it hard to find somebody to fall in love with?"

"No. God, it's easy. You don't even have to be looking for it, it just happens. It's a little like getting sick, you don't know it's happening and then you've got it. No, what's hard, it's hard to find somebody to fall in love with who's also gonna be in love with you, that's the thing right there." I could think of nothing to say to that, I wasn't even certain any of it made sense: I thought two people met and fell in love, both of them simultaneously.

"Anybody can fall in love," he said after a moment, "happens every day, but if you fall in love and it doesn't work out for you, then you've got trouble."

"Why?"

"Because you can't just fall *out* of love then. You're in it, you got no choice. Some people spend their whole lives in love with somebody that don't love them, or somebody that's just not any good for them. And then their lives are a mess."

"Like Aunt Mary Jane and Uncle Dennis?"

He didn't answer for a moment, and I thought I'd said something wrong and spoiled it all. Then he shook his head. "No, they…their problem is different. Dennis and Mary Jane love each other, they just have lots of problems, lots of trouble. And Dennis is the cause of…a lot of it, but he doesn't run around. You know what I mean by running around?" He squinted at me and I just nodded, though I wasn't at all sure.

"He doesn't have girlfriends or anything like that." He sipped his coffee and said, "You know who was smart? Your Aunt Teresa, that's who. There's the smart one. Smart and good-looking, and a nice girl, too, and she got out of all this mess by becoming a nun. Maybe that's the answer, I should become a priest."

Finally he was making sense, and I said so. "You'd be a good priest."

He laughed and put an arm around me. "That's great, I ought to tell your grandmother that one, but she's liable to agree with you, so we'll just let it drop."

After that, we roamed the museum in silence till it was nearly empty and then left. Outside, the sky seemed to have lowered itself onto the city. The clouds were dark and full and seemed to be telling me that summer couldn't last forever.

"Looks like a winter sky," my uncle said.

"Yeah," I said in disappointment.

He laughed. "I like winter. You're so busy fighting it, you've got no time to feel sorry for yourself."

Shortly after that he began going out more at night. Some of the time he was at the tavern, still more a source of trouble to him than income. He had stopped complaining about it but encouraged no conversation on the subject.

Other nights he seemed different, there was a new look in his eye, a suppressed excitement. He was filled with energy, he couldn't sit still, he paced constantly when he talked, and laughed even more easily than usual. One afternoon Uncle Mike the Newlywed stopped by after work to visit, and after he'd had a cup of coffee with Grandma, Uncle Tom took him aside in the farthest corner of the living room, beyond even the range of my spectacular hearing, and they spoke in low tones. I couldn't hear more than one or two words, but I heard Uncle Tom say "she," and then his brother gave him a pat on the back and they headed back out to the kitchen.

As they passed my perch at the dining room table, I heard Tom say, "What have I got to lose, right?"

"Right," Uncle Mike said, but without conviction.

July came in, and on a scalding Saturday early in the month, one of the hottest days I can ever remember, my uncle took me to a party at the home of a friend. I was excited: the place was "out in the country," an unincorporated piece of Cook County, and the couple who lived there had a swimming pool. It wasn't much of a pool, plastic stretched over a metal frame, no more than three feet deep, but it had a little wooden staircase to help people climb into it, and to a small boy it could have been Lake Huron.

Tom left the house in the morning "to do a few things," and when he came back I came bounding out of Grandma's house with my trunks and towel in a blue bowling bag. He was leaning against his big two-toned Buick with its metallic nostrils, and I could see that he was as excited as I was. It wasn't till I was getting into the car that I saw he had a passenger already.

I fell across the backseat getting in and heard my uncle say, "He's clumsy but he's all we've got, so we keep him."

"I think he's adorable," the passenger said. Though I'd never seen her up close, I'd recognized the dark hair and felt a thrill of insider excitement.

"Helen, this is my nephew Danny. Dan, this is Helen."

I said, "Hi," and found myself sticking out my hand. She laughed, shot my uncle a quick glance, and then took my hand.

"I've heard all about you, Danny. Your uncle seems to think you're pretty special."

"Don't talk like that, you'll give him a swelled head," my uncle said, but he was grinning. He got in behind the wheel and they looked at each other in what I thought was an odd way. He was still grinning; the girl called Helen was looking at him with her head tilted slightly, squinting at him, but there was a brightness to her eyes as though she was on the verge of sharing secrets.

"Well, let's go," he said, and we were off.

They talked in what seemed to me a strange way, starting and stopping suddenly, and smiling a great deal. They traded stories about people they both knew, and several times they returned to some time in the past when they'd known each other, and then I recalled Tom's comment to Uncle Mike at the wedding, that this young woman would have been his if he hadn't gone to Korea. At one point she turned and smiled to me.

"The poor kid's probably bored to death with all this grown-up talk," she said, unaware how I absorbed everything they said to one another.

Eventually the city gave way to trees and farmland, and I lost all interest in the adults in the front seat.

At our destination, they introduced me to May and Ed McKay, "Big Ed," my uncle called him, and it was clear they were fond of one another. I was somewhat excited to meet Big Ed myself, for there were certain similarities between the two of us: Big Ed was an orphan. What made him special for me was that he'd been sent upon the death of his parents to Boys Town, he had known the great Father Flanagan. I'd seen the movie with Spenser Tracy portraying the tough priest as a composite of General MacArthur and God, so that meeting a boy who'd called that place home was not far different from meeting Joe Louis. Ed held out his great flat hand to me and said, "Ed McKay."

I planted my small one in it and said, "Daniel Dorsey," and he laughed. He seemed enormous, a big-boned man with a large head and a round face who smiled constantly and had a habit of running one hand through hair like a wayward child's. He towered over them all and made his wife look like a pixie.

He patted me on the head, told my uncle I was "a polite kid," and then he took me off to see his pool.

It might be fair to say that my uncle and his new friend ignored me for the rest of the outing, and certainly I was unencumbered by supervision. I spent most of the day putting together a sunburn that I have never forgotten, basking in the wonder of the icy water in the little pool and pretending I could swim. I held my breath and went between people's legs, then burst to the surface in my best impression of a breaching whale.

While catching my breath I sat in the water and studied the overheated adults: perspiring faces, hair plastered with sweat, the faces going redder and redder as they drank their way through the steamy afternoon. My uncle and the dark slender Helen mingled with the guests, indeed they seemed constantly surrounded by people, all of them held in thrall by my uncle's ability to tell a story and his great good humor, and most of the men stealing a look now and then at Helen. She was beautiful, in a dark red blouse that matched the lipstick and nail polish she wore, and I saw that Aunt Mollie was no match for her.

As the afternoon wore on, the heat became palpable, the sun shimmered off walls and eventually drove most of them into the pool, and Helen came out in her bathing suit: like her lipstick and nails, like the bloodred earrings, it was crimson going purple and she was magnificent. She was darker than the others, and it seemed to me that the heat had no effect on her beyond the single damp curl that clung to her forehead.

When she moved toward the pool I was startled to see her, she seemed almost out of place amid the other pale-skinned, sweating adults, especially the men with their T-shirt lines where sickly looking skin met sunburnt forearms. I saw immediately that my reaction was not much different from the men's: I could see a dozen of them at a glance, my uncle included, and they couldn't take their eyes off her. Someone said something to my uncle and he laughed, but his look of pride was unmistakable, and I was delighted for him.

Later on there was food which I would have had no time for, had my uncle and Helen not forced a plate on me. They fed me ham and cheese and potato salad, and I encountered my first barbecued ribs, and when no one was watching I tossed the gnawed bones off in the direction of the woods, convinced that I was feeding wolves. They each gave me a bottle of soda and I took two more myself, but I could have run around the yard naked without eliciting comment from Tom and his girl. They still talked with the others, but gradually they drew off into a corner of the party and spoke with their faces close together, and my uncle had his arm around her. I saw her laugh, he seemed to make her laugh without effort, and I was glad to see he had this same hold on her that he had on all the rest of us.

I was sitting at the foot of a small tree, where I'd planted myself to enjoy my latest bottle of pop, and my uncle led Helen over and they sat a few feet away—"Where we can keep an eye on you," Tom said.

But policing his nephew was clearly low on his list of priorities, for he soon turned his attention back to the dark-haired Helen.

"Great place," I heard him say.

"I'd love to live out here, and have a house of my own, a big house with a yard."

"Who wouldn't?" Tom said.

Helen told him he didn't understand, that he hadn't gown up "in a crowded place with eight brothers and sisters and no money, no privacy."

"We never had much of either of those things," Tom said.

"I know you didn't have a lot, but if you could see that place where I grew up, if you knew my old...my father," she said, and I was certain she'd caught herself in case I was listening. "So that's what I want someday, a place of my own, with whatever I want inside it, and I want privacy, I want room. Like this," she said, and indicated Big Ed's sprawling, unfenced yard with a smile.

"Everybody wants a place, everybody wants a house, and to be away from his goofy neighbors," Tom said. "Who wouldn't want this much room? But you'll have what you want someday."

For a moment she said nothing, and then when I thought they'd dropped the subject, she said, "Everything good seems to take forever. Don't you get tired of waiting for things?"

"Yeah, I got real tired of waiting to get out of Korea. But there's, you know, some things I'd wait a real long time for," he said, and for some reason she laughed. She gave him a long look and he grinned at her. Then they both got to their feet, told me they were going to get something cold to drink, and to try not to drown.

As my two grown-ups forgot my existence, I played in the pool and explored the big unfenced yard, and eventually Big Ed decided I'd had enough of the sun and water.

"C'mon with me. My wife thinks you're gonna turn into a prune if you spend any more time in this pool." I laughed and followed him, watching the back of his big sweaty shirt. I wanted to ask him about Boys Town but shyness had my tongue. As we went inside, Ed called out to my uncle.

"Hey, Flynn! If you can take your bloodshot eyes off the beautiful girl for a minute…"

I heard people laughing and my uncle joined in, reddening slightly.

"Is it all right if I show him my, ah, what I got in the guest room?"

"Yeah, sure, that's nice of you, Ed." To me he said, "Don't get any ideas, there, champ. Our house is crowded enough with you."

I had no idea what he was talking about but I would have followed Big Ed from Boys Town into combat. He took me down the hall past the bathroom, then stopped in front of a closed door and motioned for silence.

"If we're real quiet," he whispered, "we'll catch him by surprise."

I thought he meant a dog, a big dog, perhaps, and my heart started beating faster. Big Ed watched me, milking the moment for all its dramatic potential. His eyes widened in a parody of terror and he pretended to be gasping for breath. He put his hand on the doorknob, gave me one last look, swallowed hard, said, "Here goes," and threw the door open. His big body bent down and he yelled, "Get down, kid, he's armed and danger- ous!" and then I was following Ed breathless into the room. I waited for something to attack me and couldn't understand why Big Ed was laughing so hard, and then I heard the room's tenant screech. When I looked up, I saw a monkey in the over- head light fixture.

It was a big square piece of glass with a curved bottom and the monkey was sitting in the bowl of it, one skinny hairy elbow resting on the edge and looking from Ed to me with little jerky motions of his tiny head.

"A monkey!" I heard myself say.

"Hey, you're smart—and here your uncle tells everybody you're retarded."

The little monkey was staring at me now and I felt myself grinning all over. I thought I'd never seen anything so ador- able in all my born days, and then the little fellow was reaching down beside him into the light fixture.

"Look out, Dan," Ed said.

The monkey came up firing, something small and dark, pellets of something, and I laughed.

"He's throwing his food at us," I said.

Ed grinned and said, "It *used* to be food, kid," and made a high-pitched whoop as he ducked.

Now he had my attention, and I threw myself onto the

floor as the dark missiles whizzed past my ear and struck the wall behind me at just about head level. I stayed on all fours and Ed, crouched down like a combat infantryman, looked back at me over his shoulder. He was laughing silently, his eyes tearing.

"You hit, kid?"

"No," and I was laughing with him. Our mirth served only to irritate the monkey, who redoubled his efforts by throwing larger handfuls of his excrement till the air overhead was a hail-storm of monkey droppings.

"He'll run out soon," I suggested with a note of hope.

"Nah, he's got a lifetime supply up there. He can keep us pinned down for a year if he wants to. One of us is gonna have to go for help." I must have given him a puzzled look because he burst out laughing. After a moment he ruffled my hair and said, "I wish I had a kid."

I wanted to point out that a monkey was far better in almost every way I could think of, but the hairy creature in the light fixture chose that moment to go into phase two of his offensive. He stood up with a little bouncing motion, turds in each hand, and screeched at us.

Big Ed grabbed my arm and pulled me behind an old sofa, the only real furniture in the room. Closer to the light fixture I saw a ladder, and there was a little wooden house of some sort, and I gathered these were the monkey's playthings. Scattered on the floor were the brightly colored toys one would give a small child.

The monkey was howling indignation at us and I looked up at Ed for explanation.

"He wants us to come out and fight like men. I'm not brave enough. You?"

"Uh-uh," I said, then raised my head over the back of the sofa to look at him. He glowered at us from his glass vessel, screeched and bounded down onto the ladder.

"He's coming!"

"Nah, it's all for show."

"I'd like a monkey," I said, and of course I'd never said a truer thing. I raised my head again, and found the little beast staring at me: I'd seen monkeys just like this at Riverview and at the zoo.

"Not this one, you wouldn't."

"No?"

"No," he repeated, but he was smiling at his savage roommate. "His name's Ollie. You know, like *Kukla, Fran, and Ollie?*"

"Sure." I said "Hi" to Ollie but he just glared at me.

"He doesn't answer to it. See, Ollie's a squirrel monkey. You don't want to get a squirrel monkey, partner. Get a spider monkey, they're not as cute but they're nicer. Or get a nice dog. Get a cat or a turtle. Want to look at a turtle?"

I didn't, I wanted to stay there for the rest of the day with his wonderfully bellicose monkey, but I was a guest, after all. He took me to another room where he had turtles in a big tank, and it took me no time at all to decide that they were, in the single-mindedness of their inertia, almost as wonderful as the monkey, except that I might have trouble telling when a pet turtle was dead.

Eventually, my favorable impressions of Ed confirmed, we returned to the yard and I went on as before, filling myself with pop and cake and horrible things, then cavorting amid the adults. Across the yard I saw my uncle standing with his arm around Helen, and she was leaning a little bit against him. They both looked as though it was the most natural thing for either of them. My uncle came over once or twice to see how I was doing, and he asked if Ed had shown me Ollie, but for the remainder of the day, I could have been on the far side of the moon for all the attention I drew from Uncle Tom and Helen.

It was dark when we finally left the party. I was exhausted and my skin was beginning to hurt, and the night air chilled me. I slept most of the way home, occasionally regaining consciousness to ask if we were home yet. They talked, Tom and Helen, in low, flat voices, like exhausted conspirators, and I wanted to tell them they didn't have to speak so quietly, that I was too tired to eavesdrop, but I didn't even have the strength for that. I heard only a few things.

"I don't want to talk about him, Tom," she said.

"I don't want to talk about that guy either. Some things I just can't figure, though, and you and him, you're one of them," and I understood they were talking about Philly Clark.

"He's not so bad. He's a nice looking guy, and he's smart—like you," she added, and I thought this clever. "And he can be fun..."

"Yeah, he's a million laughs."

She laughed and said, "No, he's not funny like you, but he can be fun. He's got a lot of energy, he's always got to be doing something, and that's...that's nice. It's interesting."

"He's got a lot of money," Tom baited.

"That's not it. He knows what he wants in life."

"How about you?" Tom asked, but she didn't answer him.

They fell silent for a time and I must have dozed off. A while later I woke up and she was talking about something else, apparently a trip of some sort, and she said something about not being able to decide. After a pause, I heard my uncle say, "Sometimes you got to stop thinking about it and just make up your mind. That's what you got to do." And it seemed to me that he was talking about something other than a trip.

After a long moment of silence, he added in a joking tone, "Anyway, I saw you first!" and she laughed.

I was sick that night. I threw up—I was later to tell people I'd vomited more than fifty times—but it was probably closer to four or five. I was sick, exhausted, and hurting from every part of my body that had been exposed to the sun: my back, my chest, my ears, my face, the part in my hair and my eyelids, the tops of my feet and the backs of my legs. I hurt everywhere and all at once, and I couldn't breathe properly. From hours of holding my breath under water, my chest hurt and I was unable to draw a deep breath. I believed I would be dead by morning.

At some point during the night I opened my eyes to find my grandparents hovering over me, my grandfather looking worried and my grandmother furious.

"Should we call O'Leary?" my grandfather was asking.

"We should, and have him examine their heads, the both of 'em, especially my son that doesn't have the sense God gave barnyard animals."

From somewhere outside my room I heard my uncle say, "Aw, Ma, he was having a good time, for God's sake."

"You couldn't put that suntan lotion on him, the poor thing? And what did he have to eat?"

I tried to protest that the barbecued ribs had been my undoing, having developed this notion between trips to the bathroom, but I was too weak. I felt my grandmother feeling my forehead and then I drifted off to sleep, alternately praying for death and vowing that if I lived, I'd never eat spareribs again, nor play in the sun, and I had a passing notion to swear off orange pop, but I wasn't ready to commit to it.

My near-death experience passed in the night. My grandmother gave me the silent treatment all the next day, and I suspect my uncle envied me because she spent the greater part of it in a verbal assault on his judgment. He sat at the kitchen table and smoked, and when she tore into him for bringing me home "half-naked and ready for the last rites," as she put it, he seemed to grow smaller, as though withering in her heat.

Late in the day she muttered something in his direction and I saw him laughing, and knew that if I survived the sunburn and the stomach cramps, he would likely survive his mother's anger, though I thought my chances were better. By the end of the day I was taking solid food, sitting in my undershorts and covered in calamine lotion thick enough to repel hailstones. I even had a can of pop after dinner, 7 Up, believed by my grandmother to have medicinal properties, but I did not eat a rib again till I was almost thirty.

Dog Days

I t was a summer of weddings and parties, but there was an undercurrent of trouble to it, and I believe I was, on some level, conscious of that.

We grew, all of us, more aware of the decline of my grandfather's health. I found myself watching when he coughed, to be told in an aggravated tone that it was "just a cough, not a heart attack," and to mind my business. More than once I heard my grandmother badger him about his diet, his smoking, his visits to the tavern, and he would grumble, "Woman, will you give me some peace?"

Once I heard him tell her that he was convinced his coughing became more troublesome when she was thus harassing him.

"There's no rest from your trouble, it weakens my constitution. I can feel it," and then he coughed for effect.

My grandmother didn't buy either the logic or the performance, called him "a great willful child with no more sense than little Danny in there," and stalked out of the room.

As though to demonstrate his health, he took to playing practical jokes on her: one day, for example, he called her from Liquor Town and said he was the police, that her husband had been apprehended in the commission of some crime. He delighted in imitating members of her family, his specialty being his impression of Mary McReady, the surviving member of the Behemoth Sisters. For this act he stuffed pillows under his belt and wore

Grandma's Sunday coat, put a small saucepan on his head to represent the celebrated pillbox hat, and spoke in a froggy voice, asking repeatedly if there was any whiskey in the house.

Several times that summer in 1955 I spent the day with my grandfather. Once we went to the zoo and the other time he took me to the Historical Society and I held my breath waiting for the security man to recognize me as the young miscreant who had rolled the artillery piece around and otherwise compromised the sanctity of the museum. A different man was on duty, though, and the day was uneventful, except that I was aware of things that had never been there before: my grandfather's labored breathing and his flagging energy. I'd noticed these changes during an earlier trip to the zoo, where he made frequent stops to rest on a bench, and at one point seemed to be gasping. He made light of both, said it was the heat, and since it was a wilting August day I believed him.

In the Historical Society there was an exhibit on the death of Lincoln, and Grandpa had always been fascinated by it: the museum had come by a number of Lincoln's possessions, items he'd used, items he'd carried on his person the night of his death, even the bed he'd been laid on in his final moments. On this visit, my grandfather lingered on these things for even longer than usual, till I was practically prancing up and down the hall in my need to move on to cannons and battleflags.

Late one evening I crept out of bed to use the washroom and saw my grandmother sitting alone at the kitchen table. She was leaning against the table, her arms crossed and hugging herself, and looking off into space. I decided not to bother her but she looked up at exactly that moment, as though she'd sensed my presence. She blinked at me, shifted in her chair, and asked me if anything was wrong. I went to the bathroom and when I came out again, she said, "Good night, sunshine," in a distracted voice. I remember thinking that she was probably having one of the sad times when she thought of my mother.

One muggy night we were all together for dinner, even Uncle Mike, who called himself "bachelor for the night" because Lorraine was at a bridal shower for a friend.

My grandmother served us cold corned beef and her homemade potato salad and cole slaw, and a couple of quart bottles of Meister Bräu appeared on the table. They threw open all the windows and I watched the beer bottles sweat and create little pools on Grandma's tablecloth. Her delight at having the crowd back around her dining room table was obvious and infectious, and dinner took on the trappings of a party. Everyone seemed to be talking too loud, and there were moments when everyone was speaking at once. My uncles were debating about what they called the "dog days," with Mike insisting they didn't begin till August, and Tom holding that as soon as you couldn't sleep at night without soaking the bed, you were in the dog days.

Since Uncle Mike was the nominal guest, they all took turns prodding him with questions about whether his new marriage had wrought any changes in him. Never a man to let unimportant things like conversation take precedence over his food, Mike grunted answers through his corned beef, smiled a great deal, and seemed unaware that he'd gotten both mustard and horseradish on his face.

"Are you still a slob?" Aunt Anne asked with an expression of innocent interest.

"He was the slob," Mike told her, pointing at Tom with a fork. "I was the neat one," he said through a huge mouthful of food.

"The one with the best manners, certainly," Anne said with a sly look, and everyone laughed except Mike, who looked mystified.

"Exactly," he said through his potato salad.

Grandpa held up a hand for silence and gave his older boy a serious look. "Not to bring up an unpleasant subject, Michael, but they tell me she left you." Grandpa looked at me. "The milkman, you said it was."

I must have looked shocked, and I wasn't at all sure what he meant by "the milkman," and they all laughed as I sputtered that I'd never said any such thing.

They had gone giddy for the night, and I thought at the time they were just so glad to be together once more that no one minded hearing the same stories and tired jokes. I didn't mind any of it, and found that I was now a featured performer, for they couldn't let the evening move on without rehashing the epic tale of The Chicken. Grandpa had already begun the storyteller's process of embellishing and editing, so that I'd already heard the tale half a dozen different ways, including one version in which I wept and ran after the chicken as it disappeared into the night. This led to a brief debate over whether the chicken episode was hard evidence that Grandpa had begun to lose his mind.

Grandma steered the talk to her younger children and forced Anne to tell us about the promising young man whom she'd met at a dance at St. Bonaventure's.

"A college man, he is," Grandma said, happy with any replacement for the undistinguished Roger.

"Well, he's had some college," Anne said. "He's gonna finish on the G.I. bill."

"I wanna meet this guy," Tom said. He exchanged a wink with Mike and added, "Some night when Mike's free. We can sit down with him at the table, have a beer, decide if he's—what, Mike?"

"If he's fit," Mike said through cole slaw.

"That's it, see if he's fit to be courting our sister."

"'Courting'?" Anne wrinkled her nose at them. "Nobody calls it that anymore, this is modern times, and for your information, I just met him, we're just..." Then she caught the looks going from Tom to Mike and realized they were having fun with her, and she laughed.

"I'll bring him to you guys when I've toughened him up."

"Fair enough," Tom said. Uncle Mike went on chewing.

For her part, Aunt Anne tried to pry something about Helen out of her brother.

"And what about you, Mr. Romeo? How's that new girl-friend of yours? The one I haven't actually met yet."

"Oh, no?" Tom said innocently. "Gee, Danny's met her, right, Dan?"

I nodded, feeling a member of a small inner circle.

"She's fine, Sis. And you'll meet her soon enough. When I toughen *her* up."

"We're not going to bite her, for goodness sake," Grandma sniffed.

"What's the hurry?" Tom asked. Then he gave Aunt Anne a funny smile, the smile of a fellow who knows secrets that cannot be turned loose yet.

We stayed at the dinner table so long that I received a second Pepsi, largely to keep me quiet. Eventually the talk turned to Grandpa's health and I felt some of the steam go out of the room.

"Leave me be about my health, for God's sake," Grandpa said. "I'm fine, I'm just *old,* that's what you all forget. I'm not a young buck anymore."

"He needs to go to a doctor," Grandma said, as though speaking of a person who was not present. "He's so stubborn, he never wants to listen to anyone. He needs to see O'Leary over on Damen. Maybe you can talk some sense into him, you boys. He won't listen to your sister or meself."

"Not now," Grandpa protested. "Let me eat my dinner in peace."

This proved a tactical error, for it allowed Grandma, addressing him directly now, to point out that dinner had been over for twenty minutes, and that what he ate "wouldn't keep a bird on the wing. A baby eats more than you eat, Patrick Flynn, for the Love of God."

Grandpa growled at her, something like, "Give me some peace." She turned her complaints to Tom, telling him Grandpa was eating almost nothing these days. Before Tom could say anything, Grandpa stopped him in midsentence with, "I still drink that eggnog thing of hers *every morning of my life*," and this seemed to mollify Grandma and to impress Tom.

"Yeah? Still, Dad? You still drink the eggnog?"

"I do. Ask Danny. Tell them, Dan, tell them how I brace myself against the sink there and force it down. A lesser man would toss it down the drain and lie about it."

"He does, he drinks it," I said. "He says it's terrible."

"You keep still," Grandma said. To her husband, she said, "You need more than a glass of eggnog."

"I thought it would give me eternal life. If it doesn't do at least that much, I'll drink it no more."

"Maybe I'll make a bigger glass of eggnog."

Grandpa stared at her for several seconds and then speared the last piece of corned beef from the platter and forced it into his mouth. Only half made it inside his mouth, and he made a fine show of chewing it with the tail end still hanging outside and mumbling how good her food was, and I had to laugh. My grandmother stared at me with regal contempt, then shook her head at Grandpa.

"You can make all the jokes you want, you know I'm right," she said.

She gave me a hard look. "And he's not that funny." Still shaking her head, she gave a little nod to Aunt Anne, and the two of them began to clear the table.

Uncle Mike gave us all a contented look and allowed as how Lorraine was great but couldn't cook like Grandma. This seemed to lift my grandmother's mood, and a moment later I heard her humming in the kitchen. Mike left to pick up "the wife," as he called her, and I moved, uninvited or no, into the living room with Tom and Grandpa.

I listened to the scratchy sounds of Tom and Grandpa lighting up their cigarettes, and my grandfather brought up the subject of the Cubs, the hapless Cubs, who by that point in the summer of 1955 were an object of pity or horror, depending on how fervently one followed them. Their ineptitude thus far had been broken only by the emergence to center stage of "the colored boy," as my grandfather quietly called him, Ernie Banks, the only bright spot during the previous season of disaster and on his way to shake a few long-cherished Chicago notions about how well black people might play baseball.

My grandfather was off on a rant this evening and Uncle Tom let him run with it. Grandpa went on at length about the misguided efforts of the Cubs' ownership, then launched into a sort of Ode to Dead Pitchers, narrating the achievements of Grover Cleveland Alexander—"Who could pitch better drunk and puking up his guts in the bullpen than these fellas can pitch cold sober"—and someone named Mordecai Brown—"He had just the three fingers, and he could make the ball go anywhere he wanted."

Uncle Tom sat across from him, nodding and smiling, occasionally looking to see if I was paying attention. He smoked and listened, and it struck me that Tom had heard Grandpa's baseball views before, and knew by heart the list of Grandpa's dead Cub heroes. But there was something in his face that said it was somehow important for him to listen to his father talk about baseball on this steamy summer night, to listen as long as Grandpa needed him to.

Unraveling

Less than a week later I heard that Uncle Dennis had gone to the emergency room at St. Joseph's. They told me at dinner, then excused me and went on talking about the disaster he'd become: he owed everybody, cadged drinks and placed bets he couldn't cover, then placed further bets, some of them apparently quite foolish, in an attempt to come up with cash in a hurry. He was apparently drinking more than ever, and I heard my uncle speculate that Dennis would lose his job before long.

Short of death, no one in my world had ever suffered through such a string of disasters. More importantly, no one had been sent to a hospital by another person's malice. I was horrified. By this time I think I knew I didn't like my Uncle Dennis very much, he reserved the large part of his charm for other adults, but he was still my family, and it came as a shock to me that one of my own circle of grown-ups could have his life come crashing down around him. That night I dreamt that dark, shadowy men were pursuing Dennis down an alley; he was crying and there was no one to help him.

The darkness had taken us by surprise and we were hurrying up Clybourn when a vaguely familiar man in a suit stepped out of a gangway a few yards ahead of us and planted himself in the middle of the sidewalk, as though astraddle a narrow bridge. From the corner of my eye I saw Matt go stiff-backed as he recognized his father. I heard Matt mutter a greeting and I was about to speak but something in Dennis's face silenced me. He was smiling but there was nothing happy in it, and he peered at us as though watching for something. He still wore a small piece of bandage at the corner of one eye, and I told myself not to stare at it.

"What're you doin' out when it's dark?" he said to his son. He brushed back his suitcoat—he was always in a suit—and thrust one hand casually into his pants pocket, then rocked slightly on his feet. In the distance I could see the lights of Riverview, and the Para-Chutes dropping their screaming loads, but they might have been many miles away. For some reason I remember noting that the street was nearly empty.

His squint focused first on Matt and then on me, a long look that seemed to carry a dull malice, and I felt the need to say, "Hi, Uncle Dennis."

He snorted. "Never mind 'Hi, Uncle Dennis,'" he muttered, and I could barely understand him. "Your grandma's gonna have your hide. And *you*," he said to his son, and then stopped. He wet his lips and rocked a little to one side and nodded, as drunk as I'd ever seen an adult, and I took a little step back from him. He was nodding at Matt now and when I looked at my cousin, he was watching his father with an open fear that I'd never seen before. I saw Matt take his hands from his pockets, slowly, and then let them dangle because he didn't know what to do with them.

"We were at Jerry's house," Matt lied, and I nodded to it without hesitation. "I'm goin' home now, Dad."

This seemed to derail Uncle Dennis, and he just nodded and squinted at his son for a moment. He wet his lips again and I noticed that his face was wet with perspiration, and now

I could see that the gray suit was a mass of wrinkles. Our eyes met and I tried on a smile without much behind it. Dennis turned his attention to his son.

"C'mere."

Matt took a step forward, his head bowed slightly. For a second Dennis stared at him and I could hear the man's moist breathing, and then he snorted again. He looked at me and said, "You c'mere, too."

I moved to within a step of Matt and watched as Dennis went foraging into his pockets. His gaze moved to a passing cab on Clybourn and he tried to sing something, then pulled out a handful of keys and change and bills. Coins fell to the sidewalk and a dollar bill seemed ready to fly to freedom, and I saw that Matt had relaxed.

Uncle Dennis's liquor-stiffened fingers fought with the money and then he was holding out his fist filled with change. He told us to hold out our hands and then poured the coins into our palms, going from hand to hand till it was all gone. As he distributed his pockets full of change, some of it went bouncing out into the street.

"You dropped..." Matt started to say but his father stopped him.

"I don't care, never mind. Just money, all it is, is money. I got money, I don't crawl around for a quarter." He dropped the last of it into Matt's open hand. "Put it away. Go buy some candy tomorrow, or—I dunno, whatever you want. Now get outta here, the botha you."

"Thanks, Dad," Matt said, and I echoed him, putting the money into my pocket.

My uncle stepped aside for us and we marched in lock-step up Clybourn till we were close to Matt's house. When I looked back, I could no longer see Uncle Dennis.

"He's gone," I said.

"He's goin' to the tavern. He always does," Matt said. I saw that he still held the coins in his tight fist, and now he looked at the money as though deciding what to do with it.

"Is he gonna be mad when he comes home?"

Matt looked back the way we had come. "He is sometimes, and then they fight."

"Maybe you'll be asleep," I said.

"You can't sleep through it," he said in a dead voice. "I gotta go." He didn't look at me. Then he turned and crossed Clybourn toward the projects, and I went home to face Grandma.

We were in the tiny corner playground, where we'd been digging a matched pair of tunnels in the sandbox. We carefully soaked the sand with water from a drinking fountain, then went to work on our excavations. Matt dug too far into the sand, where the water hadn't reached, and his tunnel wasn't holding. He made a little exasperated gasp, then moved around to get a better angle, swinging his legs around in my direction. His foot caved in part of my tunnel and I pushed his leg away.

At exactly that moment, the ceiling of his tunnel collapsed. He muttered a curse, wheeled around on his knees, and threw a handful of sand in my face. It went into my hair and I got some in my mouth and my eyes. I swore at him and scooped some in his face, and then he was on me. We fell backward into the sand with him on top, then rolled around. I think he was punching me and I slapped at him. I couldn't flip him off me, but I pulled his hair and gouged at his face and his ear, and as we rolled closer to the wooden side of the sandbox I tried desperately to push his head into the wood, it seemed the most urgent thing in my world to smack him against it. Then we pulled free from one another and I tossed a great double handful of sand in his face. He threw a blind punch that caught me in the mouth, and then we sat back on our haunches and sobbed.

A man came over and told us we shouldn't fight, and Matt yelled at him to go scratch, then got to his feet and stalked out of the park. I watched him go, the back of his yellow shirt caked with wet sand. If I live ten centuries I will always see him that way, head down and crying and filthy. The man was telling me to wash the blood and sand off my face but I watched my cousin and felt as though I'd committed terrible sins.

I ran across him about a week later. I was roaming around Lincoln Park with Rusty, who had hit upon the notion of catching fish in the lagoon with a net. I'd never seen anyone catch anything in the park with a net and so was half-convinced it was illegal, but if there had been nothing challenging about it Rusty wouldn't have been interested. We were circling the water, looking for the best spot to catch fish, and Rusty had just spotted what he insisted was a crayfish in the shallow part of the water near the pond's concrete border. I peered into the water at the creature, impressed by its oddness. It was ugly and brown, and could have been a crayfish or alien life from a distant galaxy, since I had no idea what a crayfish looked like, and as I admired this crustacean question mark I heard a familiar voice saying my name.

I turned and saw Matt on a bench, alone. Rusty said hello and asked if he wanted to fish. Matt just shook his head and looked at me. There was no reproach in his eyes, just a kind of sullen challenge, and when I moved closer to the bench, he just looked out at the water. I joined him on his bench.

"What are you doing here by yourself?"

"What's it look like?" He looked at the water and I studied his face. He sounded as though his nose was stuffed up, and there was a redness around his eyes, so that I believed he'd been crying.

"What're you lookin' at, stupid?"

"Nothin'." I looked away for a moment and wondered if after all my cousin no longer liked me. I tried to seem interested in the rowboats out on the water but was drawn again to his face, to marks I knew I hadn't made.

"I said what're you lookin' at?"

"I was just lookin' at your face."

One cheek was scratched—that was probably me—but he wore a dark red welt on the other, and one on his arm.

I pointed to his cheek. "Did you fall?"

He turned and frowned. "What? No, I didn't fall. And it sure ain't from you."

"You got in trouble?"

He nodded and watched Rusty fiddling with the net.

I tried to fill the cold silence with talk, unconnected chatter, mindless observations, I wanted to know that things would be as they were. He made his short responses in a flat voice and finally stopped answering altogether. I looked at him and he was staring out at the stark little islands less than twenty yards away, and I could read his thought.

"We should hide out there one night," I said, not believing for a second that we'd ever get away with it.

"I'd like to live there," he said.

"You couldn't live there," I pointed out. "There's nothing to eat."

"I wish I could. I'd stay there forever."

"There's other islands that you could live on."

"I know. There's real big ones out in the ocean. I want to live on one of them someday, someplace far, so nobody can find me."

"You'd be afraid."

"No, I wouldn't. I'm not afraid of anything anymore," he said, and the way he said it, calmly and with no hint of a child's cockiness, told me it was probably true.

Brain Fever

They were all fond of talking about my grandfather losing his mind, but it was clear to me that the person in that house closest to madness was Tom. I knew that his state was attributable entirely to love but understood little about it.

For several weeks after Big Ed's barbecue my uncle was as cheerful and funny as I'd ever seen him. One day he came in with Uncle Mike, laughing and joking with Grandma and raising the noise level in the house. She feigned irritation with him, pretended to take his temperature, and I watched in delight, for her joy at her son's happiness was plain. When he started coming my way Uncle Mike yelled for me to take cover.

"He's lost his mind, Dan." To Grandma he muttered something and I heard only the word "girl." A slight shadow seemed to cross my grandmother's face but it was gone as soon as it had come, and then she shrugged.

His newfound romance meant he was frequently not around to spend time with me, and there were other times when his preoccupation with Helen cut him off from me, so that I was sour with jealousy over this new girl, but I benefited in other ways. If he was seeing her that night, he frequently took me out in the afternoon, just to fill the time till he could get shaved and dressed and douse himself in a cloud of talcum powder and Vitalis, and at these times he was chatty and attentive and full of energy. And, try as I might to maintain my hostility toward her, on those occasions when I saw Helen she went to great pains to talk to me, as if my good opinion of her were as important as anyone else's.

It seemed to me that Tom saw her constantly—"He's out with her all the time," I heard Aunt Anne say—but apparently he couldn't or didn't see her enough to suit him. When he couldn't, he was quietly sullen, and his anger hung about him like smoke. One Saturday night he sat with his parents watching the fights and saying nothing. For a time his parents attempted to draw him into conversation, but he answered their questions with a brief comment or a nod, and they soon fell into a stiff silence, shoulder to shoulder on the long couch. More than once I looked up and saw that he wasn't even looking at the TV set. I saw Grandma shoot a surreptitious glance his way, and there was fear or worry in her eyes.

The next day he spent almost an hour on the phone. I spied on him from the dining room and noted how he never actually used her name, which seemed to make it even more obvious that it was Helen. He chain-smoked and filled the kitchen with smoke and spoke in a hard low voice. At some point in the conversation he became upset, and I could almost hear her attempting to placate him.

He held the phone to his ear in silence, his attitude expectant, and eventually the angry tightness left his shoulders, she'd said the right thing. When he spoke again he was in a more casual tone, and he was pressing her for a date, rebutting whatever excuses she made about other obligations, and soon he was laughing.

"See? You know what you really want, right? You want to go out with me."

She seemed to buy this, and the conversation took on more relaxed tones. Eventually I heard him tell her he'd pick her up the following night. When he got off the phone he was smiling. I went back to playing on the far side of the dining room, and when he came in from the kitchen he made a point of getting down on his haunches.

"So when you get through with all this important stuff here, what're you gonna do next?" I told him I had nothing to do: Matt wasn't around, Rusty had gone to a picnic with his mother, and Jamie had chicken pox.

"In the summer? Chicken pox? Aw, the poor kid. Well, why don't you and I go somewhere," he said, and I told him it would take no time at all to kill all the soldiers in my fort. We spent the afternoon at the movies, watching Tyrone Power first in *Yank in the RAF*, and next as an unlikely but successful Bengal lancer.

In days to come I saw to me that this most mysterious of all adult states brought its share of trouble. From Tom's reactions I was not convinced that it was the most salubrious thing for him. The relationship itself was hard for me to follow or fathom, for it seemed at times to speed on like a runaway train and at others to come jarringly to a halt. I had witnessed Uncle Mike's slow and stolid courtship of Lorraine and heard about other people's involvements, but nothing I'd seen prepared me for the suddenness of these changes.

Tom and Helen fought, apparently on their dates and on the phone as well, and more than once he caught me in mid-step as I entered the kitchen when he was on the phone. He waved me out without so much as a glance in my direction, and I backed out without murmur, for the look on his face told me that room was a hard place to be.

I wanted someone to sit down with me and explain exactly the way of things but knew better than to ask. One morning I caught Aunt Anne alone in the living room. She was paging through a magazine with a bored look, and she smiled when I came in.

We made some small talk and then I went fishing.

"I hope I never have girlfriends when I grow up."

She gave me an amused look and said, "Well, I hope you

do. Unless you decide to become a priest, which would make Grandma go dancing down Clybourn."

I was momentarily distracted, for the image of my grandmother doing a sort of rhumba through the neighborhood was rich with promise. Then I returned to reality.

"I think people who have girlfriends and boyfriends fight a lot, I think they're mad at each other all the time."

She started to answer, then paused, her eyes resting for a second on some distant object, and when she spoke I knew she was speaking to us both.

"Well, that's true sometimes but not always."

"Uncle Mike and Aunt Lorraine used to fight a lot."

"But that was just because your uncle…Aunt Lorraine really wanted to get married—besides," she broke off, "they don't fight at all now."

"How about Uncle Tom and Helen?"

She looked away. "Yeah, they fight a lot. Sometimes it's not good if both of the people are hot-tempered, because then you're liable to fight over everything. And both of them are."

I went for the home run.

"Are they gonna get married?"

"Well, we'll have to wait and see," she said, and I understood exactly what she thought.

Gradually I was able to piece together what few crumbs they fed me, what I overheard and saw, what I could infer, and I thought I had at least the history of this strange thing, if no understanding of it.

As near as I could make out, my uncle had met Helen just before he'd gone off to Korea but they'd had no time to get anything started. While he was overseas, she'd begun seeing Philly Clark in what was to become an on-again, off-again relationship. Tom had come back from Korea and for a time played the field. But a comment I heard him make to Aunt Anne told me he'd just been biding his time.

"That's the one I been waiting for since I got back, Annie," he said.

Tom had seen Helen a few times on the street or at social gatherings, and at around the time of the Paris-Shanahan wedding, when Helen and Philly had been in the midst of one of *their* frequent fights, he'd made his move. For a time all had gone well. Then something had happened to alter the picture, to complicate life, and Tom and Helen battled their way through a steamy July and into August. And though no one ever explained it to me, no one so much as mentioned his name to me, I understood that Philly Clark was the cause. Helen was seeing both of them.

An incident occurred at about this time, a small thing that for some reason stuck in my mind. We were standing in front of the hot dog stand on Clybourn and Oakley, a half dozen of us fighting oppressive heat on an overcast afternoon. My friend Jamie got into a shoving match with a boy named Alvin and soon they were grappling on the sidewalk in matching head-locks. They rolled onto a patch of bare dirt and the rest of us crowded around, eager for the diversion but nervous at the violence. Suddenly I was aware of hands on me, large hands that threw me effortlessly to one side, and a large figure moved past me toward the combatants.

"Come on, break it up, let 'im go," the voice said, and I saw that it was Philly Clark.

"Let 'em fight," another guy behind me said, and a third voice agreed with him.

"Fight's over," Philly Clark said in a tone that was as much intended for his companions as for us, and he pulled Jamie off the other boy.

Alvin kicked at Jamie and Jamie tried to kick him back, but by now Philly Clark was swinging him through the air.

"Here, you take Dempsey and I'll get Tunney," he said, and deposited Jamie in the arms of one of the other men.

A moment later two angry boys, sniffling and sweating and now covered with sidewalk grit, stood a couple feet from one another and Philly Clark stood between them like a giant referee.

"What're you fightin' for?" he asked but didn't wait for the answer. "This is stupid. You guys got your whole life to fight. Wait'll you grow up, you'll get to fight all you want. They might even put you in a uniform and let you have a gun. Now shake hands."

No child ever shook at the first invitation, and these two had made each other miserable enough that a truce wasn't very appealing yet.

"I said shake," Philly said.

"You should let 'em fight," one of the others said.

"Yeah, you wanna see a fight?" Philly asked him but I could tell there would be no more fights on this corner today.

Eventually Jamie and Alvin shook, grudging and sullen, and then Philly Clark made them do it over because "your heart ain't in it. Besides, you look like a couple of dimwits." And then he had them laughing.

He looked at them and then at the rest of us and I saw his hand go into his pocket. Then he noticed me. He frowned slightly and pointed his chin at me.

"You're the Flynn kid. Tom Flynn's nephew, right?"

I decided my actual lineage was too complicated to discuss so I agreed that I was a Flynn.

He looked at me and then put both hands in his pockets. He stared for a moment up Clybourn Avenue and then made a little shrug.

"You guys go get a pop or something, all you guys." He took out a handful of change, more than a dollar and held it out. He was looking at me.

"Here, you, Flynn. You take care of it. I'm holding you responsible. Everybody gets some, okay?"

I nodded and said thanks.

"And no more fights, right?" Now we all nodded, willing to swear off violence forever if it meant a steady income.

As we walked away, Philly Clark called out to us once more, or rather, to me.

"Hey, Little Flynn. Tell your uncle I said hello." He said it without any rancor, and I nodded but knew I'd never do any such thing. I knew there were undercurrents here far beyond my understanding and I would convey no messages from Philly Clark, no matter what they were.

Twice during that last hot month of summer Tom and Helen took me out with them, once for a hot fudge sundae at the Sweet Shop on Roscoe and another time to North Avenue Beach. On these occasions they talked at what seemed to me great length, often of vague things such as The Future and Settling Down, and soon managed to forget I was there. In truth, I paid little attention to most of their talk, coming out of my trance only when a change in tone told me the talk had gotten serious and, therefore, worth listening to.

At the ice-cream parlor, I could not follow the heart of their discussion, but it seemed to concern whether it was time for them to change their relationship somehow. They spoke in euphemisms and abstractions till their talk was a rhetorical maze to me. I heard him say, "We've got to get serious about things, it's time we started doing some thinking," and she would say, "We're serious enough, you do enough thinking for the both of us." A moment later she suggested that we go up to Lincoln and Belmont and look in the stores, and I could see that she'd taken control of the conversation for the moment.

The other time, at the beach, they resumed this discomforting debate that always seemed to make them both unhappy and made me want to be somewhere else. It was dusk and we'd been at North Avenue Beach since the mid-afternoon, and they both seemed tired. I dug a great tunnel in the sand and made endless trips to the bone-numbing shallows to fill a shapeless paper cup with water for my tunnel. They were sitting on a blanket and she was looking out at the water, where a lifeguard was arguing with a group of teenagers attempting to put an innertube in the water.

Tom never took his eyes from her profile. He seemed to be talking about making decisions, said it was about time.

Helen shook her head.

"We got plenty of time," and he was shaking his head before she'd finished her sentence.

"No, at least I don't. I spent long enough running around in circles. For God's sake I spent two years of my life in Korea."

"That's why you're in a hurry for things," she said. Now she looked at him and smiled.

"No, not for things. I can wait for all that stuff. But sometimes people got to make choices, they got to make decisions."

Helen looked back at the water. "That's what my Ma did, she was in a big hurry for everything, and nothing ever turned out good for her."

He leaned over and put a hand on her bare shoulder. "Nah, she got you. That's something, isn't it? She got you out of the deal."

She smiled and when I came back from my next trip to the water, he was laughing, animated, joking, and it seemed something had been settled. When we headed for the lot where he'd parked his car, I straggled behind them.

"That's the one thing I don't follow, is you and him. I can't see it," I heard my uncle say.

She shrugged. "He's not like you think. Just like you're not the way he thinks. Anyway, I've known him a long time."

Tom made a little snorting nose. "That don't mean you know what he's like."

She gave him an irritated little shake of her head and was about to say something when he said, "All right, I'm outta line. I'll change the subject. I'm hungry, how about that for something to talk about?"

Now Helen laughed and I saw they were finished with the subject of Philly Clark. I fell farther and farther behind them, stopping to shake sand from my canvas shoes or watch a pair of squirrels fight in the high branches of an old fire-scarred oak, and when I finally reached the car, my uncle was standing with one foot just inside the door and Helen was already sitting in the front.

"Thought you changed your mind about coming home," he said to me. He gave me a smile to show he wasn't irritated, then added, "When you get home, you got to shake your whole self out on the back porch or Grandma won't even let you in. She'll make you sleep on the porch."

I told him that sounded like fun, and he laughed.

On the way home I noticed how she looked out the window. In profile she looked sad, and though she talked with Tom and even laughed once at something he said, it was clear that she was distracted by something.

A little over a week later, something happened between them, and no one would speak of it, whether in my hearing or in what passed for privacy in that crowded house. The family spoke in subdued tones as though more trouble might find them.

That Sunday morning we went to Mass, my grandmother and I, and Tom joined us toward the end of the sermon. Grandmother gave him a look of pure worry, then quickly turned away. He was pale, the circles under his eyes gave him a tired look, and for a brief moment I fancied that I knew what he'd look like in middle age. For the rest of the day he was quiet, gave me the briefest answers to my questions, and eventually my grandmother told me to leave him alone.

Later that week, on an impulse, I asked him if he would be seeing Helen soon, and he looked down at the floor for a moment, then said, "No," and nothing else. At dinner that night, while Tom was working an evening shift at the tavern, Grandma explained in obvious discomfort that Tom and Helen weren't going to be seeing each other anymore.

"Is he sad?"

"Oh, I'm sure he is, you're always sad when you break up with a girlfriend. But not for long," she said as though to convince herself. "There's lots of girls that would like him."

For a week or so he was as silent around the house as I'd ever seen him, he looked physically ill, and no one broached the subject of the girl to him. No one with sense, that is, but my Uncle Mike came over one night, took him aside and expressed in a raspy whisper that could have been heard anywhere in the house his intention to "make you see reason and stop acting like a kid."

Tom pulled him by the shirtfront into a bedroom and the door closed on them, but for a long time we could hear their angry exchange, Uncle Mike telling Tom he was childish, full of silly ideas, wanting what he couldn't have, and Tom growling his responses so that I heard only one, the one when he said, "A guy that went out with one girl his whole life ain't exactly the book of knowledge on women."

A short while later, Mike emerged, looking drained, the two high red points in his cheeks showing the leavings of his anger. Tom emerged a moment later carrying a sweater, announced that he was going to "check on things in the saloon," and left without making eye contact with any of us.

"Why did they fight?" I asked my grandparents.

"Ah, all brothers fight, now and then," Grandpa said, trotting out the ancient gloss, but there was a crushed look in his face and I turned to my grandmother.

"Because one of them has...he has things on his mind, and the other one doesn't know enough to leave him alone." She looked away, her lips moving, and I think she was calling her elder son "a great half-wit."

Runaway

For several weeks I did not see my cousin. I played with Rusty but I found myself wondering about Matt, about the troubles in his home. I missed him, and I wondered if things would ever be normal again between us. Several times I went to his house in the projects and called on him, but no one answered.

It was just short of dinnertime one evening toward the end of that summer; I had just come back from Hamlin Park when my grandmother took a panicked call from Aunt Mary Jane and called me into the kitchen.

"Have you seen Matt?" she asked, and there was fear in her eyes.

"No."

She said something into the phone and then handed it to me. On the other end, my Aunt Mary Jane told me Matt was missing, and I heard her effort at self-control. She asked me if I had seen Matt either that day or the previous night, and I felt a small surge of horror that he had disappeared at night. Calmly, as if leading me through a difficult exercise, she asked if I knew any of the places he liked to visit, the boys he roamed the neighborhood with. I told her everything I could and when I was finished, she fell silent for a moment, and then spoke.

"Danny, listen to me carefully. If you should see Matt, or talk to him or anything, it's very important that you tell your grandma or someone there and…and if you do talk to Matt, tell him that we all love him, and that there's no reason for him not to come home. Tell him that, Danny, that everybody in his house loves him."

"I will," I said, and understood that my aunt had just told me what Matt had run from.

Aunt Mary Jane's call turned our household inside out, and my grandmother, just home from the knitting mill herself, dropped her dinner preparations and got on the phone to various people in the neighborhood, telling them to watch out for Matt: she called the firehouse and the Certified and the woman who ran the dry goods shop up Clybourn where Matt and I liked to look at the toys. When Aunt Anne and Uncle Tom came home from work, she told them what had happened, and within ten minutes both of them had gone out to help look for my cousin.

For my part, I sat in the living room and tried to watch television and not think of my missing cousin or his tormented mother. It proved impossible.

The world was on the cusp of change just then: the abduction and subsequent murder of a St. Louis child the previous fall had told the nation that the simple times were gone, something new and dark and unforeseen had emerged in the cities, and more and more parents were refusing to allow their children to roam the streets as they once had. It was for this reason that I had never let my grandparents or the other adults in my life know just how far I roamed in my summer explorations with Matt or Rusty. A hundred times over the past year, my nervous adults admonished me to be more careful, never to talk to a stranger, never to accept a ride with one, never to walk anywhere without my playmates. There is no cure for foolhardiness, and their warnings did little to constrain me from my wanderings and "explorations"—especially in the company of my bolder playmates—but they made an impression on me nonetheless.

296 ∾ Michael Raleigh

My family had no misconceptions about what had driven Matt from his own house. I had heard my uncle mutter, "That crazy drunk," as he went out. At first it seemed clear to me then that Matt had not been kidnapped and was therefore safe, just hiding, but the frantic nature of the search for him began to wear down my composure. I sat staring at the small bluish television screen and fear began to gnaw my stomach, for it suddenly came to me that a child on the street, running from his parents, could still be taken easily by strangers.

I remembered Matt's angry, injured face that day at the lagoon, and I knew not only what my cousin had decided to run from, but where he might be. I saw that place in my mind's eye and grew cold, for I did not believe a small boy who spent a night alone in such a place could live out the night. And as I fretted about him the image returned to me of the two of us rolling and clawing in the sandbox, and of my desperate, heart-bursting attempt to hurt him.

I began to cry—quietly, I thought—but my grandmother, bravely attempting to catch up with her dinner routine, heard me and came in.

"Oh, they'll find him, sweetheart." She brushed the hair from my eyes and I could almost hear her wishing she believed it.

For a brief moment I was ready to blurt out what I thought I knew, but guilt immediately silenced me: my cousin did not want to be found, to be taken back to the place where his father was waiting, not the handsome, witty Dennis of weddings and family gatherings but the dark-faced drunken man I'd now seen more than once.

"Do you want to play in the yard till dinner's ready?" she asked, and I grasped eagerly at this straw.

Five minutes later I was headed up Clybourn, no doubt in my mind where I was going. I quickly developed a cover story in case one of my relatives or one of Matt's came upon me: I was helping in the search, my Uncle Tom was right around the corner. As it happened, they had probably scoured that stretch of the street long before, and so no one saw me.

I walked forever. Traveling first on Clybourn and then on Diversey, I stayed on the shaded side of the street and continually looked over my shoulder to see if I was followed—by strangers or relatives. Twice I stopped to rest, and once, having convinced myself that I'd gotten somehow turned around, asked a cheerful-looking older woman if I was headed in the direction of Lincoln Park.

She looked me over and repeated "Lincoln Park?" with alarm. Then she said, "Well, yes, you are," and I moved on before she could ask the question in her eyes.

It was still light out when I reached Lincoln Park, but the sun had gone behind the taller buildings and the air that close to the lake had a bite to it. I had started out hungry, and now I was thirsty and I thought I could feel a blister forming on my heel. To make matters worse, I had to go to the bathroom, but I had heard enough dark tales from older boys about the shocking things that were known to happen in a public toilet, and so ducked into the dense bushes for a moment, terrified that someone would surprise me in the midst of my urgent business.

It seemed to me that the sky lost its light quickly, and when I reached the lagoon, I was frightened to see several men sitting by themselves on benches, and one noisy group of older boys. There were also several couples in a grassy area just beyond the eastern edge of the pond, and I decided that nothing could happen to me if I stayed in sight of them.

I made a long circuit of the pond, my eyes fixed on the dark little islands, and gradually made my way to the spot where Matt and I had sat and stared out at them. I could see nothing but the trees and the great dark knots of shrubbery that came down to the water's edge, no movement, no sign of a child. For a moment I peered out at the islands and then I called out to him. There was no answer, and I grew self-conscious, convinced by now that every adult on the North Side was watching me. I called him again and was struck by the absolute certainty that he was not on the island. I began moving off to my right, and then stopped. At the edge of the wide sidewalk was a pool of water, where someone had come out of the pond. I could even see his tracks, at least those closest to the water, a child's footprints, and they led off behind the benches and to the east, and now I knew where I'd find him.

It seemed important not to let him see me first, and so I climbed the faint little track up the side of the hill, coming out at the top a few feet short of the big granite monument and the green giant on horseback. A few yards down the monument I could see a couple of teenagers wrapped around one another, oblivious to the existence of the rest of the universe. I looked around and realized that if I didn't find my cousin, I didn't want to be in this place.

Something moved in one of the tall stone windows and frightened me, and as soon as I'd seen it, it was gone. I moved forward a couple of paces and saw him, squeezing himself up against the wall to avoid detection, mine or anyone else's, and then I went to him.

"Matt?" He said nothing and I moved closer and repeated his name, and this time he peered out at me with a look that mixed relief and betrayal.

"What do you want?"

"They're all lookin' for you."

"Who's with you?"

"Nobody."

"Yeah? So how'd you get here?"

"I walked."

"You're full of it."

"No."

He tried to stare me down but he was shivering, and I realized that his clothes were soaked.

"You're all wet."

"No lie, Sherlock."

I came forward and sat on the stone bench next to him, and the water from his clothes got the seat of my pants wet. Beside me, he stared straight ahead and shook with cold and God knew what else.

"We better go."

"I'm not goin' anywhere. I'm staying here." His gaze moved out to the islands. "I was out there, I was on it, that island." He tried on a sly smile but he was shaking, and his eyes were red with crying.

"What was it like?"

"It's muddy and there's garbage out there. I thought maybe there'd be animals but I didn't see any. I got my clothes all wet."

"So now what are you gonna do?"

"I'm gonna run away."

"You can't. You gotta come home. You'll catch it."

"Like I don't catch it already? I'm not goin' back, and nobody…"

When he stopped, I looked up and saw him staring at something behind me. I turned and saw Uncle Tom. He was standing only a few feet from us and had the look of an outsider. I felt Matt move beside me and I put my hand on his arm.

"No, don't. Wait."

"You didn't walk here."

"Yeah, I did, I swear to God."

My uncle came closer and nodded and said, "Matt." He shot me a quick irritated look and then faced Matt, wiping his hands on his pants.

"You okay, Matt?"

Matt nodded and looked away and Tom came to within a few feet from us.

"You guys goofy? Don't you know you could both wind up dead, running around by yourselves down here?" He fixed me with a quick look and said, "*You*. You're in trouble." My heart sank. I decided I had nothing to lose and so asked him how he'd found me.

"Yeah, that's a good question, ain't it? I looked all over the goddamn neighborhood for you, and then I thought of that maniac Rusty, I went to his house. He thought you might be here." He glared at me and spoke slowly, and I expected to see steam coming out of his ears. "He told me you guys came down here to this place. A lot. And you found Matt here once. Like now."

I sighed and moved closer to Matt. I was fairly certain he'd bolt in a second, and I didn't know what I'd do then. Matt looked over his shoulder out at the lake. Despite the diminishing light, I could make out boats still out there. A soft wind was coming off the water, and I could smell the fish smells from North Avenue Beach.

My uncle sighed and said, "Your ma's looking for you, Matt. Everybody in your family, everybody in my family, they're all looking for you. Come on home with us."

He shook his head and said, "I'm not goin' back there. I'm not," and I heard his voice start to break. "I'm not gonna live there anymore," he said, and began crying.

"Take it easy, take it easy," my uncle said. He watched Matt for a moment, blew his breath out in a long sigh and said, "Okay," and I could see him thinking on his feet. "Tonight, you stay at our house, or with one of your aunts—maybe Ellen."

Matt considered this for a moment, shivering, and then said, "I want to stay with Danny."

"Danny? Danny's gonna be livin' in the street," he said, and Matt actually laughed. His face was wet, his nose running, he looked as though he'd been beaten up, but he was laughing. I looked at Tom and saw him studying me, giving me an odd look.

"Let's go home," Tom said.

"Okay," Matt said, and we got up together. Tom took off his light jacket and put it around Matt but said nothing to me.

At the edge of the pond my uncle stopped and looked out at the water. "I was afraid I'd have to go looking for you out there."

"Matt was out there," I said, hoping to force him to acknowledge my existence.

"On those islands?" He looked at Matt in wonder. "There's nothing there but old beer bottles, they're just a couple of nasty, muddy little lumps of ground."

"How…" I began.

He gave a short laugh. "How do I know? I been on 'em. A long time ago. We used to come down to the park at night and take the rowboats out."

"They let you?"

"Nah. But they didn't lock 'em up. They locked up the oars, so we came down with boards and pieces of wood, a dozen of us."

"You didn't get into trouble?"

"Yeah, I did, I caught hell. You know George Bauer, the old cop?"

"Sure." George Bauer was a retired policeman who frequently visited our Cub Scout Pack to give instruction on first aid. We loved his visits, for his stories were chilling, his anecdotes dripped blood. My favorite involved a Chinese man—"A Chinaman," Officer Bauer would say—who bit his tongue off in a boating accident.

"I rowed my boat to the shore," Tom said, "because one of the guys had to get home, and Bauer was waiting for us. The other guys made it into the bushes but he grabbed me and wanted me to tell him the names of everybody out on the water. I wouldn't tell him, I mean my brother Mike was one of 'em." He looked at me, "and your dad. So he beat the crap out of me, then I got away and ran home, all the way home from Lincoln Park to the old house on Sedgwick. Anyhow, there's nothing nice on those islands."

"They're all mud, they're not like you think they're gonna be," Matt said. After a long moment, he added, "Everything's like that."

"Nah. Not everything. Let's go, guys."

We walked back to the car in silence, and my uncle let Matt get in first, then gave me a long look.

"Now we all know what we've been afraid of for a long time: that you're dumb as a doorknob. You coulda got yourself killed down here—the botha you." To me he added, "You'll be lucky if your grandmother ever talks to you again," but I saw the trace of a tired smile forming as he walked around the front of his Buick.

Indeed, my grandmother greeted me with a look that could have shriveled my vital organs, and for a long time after they sent me to bed I could hear her rumbling to herself about what I'd done, catching only a phrase here and there, most of them ending with "for the love of God." She called me "the little *amadan*" and "that little wild crazy thing," and once I heard her ascribe my lack of common sense to Grandpa and his entire long line all the way back to their tribal days, "When the lot of you were madmen and pagans living in the trees," but by breakfast she was speaking to me.

Matt spent the night at our house, and in the morning Aunt Mary Jane came for him while we were sitting on opposite sides of an improbable stack of Grandma's pancakes. At first Matt fought her, saying he didn't want to go back, but she calmed him down and told him things were all right now. She said his father was sorry. Eventually he calmed down, and when break-fast was over they left.

Uncle Mike was over, talking quietly in the living room with Tom, and they stopped talking when I went to the living

room window to watch Matt go home. Uncle Dennis was outside. He was pale, with dark circles under his eyes and a pleading
look in them, and when his son came down the stairs, Dennis
moved to meet him. He said something to Matt, and Matt nodded, still looking down, and then Uncle Dennis hugged him and
I thought he was crying.

I waited till they were pulling away in Dennis's red Dodge
and then looked at Uncle Tom.

"Will things be better in Matt's house now?"

Uncle Mike opened his mouth but Tom headed him off.

"Sure, they will," he said. "They'll be okay now."

The Announcement

About a week later, Tom and Philly Clark chanced to meet in a tavern on Barry. Several drinks and a few well-chosen words later, they nearly traded punches. I listened to Aunt Anne and my grandmother discussing the encounter. I heard what they said and added what they'd probably left out and drew my own sanguine conclusions. I took this first angry encounter as a portent of what was to come: a long campaign, at the end of which my uncle would have won his girl back.

Three days later Aunt Anne, her face pale, stunned me with her announcement that Helen was going to marry Philly Clark.

"They're not really engaged yet, you know. There's no ring. She doesn't have a ring," my aunt said in a hollow voice. She seemed to take consolation from this business of the ring but I didn't understand what a ring could have to do with anything. I felt the breath leave me, my disbelief made me giddy. I thought with hatred of the tall, cocksure Philly Clark, handsome and as lucky in his life as anyone I knew of. It occurred to me that Philly couldn't marry the dark Helen if he were dead, and I even considered praying for a virus of some sort to take him; I was certain that measles would do it, for Grandma had told me measles was dangerous for grown men. A sudden rush of guilt swept over me and I found myself apologizing to God for praying that Philly would die. Instead I found myself praying that perhaps he'd change his mind about Helen, find another girl, perhaps, or even become a priest, but I couldn't muster much confidence in Philly's vocation to holy orders.

For days afterward I went out of my way to show Tom extra kindnesses till I believe I was driving him crazy. He said little to anyone, his presence ghostlike in the house. Gradually he fell into his normal routines but something was gone from his face and I waited anxiously for it to return. At night in bed I prayed for him to be all right again and had no idea what it would take. If he hadn't been my favorite I might have been irritated with him, for it seemed to me an overly dramatic reaction to the loss of a girlfriend.

Labor Day

Sometimes a name, a few bars of an old song, a faint scent on the wind, can call up moments and people long gone. Mention Labor Day and I will forever see my Uncle Tom on a pitching mound in the forest preserve, covered in sweat and smiling a murderous smile. Every eye is on him, and something close to quiet has come upon the spectators, a hundred or more of them. Philly Clark is forty feet away, a bat in his hand and my uncle's imminent death on his mind, it is a moment they've ached for, and the two of them are frozen forever in that pose. In memory's eye, my uncle goes into his windup and Philly Clark waves the bat, and at the prime moment when the ball leaves Tom's hand, a boyish look of perfect happiness comes over his face, and Philly's eyes widen. A half mile in the distance, a slender wisp of smoke rises from the trees, unremarked by anyone, growing thicker, taller, just moments from calling all attention to itself.

Part of a child's world dies on Labor Day. I have seen more than fifty of them, Labor Days, learned to appreciate their dark significance: the last pretense at summer, a boy's final moments of freedom. A child spends three months carving a fictive world for himself, and on Labor Day it collapses with the setting sun. But the Labor Day that sealed the summer of 1955, that Labor Day I will always remember and measure the others by— unfairly, for they will all suffer in the comparison.

Several times each summer our parish gathered in the sunshine in a forest preserve now completely engulfed by the city proper. Over the years I have come to understand the darker reputation our forest preserves hold, as places where underage romantics convene to playact at love, where young drinkers come to carouse and bay at the moon; hoboes and homeless have camped in these woods, and they have seen crime, with more than one body being discovered in the underbrush by picnickers. But to us in that simpler time, the forest preserves were a place for fun. That year there had been no neighborhood or parish picnics for us in the forest preserves, and so I was almost giddy to learn that there was to be a Labor Day picnic. My grandmother and Aunt Anne put together a lunch that would have fed us for a week, my uncles dredged up a heavy red fossil of a cooler and filled it with beer and bottles of soda, and we jammed ourselves into Tom's car. Both sides of my family would be there, as would most of the neighborhood, and that meant I'd see Matt as well as Rusty, and my imagination was taxed by the day's possibilities for mischief.

Perhaps it was just that anticipation of unsupervised criminality, or denial that my summer was coming to an end, but any semblance of my patience had flown: I thought the car ride out would kill me, that my own chest would explode with the tension. The adults were no help: my grandmother seemed unusually giggly, Tom and Anne sang with Fats Domino on the radio, my grandfather gazed out the window and smiled at it all. He didn't seem to be coughing as much.

After a week of cloudy skies, the sun rose hot and high and unchallenged, and it could have been the Fourth of July. We found our perfect place beneath a pair of small trees, the self-same trees we always sat under, and as we set out our blankets and baskets and coolers, people came by to greet us, particularly my uncle. I saw quickly that mine were not the only giddy adults at the picnic, and I have no doubt that I was seeing not only the silliness of the end of the summer but the effects of liquor in the morning sun.

I noticed an edge to many of them, too, especially the young men. There would be a baseball game that afternoon, there was always a baseball game, and this one had now taken on a special meaning, as it would match two neighborhood teams with more than baseball between them: Philly Clark's team would play my uncle's team. The excitement hung in the air like a cloud of bright contagion.

The Dorseys were camped not far from us, a noisy sprawl of blankets and boxes of food and cases of beer, and when I came calling for Matt they yelled out my name as though I was a celebrity. My Aunt Mollie called out that she heard I was living in Lincoln Park now with the squirrels, and they all laughed.

Matt was glad to see me, but guarded, and I sensed that he was unhappy about something. As we talked, Aunt Mary Jane laid out sandwiches and a plastic bowl of potato salad, and Matt's eyes wandered over to the baseball diamond, where Uncle Dennis was hitting fly balls to a couple of other men. Matt watched his father for a while and then said, "Let's go someplace."

We found Johnny Butcher, one of Matt's friends, and my classmate Jamie Orsini, and busied ourselves climbing trees and playing games until Rusty showed up. We greeted him from aloft, each of us in a different section of tree, and he waved to me. He was beaming, and there was a bright glint in his eye that bespoke the possibility of high adventure and wanton destruction. In a matter of seconds we clambered down and Rusty had us clustered around him, a tight circle of young disciples. He was carrying a khaki pouch with a stencil that said U.S. ARMY, and when he sat down on the grass and displayed this cache of treasures, he secured our attention as well as our loyalty. Inside, he had a magnifying glass, stick matches, a pocket knife, a small hatchet, a folding spade, a vial filled with a gray substance that proved to be homemade gunpowder, fireworks great and small, a number of plastic containers and what appeared to be a lifetime supply of Lifesavers in half a dozen flavors. Rusty passed some of the candy around, then sat down cross-legged and held up each item like Balthazar at the manger, explaining what he thought it might do for our entertainment. He proposed an expedition into the dark heart of the woods where, he said, a dead body had been found no less than a year ago.

"Why should we do that?" I asked.

He gave me a puzzled look and said, "We might find another one."

This made eminent sense. Failing to find corpses, Rusty said we could conduct a series of sylvan experiments designed to teach us the power of modern man's ingenuity and bring terror to the forest creatures.

I learned many things in the woods that day, not the least of which was our own infinite capacity for destruction. In the course of the next four or five hours under Rusty's single-minded leadership, we dug holes, chased birds, hacked at trees, set fire to a dead rabbit, constructed wooden edifices of dubious intent, tossed lit firecrackers into the hollow trunks of trees. We attempted to use the magnifying glass to set a colony of red ants ablaze, succeeding instead in sending the irritated insects swarming up the legs of Matt and Johnny. We dug deep holes and covered them with twigs and brush to trap unsuspecting forest beasts, and I have no doubt that two or three years later a hiker or forest ranger sprained an ankle in one of our traps. Oblivious to the laws protecting such things, we cut down a dozen saplings and constructed a lean-to as a headquarters, protecting our little shack with a thin circle of gunpowder from Rusty's vial, to be lit in case of intruders. From this camp, we went into the brush, using Rusty's plastic containers to store for later use the spiders, crickets, earthworms, and other feral creatures who blundered our way. In the end, the candy gave out,

the heat in our lean-to grew oppressive, the mosquitoes counter attacked, and thirst got the better of us. Johnny Butcher suggested that we set fire to some of the trees, but Rusty silenced
him with a look of boundless contempt.

"Start a forest fire? You wanna break the law?"

In the end, we returned to civilization, filthy and sweating,
lumpy with mosquito bites and aburst with secrets, each of us
going to his family's blanket to eat. As we parted, Rusty whispered to me that in the afternoon he would find something to
blow up.

"Blow up?" I echoed.

"Sure, but I don't wanna cause no trouble."

Back in the bosom of my family's blanket, I gulped down
soda but had to be force-fed lunch, then sat restrained by my
grandmother so that my food could "settle," as she put it.
Grudgingly I sat on the blanket and listened to the Birely's
Orange gurgling around the bologna sandwich inside me; a few
feet away my grandfather and Uncle Mike dozed in the sun.
Uncle Tom was already out on the dusty baseball diamond,
fielding grounders and chattering to his friends. From my forced
place of rest, I scanned the rest of the picnic: most of those close
to us were either family or people from just up the street. In
the distance I saw others, people who lived a little farther away,
some of them from the opposite side of Riverview, or "across
the river," as my grandmother liked to say. And at the very
limits of my vision, on a long blue blanket, I could see the girl
named Helen, once again startling in her red bathing suit. Beside
her was Philly Clark. He appeared to be talking to someone else,
and I wondered if Helen knew yet that my uncle was there.

I studied them for some time, puzzling over their appearance together. From all that I'd heard, it seemed to me that
their romance, mistake that it had obviously been, was now at
an end, and I wondered that they didn't realize it. Then I saw
Philly turn slowly, his eyes scanning the crowd as he spoke to

his friend, his gaze coming to rest eventually on my uncle out on the diamond. I fancied that I saw malice in his eyes. At least Philly knew it was over.

There would have been a crowd to watch a baseball game anyway, the last ballgame of the long summer, the last day for these adults to stand in the sun and sip at their beer and forget about the factories and shops and warehouses that provided them with both employment and servitude. And of course they would have been gathered to watch this particular game, a continuation that it was of many other games between these two teams. Their sports rivalry had come to match the one in their everyday lives, but it was the baseball games that seemed to distill whatever poison they shared between them. So these little baseball wars were a special feature of the parish picnics.

But it was obvious to me that this crowd had gathered to watch something else, that word had spread of the "problem" between my uncle and Philly Clark.

I remember little of the game itself: I can say that, like most of its fellows, it was low-scoring and close. They were good teams, well-matched. Unlike other sandlot teams I was to see over the years, Philly's team and Tom's both boasted real pitchers as well as several men who had starred in American Legion ball, and each could field a squad that could actually catch the ball.

I once saw Uncle Tom's team beat a team of big muscle-bound strangers by a score of 22 to 3, but on this hot Labor Day they led Philly's team 3 to 2. It was the top of the seventh inning when the issues festering in them all finally surfaced. It had been a quiet game, with almost none of the loose-lipped bravado and taunting that marked most of these games. Players known for their mouths were strangely silent, and they displayed their tension toward the umpire rather than each other. The strange quiet grew till it engulfed the spectators as well, and finally it touched the play on both sides. In the sixth, Philly's men made several uncharacteristic errors to let in the tying and lead runs, and in the seventh, Joe Burke, Tom's usually competent pitcher, gave up a single with one out and then seemed no longer able to find the plate. His teammates barked abuse at the umpire, an unfortunate older man accustomed to umpiring softball games, but their hostility did not help Burke. He walked the number two hitter in Philly Clark's lineup, then gave up an infield hit to the third batter, loading the bases and bringing up Philly Clark, the best hitter on their team and probably on either.

Now the onlookers found their voices and the players regained their edge, especially Clark's people, who laid down a verbal assault of taunts thick as fog. My uncle's team gave it back, and a casual observer would have thought he'd stumbled upon the Yankees and Dodgers in a grudge game.

The noise unnerved Joe Burke. He peered in at the jeering Philly Clark and missed badly with his first pitch. Philly laughed and said something to Burke, then yelled out to my uncle at his shortstop position. I saw Tom's face darken but he said nothing. Joe Burke put the next pitch right down the middle, a gift, a Labor Day courtesy, and Philly sent it high and far into the trees on the far side of the diamond, farther than I'd ever seen anyone hit a baseball outside of Cubs' Park, a howitzer shot. But foul. A great whoosh of air left the crowd and the ones from Philly's side of the neighborhood crowded the foul lines and cheered him on. I saw him shoot another look at my uncle, an insufferable look of confidence, conquest. A few yards away, still on her blanket, I saw the girl Helen. She wasn't watching, she was picking at blades of grass near her blanket, her body stiff, and now I understood. I looked at my uncle who had not once looked her way, and finally understood.

Philly scalded another pitch past third base, just foul, and told Joe Burke to let him have that one again.

Then my uncle came to the mound. For a moment he spoke to Joe Burke, then stepped back and signaled the infielders to come in for a meeting. Uncle Mike trudged in, bear-like, from first, the long-armed George Friesl from third, Don Verschor from second, and Ernie Scholtz, the little catcher. The meeting quieted the crowd and the little cluster of sweating men in the center of the dirt field held every eye. I knew little of baseball, only that they were in trouble, with all bases occupied and a good hitter up. I understood that even if they got Philly out, there would be another hitter, and that it was unlikely Joe Burke would make it through the inning.

They spoke for a moment and then the meeting was over, and as the others returned to their positions, Joe Burke moved to shortstop. Tom had his arm around Uncle Mike and was speaking to him in a low voice, and Uncle Mike looked unhappy. Tom walked him part of the way back to first, and as they came nearer to me, I heard Tom say, "I'm countin' on you, big fella." Uncle Mike nodded once, then shot a quick, guilty look in the direction of the baserunner on first. He took his position, resumed his half-crouch and looked rigidly ahead of him.

Uncle Tom walked back to the mound and showed everyone the ball so that there could be no doubt what was happening. I was near delirious with joy, it was the stuff of daydreams and movies: Grover Cleveland Alexander—Grandpa's hero—aging and hung over, trudging to the mound to strike out Ruth, Gehrig, and Tony Lazzeri. My uncle would strike out Philly Clark and whoever they threw at him next, for clearly God watched the baseball diamonds below.

The noise grew and Philly Clark was nodding at my uncle as though he'd expected this all along, and then he barked something at Tom that sounded like, "You're a joke," and my uncle said nothing. Behind me I heard people wondering what was going on, what my uncle had in mind. I heard someone say "bad blood" and somewhere my grandfather could be heard calling Philly "that goddamn bum," and I wondered why he sounded so despondent.

Tom went into a stretch and the runner on third, an irritating little dark-haired man, began the time-honored jitterbug of the baserunner, calling out to Tom, faking a dash toward home, laughing, running with little mincing steps and diving back toward the base. Clark called for my uncle to pitch and Tom threw one that was shoulder high and called "ball two."

Philly grinned. "Whatsamatter, Flynn? Nervous? You look like you're ready to piss in your pants."

Some of his teammates hooted. Tom just went into his stretch. The little man on third danced twenty feet toward home and Tom turned as if to pick him off, then just waved at him in disgust. He faced the mound, looked in at Philly Clark, went back into the stretch, then wheeled to third, and the baserunner froze. I could see the shock in his eyes. They had the little man caught in a rundown, eventually tagging him out. The runner on second moved up to third, but the man on first remained there, claiming loudly that Uncle Mike had held him by his belt.

Uncle Mike stormed toward the umpire. "Did you see it? Did you see me hold him?"

"I didn't see nothing. I was watching the rundown."

"Okay, then."

Uncle Mike stalked back to first and exchanged hot looks with the base runner. Out on the mound, my Uncle Tom looked relaxed. He tossed the ball in the air and waited for his fielders to settle in, then looked at Philly Clark.

"Well, now it's interesting, Philly. Two outs."

"Throw the ball and shut up, Flynn."

Tom nodded, looked at the two baserunners, winked at Uncle Mike and threw a fastball at Philly Clark's chest. Philly swung the big bat in self-defense, fouling the pitch armlessly. His movement sent him stumbling backward from the batter's box and he almost went down on the seat of his pants. For the first time, Philly Clark did not seem elegant and confident.

He glared at my uncle for a long moment. "Over the god-damn plate, Flynn, or I'll come out there."

"Ah, quit your complainin'. Nobody told you to swing at it. You don't know the strike zone from your behind. And you swing like a broad." The crowd had fallen silent, breathless, they could have been corpses.

Philly muttered something I couldn't make out and took his stance once more. He took his graceful practice swing and yelled, "Over the goddamn plate this time."

"Take it easy," my uncle said. "I'm gettin' all nervous."

Then he went into his stretch, looked once at each baserunner, and threw another fastball. It was never a strike, never had a chance to be a strike, and the umpire had the sense to leap away as the pitch sailed in high and tight toward Philly Clark's long chin. The ball missed him, but he fell back as though shot, and the bat sailed fifteen feet behind him.

People were yelling and cursing, and I heard some of Tom's friends hooting and laughing and calling out to Philly Clark. The umpire yelled in a trembling voice for Tom to be more careful. Out on the mound, Tom shrugged and held up his mitt for the ball.

Philly Clark got to his feet and took a couple of steps past the batter's box. He pointed with the fat end of the bat.

"You tried to hit me, you sonofabitch!"

"No. If I try to hit you, you'll get hit. You're just jumpy up there, Philly. Got to calm down if you want to be a hitter."

"You little Mick bastard, you hit me and I'll come out there…"

Tom stepped toward the plate. "And what? And do what, asshole? Never seen you hit anybody but women. You gonna beat up my sister, Philly?"

Tom looked around, feigned panic. "Hey, somebody keep an eye on my sister, Philly Clark's pissed off."

Philly looked to be on the verge of coming after my uncle, and Tom waved his mitt at him.

"Get in the box, tough guy, I got one more for you."

Clark stepped back into the box and took that long practice swing that I will see in my mind's eye till the day I die: Philly holding the bat out one-handed, the business end pointed directly at my uncle, then bringing the bat back, two-handed. I can see the bat poised just behind Philly's right ear, moving slightly, rich in menace, and then the scene plays itself out once more.

My uncle stood with his glove touching his leg for an extra measure of time and then went into a full windup, ignoring the baserunners. I watched him coil back into himself and uncoil as he released the ball, I saw the strain as he put his body into the pitch and his face as he released the ball. I would never see his face again as it was at that moment, dark with effort and anger and the catharsis of his moment, and in his eyes I saw something a little like hope as he followed the hot hard flight of the ball.

The pitch sailed directly into Philly Clark, giving him no time to dive, only to turn a shoulder and take the missile high in the small of his back. Now he did go down, and I watched him roll around in the dirt for several seconds. Gradually he got himself up on one knee and stared out at my uncle.

On the mound, Tom took a step back and folded his arms. I saw him mouth the words "Ball four."

"You little shit!" Philly snarled, and he was charging the mound before anyone could restrain him. I opened my mouth to warn my uncle and then someone grabbed me, my Aunt Anne, and I realized I had been running out onto the diamond.

She yelled, "No, Danny!" and pulled me back. With her restraining arm still across my chest, I watched and now I saw what the meeting on the mound had been about.

At the exact moment Philly Clark rushed my uncle, his men on first and third both moved to join the fight and they both went down at the same instant. On third, George Friesl wrapped his gibbon arms around the baserunner and flung him facedown into the gray dirt at his feet, and the runner on first wasn't two steps off the base before Uncle Mike put a beefy forearm to his head, and the man's knees buckled. A half second later the batter warming up behind Philly dropped his bat and followed Philly out, but Ernie Scholtz tripped him, and Philly Clark's friends seemed to be hitting the ground all over the field. Both benches poured men out into the brawl but the heart of the fight took place on the mound, and I watched till I feared my heart would burst and I'd be the lone fatality.

Philly Clark was on my uncle like a cat. He hurled his big body at Tom and they both sailed several feet off the mound. They raised a cloud when they landed in the dry dirt, and I saw four fists pounding away as they rolled over and over. For a moment Philly Clark appeared to engulf my uncle, and then they were rolling once more and I saw that Tom was still battering at the bigger man, holding onto Philly's shirt with one hand and whacking away with the other. They separated, scrambled to their feet, and I saw that both were bleeding and filthy. Blood seemed to be coming from Tom's nose, and Philly was cut over an eye. They stepped back, circled, joined, and threw more punches, then danced out of range. The blood made it different to me, I was terrified, I grew nauseous. I'd never seen men fight. I was certain my uncle was going to die. Philly threw several punches that missed as my uncle bobbed and moved his head, and then Tom landed a quick punch. They circled and I could see the rage in their faces, and their eyes: there was something like surprise in Philly's, and an urgency in my uncle's that I didn't understand. They threw more punches and backed away, and both were panting. As they circled and sucked in air, my grandfather and several of the older men slid in between them, and I saw my grandfather put his arms around Tom, his back to Philly Clark.

A few yards away a general brawl was in progress, perhaps a dozen on a side, and a dozen more trying to break it up. They made their own dust cloud and it grew thicker and higher till some of them were obscured. It was thrilling to see and horrible, made worse by the familiarity of most of the combatants. Men went down and appeared again on their knees, shielding their heads. In the thick of it I could see Uncle Mike, his big arms pumping, and Uncle Dennis throwing sharp, quick punches. He was snarling, and as I watched, I saw Dennis pull a man down by his hair.

In the distance I heard a siren, and at the very rim of the roiling mass of fighters I saw the two heavy-set, hot-looking policemen who had been at the picnic all day. They were pulling men from the fight and pushing them away, but the fighters seemed to charge right back in, as though the police had no say in this matter. I saw one of the policemen lose his cap, and the other fell on the seat of his pants, looking annoyed.

The big fight seemed to feed on its own energy, and out near the pitcher's mound, my grandfather and his companions were having difficulty keeping Philly and my uncle apart, and I wondered if grown men could fight in the hot sun forever. Then the park exploded.

I have always believed that a slender column of smoke hung in the air throughout the fight, that I'd actually seen it, as several others were later to claim. But when the cold light of reason strikes, I will admit that I couldn't have seen it, that there was no column of smoke, at least not beforehand. What I did see, and hear, and feel, was the explosion, for explosion there was. Indeed.

The concussion rocked the park and screamed for attention, and to this day I'm not certain the fight would have been stopped but for this intrusion of noise and shock and smoke. It was the loudest single noise I heard in all my life and it froze the fighters in mid-assault—some of the younger ones had, like my uncle, served in Korea, many of the older ones in the two World Wars, and an explosion was never entirely good news— all heads turned just to the north, and *now* there was a column of smoke, and with it a rain of sorts, a dark noisy rain of objects and moisture that we could hear spattering against the leaves. I watched it in wonder, my consciousness still held by the violence of the fight and the danger to my uncles, but somewhere in my head, in that dark compartment where the arcania of boyhood is kept, a voice whispered "Rusty." I looked at the smoke and realized we were witnessing Rusty's personal celebration of Labor Day.

I heard someone ask, "What the hell was that?" and then half a dozen theories, including an explosion of natural gas and an old artillery shell.

Uncle Martin searched the sky, muttered that there'd been no siren, and I realized he believed us under attack.

Police cars came rumbling across the field and right onto the diamond, as if in official City of Chicago tribute to Rusty's efforts, and half a dozen police officers waded in among the fighters to restore peace, though I believe Rusty had already done that. I saw two of the cops walk a few yards toward the woods, peering in the direction of the explosion.

My grandmother and Aunt Anne and I rushed over to where my grandfather stood with an arm over Tom's shoulder. They looked like a fighter and his aging manager. A lone police officer had reached this part of the fray and Philly was loudly proclaiming his intention to finish it, though he made no move to get around the short, gray-haired cop. My grandmother was nearly undone by it all.

"Look at your face, Thomas, oh, God help us!"

Tom put a couple of fingers to his nose and shrugged. "It's a bloody nose, Ma. I'm not gonna die."

"Don't tell me about bloody noses. There's blood all over your face." White with rage, she pawed at the mess of blood and dirt, muttered about "brawling in front of God and everybody," said something about "shaming his family" and then took her revenge, every mother's revenge. From nowhere she produced one of her small delicate handkerchiefs, wet it with saliva, and proceeded to mop up Tom's face with spit, as a billion mothers have done since the days of caves and clubs and as they will continue to do till the Almighty bids them stop.

Tom winced and stepped back. "For Christ's sake, Ma, I'm not ten years old." He wiped the side of his face with his hand and looked at me.

"I'm sorry, kiddo, you shouldn't see this. Grown men fighting like…animals," and on the last word he thrust his chin in the direction of Philly Clark.

Both men looked worse-injured than they were: Philly's cut rode the bridge of bone over his left eye and bled with the theatricality of a scalp wound. He also had a swollen lip, giving him a slightly monstrous aspect. Blood from Tom's nose had been smeared all over his face, making it appear as though he had multiple cuts. Their sweat made mud of the infield dirt so that both men looked like coal miners.

More police officers came over to sort out the brawl and my grandmother tugged at my T-shirt.

"You don't need to be listening to any of this nonsense. Go on and play with your friends. Find…find Matt, why don't you."

"All right." I took a final look at my uncle, who was calmly cleaning his face with a handkerchief and listening to a policeman, and then went to find not Matt but Rusty. Alone, I made my way into the trees, keeping to the path and moving in the direction I thought the explosion had come from. Eventually I found the spot.

Even if the path had not led me there, the stench would have told me where it was. I found myself in a small clearing, originally laid out as a campsite or a spot for a barbecue, with an ash-filled pit in its center. We had passed this spot on our earlier exploration, and found it held no promise of adventure. Set back from this camp area was—or had been—an outhouse, a small, foul-smelling wooden structure painted a dark red, with doors on two sides for the two genders. Inside each door was, or had been, a plain bench with a hole in the center, and below the hole was a deep, foul, wet pit filled from years of use with a festering brown stew.

Approximately a third of this little shack still remained, largely on the women's side. I did not venture forward to inspect it, or peer into the dark hole, for I could see the contents of the old outhouse still dripping down from the tree limbs overhead, and the whole place, trees and all, smelled like a great outdoor toilet. A wisp of gray smoke still rose from the floor of the shack, and pieces of rotting, shattered wood had been spewed across the clearing.

If not for the rank smell, I could have imagined that I'd happened upon the aftermath of a great battle, replete with bombs, rocketry, and the roar of heavy cannon. All that was missing was life. Nothing moved in the clearing, and for a moment I wondered if Rusty had killed all the wildlife in the area. Then it struck me that there was no sign of my friend, either, and my heart dropped like a stone. I moved toward the shattered outhouse, holding my breath and praying that I would not find his lifeless body floating in the pit. As the fear grew in me, I called out to him.

"Rusty? Rusty, are you alive?"

A few feet from the outhouse I saw something green and realized it was his knapsack. I began to breathe faster, I am certain I was about to cry. "Oh, Rusty," I said, "you killed yourself."

Something moved in the brush beyond the clearing. It moved toward me. It was dark and alien, the creature I'd always known would come for me in the end, and even as I backed away it fixed its terrible eyes on me and croaked in its evil, flesh-eating voice. I stepped back and the thing croaked again, and this time it called my name.

It said, "Hi, Dan. Didja hear it?"

I don't believe I said anything for awhile, and my apparition was forced to repeat itself.

"Didja hear it go? Huh?"

I could not answer at first but giggled, a great rush of joy washed over me that he had not blown himself into individual molecules to be scattered by the late summer wind throughout the woods.

Then I told him I'd thought he was dead.

He shook his head. "Nah."

"You're all..." In truth his face was nearly unrecognizable through its mask of dirt, smoke, ash, and what had to be the wet leavings of the demolished outhouse, lashing out in its final moment at its tormenter.

"Yeah, I'm kinda dirty." He examined himself and shrugged.

I looked closer and saw blood on his face and arms. "You got hurt." He frowned and we examined his wounds together.

"Aw, man, slivers. I hate slivers."

Slivers they were, half a dozen of them in his hands, forearms, cheek, even his forehead. I helped him pull them out, these tiny missiles from a beaten adversary, and he looked at the little wounds.

"I'll tell my ma I fell into a thornbush."

I scanned his face quickly, became aware of his awful odor and faltered over how to tell him of his next problem.

"You got...you-know-what on you."

"I'll tell my ma I fell into dog shit."

"On your face?"

"I'll wash some of it off. There's that little stream we saw."

He glanced over at the smoking outhouse and wet his lips. I remember thinking it took courage to wet his lips—I wouldn't have touched my tongue to any part of that face.

"Didja hear it where you were?"

"Sure, they all did. But there's cops, a lot of cops, they might come looking for you."

"A lotta cops?"

"There was a big fight, you missed it. My uncle and that Philly Clark."

"Really? Did your uncle pound him?"

"Yeah, but the cops came 'cause everybody else got into the fight, there was a hundred of 'em in the fight."

He looked down at the ground and pulled at his lip. "I missed a fight, huh?" He sighed and looked back at the outhouse, then smiled at me through the layer of crap on his face and gestured toward his masterwork.

"It's pretty neat, huh?"

"It's great. It was real loud."

He nodded and stared wide-eyed one last time at the outhouse. He sighed. "It's the greatest thing I ever did."

"I know."

I accompanied Rusty down to the little stream where he washed some but not very much of the offal from his face, and put water on a few of his cuts. I wondered aloud whether one could drink from the stream and Rusty quickly shook his head.

"It's poisonous," he said with a knowing look.

"Oh," I said.

When we finally emerged from the woods we were greeted by my Aunt Mollie, who had been dispatched by Grandma Flynn to look for us.

"Your grandmother thinks you fell into a river or something. What happened to your friend?"

We exchanged a quick look. "He fell into a thornbush. And some dog poo."

"Aw, you poor kid."

"No, I'm fine," Rusty said, and went to find his mother.

We passed Uncle Martin, who appeared to be haranguing a group of older men with a theory.

"A torpedo?" I heard one of them say.

"I served on a tin can in the first war, and I'm telling you there's nothing that sounds like a torpedo."

Mollie chuckled and shook her head, then took me back to the blanket where my grandmother and Aunt Anne appeared to be forcing Uncle Tom and Uncle Mike to eat sandwiches. The two men looked up at us, embarrassment showing through their bruises.

"How you been, Mollie?" Tom asked, looking mortified.

I looked up and saw Mollie bite her lip. She was frowning but it seemed she was holding back laughter. "I'm fine, Tom. Are you...all right?"

"Oh, sure." He looked to me for a diversion. "So where you been, kiddo?" Tom asked, and I heard him trying to sound normal.

Mollie nodded and took her leave of the Flynns. She bent over and whispered in my ear: "Please don't grow up to be crazy."

Then she walked away, a thin confident girl in a sundress who made a striking contrast to my bruised, abashed uncle.

He looked her way for a moment, then at me. "So you been playin'—nah, you went to see what that was in the trees, didn't you?"

"Yeah."

A little smile appeared on Tom's face. I thought it looked odd against his injuries. "So? What was it?"

"Uh, it was this explosion."

"Yeah, we know that, we heard it. What exploded?"

"Um, you know, an outhouse?"

"Oh, for the Love of God, an outhouse!" Grandma exclaimed.

Tom looked at Mike, then back at me with raised eyebrows.

"They don't explode, usually. How did this one explode? No, you don't wanna snitch on your friend. It was that Rusty, right?" I looked from him to Uncle Mike and saw them both fight to keep the moment serious.

I nodded.

"He blew up an outhouse? No kidding?"

"Yeah. It was wonderful."

My grandmother began muttering about the world going all to hell with children running wild in the streets and blowing things up. Uncle Tom looked at me with his battered-pug's face and started to tell me that someday Rusty was going to kill himself, and he couldn't finish. He began laughing, his body rocking with it, and tears came into his eyes. Uncle Mike was laughing now, and my aunt and Grandma tried to keep a straight face and I heard her say, "A pair of little idiots," and then they were all laughing at me. For a moment I watched them, slightly embarrassed at being the object of their humor. Then I saw how good it was to hear them all laughing for the first time in many weeks, and I joined them.

It was dusk when we left the park, and no one said much in the car. The air was rich with the smells of charcoal sizzling through the grease drippings, and through it I thought I could still make out the pungent scent of Rusty's masterpiece. I reflected on all I'd seen and done that day and blurted out that it had been a really fine picnic, and they all started to laugh again, and this time I had no idea why.

Aftershocks

School resumed and this year Matt and I were to be in the same room, a change we both greeted with undisguised joy. At first it proved to be the cause of no small degree of trouble, both for the teacher and then for the two of us. Her name was Miss Bobek, and I was to learn much from her: she was, first of all, a handsome young woman, with large blue eyes and dark hair, and this taught me that a pretty woman could still make herself quite unpleasant if she devoted the proper time and energy to this end. I was also to learn that a pair of wild, industrious third graders were, in the long run, no match for an adult who possessed both a dour disposition and the patience to use it well.

For that first few weeks of the year we were the little mad-men of the third grade and took pride in the small victories we earned over Miss Bobek. As time passed, however, she wore us down like a body puncher, greeting each new assault on the decorum of her classroom with a counterattack of her own. She swatted each of us more than once, sent us to see Sister Phillip-the-Principal, stood us like unrepentant bookends in opposite corners of the room, sent notes to our families implying a family disposition toward criminality and handed out punishments that would have daunted the martyrs.

I caved in first and, uncharacteristically, Matt followed soon after, though his classroom demeanor was punctuated by sudden, ferocious temper tantrums, and moments when he wept as though he would never stop. At such moments Miss Bobek blinked in stunned surprise, sat back and gave the class instructions to proceed with some assignment or other, then took Matt out to the hall to calm him down. I thus learned that she was neither coldhearted nor mean-spirited, just a humorless young woman with an iron resolve that no one would take over her room. After these outbursts my cousin would apply himself, red-eyed, to his work, and I would watch him and worry. I wondered if a small boy could go crazy.

If Matt's unhappiness was plain to all, mine remained hidden. As night began to fall earlier and the air grew colder, it seemed that there was much to worry about. Changes had taken place around me that I could do nothing about, and I was convinced that more trouble would come. I no longer imagined that any of these things were my fault, perhaps because they were clearly real troubles, not shadowy creations of my imagination. Three people in my life had been visited by trouble, my grandfather, my cousin, my uncle: I thought about these dark changes late at night and prayed to God to take them away, to make them better.

My uncle made a great show of spending more time with me: we continued to go to the movies often, sometimes twice a week: he seemed to lose himself in the glow of the screen. He enjoyed having me along but was quieter now. Left to his own designs on the way home, he would have listened to the radio, but I wouldn't let him. I hit him with volley upon volley of questions, many of them sincere and based on things in the films that had shot completely over my head—I never understood, for example, the delicate relationship between Gary Cooper and his two women in *High Noon*—but for the most part I was prodding him out of his silence, for it wasn't his nature and it made me a little fearful.

He went out more at night but was not necessarily enjoying himself. For one thing, he was spending more time at the tavern, and my grandmother explained that it was because of a lack of help.

"You can't trust anybody these days. They'll rob you blind."

I had no idea who "they" were but understood that my uncle had a problem. The bar's earlier troubles had intensified and my uncle now had serious trouble with two of his four partners: one was drinking excessively and costing them business and another was deep in debt and "borrowing" from the till so often that the bar made no money on some days.

One night I caught a snatch of conversation between Tom and my grandfather. Tom was telling him that Dennis had come by the saloon, and Tom "had to give him a sawbuck."

I came into the room and they both fell silent.

On a Friday night soon after, I was drawing one of my dinosaur masterpieces when I heard about my Uncle Dennis. Aunt Anne had come rushing in from work and told Grandma and Grandpa.

"Dennis is gone," she said. She remembered me, looked my way, then dropped her voice. "They think he left town."

I wrestled with this and gave up, though the words were simple enough: my Uncle Dennis was gone, someone had seen or spoken to Mary Jane, and Dennis was gone, long gone. I stopped drawing and looked from one of them to another for a reaction that would make sense of it for me. My grandmother shook her head and looked away, and Grandpa muttered something about Dennis. Aunt Anne looked at me and gave me a rueful look.

"You didn't know, did you, honey?"

"No. Where did he go?"

She opened her mouth and shut it again, and I wondered

what could be so difficult about this. I was also puzzled about what it all meant: surely he wasn't dead or they'd be acting differently, so what did it mean that he was "gone"?

She came into the room and knelt down; she smelled of perfume and spearmint gum and I could smell the big grocery store on her, the smells of the A&P and the National and the Kroger.

"Sometimes when people aren't happy, they do strange things, they act funny."

"What did Uncle Dennis do?"

"He left home. He's gone from his home, he's been gone...a few days, and they don't know if he's coming back."

I thought fast, they were all stupid. "Maybe he's hurt somewhere."

"No, somebody would have called Aunt Mary Jane."

I remembered a movie I'd see once with my uncle. "Maybe he got hit in the head, and he can't remember anything."

"No, honey, it's...not like that. He took his money and some of his stuff, and he...he just left. He owed money to a lot of people, and some of them are bad people, so I think he was afraid."

"He's sick, that one," Grandma said.

"*Ma*, come on."

"Well, he is."

They moved into the kitchen to finish their discussion and make phone calls to the Dorsey side, and left me to ponder this revelation, that an adult could leave his family, apparently without warning. I felt pressure in my chest, a rising wave of panic. It was some time before I could think clearly. I sought to dress this news in more logical terms: I imagined that my uncle Dennis was dead, his body in an alley somewhere, but I soon realized that he was not dead or we'd surely have heard that. I don't know how long it took me to realize the true significance of this, what this meant for Matt: that he'd lost his father. A image struck me, dark and sudden, of a small boy sitting alone in a room waiting for his father, and I left the room so they would not see me if I cried.

I didn't see Matt in school for most of the next week: I was told he was at Grandma Dorsey's, that he was "a little under the weather"—as perplexing an expression as my family ever came up with. At night, I found myself wondering about him, imagining all sorts of cataclysmic life changes for him, now that he had no father: he would never have a Christmas again, they'd have to take him out of school, he'd have no home.

When he returned to school I saw how the other children watched him, noted how Miss Bobek tried in her impassive fashion to cut him some slack. Matt never spoke of the turmoil in his life, but he was quiet in that tight-lipped way that I'd come to know. I treated him gingerly, shared things with him, tried with mixed success to make him laugh, backed off when he grew angry. But even his anger was muted, something in him seemed to have burned itself out, and I wondered if he would ever be himself again.

I told myself that now he would no longer be subject to his father's rages, that no one would hit him anymore, but I knew what Matt would have said, given a choice between this new life and the one that had gone forever.

At about this same time my Uncle Mike announced to the family what he and Tom had heard: that Philly Clark and the girl called Helen had set a date, they were to marry in March. I understood that somehow this made the girl's choice final, and I could see the effects in my uncle's face. He said little, smiled little, spent more time at the bar.

One night, desperate for some response, some reassurance that he was all right, I crept into the bathroom as he was combing his hair. There was a thinness to his face, as though he'd just gotten over an illness. Then he looked my way and I asked him if the bar was making lots of money.

He gazed at me for a moment and then made a little snort of laughter. "You're a good kid. No, the bar's not making lots of money. The bar is...the bar's going down like the old *Arizona*. It's a bust. And...I'm a bust. I gotta get out of it before I lose my shirt."

That night, I was unable to shake the picture of my uncle standing on street corners begging for money, or walking up Clybourn Avenue looking for work, as I'd seen men do. I thought of my uncle's world of troubles and my cousin's harsh life, and felt a small boy's rage that I could do nothing to protect either of them. There seemed to be no end of trouble for people I cared about. I started to cry, and fell asleep amid dreams of doing great violence to faceless menacing adults.

I watched my uncle carefully now, noted how all his energy seemed to have drained from him. One morning I told my grandmother I thought he was getting sick. She said, "He's got a lot on his mind, the poor boy," and she didn't look at me.

I watched the adults of that house walk on eggshells when Tom was around and thought I'd die if somebody didn't talk to me about it. But my grandfather couldn't be drawn out on the subject, my grandmother answered me with platitudes I didn't even understand, and Aunt Anne told me, "You're too young to understand this stuff now."

On a Saturday in the middle of the night I woke to my dark room and listened to the wind sweeping Clybourn Avenue. I thought of my uncle and it was no trouble at all to see him now as Uncle Dennis. There seemed to be no limit to what an adult could do in the throes of unhappiness, it was clear to me that he might die, and the pain was suffocating.

I sat up in bed, panting and listening to the pounding in my heart, and I wanted to scream.

I crept out of my room and padded through the hall till I was outside his bedroom. For what seemed a long while I stared at his door, trying to hear over the pounding of my own heart and listening for some hint that he was in there breathing. He suddenly seemed vulnerable to me, in need of protection. Strange things make sense in the middle of the night, and I settled onto the floor outside his bedroom to act at least as his sentry, if not as his guardian, Cerberus in flannel pajamas.

Sometime later he emerged to use the bathroom and tripped over me where I had fallen asleep.

"Jesus," I heard him say. "I almost broke my neck, and yours, too. What're you doin' on the floor?"

"I'm sorry," I said, and scrambled to my feet, embarrassed.

He brushed hair from his face. "What are you doing here, Dan?"

"Nothing."

"Why were you sleeping outside my door?"

In the candor of a sleep-dulled brain I told him, "I wanted to make sure you were all right."

"Sure I'm all right. What're you talking about?" He squinted at me and I just stood there, dumb with the need for sleep and past caring how foolish I seemed.

"I'm fine, Dan," he said, and seemed about to say something else when he just told me to go back to bed. I did as I was told and he went on to the bathroom. I was already wrapped in the covers when he came into my room. He tapped me on my head and whispered, "Anybody in there?"

I pulled the covers back and he was shaking his head. "I don't know how you can sleep like that. I'd smother. Come have a talk with me," he said, and I slid out of bed. I waited while he went back to his room to fetch his pajama top and then followed him out into the living room.

He brought me a couple of cookies on a small plate, and a glass of milk, and then he turned on the TV. I gave him a look and he shrugged.

"What Grandma don't know won't hurt her."

He fiddled with the channel selector and found an old

movie about jungle explorers, then came and sat down on the couch with me.

He nodded toward my milk. "Spill that and we're both on bread and water."

"I won't."

He watched me for a moment, then said, "You're okay?"

"Yeah."

"You didn't have any nightmares or nothing like that?"

"No, I'm fine."

"Good." He nodded toward the television. "Jon Hall here has got troubles, though. Look, he's got natives after him and he runs into a man-eating vine. And I think his shorts are itching him, too."

I laughed and he patted me on the shoulder. I could see he wanted to say something more but for a while we both watched the mindless old movie, in which Jon Hall did seem to have troubles to rival Job's, and gradually I saw that Tom was no longer even looking at the television. He was staring at the far wall.

I never saw him cry, and I knew I wouldn't see it now, nor any other sign of capitulation or despair. But he sat a few inches from me and couldn't have presented a clearer portrait of defeat. He needed someone to help him through this time, an uncle of his own, though I couldn't envision Uncle Martin or Uncle Frank being anything but a bottomless source for more trouble.

For a few seconds I fancied again that I could protect him, I would be his last line of defense against the catastrophes that seemed to be gathering in his near future. I stared at him and told myself as long as I was around, as long as I could keep near him, I could protect him, I could pray, I could call in favors from God the way soldiers in the war movies called in air strikes and artillery support. I listened to his silence and wished the movie would go on forever.

I was planning all the things I could do to protect him from the capricious world of adults when I noticed that he was looking at me and shaking his head.

"I must be in pretty bad shape, huh? I got a eight-year-old boy sittin' up nights worrying about me. So whattya think, Dan—you think I'm gonna jump off a building?"

In truth I thought he'd die in his sleep or slip off life's deep end like Uncle Dennis, but I couldn't put either of those thoughts into words. I shook my head.

"But you're worried about me." He sighed. "Things happen to you in life, they can turn you into a bum if you don't watch out. I'll be all right, Dan, Jesus, I feel like an a...like a jerk making you worried about me. I'll be okay, I just need to..."

And then I opened my mouth without ever planning to, I opened my mouth and started talking and couldn't stop.

"You should go away," I heard myself saying. "You should go someplace far away where nobody can bother you, and you should wait there, and you could come back when everything's different, you could go away till you feel okay again and start everything over."

When I finished I met the surprise in his eyes and felt horror at myself, what I'd said, the implications of my own words. He looked away for a moment, then made a long slow shake of his head.

I watched him and I know I was about to slink back to my bed when I realized that he was silently laughing. His face was red and his eyes were shut, and a low hiss was the only sound that escaped him, but he was laughing that sibilant laugh he shared with his father. I looked up at him, feeling utterly stupid, and he saw, and put an arm around me.

"I'm not laughing because you said anything dumb, I'm laughing because you said what I was thinking." He gave me a long look of affection. "Maybe your Uncle Mike is right about you."

I blinked, confused. "About what?"

"He thinks you're not human. Thinks you're some kinda creature from space, like in those movies you and me go to. He says you got ears like a cat, you can hear through doors and walls, and he thinks you see everything, he thinks you show up whenever anything is gonna happen, good or bad. And he thinks you can read minds."

"I don't think I can read minds," I admitted, and I wasn't sure about my propensity to materialize at dramatic moments, but I was willing to admit to the other things. I was fairly certain I did have the hearing of a jungle animal, and all children think they have the eyes of eagles. After all, they notice everything, forget nothing.

"Well, you read one mind just now."

I started to smile and then his meaning dawned on me and a hard knot grew in my throat. "You're going away?"

"I think I am. Sometime after the holidays. But don't get that look on your face, I'm not leaving. I'm just…taking a vacation."

He was staring at the television. I looked at the screen for a moment, where Jon Hall was now in quicksand, and my brain was seething with suggestions. It was his turn to read minds.

"No, I'm not going to Africa, kiddo. Nothin' that dramatic."

"It would be neat."

"Tell you what, I go to Africa, I'll take you with me. No, I'm just gonna get in my car and take a long drive, see some of the country, and think for a change." He looked straight ahead as he spoke, and I understood he was talking to himself, that no response was necessary.

"It's why people stay in trouble all their lives. They never get a chance to step back and take a look at what's going wrong, at maybe what they're doing wrong. But I'm gonna. I don't know if I'll come up with any answers, but I'm sure not doing any good right now."

He lit a cigarette and blew smoke into the blue glow of the old movie, and now that he'd put words to his feelings I wanted to talk him out of it, to tell him it was the silliest idea I'd ever had, that adults didn't do this sort of thing. He said nothing more for a time and I told myself that he was leaving me.

Without a word, for I no longer trusted my voice not to break, I got up and moved toward my bedroom door.

"Hey, Dan. Wait up." He came toward me, shaking his head, and put a hand on my shoulder.

"You don't trust nobody yet, you don't know what to believe. I told you, you got people all around you that you can count on. And I'm one of 'em. I'm not your Uncle Dennis. I say I'm coming back, I'll come back."

I held my tongue for a moment, then blurted out, "What if you get killed in a car crash?"

He made a wry face. "Gee, thanks, that helps a lot. I'm not gonna get killed in a car crash. Now go to bed, and don't say nothing to your grandmother about that car crash stuff, you'll make her nuts. She's gonna be nuts enough as it is."

And so it was that one cold morning in late February, he got into the Buick and took off down Route 66 where they were all going back in 1956, and was somewhere in New Mexico when Helen and Philly Clark were married, a big wedding at St. Andrew's Church, with a lavish reception at an ornate hall on the Northwest side.

Tom sent me postcards from New Mexico and Arizona and Texas, and I brought them to school to show my friends the proof of this man of the Flynns who actually traveled around the country. Privately, I waited daily for word of his death, and my grandmother was no help whatsoever, asking repeatedly what a young man alone could possibly do by himself for all this time, and predicting that some dark-hearted stranger was going to "knock him in the head and take all his money."

Almost a month after leaving but just short of my ninth birthday, he pulled up in front of the house in the now-dusty Buick and emerged with his suitcase and bags of souvenirs, many of them for me.

That night I sat at his feet and listened as he told his parents what he'd done, the things he'd seen. He spoke of Indians in walled towns, the Grand Canyon, the Mississippi River, the mountains, he'd seen antelope and cactus and eagles and a coyote. They took it all in, my grandmother looking as though she'd found herself in the presence of Marco Polo. I fell asleep before he was finished.

The following day he went to the tavern and allowed his partners to buy him out for what amounted to little more than pocket change. Afterward, he seemed relieved.

Around the house he was almost himself again but quieter, calmer, and I was uncertain that this change was for the better. He treated me the same as he always had, and if anything we spent more time together, more museums, more trips to zoos and parks, more movies: his trip through the Southwest had done nothing to dull his taste for westerns, and if there was a western out in the spring of 1956 that we missed, it was not for lack of effort on Tom's part. But there was a tight-lipped quality to him now, a part of him no longer accessible, and it made me uncomfortable. In my darker moments I found his behavior foreboding.

He seldom went out with his old friends now, though he eventually began seeing women again. About these women he told us nothing—not me, nor his parents, nor his sister and brother. When I asked him once if he had a new girlfriend yet, he silenced me with the same look I'd gotten from asking him about Korea, then said, "When I got something to tell you, champ, I'll let you know."

Sometime in late April he began seeing a young woman that no one seemed to know anything about. He told us only that he'd met her at a dance and that he'd "seen her around." He never brought this new girl home, was careful not to introduce her to old friends, and this all served to vex my grandmother as nothing else could have. She took to muttering to herself, giving voice to her darkest fears about the dangerous sort of women he was wont to take into his heart.

She referred to the mystery woman as "that one," and once I happened into the kitchen when she was cutting onions and peppers and muttering to herself about her son. She called him "a lost boy, just a lost boy."

Just before school let out for summer, he capitulated to several months of badgering by his mother and Aunt Anne and brought the new girl home after warning us one and all not to make her feel as if she were on display.

"She's not some thing in a zoo, all right?"

"Oh, I'm sure we'll all like her, the poor thing," Grandma said, her doubts manifest in her voice.

For the first time in my life, I combed my hair without an adult telling me I needed to.

The new girl proved to be Mollie Dorsey. The two of them, Tom and Mollie, stood just inside the door as though unsure whether they were entirely welcome, their faces showing a mix of delight, relief, guilt at weeks of outright, bald-faced lying. I couldn't catch my breath, my ears seemed to be ringing. My grandfather kept saying, "I knew something was up, I knew it," and my grandmother, speechless for just this rare moment in her long life, threw her head back and laughed, eyes shut and mouth wide, just as she looks in the picture.

I felt as though a loose piece of the firmament had just slid with a neat click into its natural place. I wanted to proclaim to anyone within earshot that it had all been my idea, though I knew something quite different had taken place. I understood in a vague way that this marvel would never have happened if my uncle's life had kept to its original course. For a time I was uncomfortable with this knowledge, wondering if he viewed this new phase of his life as a second-best choice, a poor second. It was not till many years later that I learned from my own life that a happy man understands the pointlessness of looking back.

Epilogue

I greeted the summer of 1956 with a child's willful assumption that life would now be a settled, patterned affair, ignoring all the contrary evidence around me. In April my grandfather had gone in to the hospital for a brief time, and in June he went out to the Hines V.A. Hospital. He would be in and out of Hines several times before the end. At the beginning they took me with when they visited him, though I wasn't allowed into the ward itself.

A couple of times with the help of a sympathetic nurse, we contrived meetings on a back staircase where I gave him pictures I'd drawn and told him of my latest adventures. He gave me Chiclets and Lifesavers, told me not to let Grandma see them because she'd say, "They'll rot your teeth," and made me laugh when he asked if I'd seen The Chicken. Once, as I waited out on the hospital lawn while my grandmother and Uncle Tom went in to visit him privately, I chanced to look up and saw him in a window, watching me. When he died late that summer, we were all tested for tuberculosis.

My grandmother recovered slowly from his passing, and I understood enough of death now to worry about her. Soon enough, however, she had returned to her hard but comfortable routine of work at the knitting mill and keeping her house. She seemed to spend more time in the kitchen over her tea, in the company of only the big yellow radio. In the fall of 1956, my grandmother stunned the entire gathered family at dinner with the announcement that she was going to New York to search for her lost brother. A Greek chorus around her dinner table told her she was insane.

"Mom, that's nuts," Anne said.

"Ma, you're not going to New York," Uncle Mike said, and Grandma wheeled on him.

"And who died and left you boss in my house, young man?"

I saw Uncle Mike wince, and when he opened his mouth for another ill-considered response, Aunt Lorraine put a restraining hand on his arm, to match the one she doubtless wanted to clap across his mouth.

Beside me I heard Uncle Tom mutter, "Ah, Christ."

She looked from one to the other of them, little red points of anger in her cheeks. I offered to go with her if I could be excused from school. She ignored me, staring down the table at Tom till he said, "No, kiddo, she's already got her dance partner picked out."

"Indeed I do *not* need a dance partner," Grandma said, but I could tell her heart wasn't in it. He looked at his new wife, Mollie, who just nodded once.

They were gone for a week in October, and when they returned from New York my grandmother was quietly self-satisfied. All she would tell anyone was, "We found him, the poor soul, and he's all right." Tom said nothing: she'd sworn him to secrecy.

In that childhood visited by a hundred terrors, one eventually came to stand out: that all the people around me in those days, all the people I loved best, would die and I'd survive them. I hated the thought, fought to suppress it whenever it visited

342 ∾ Michael Raleigh

me, refused to admit the possibility that I could outlive them all, and more than once I wished for an early death, preferably something combining heroism with high drama. At the time, I was bombarded like all Catholic schoolboys with instructive stories of the saints, I knew the names of a hundred of them, the cherished causes for which one sought their individual help, I knew their lives and their deaths, hardships and bloody torments, but of them all, the one whose end called out to me was St. John, the Evangelist.

The image of that ancient saint—companion and even friend to Jesus, comrade and co-adventurer with the other doomed ones in that embattled band of dreamers—he alone living to an improbable age, much of it spent on a sun-baked island in exile, caught me and held me and would not let go. I wondered about this solitary old man, about his memories, his private moments, his nights, whether he was bitter to have witnessed the passing of his whole world, to have outlasted them all; whether this solitude among strangers was sufficient to shake his faith and render meaningless the way he'd lived his life.

Age has done nothing to enlighten me about those other holy souls the nuns tried to teach me about, but I cannot help feeling that I understand the old saint on the island, however imperfectly. I have outlived almost all of them, you see, the Dorseys and the Flynns. Almost all the laughing faces in "The Photographer's Nightmare" have gone: grandparents, uncles and aunts, the lot of them assembling in another world, Uncle Martin no doubt looking the Creator in the eye and grumbling, "Not much of an afterlife, is it, your lordship?"

A handful remain from that time: my Uncle Michael, stolid and grumbling and arthritic, out in the suburbs with his unswervingly cheerful Lorraine. He is content with his lot though baffled by life in general, uncertain why he outlived his family.

My Aunt Teresa currently serves her church in Guatemala, where she is a sort of principal in a school for the poorest of the poor. I saw her a couple of years ago when she came home for a short rest. Still the pretty nun though now in her sixties, she allowed me to take her to lunch. She writes me often, taking a few moments from the seemingly endless labor of a nun's life in a poor country. She jokes that this work is nothing to her days among the poor in Chicago.

Nor is she the sole person from my past to be found in the jungles of Central America, for in the verdant, steamy heart of the Costa Rican rain forest is Rusty Kilgallen. Contrary to my imaginings, he did not turn out to be a dazzling weapon for international terrorism but a renowned herpetologist. As I write this, he stalks through the jungle in search of a rare snake whose venom is an almost perfect toxin. I still mistrust his motives.

Tom is gone, of a heart attack at the age of fifty-one. Once a year I drive up to the northwoods country in Wisconsin to visit his widow, who chose never to remarry. Mollie has come, in old age, to resemble no one so much as her elder sister, my late Aunt Ellen—tough-minded, independent, a woman who has seen the elephant and found nothing to be afraid of. Like the many Irish wakes of my youth, these visits to Aunt Mollie's house are not entirely somber affairs. She makes me tea and we talk of those old days and the Flynns and Dorseys and most of all, of our mutual favorite, her late husband. Then I take her to dinner: we find ourselves a private corner in a Wisconsin roadhouse and she proceeds to drink me under the table, all the while spinning the old tales I still need to hear, my reassurance that he found happiness in a short life.

Years after all these events of my childhood I was to see my Uncle Dennis once more. I was hurrying down Clark Street and heading for the Loop, and I passed a corner where three men were arguing. They were drunk and poorly dressed and seemed to be discussing money, and from the desultory way they pressed their claims, it was an argument they'd had more than once. One of them, the shortest, broke away from the others and began stalking, eyes asquint in the wind, in my direction. I recognized him instantly, the haunting gray eyes would have given him away behind a mask. He was hatless and gray-haired, his face burnished a dark red by drink or the elements, and he gave no sign that he knew me. As he passed, one of the other men called to him: the name he used was "Lacey."

In the summer of 1971, Philly Clark, thrice married and divorced, was found dead in the trunk of his Lincoln Continental in a parking lot at O'Hare. He had been shot. There seemed to be little surprise among people who knew him and the darker associations of his life. For years people had spoken knowingly of his connections, and there was speculation that Philly's unfortunate combination of ambition and a taste for gambling had hastened his end.

Someone from the old neighborhood told me that Helen had moved away but I never believed it, for the people I knew in those days didn't leave Chicago unless they were drafted. And indeed I believe I saw Helen once after that time, many years later, though I am still uncertain it was she. I was waiting for a light to change and the Belmont bus moved by me and I caught a glimpse of a face in a window. I saw her for no more than a fraction of a second but recognized her immediately. She looked like any of the other women on the bus, a dark-haired woman in a scarf, just one more working woman going home after a day in an office or a factory or a warehouse.

After all the years, one detail in the old photo still obsesses me: the blurred running figure entering the photo through its right-hand margin, as though invading the picture from an adjoining frame, my cousin Matt. He is smiling in the photograph, excited, almost dancing into the cursing photographer's line of vision. I have all my life been troubled by that smile, the smile of a boy unaware that his life will unfold in a way far different than he imagines. At some point in the 1960s we lost contact and he left my life for many years, so long that at one point I caught the tail ends of rumor that he was dead, the victim of liquor or his own temper—in one version, killed in a fight, a John Doe somewhere in the potter's field corner of a distant cemetery, ignominious, insulting end, a street person's death. Both Dorseys and Flynns accepted this as horror but no surprise: he was, after all, his father's son, and for a time I believed it.

But more from a native intractability than anything else I began to allow myself to doubt, and eventually faint hints reached me, other versions of his story and a chance sighting, no proof for any court I knew of but enough for me to believe that he still lived. The year was 1977, and I had reached my own dead-end, a gray time when I no longer seemed to see a point in my life. I remembered my grandmother's tight-lipped trip to New York and decided that I could do a lot worse than look for Matthew Dorsey, whether he wished to be found or not.

It took almost two years, but I found him—twice, for he had no wish to return to any part of the life he'd known. My search took me first south and then west, and into the back streets of a half dozen cities. I spoke with priests and social workers and street people and sought his face in flophouses and parks, and at one point found myself following a pair of traveling carnivals on his track. Somewhere toward the end I realized that I was searching for my own good more than his, but I found him. I will say neither that I saved him from the street nor turned his life around nor brought him to a dramatic religious conversion, just that I found him. The day I finally caught up with him was a painful one for us both: he had not wanted to be found, and I had not been expecting to see the sick man he was. I stayed with him for the better part of a week, and managed to get him to see a doctor.

We spoke over the phone more than once after that, and for a time I had an address for him. I have not heard from him now in six years but I believe him to be alive, and he knows where to find me.

The stores on Clybourn Avenue are shuttered, some of them torn down, the big laundry closed. Riverview is long gone, a clanking ghost invisible to all but a handful. The rambling house at Leavitt and Clybourn still stands, though probably not for long: when last I drove by, a small rear staircase had collapsed and a piece of plywood had been thrown across the hole to prevent anyone's using the stairs. The long porch that girded the house and gave it its airs and small pretensions now sags in several places, and the dark underside, the old damp beams and joists that hold it all up cannot be much better. It is still white, now a dusty, uneven white, the color of old bone, and clings stubbornly to a certain dignity. I stopped my car and studied it. In the living room window, where as a child I watched the street on rainy mornings, a small round Hispanic face watched me. I waved and she waved back, just a shy wiggle of her fingers.

For four decades and more I have held my picture to the light, half wondering if I might notice some new detail, never before remarked, a new face in the shadows, and failing that, studying once more the faces of those long dead. I understand that a part of me attempts in this way to breathe life into those faces, break the seals of time.

I watch them at this moment in their lives that found them laughing, cocksure for just that wisp of time that they all had life by its knotty tail, and I wonder what they would make of Daniel Dorsey. I have, after all, never made a great success of anything, never quite established a career as a painter, "never made a buck," as Uncle Mike would say. My wife, herself a tale, in and out of my life for twenty-five years, calls it a foolish question. She's right, though like my grandfather in that distant tug-of-war marriage, I won't let her know. But approve of me or not, to them I'd still be one of their own, come hell or high water. A stranger studying my photograph would probably see just another family, one that never quite achieved anything, made no mark at all in its world, left no footprint, a family like the millions of others that populate the cemeteries. This unenlightened stranger would be unaware that he was gazing at the face of royalty.

Michael Raleigh is the author of five critically
acclaimed novels, including *The Riverview Murders*, which
won the first Eugene Izzi Award. He has received four
Illinois Arts Council Grants for fiction. He teaches
English at Truman College. He lives in Chicago
with his wife, Katherine, and their three
children, Sean, Peter, and Caitlin.